Lily's Journey

TANIA CROSSE

Allison & Busby Limited
13 Charlotte Mews
London W1T 4EJ
www.allisonandbusby.com

Hardcover published in Great Britain in 2009.
This paperback edition first published in 2010.

A CIP catalogue record for this book is available from
the British Library.

10 9 8 7 6 5 4 3 2 1

ISBN 978-0-7490-0860-4

Typeset in 10.5/14.75 pt Sabon by
Allison & Busby Ltd.

The paper used for this Allison & Busby publication
has been produced from trees that have been legally sourced
from well-managed and credibly certified forests.

Printed and bound in the UK by
CPI Bookmarque, Croydon, CR0 4TD

TANIA CROSSE was born in London but at a very young age she moved to Surrey, where her love of the countryside took root. She always enjoyed reading and has composed stories ever since she could hold a pen. After studying French Literature at university, she devoted twenty years to bringing up her three children. But her passion for writing never left her and, side by side with her in-depth historical research, she began to pen her novels in earnest as her family grew up, focusing on Tavistock and the surrounding area of Dartmoor from Victorian times to the 1950s. Tania and her husband live partly in Berkshire and partly at their cottage on Dartmoor, where Tania retreats to write and absorb the atmosphere of the places that inspire her.

Available from
ALLISON & BUSBY

Hope at Holly Cottage

For my brother and his wife,
two very brave and amazing people.
And, as ever, for my wonderful husband,
for his love and his unfailing support.
Thank you for always being there.

Chapter One

Out of the darkness there came a wavering pinpoint of light. It was difficult to tell in the disorientating pitch black, but it appeared to be wavering in my direction.

'Just be careful it isn't a Dartmoor pixie,' the railway guard had winked at me as he got back on the train. At least, I think he had winked. I couldn't really see in the yellow glimmer from the storm-lamp that swung from his raised arm, but his voice had portrayed some amusement. He had been concerned at leaving me alone on the isolated station. Well, I say station, but it only bore the name of a halt and from what I could make out, it was nothing more than a raised platform with a small hut at either end. I told the guard someone was meeting me and watched as he retrieved the oil-wells from the two lampposts, plunging the halt into almost total darkness.

'Last train has to do this, see,' he explained, and when there was no sign of another living soul, he made the train wait, which amazed me. You wouldn't find that in London! But we were miles from London. Miles from anywhere, or so it seemed.

And then it appeared that someone really was coming and the guard hopped back on board. There was the usual squeak and lurch and hissing of steam, and the two carriages of the little moorland train moved off into the night.

I watched it go, the red light at the rear fading into the blackness. It was as if my last contact with civilisation was being borne away for ever, leaving me behind, and I suddenly felt very alone. I shivered as the cold November wind licked about me, and I began to tremble. I had seen where I was going on a map, but just then I didn't have a clue where I was. Just somewhere in the middle of nowhere. And so I turned my attention back to the single white light in the distance. It was growing brighter. Drawing nearer. The train guard obviously hadn't really thought it was a pixie, but I could have believed it was. I still couldn't see who – or what – was carrying the light.

And so I waited. It had been a long day. I was tired and just wanted the journey to be over so that I could go to sleep. But now my heart was racing.

At last I could just make out the silhouette

of a man, a darker shadow in the obscurity that surrounded it. I stood perfectly still. Like a statue.

Could it be that the figure coming towards me, this total and utter stranger who I had never known, really *was* my father?

The light was almost on me now, and I could hear footsteps on the gravel that topped the narrow railway halt. The beam of light struck my face, blinding me, and I instinctively swivelled my head away, eyes tightly shut. I felt like a cornered animal, vulnerable and afraid, and turned back to defend myself, shielding my eyes from the dazzle.

'You Lily?'

I still couldn't see anything beyond the flare of the torch, but I heard the voice, clear and gruff. At least it wasn't that mischief-making Dartmoor pixie.

'Yes,' I answered boldly, not wanting him to know that I was as nervous as a frightened rabbit.

'I'm your father. Follow me and keep up, or you'll do your ankle on the rough ground.'

For a moment or two, I didn't move. What had I expected? Some joyous reunion? A hug? He was already walking away, shining the torch in front of him instead of into my face so that my vision had the chance to adjust. In a panic, I picked up my luggage and ran to catch him up. I wasn't going to be left behind in this wild, inhospitable place. I was cold, not just with the damp and the wind that laughed at my city clothes and blew up inside my fashionably full skirt, but with a coldness that had penetrated my heart.

It wasn't easy, carrying the heavy case. I'm of a slight build and not terribly strong. Jeannie, now, she could have managed much better. Ah, Jeannie, my dear friend in London. I had only left the city I loved that morning, but already my life there seemed an age away and I had to force myself to imagine what Jeannie's reaction to the situation would have been. She'd have winked and whispered *bloomin' 'eck* under her breath. I felt a smile twitch at my lips, and the strength of our long friendship sparked inside me.

'Do you think you could slow down?' I called. 'This case is heavy.'

The figure halted and paused for a moment before turning back. I braced myself, instinctively expecting some sharp rebuff, but he merely grunted as he reluctantly took the suitcase from me without uttering a word. He was still a featureless, black form, shoulders hunched, as I trudged on behind him. My eyes were trained on the ever-changing ground illuminated in the shaft of torchlight. We were walking along an uneven, grassy track, totally unsuitable for my shoes. I only had the one pair, a sensible court shoe with a broad one-inch heel. Comfortable enough for me to be on my feet all day at work, but useless out here. The grass suddenly became earth. Muddier and muddier until we came to a point where the entire width was flooded. My father walked straight through without slowing his pace. I tried to step round the side, hoping my feet would find some drier ground as I couldn't see in the dark. Instead, they slid on deep sludge that squelched over the top of my shoes. I could feel the cold slime seeping through my nylons and between my toes.

The path became firmer. Just as well, as my feet were slithering inside my shoes. I thought I could distinguish the inky hulk of a building on the left, and fifty yards or so further on, another which appeared to be below me. There must be a drop, so I was careful to follow exactly in my father's footsteps. Then he turned sharply between two stone walls and the wind whipped across my face as I followed in his wake. The walls on either side must have funnelled the air-stream through the narrow gap, and I shivered inside my gabardine raincoat. I realised, though, that we were walking between some buildings, cottages I assumed, and a second or two later, my father opened a door to the left. I wanted to get inside out of the cold, but the moment had come when I would see Sidney Latham face to face.

I shut the door behind me. It was scarcely any less dark, and I waited for a light bulb to burst into life, bright and comforting. But my father's silhouette was fiddling with something on what seemed to be a table. I heard the rasp of a match being struck. It flared, small and yellow in the gloom, and as an amber glow diffused through the murk, it dawned on me with astonishment that he had been lighting an oil-lamp.

'Stop dithering by the door, girl, and come in,' he growled.

I was taken aback. Who did he think he was? I felt like answering back, but thought better of it. I didn't want to start my new life on the wrong foot.

'I'll just take off my shoes,' I said instead. 'They're muddy.'

'No need. You'll soon learn you can't keep mud out. Stone floor. Just mops over. No lino or fancy rugs like you're no doubt used to.'

'I'll take them off anyway,' I insisted, determined not to be intimidated.

'Suit yourself,' he shrugged.

I stepped forward in my squelching, stockinged feet. It felt quite revolting, and the stone floor was so cold despite the surprisingly warm atmosphere. My father had lit a second lamp, turning it up so that the place flooded with a flickering, jaundiced radiance. We were in a kitchen. It was fairly small, perhaps ten foot square. Even inside, the walls were bare stone. They looked as if they had once been whitewashed, or perhaps it was just the light. A plain dresser with plates and cups and saucers stood along one wall, and in the centre was a simple wooden table with two rustic chairs. My father had his back to me, and I realised he was attending to an old cast-iron range. I was fascinated and yet horrified at the same time. I felt I had stepped back a hundred years.

'Let's see you, then.'

If his bark was curt and unfriendly, I wasn't going to let him see it had upset me. I tilted my chin as I came into the light, head held high and my eyes meeting his. He had a stern face, weather-worn and clean-shaven. He wasn't particularly tall or broad, and clearly had no intention of removing his flat cap. He wore workman's clothes and altogether looked like someone out of the 1930s depression photographs I had seen in a textbook at school. It was his narrow, mean mouth I noticed most, and his small eyes that looked me up and down. They stopped at my feet, and he failed to conceal a snort when he took in the mud-smeared toes. I saw him glance over his shoulder at the shoes I had placed neatly by the door.

'Those are no good,' he scorned.

'I can see that,' I bristled back. 'But they're all I've got. I'll have to buy some more suitable ones. And some Wellingtons.'

'Hope you've got some money, then.'

'Yes, I have. So you needn't worry about that.'

I made my voice as abrasive as his. He blinked at me, but I held his gaze and he nodded slowly. We were getting the measure of each other. I had the distinct impression he wasn't going to make my life easy.

'Bring one of the lamps,' he commanded a little less brusquely. 'I'll show you your room. Someone had left an old bedstead in one of the cottages, and I got a mattress from someone in Princetown. Their son was killed in the war and they've just got round to clearing out his room.'

'Poor people,' I answered with compassion. 'War goes on affecting people's lives long after it's over, doesn't it?'

As I spoke the words, I realised how relevant they were to my father. And so I pronounced them with slow deliberation, catching his eye and hoping he would realise that I understood. Perhaps it would help break the ice. But he pushed past me and taking up my suitcase, stomped up the narrow staircase. I followed, bringing the oil-lamp as he had instructed.

My room was on the opposite side at the top. It struck so much colder than downstairs in the kitchen, and it smelt musty. I put down the lamp on a chest of drawers. That was all there was, and the bed. The floorboards were bare. It was like a prison cell.

'The mattress sags but it's clean and dry. I got you the drawers from the same people.' He deposited my case on the bed and then went over to light the candle in a cracked china holder next to where I had put the lamp.

'Thank you,' I said without expression. 'I'll pay you for everything, of course.'

'No need. Didn't cost me anything. Now you just unpack what you need for tonight. You'll see better to do the rest in the morning.'

He took up the lamp, leaving me alone with the feeble, vacillating flame from the candle. I heard him plod down the stairs and then all was quiet. So quiet. I'd never experienced such silence. It hummed in my ears. Mocked me. I sat down on the bed and let my eyes take in the room. Cold, stone walls. Torn curtains at a small window. It was so different from the cosy, friendly home I had left behind in London. My chin quivered and I wanted to cry. Where were the buses and the traffic at the end of the road, the streetlights, and the knowledge that there were people all around? Where was Jeannie, and where was my mum?

Her face flashed before me. Not the face creased with laughter at Arthur Askey's jokes on the radio, her eyes running with tears of mirth. Or the smile that greeted me each morning and tucked me up at night. But the motionless face, the mask of grey marble, sightless eyes closed, that lay on the crispy white hospital pillow.

I leapt to my feet, dashing my hand over my eyes. I couldn't turn back the hands of time. It was no good having regrets, and after all, it had been *my* choice to come and live with the father I'd never known I had. Surely it must be better than going into the children's home I had been threatened with.

'You're only fifteen,' the officious dragon from the local authorities had said. 'You might have left school and have a job, but the 1948 Children's Act makes you our responsibility until you're eighteen.'

Well, there had been no way I was giving up my newfound independence to go into a *children's home*! So I had told her what my mother had revealed to me in the letter, proving it with my birth certificate and the adoption papers and pretending that I had always known all about it. And so now I was here.

I glanced around the room again. I could make it more welcoming with a couple of rugs and some new curtains. I was handy with a needle and could perhaps make a pretty cover to hide the rusty bedstead. The bedclothes were topped with a heavy, somewhat old eiderdown, so a new counterpane to throw over it would make a difference. I had brought with me a couple of my mother's figurines that I could display on the window sill, and I would add to them in time. Make the room mine.

I peeled off my wet stockings and changed my flowing skirt and petticoat for some slacks, the only pair I had but they were clearly going to be of far more use. I had put on my twin-set and pearls that morning, wanting to look my best. I was convinced that my father would deride their unsuitability, so I put a thick cardigan I had knitted myself over the top. I took a deep breath and padded down the stairs in my bare feet, candle in one hand and slippers in the other.

'Where can I wash my feet, please?' I enquired in a polite but confident tone.

'Bowl over there,' he nodded, 'hot water in the kettle and cold in the bucket. I've washed your shoes inside and out. They should be dry by the morning.'

I felt encouraged. That was certainly more civil, so perhaps I had been mistaken in my original impression of him.

'Thank you. That's very kind.' I gathered everything he had indicated to wash my dirty feet and since I couldn't see a tap or a sink anywhere, I asked innocently, 'Where do we get the water from?'

'Leat on the other side of the track. By the entrance to the old quarry,' he answered. 'I suppose you expected running water and electric and gas, did you? Well, my girl, if you want to live with me, you'll have to put up with what's here. I live by nature, the way God intended. None of your lazy, labour-saving devices here. The water runs, though. Straight off the moor.'

The muscles of his face moved into a sardonic grimace and I cringed. My initial reaction had been right after all. I didn't know how I was going to stand living with him, but for now, I had no choice.

'Is that safe?' I asked, attempting polite conversation as I dried my feet and wriggled them into my slippers.

'That leat has served people living here for over a hundred years. It's been good enough for me, and it'll be good enough for you.'

Well, that had fallen on stony ground. I felt like telling him not to be so rude and ill-tempered, but I held my tongue. It wouldn't serve any purpose to make matters worse. I had seen the Devonport Leat marked in blue on the OS Map of Dartmoor I had bought, so I had guessed that a leat was some sort of stream. Possibly man-made to divert water for some purpose. But I didn't fancy drinking water from a stream any more than I fancied sleeping in a dead man's bed.

'So what do we do for a lavatory?' I ventured.

'Pot under your bed,' came the short reply. I might have known! 'Empty it wherever you want. There are some old earth privies out on the tip if you prefer.'

'Right. Thank you.'

And thank God I had used the facilities when I had changed trains at Yelverton Station so that I didn't need to go just yet. My father was ladling something out of a saucepan on the range, and he put the two bowls on the table before standing behind his chair, head bowed and hands clasped. I frowned, and then the penny dropped. A good, staunch Methodist, the local preacher had stated in the reference the welfare people had requested. I stood to attention. My mother had been Chapel, but she had never insisted that I went with her once I was old enough to stay behind on my own. But I had no objection if my father wanted to say grace.

We sat down afterwards and he cut some chunks of bread and poured out some tea. I had to explain that tea makes me sick, to which he replied that he didn't keep coffee in the house so, unless I wanted water, I'd have to go without. As it happened, I wasn't fussed, and was more concerned about the greasy stew that was staring up at me from the bowl. It looked unpalatable and I wasn't sure I could stomach it, so I didn't mind that he had given me half a bowl as opposed to his own full one.

'So who else lives here?' I dared to ask as I tried to force down a second spoonful. It tasted disgusting, all fat and gristle.

'Didn't that Ellen teach you not to talk at mealtimes?' Sidney Latham snarled.

I'd had enough, and it riled me to hear my beloved mother referred to in such a way. I was tired, and I wasn't going to let this bully have the upper hand. 'No, she didn't. You may not have noticed but this is 1952, not the Dark Ages. I will be polite and I won't talk with my mouth full, but there is nothing wrong with talking over a meal.'

I felt the crimson flaming in my cheeks, but I would stand my ground. Even in the uncertain light from the oil-lamps, I could see his face turn puce and his mean mouth knotted. But his anger must have quickly subsided, though he said nothing and I felt obliged to break the ensuing silence.

'This has all come as a terrible shock to me,' I began openly. 'I was too young to remember anything about what happened, and you know I only found out when Mum – Ellen – died. So I do hope we can live happily together.'

My father was studying me with penetrating eyes, but to my relief, after only a few seconds, he went back to his meal, dipping a chunk of bread into the swimming yellow fat. He chewed on it and swallowed, taking his time.

'All the other cottages are empty,' he finally replied to my earlier question. 'Last people moved out a year or so ago. And that's how I like it. Nice and quiet and no one to bother me. So if you don't like it, Copper Knob, then tough.'

I had felt somewhat concerned at the knowledge that we were the only inhabitants at the remote moorland hamlet. But my apprehension was obliterated by the anger that swept through me like a roaring breaker. Copper Knob! I'd been teased often enough at school, but had learnt to rise above it. The fact was that I wasn't really a redhead at all! My hair was a strong, gilded blond that in certain lights took on a sandy shade that some ignorant people saw as a prompt to ridicule. Normally I shrugged off any mockery, but just now it spurred my fury.

'Oh, I think I can put up with it,' I snapped back, ignoring his personal insult. 'And by the way, this must be the worst food I've ever had the misfortune to taste. It's worse than school dinners!'

'Think you can do better, then?'

'Infinitely. I told you in my letter I'm a good cook. Mum taught me well.'

'Then you'd best prove it. If you can manage the range,' he sneered.

'Well, if *you* can, then I'm sure *I* can, too.'

'Hmm,' he grunted. 'We'll see. Well, you can make yourself useful and wash up if you don't want to eat God's good food.'

'I'll have some bread first if you've no objection. Do you have any cheese or anything to go with it?'

He glared at me for a moment, but then jabbed his head at a small cupboard in the corner by the door. It had a mesh door, and when I opened it, I saw it was lined with sheet metal, lead I presumed, and had two marble shelves. It felt amazingly cool, and I supposed was the equivalent of our cold pantry.

'In the blue dish,' my father's voice directed me. 'None of your factory rubbish. Straight from the farm.'

I brought it out and set it on the table. My knife slipped into a soft, white substance that spread almost like butter. It tasted good and surprisingly strong. I said so, trying to break the tension.

'If you want hard cheese, you'll have to buy it in Princetown,' Sidney told me, his voice less testy. 'There's Bolts and there's Bottom Finch's. Bolts is the one on the corner. Called The Mart as well, it is. They sell everything, including shoes,' he added pointedly. 'But if that doesn't suit madam's taste, you'll have to go into Tavistock. And you'll have to go there to get a job. You won't find much work in Princetown.'

I nodded. There was much I had to learn, and I'd have to get used to being a stranger in an unfamiliar place. I didn't suppose my father's reclusive and abrupt manner had ever endeared him to the local people, so I would have to make my own impression on them. I found it hard to believe this unpleasant, abrasive man was my father, and yet what should I have expected from someone who had abandoned me as an innocent child?

I did the washing-up in a bowl on the table while

my father sat in an old easy chair by the range and watched me with eagle eyes. It was so peculiar not having a sink with taps. I dreaded to think what we would use as a bath. Perhaps we didn't. Back in London, we had a plumbed-in tub. Admittedly, it was in the kitchen of Miss Chalfont's basement flat at the bottom of the house, and the hot water came from a gas-heater on the wall. Once a week on Friday night, my mother and I had the use of it, and Miss Chalfont never seemed to mind.

My thoughts were wandering back to London again as I dried the crockery and replaced it on the dresser. I felt exhausted, not just from the long journey but from the dubious welcome I had received. Perhaps everything would seem better in the morning.

'I'd like to go to bed now, please, if you don't mind.' The fight had suddenly drained out of me and I reverted to my normal polite self. 'Where do I do my teeth?'

'Here. Spit into the washing-up water and I'll throw it out later.'

'Oh, right.' It didn't seem very hygienic, but I was too tired to care. It crossed my mind that I should purchase an old-fashioned jug and bowl for my room, if such a thing could be found in 1952. 'I'll just get my toothbrush,' I said, and then remembering how cold the bedroom was, I added, 'Can I fill my hot-water bottle, too, please?'

'You can, but I'm not stoking up the range just for a hot-water bottle. You'll have to make do with water from the kettle as it is.'

'Yes, that'll do. Thank you.'

I ran upstairs into the freezing room to collect what I needed, and my eye fell on the chamber pot. As there was no water upstairs, I would need to use it now if I wanted to wash my hands afterwards. I squatted down over the pot. It felt horrible and degrading, but I guessed I would just have to get used to it. Down in the lovely warm kitchen again, I washed my hands and cleaned my teeth, and then stood in front of my father, clutching my lukewarm rubber bottle.

'Goodnight, then,' I said tentatively, wondering if I should give him a peck on the cheek.

'I'll be up myself soon,' was his answer. 'I go to work early.'

With that, he opened the well-thumbed Bible on his lap and began to read. I took that as my dismissal and took myself back up to the bedroom. I swear it was no less cold than if I'd been standing outside. I changed into my nightie with lightning speed, pulling my thick cardigan back on over the top before diving into bed. I cuddled the hot-water bottle, but it gave off so little warmth that I was still chilled to the marrow. I felt so wretched that it reminded me of Jeannie's words when I had told her where I was going to live, and we had pored over the map. Dartmoor had seemed huge with very few villages or even roads.

'Blimey,' she'd whistled. 'Nearest place Princetown, you say? Well, that looks a *bit* bigger, I suppose. But bleedin' 'ell, Lily!' she'd suddenly cried. 'Dartmoor Prison's at Princetown! 'Ere, you sure your old man ain't been in clink and that's why 'e's been away all these years?'

At the time, she had made me rock with laughter, but now it didn't seem the least bit funny. I felt as if *I* was the one who was in prison as I shivered beneath the heavy, scratchy blankets. I heard my father come to bed in the other room which was probably much warmer than mine being above the kitchen. Although my eyes were pricking beneath their closed lids, I couldn't sleep. I tossed and turned. I just wanted my mum. Oh, please come back! I felt my mouth twist into an ugly grimace, but I couldn't stop it as the familiar, cruel pain raked my throat. Mum had gone, and the only time I felt really close to her again was when I read the letter. She had kept it from me that she was ill and that despite taking medication, she could go at any time. And yet she had found the strength to write to me, explaining everything and leaving the letter in the safe hands of Dr Robbins to give to me on her death. If I read it again now, perhaps it would help.

I fumbled with the matches and managed to light the candle in its holder on the floor as there was no bedside table. The flame was so tiny I could only just see my way to pad across the room and grope around in the shadows for my handbag. I found the letter easily enough, and climbed back into bed. I had to lean over the side to let the candlelight fall on the pages. My eyes struggled to see the shaky writing and my fingers were already becoming stiff with cold, but I knew I *had* to read it once again. Without the letter, alone in this isolated, godforsaken cottage with only the fractious, unloving stranger who was my father for company, I would have wanted to curl up and die.

Chapter Two

My dearest darling Lily,

When you read this, I will be gone from you for ever. I know it will be hard for you, but you are a good, strong girl and you will cope without me. But now I must make it even harder for you by telling you something I should perhaps have told you long ago.

No mother could ever have loved her daughter more than I have loved you, but I am not your mother. That blessing fell to my real daughter, Cynthia, who perhaps I shall, by now, have met again in the afterlife. So, yes, I am your grandmother, and my dear John was your grandfather. That you came to us late in our lives was, you see, a lie.

Your mother married a man called Sidney Latham, a very dour chap John and I never took to. They had two children and then, in July 1937, a third. You. All three of you were such little angels. Then war was declared, and Sidney joined up straight away. Because you were all so young, Cynthia was allowed to go with you when you were evacuated. But she didn't like the country and when the bombs didn't come, she brought you all home. That was a mistake. When the raids finally started, she applied for evacuation again, but it was too late. The house next door got a direct hit. Part of your house collapsed. Cynthia threw herself on top of you. It saved your life, but Cynthia and your brothers were killed.

You were three years old. Of course, John and I took you in with Sidney away fighting for his country. But he asked us to adopt you officially. So we did, changing your name to ours, Hayes. You were our little Cynthia come back to us, you see. We loved you so much. You were very traumatised at first, and had terrible nightmares, about being buried in the rubble, we supposed. You called us Mummy and Daddy, and that's how it went on. We moved to a new area, Battersea, so that nobody knew the truth, not so easy in the war with the housing shortage. I even lied about my age to Dr Robbins. He thinks I was born in 1890, not 1880. Good job I don't look my age. And then, when dear John was killed, you and I relied on each other so much that it seemed best to carry on as we were.

Leaning over the side of the bed was making my back ache and so I paused for a few minutes to lie back on the lumpy pillow. I closed my eyes, remembering the man I now knew had actually been my grandfather. I had loved him dearly. I remembered the way his moustache tickled when he kissed me goodnight, and he always wore a collar and tie. Always. Even to dig our little back garden. I was seven when he was killed by a doodlebug when he was on ARP duty late in 1944. After that, it was just Mum and me against the world, huddling together in the Anderson shelter during raids until the war was over. Grief clawed at me at the memory, and I hauled myself over the edge of the bed again to read the rest of the letter in the flickering candlelight.

When your real father came home after the war, I thought I would have to tell you the truth. You were only eight and I thought you'd soon get used to the idea. But to my amazement, Sidney wanted nothing to do with you at all. I thought at first it was just his grief over Cynthia and the boys, and he had been fighting for all six years of the war which must have taken its toll on his nerves. Physically he'd survived unscathed, which was a miracle. But he disappeared. I heard nothing from him for nearly two years, and then I had a letter. He said he had made a new life for himself in Devon. There was no other woman involved, but he was living in a tiny, isolated hamlet on Dartmoor. He had been taken on as a labourer at a quarry and just wanted to be left alone in peace. He gave an address, but it was never to be used except in an emergency.

Well, you can imagine I was disgusted at his attitude, not wanting to know his dear little girl. And you were my treasure, the only thing I had left in the world after John was killed. So I never tried to change Sidney's mind and reunite you. I never replied, and I never told you the truth. Not until now. I don't know if it was the right thing to do. Please forgive me if you think I was wrong. If you look in the little writing desk in my bedroom, you will find an envelope with your name. In it are your father's address and all the documents you will need. You will see I have arranged my own funeral. All paid for. It is true there is no other family, but please tell my friends at chapel.

It is up to you what you do now. The war has so much to answer for, destroying people's lives, families. There are probably thousands of children being raised by people who aren't their real parents. You are just one. But a very special one. I know you will do what is right for you. You will never know how much you always meant to me. Don't be sad. You gave John and I so much happiness when it seemed all was lost.

Goodbye and God bless, my dearest child,
Grandma Ellen.

There. I had read it again. It hurt so much, but whenever I found the courage to go over the lines that had caused my mother – grandmother – such pain to write, in a strange way it brought me comfort. It was as if she was speaking the words to me, her voice in my head. It would always be there.

I folded the letter, carefully replaced it in the envelope with the other items that were so precious, and slipped it under my pillow. I blew out the candle, filling my nostrils with the sharp sting of snuffed-out wax, and snuggled down in the cold bed.

I still couldn't sleep. I felt so empty, as if nothing would ever fill the tearing void my mother's death had gouged out of my soul. I sighed and turned over for the umpteenth time. The wind sighed with me, and I listened to it breathing around the solid stone walls of the cottage. There were other sounds I couldn't identify, sounds of the night in this strange, alien world that had no flushing toilets, no electricity and no distinctive smell as I turned on the gas to boil the kettle in the morning. No Jeannie, and no Mum. Just an aching, broken heart.

The tears came again, drenching my pillow. I began to wonder how long you can go on crying for. Do you run out of tears, or can you go on crying for ever? I didn't find out. At some time in the small hours, I drifted away on a wave of exhaustion.

* * *

A vigorous rattling noise woke me from a deep, heavy slumber I wasn't yet ready to leave, and all the misery of the previous evening swamped over me once more. The rattling came again, short and staccato. This time I guessed it must be my father raking the grate of the range. We'd had a coal fire in our sitting room in Battersea, and I was thankful I was used to lighting it, so that my father couldn't accuse me of total ignorance. I'd show him, I vowed determinedly.

It was still dark so I had to light the candle again to look at my watch. Half past six. No wonder my father went to bed early. When did he get up, I asked myself. He had told me he walked to his work at Merrivale Quarry. I had seen it on my trusty map. You could see across to it, he had said in one of the few less taut moments of the previous evening.

I stretched my eyes and yawned. I might have gone back to sleep, but I didn't want my father jeering at me for being a sloth. The icy air wrapped its fingers about my skin as I tore off my nightdress and pulled on my clothes of the previous day. I could have a wash later.

I set my jaw as I came down the creaking stairs. My father was busy shaving, his face white and lathery making him look like a disgruntled Father Christmas. He scarcely glanced at me as I set the kettle on the range. I could feel it was cold and I frowned.

'Wretched thing's gone out,' he grumbled, 'and I haven't got time to light it again. So you'll have to do without.'

It was as if he wanted me to suffer, so I shrugged carelessly. While he went back to shaving, I cautiously tested the temperature of the firebox door and opened it. The banked-up coal inside was black and lifeless. Without a word, I dragged it back into the bucket that served as a scuttle, re-laid the fire with twisted newspapers, some kindling and a thin layer of coal, and within a few minutes, had it going again. I knew it would take some time to establish a good heart, and I wasn't used to the controls and air-vents, but I wasn't going to let it have the better of me.

'Clever clogs.' My father's voice behind me was scathing.

'I'm not as stupid as I look. For a redhead,' I threw in for good measure. 'And I'll soon get the hang of cooking on it, though I can see using the oven might be more tricky.'

'We'll see.'

Well done or *thank you* might have been nice. I stayed by the range, giving it my full attention so that the fire wouldn't die on me. But I seemed to have judged it perfectly, and was able to boil the kettle in time for my father to have a cup of tea before he left for work.

What a relief when he'd gone. I felt the tension empty out of me and I sank back in the old armchair. It had a peculiar smell and the horsehair stuffing was hanging out in several places. It was quite comfortable, though. If I'd had a mug of nice hot coffee to sip, it would have been bliss. The muffling silence swirled in my head again, and I wondered if I wasn't mad to stay here. I could quite easily pack up my night things and find my way back to the railway halt, but there weren't many trains each day so I might have to wait for hours. If I went back to London, I could perhaps take up Jeannie's parents' offer of going to live with them if the authorities would accept it as an alternative to the dreaded children's home.

My grandmother – oh, dear Lord, I could still only think of her as my mother – had never entirely approved of my long-standing friendship with Jeannie. Especially when I had followed her example to leave school at fifteen and go to work at Woolworths! Jeannie wasn't particularly bright at school and came from a barely literate background, whereas, although not highly educated, my family were intelligent and hardworking. I was always top of the class and my *grandmother* had seen the education I could have had as an opening to a glittering future. My English teacher had observed my natural love of books and had encouraged me to read far beyond what was required in the classroom. I had the ability to take the brand new O- and A-level exams, everyone had said. But no. I had wanted to share what I saw as Jeannie's new freedom. She was the salt of the earth, was Jeannie, genuine to the core, and she made me laugh. She had been a tower of strength and I couldn't have got through the loss of my mother without her.

I hadn't taken up the offer because Jeannie's family shared their house with two others, all crammed into four rooms and with only one small kitchen between them. They were all relatives who had been bombed out during the war and were still waiting for new housing. There was always washing draped all over the place trying to get it dry, and somehow they'd installed an extra gas-cooker on the landing. It was absolute bedlam, and I hadn't fancied it. But more than that, I wanted to meet with this estranged father of mine and find out all I could from him about my real mother and my brothers. *Then* I could make up my mind whether or not I wanted to stay.

I had a quick wash in the bowl my father had used to shave, and then, as daylight was filtering through the shabby curtains, I drew them back. I stared out at a chalky veil that blotted out everything beyond a few feet of the house. Damn it. I had wanted to explore, but I wasn't foolish enough to think I could find my way around in this! So after helping myself to some of that lovely cheese spread on a chunk of bread, I went upstairs to unpack.

I made my bed and taking the envelope from beneath the pillow, sat down on the edge of the mattress to study its contents again. I didn't reread the letter, but I scrutinised the photographs Ellen had left me. There were several of my brothers but only one pathetic image of my mother, faint and out of focus so that I couldn't properly distinguish her face. What was she like, this woman who had given her life for mine?

I was suddenly on the verge of tears again and it was less painful to let them come than to hold them back. They trickled at first, then came in a torrent of big fat pearls that ran down my nose and dripped from my chin. I cried for my brothers and for Cynthia, for the boy who had died so that I could have his bed. For John Hayes and for the dear woman who I could only ever look upon as my mother, Ellen Hayes. But most of all, I cried for me. For Lily Hayes, and the life I had lost. It was selfish when everyone else was dead, but at that moment, I could only think of how miserable I was and that no one else could be suffering as much.

But you don't weep for ever. I'd learnt that over the previous few weeks. No matter how dark your depression. And afterwards, it changes from black to grey. For a while, anyway.

I went back downstairs. It was just *so* quiet. If only there was a radio, I could listen to *Music While You Work*. Mum had loved that, and she never missed an episode of *Mrs Dale's Diary* or *The Archers*. But there was no such luxury as a radio in Sidney Latham's life so I decided to ferret around his house instead. It would be a relief if I could find something that could endear him to me. Just a little. A photograph of my brothers or myself, or especially a clearer one of Cynthia than I had. But there was nothing personal in the kitchen at all.

Then I remembered the other door in the tiny hallway and found myself in a sort of parlour. It was icily cold and smelt of damp as if the fire hadn't been lit for years. Two armchairs stood to attention at either side of the hearth, both in better condition than the one in the kitchen. When I banged the cushions, a pall of dust rose into the air. On a small table lay Sidney's Bible of the previous evening and a prayer-book. There was a picture of him and some other soldiers in their uniforms. *They* were smiling, but my father wasn't. What had happened to him in the war? He seemed a man without a life. A ghost. Existing for no purpose. I wondered what he did with himself when he wasn't at work.

Later on, I opened the front door and stepped outside. The fog didn't seem so thick, so surely I could explore just a little without becoming lost?

The air hung as still as death in glacial droplets that clung to my eyelashes and penetrated my skin, so I nipped back inside for my gabardine, pulled my beret onto my head and wound my itchy scarf around my neck. And then I set off, feeling a little like Stanley and Livingstone.

From the outside, it looked as if there had originally been a row of four tiny cottages, but that the one my father was living in was in fact the middle two knocked into one. I peered through dirty, rain-streaked windows into one of those adjacent to it and, in the gloom, could just see the one downstairs room. It was the same with the other cottages just opposite that formed three sides of a square. They looked so sad, enshrouded in the pearly mist, abandoned, a door dangling from one rusty hinge, a broken window pane, peeling paint. In some cases, the roof had fallen in.

I crept inside one of those that had no door at all. I felt like an intruder. It was damp and echoing, the range, identical to the one I had left glowing cheerfully in my father's cottage, cold and with ash spilling out onto the floor. The stairs complained beneath my weight, and I wondered who had lived there. Had they been happy, a little community on the lonely moor? Or were their lives touched with sorrow? I certainly felt an emptiness, or perhaps it was my own grief slithering into every nook and cranny.

I made sure I had my bearings, and by making a mental note of which way I was facing, I ventured a little further. The muffling blanket of eerie mist sent a chill down my spine, and yet I was fascinated by it. I crossed over what must have been the track I had followed my father along. I found the leat and the spout where the water tumbled in a silvery cascade to the stones below. It was set at the right height to place a bucket underneath to catch it. The water was clear and sparkling. I dipped my fingers in it and dared to suck them. It tasted fresh and pure. Perhaps it was safe to drink, after all.

The entrance to the old quarry, Sidney had said. I tried to think of him as my father, but it didn't feel right. I longed to be able to call him *Dad*. It would have been comforting. But *Dad* still meant dear John Hayes, and not the ill-tempered ogre who was a stranger to me.

I stepped forward warily. Not from lack of courage but because I assumed a quarry could be a dangerous place. It was exciting, sparking my imagination, but I didn't want to break my neck or my ankle, and let Sidney have a field day with snide remarks about my being a waste of space. The ground rose on either side of me like a mountain, grey-green grass and pewter rock towering skywards and forming a narrow canyon. And yet I sensed I was walking on rising ground. It was muddy. My shoes weren't properly dry yet and I didn't want a repeat of last night, so I trod carefully, so carefully that when I saw the quarry proper, it took me by surprise.

I stared, dumbfounded. It was a thing of magic and power, a mystic vapour drifting from the sheen of dark, slate water. How deep was it? Fathomless, perhaps. I could imagine the sword Excalibur levitating from its secret depths. On the far side, the sheer rock face soared vertically, the summit lost as it stretched up into the foaming shroud that cloaked the moor that day. I had the impression that the mist was revealing only a small part of the granite wall which was scarred in clear vertical and horizontal lines. I was mesmerised, astonished that a quarry could have such a profound effect on me.

'Awe-inspiring, isn't it?'

I nearly jumped out of my skin. The silence and the deadening stillness had wreathed itself about me, and I had believed I was alone. It was disconcerting and yet I was thrilled by it, a new and overwhelming experience for me, as if no other scrap of humanity existed. So to hear a man's voice not far behind me when it appeared there was no one else for miles around set my heart pumping. If he was of ill-intent, nobody would hear my screams.

I turned round, ready to defend myself. The man was picking his way towards me, hardly the action of an assailant. He was dressed in a black overcoat of a loose, raglan style, and below the hem were black suit-trousers with deep turn-ups and polished black shoes he was trying not to muddy. Beneath his trilby hat, I could see gunmetal grey hair, and his face was lined. His eyes, a chestnut brown as he came up to me, were mournful, and I didn't feel afraid any more.

He stopped beside me, and his glance swept across the quarry. 'Took the lives of my father and my grandfather,' he murmured distantly. 'Both afore I were born. And both died here in my mother's arms.'

I held my breath. This wasn't what I had expected. The sorrow in his voice was so moving. Shattering. 'Goodness, I'm so sorry,' I said lamely. But I *did* feel for him. I knew what it was to grieve.

I heard him inhale deeply. 'Oh, it were back along many a year. I'll be sixty come the spring. And I never knew either of them. My mother, though, she died last week. Funeral's this afternoon. While I were coming to Tavvy, I thought I'd come up here for old times' sake. I were born in one of the cottages, you see.'

'Really?' I was genuinely intrigued, and I liked his accent. It was like the train guard's. And I gathered that by *Tavvy*, he meant Tavistock. But I knew what he was going through. Ellen Hayes's funeral had been the worst thing. Throat closed so that I couldn't sing her favourite hymn. I felt I had let her down.

'I'm sorry about your mother,' I added with compassion. It was strangely comforting, knowing this man was sharing my own raw grief. 'I lost *my* mother a few weeks ago.'

'Did you?' His eyes were large and opened wide, like saucers. Handsome eyes. I imagined he had been handsome in his youth. 'You're very young to lose your mother. What a tragedy. At least mine were very old. Eighty-four. She remarried. Had a good life. My step-father were a doctor. A lovely man. Died just a few years ago, so this afternoon, they'll be together again.'

I nodded solemnly. 'I suppose none of us can complain if we get to be eighty-odd. My mother was seventy-one. She would have been seventy-two just before Christmas.' I saw him frown, and realised I needed to explain. And somehow it helped, telling this stranger. 'It turned out she was my grandmother. I didn't know until she died. My mother was killed in the London Blitz when I was a baby. That's where I'm from, you see.'

'I'd guessed you're not local,' my new friend smiled. 'No accent, see. I somehow grew up with one. Much stronger than my mother's. She always said it were born in me. From my father. But, forgive me, what are you doing here, all alone on the moor, if you're from London?'

My mouth puckered involuntarily. 'I'm living here now. With my real father.'

'What? Here? At Foggintor?' He sounded incredulous, and I nodded again, this time with a wry smile.

'Yes. In one of the cottages. The double one.'

'Good God, I thought they were abandoned years ago.'

'I think they were, more or less. The last people moved out over a year ago, but it had just been them and my father since soon after the war.'

'And now it's just you and your father? And from what you say, you can't have known him afore?'

I raised an eyebrow. Quite astute, my gentleman of the mist. He seemed kind and I trusted him. 'Not before yesterday, no.'

'Yesterday? Goodness. What do you think of him, then?'

'He's a bit grumpy,' I answered evasively.

'Well, good luck.' He gave that rueful, understanding smile again. 'Tell you what, though. You should look up my half-brother in Tavvy. Dr Franfield, he is. A doctor like his father. He's got children your sort of age. You'd like them. Plymouth Road, they live. I could even meet you again there. I visit quite often. Live in Plymouth myself, see. Never married. Injured in the Great War, like, and even my step-father couldn't put back...' He suddenly clammed up as if he had said too much, and his smile stiffened. 'Anyway, you remember that. Dr Franfield. And I must be going. I mustn't be late for my mum's funeral, God rest her soul.'

'I hope it goes...as well as a funeral can,' I ventured.

He gave a jerk of his head, his eyes bereft as they cast a final glance across at the majestic walls of the quarry. 'Thank you. And I hope everything turns out well for you. It's a privilege to live on the moor, you know. It's a living thing. It breathes at you. There's no escaping once it creeps into your blood. You'll see.'

I blinked at him and nodded. I watched for a moment or two as he retraced his steps, then I turned back to the quarry. The ivory gauze was floating down like swans' feathers, wiping out the stone walls as if they had never been. Just like my phantom friend. I spun round. I didn't even know his name. His shadow was dissipating into the ether, and he was gone.

I remained, staring into nothingness. Was he real, or was he a figment of my imagination? A Dartmoor pixie in disguise? Who knows? But I had felt sorry for him. And it had somehow eased my own grief. I wondered quite what had happened to him in the Great War that he seemed to imply had prevented him from marrying. Another war. What a terrible thing. We still had Korea even now.

I shivered as the dampness of the mist penetrated my bones. And turned for home before I lost my sense of direction.

'I saw the old quarry today,' I told Sidney that evening. 'It's impressive, what I could see of it.'

I had tried to make an impression on him, too, washing over the muddy floor, cleaning the windows and generally scrubbing life into the two downstairs rooms.

'Don't you ever go in there again!' was all the thanks I received for dusting the parlour.

My tongue was burning with an angry response and I clenched my teeth to keep it inside. Instead, I made my father a cup of tea. I had skimmed the fat off the stew, sifted out the gristle and added some extra carrots and onions I had discovered in the walled garden by the track. Presumably Sidney had grown them, and I knew all about vegetables. We had obediently dug for victory during the war. The meal tasted altogether better, but Sidney made no comment.

'How do you extract the stone?' I asked, expecting my interest to please him. I wasn't going to tell him about my mystery man, though. He might not believe that anyone would venture out so far in that dense fog just to look at a quarry. I doubted

Sidney would feel the intense emotion I had shared with the stranger.

I was right. 'What do you want to know for?' he growled.

'I'm just interested. Nothing wrong in that, is there?' I tried not to sound as cross as I felt, and thankfully Sidney appeared not to take umbrage.

'We use pneumatic drills nowadays,' he answered, although still somewhat curtly. 'They were never used here at Foggintor. It closed before they came into use. They had them at Swell Tor, though.'

'Swell Tor?'

'You passed it on the train. Closed in 1938, I think, well before my time. That was when most people left here.' He took another mouthful of stew so that I thought the conversation was closed, but he swallowed and smacked his lips before adding, 'One or two stayed on, though, working at Merrivale. And some families came from Plymouth to escape the bombing, but they went back as soon as the war was over.'

The war again. I wondered what they had made of the remote hamlet and its living conditions after city life. Just like myself. But if it was a choice between that and being bombed, you'd put up with it. I knew. And the image of Ellen and I singing in the foul-smelling Anderson shelter to chase away the demons as she put it, flashed across my brain. It was a memory I had once wanted to dispose of, but now I wanted to hold onto that closeness we had shared. The closeness of fear. And of having survived together.

It was the most talkative Sidney had been, so I decided to take advantage of his marginally improved mood. 'So, you drill out the rock, then?' I prompted.

'Drill holes along the natural fault lines and then blast it. You need to be highly skilled to deal with the explosives. I don't do that. Just the drilling and what have you. It's hard, dusty work. So does that answer your question?'

He poked his nose towards me, eyes glowering, and I shrank away. Not from fear, but from disgust. I thought he'd be glad of my company and my interest. I was his daughter. There was so much I wanted to ask him, and I felt I had a right to do so. And so I braced myself and demanded, 'Why did you come here? To Dartmoor? Did you particularly want to work at a quarry, or did you fall in love with the moor?'

To my amazement, his face inflated at the simple question, the veins in his neck standing out like ropes. He looked like a red balloon about to explode. If it hadn't been so frightening, I would have been fascinated.

'No!' he suddenly bawled. 'I came here because there were no nosey people asking questions!'

If he had hurled a brick in my face, he couldn't

have hurt me more. Surely it was only natural that I should want to know all about him? As I lowered my eyes, I felt slightly sick. I was at a loss to know why my mother – who was dear Ellen's daughter and surely as lovely – had married such a spiky, bitter man. One who would go on to abandon his only surviving child for no apparent reason. I hadn't wanted this to be a fight. I wanted it to be an adventure, a new beginning. I *wanted* to relate to Sidney in some way. To find some tiny, tenuous link between us, but he evidently wanted us to remain strangers.

Sidney had already finished his meal, but I was only halfway through mine. I was so upset, though, that I couldn't eat any more, so when Sidney got up and stationed himself in the armchair with his Bible, I began to clear away the dishes and washed up, glad of something to do. I glanced across at Sidney. Was he reading a passage about forgiveness, inspiring himself to forgive me for my impertinent questions? But what had I done except show interest in his life? He was my father, when all was said and done!

I chewed my lip. All I had discovered so far was that he was a twisted, mean-mouthed recluse who drilled holes for a living. I would have my work cut out if I was ever going to learn anything about my mother and brothers from him. Perhaps I never would. I wasn't even sure if I would stay around long enough to find out.

Chapter Three

I slept better that second night, perhaps because, once I was in bed, my thoughts went not to Sidney but to the stranger, my apparition of the quarry. Had I really spoken with him? His had been a sad story, but, unlike Sidney, his unhappiness hadn't turned to bitterness. I wondered why he lived alone in Plymouth when he clearly loved the moor. Born here. In which cottage, I mused. I imagined him as a toddler, taking his first faltering steps in the mud and never knowing his father. How long had it been before his mother had found love again? I really did hope the old lady's funeral had gone well. That it had brought the family more comfort than Ellen's had to me. Dr Franfield and his children. They all had each other. I only had Sidney Latham.

I didn't get up when I heard him in the morning, but lay in bed, curled up against the cold, allowing my resentment to brew up inside me, counting the minutes until I was sure he had gone. Then I snuggled my feet into my slippers, pulled my thick cardigan over my nightdress and scooted downstairs to the warmth of the kitchen. The range firebox had been banked up with coal, smouldering quietly with two tiny spirals of grey smoke scrolling up towards the flue. Today, Sidney had judged it perfectly, as I imagined he usually did, yesterday's failure being uncommon. Everything had been left neat and tidy. Precise. The Bible on the chair was the only reminder of Sidney's presence.

I moved it as I sat down to repeat my breakfast of the previous day. The National Loaf bread was turning stale, and I wondered when Sidney did his shopping. On Saturday afternoon, I assumed, as he worked in the morning, and in this Princetown I had heard about. I found it hard to imagine a substantial settlement in such a remote place, but I supposed it had been developed to accommodate the prison and all its staff.

The water in the kettle was still warm, so I gave myself a quick wash and ran back upstairs to get dressed. It was fully light now and I went to the window to draw back those tatty curtains.

I think I will remember that moment for ever. Dartmoor, revealed in all her spectacular glory. To my left, the view was partly obscured by the sunken building I had noticed on my arrival, a house of more stature than the cottages and with the overgrown remains of what once may have been a pretty garden. But beyond that, the land stretched out to the sky, as if its soul was reaching up to the heavens and out into eternity. And it was green. Green and brown.

I had seen my first green fields as the train had steamed away from London and into the countryside. Flat and enclosed with bare autumn trees spreading their dark fingers into the rain. Cows were moving creatures, not static pictures in a book. Later, the land had undulated. I had seen sheep on hills, a tractor ploughing in rich, red earth. But this was different. It was sage green, bottle green, jade and emerald, bronze, cinnamon and burnt sienna. It rolled out at my feet with no trees or tall walls to impair my feasting eyes, a long dip that lifted to the horizon in a sharp ridge. Beyond its tip, to the right, far, far away, the blue hills of what must be the moors of Cornwall merged into the great dome of the sky.

Here, over Dartmoor, silvery shafts bore down like searchlights from holes in the dapple-grey clouds, striping the sky. And then, further down, a wisp of white smoke was puffing along a dark, horizontal line skirting the base of the ridge. Of course. The little train that coiled its way up to Princetown on the tortuous route I had seen on the map but had not been aware of as I had travelled up in the dark.

I was enthralled and threw on my coat, not waiting to plait my hair but allowing it to flow about my shoulders, Veronica Lake style, as it did naturally. Outside, the sky was clearing, so different from the blinding fog of the previous day. The unearthly mystery had given way to a bright sparkle. The landscape was breath-taking, begging to be explored. It made me feel nervous, excited and serene all at the same time. Lifting my spirit and giving me strength.

I hurried over to the quarry and found myself looking across a massive granite amphitheatre, ten times the size of what I had glimpsed in the mist. The lofty walls rose like a mighty fortress, opening up to a further, even more immense quarry to the right. But I wouldn't investigate further for the moment. Just now, I wanted to gain a more general picture of my surroundings and, retracing my steps, I walked back to the humble cluster of empty cottages. I glanced further along the track, beyond some other derelict buildings nestling in a dip that I hadn't noticed yesterday in the fog. To my astonishment, I spied a hundred yards or so away a large house that was very much in good repair with smoke wafting from the chimneys. Other outhouses, a tractor, two or three enclosed fields declared it a working farm. So we had neighbours after all!

Way beyond it, distant hills rose to sharp summits, not rolling gently but in strong, dramatic lines. A couple of vehicles, resembling ants at that distance, were passing along what must be the main Tavistock to Princetown Road. Beside it was a long, low building that roused my curiosity, and further along on the opposite side, I could make out what had to be Merrivale Quarry where Sidney worked.

I walked along to the farm, stopping to lean on a gate in a stone wall to watch a stout black horse in a field. When I clicked my tongue, he ambled over, ears pricked forward, and he lifted his head over the gate to blow down his nose at me. I was uncertain, but he seemed friendly enough, so I dared to lift my hand, slowly so as not to startle him, and stroked the long white patch down the front of his head. It felt warm and smooth beneath my fingers.

'Hello, young maid. You'm not lost?'

I turned and looked into the gnarled face of a small man with bandy legs and an old and ripped waxed coat. His tweed cap had seen better days, too, and his gumboots were thick with sludge. But he had a kind smile and faded eyes, and he had spoken with that lovely local accent.

'No, not really,' I told him, feeling confident in my newfound belief that the moor and everyone on it was to be trusted. 'I'm Sidney Latham's daughter. I've come to live with him. I'm out exploring.'

'Aaah,' the old fellow drawled, removing his cap

and scratching his bald pate. 'Didn't know 'er 'ad a darter, like.'

I paused for a second while my brain deciphered the dialect, but I thought I understood. 'Oh, well, we've been sort of estranged,' I explained with a smile. 'I was brought up by my grandmother in London, but she died a few weeks ago, so now I'm living here.'

I had decided on the spur of the moment that it was best to say the truth but to keep it to the barest minimum. The farmer nodded and replaced his cap. 'London, eh? Never bin mesel'. Not used to the country, eh, then?'

'No. A total stranger, I'm afraid. The horse is lovely. What's his name?'

''Er's a she. Poppy. Belongs to my darter. Tell you what, us was just 'bout to 'ave a cuppa. You wants to come in?'

'Oh, yes, please.' I followed him eagerly towards the farmhouse. I felt I had arrived, making new friends on the doorstep. I was waiting behind the old man as he pulled off his boots by the door, when a mewing cry from high above caught my attention and I looked up to see a huge brown bird circling overhead. I'd never seen anything like it. 'Gosh, what's that?' I gasped in wonder.

The farmer cocked an eyebrow skywards and grinned. 'Buzzard. S'ppose you've never seen one afore. Lookin' for 'is dinner, likely. Common on the moor. In singles, or pairs, usually. See the shape of the wings? Not like a rook. Wings like fingers, old rookie. Eh, Nora!' he called as I followed him through a small porch and into a ramshackle room. 'Got a visitor, us 'as!'

It was just as I imagined a farmhouse kitchen should be, and a woman with a beaming face and a pinny tied about her rotund figure looked up from mixing something in a bowl on a huge table.

'This is Sidney's darter, come to live with 'en. Sorry, maid, didn't get your name.'

'Lily,' I smiled back. 'Only it's Lily Hayes, not Latham. A long story.'

'Well, I never,' the woman called Nora shook her head. 'The old devil never told us he had a daughter. Well, you've met Father here, that's Barry. Barry Coleman. My husband, Mark, and Father run the farm. We've three children, two girls and a boy. All younger than you, mind. Go to school in Princetown. You going to go there?'

'No. I left school in the summer,' I explained, noticing that she was easier to understand than her father. 'I used to work in Woolworths in London. I'll be looking for work here, but I'm taking a few days to get to know the place first. Because of the fog yesterday, I've only seen the quarry so far.'

'It's 'cuz of the quarry that us is here,' Barry

nodded. 'My grandfather worked there and took on this farm – Yellowmeade us is called – when 'er retired. Then my father were a quarryman, too, but when the quarry here closed in 1906, 'er took over the farm, like. Could've gone to Swell Tor or Merrivale, but 'er preferred farmin'. Then it were my turn, wa'n it, and me an' the missis ran this place for years. She died back along, an' now Mark an' me runs it.'

'Coffee do?'

'Oh, yes, please. My father hasn't got any, and I can't drink tea.'

'With cream from our cows? Two Devonshires we've got for our own use,' Nora announced proudly. 'Keep them in the barn in the winter. Your father buys his milk from us, and his butter and cheese. Make it myself, I does.'

'Oh, yes, I've tasted it!' I enthused, taking the mug of coffee. 'It's delicious!'

'That's livin' in the country for you. Best place on earth, Dartmoor.'

'From what I've seen, it's stunning. I'm going to go exploring!'

'Well, you take care, maid. Moor's a dangerous place if you doesn't know it. Always take a compass an' a map. An' watch that sky. Mist can descend just like that. An' beware of bogs. D'you know what bog-cotton is? I'll show you later. If you sees it, take care. An' black Scottish bullocks. Bin known to charge. Most other cows roamin' on the moor is all right, unless they've got a calf.'

'Oh, dear, I think I've got a lot to learn.'

'Father'll put you off,' Nora chided fondly. 'It's not that bad. Really beautiful.'

'Best to be warned, I always say. This maid'll find it very different from London, I dare say.'

'I'm sure she will. Piece of cake to go with that, Lily? I don't know. We go for months without visitors, and then we have two in a row, first Artie and now you.'

'I 'opes the funeral went well. Lovely woman, old Mrs Franfield.'

My ears pricked up. I hadn't imagined my mystery man after all. 'Oh, is that the man who came up here yesterday? He was born in one of the cottages, he said, but his father had died at the quarry before he was born?'

'That's right. Artie Mayhew. 'Is mother, the lady what's just died, she remarried and they went to live in Tavvy, 'er new 'usband bein' a doctor, like. But they used to come up here often, and Artie and me would play together, though 'er's a bit younger. Now, the doctor's father were a wealthy man.' Barry Coleman sat back in his chair and I gained the impression he loved to tell a tale, especially one that involved reminiscing. ''Er ran what us'd call now a big antiques business in Plymouth. Artie were really interested an' went to work for 'en. Eventually, 'er in'erited the whole affair, but it were bombed out in the war, an' 'er lost almost everything. But 'er managed to build it up again, just a small place now. With 'is mother and the doc's 'elp. Very close family. I be sorry the old lady be passed on. But I can't sit 'bout talkin'. Work to do. You like to come with us, maid?'

'Oh, that's very kind,' I said reluctantly. 'I'd love to some other time, but I think I ought to go into Princetown. There's a few things I need.'

'Some other time, then. But I'll come out with you and point out bog-cotton.'

'Thank you. And thank you very much for the coffee and the lovely cake, Nora.'

'You're welcome any time, my dear. I'm sure we'll see you again soon.'

I went outside with Barry and he duly showed me the distinctive plant. 'You remember that,' he said firmly.

'Oh, I will. And thank you. Oh, what's that building over there, by the way?' I asked, pointing into the distance.

'Used to be a school. Nora went there. Closed back along. The Yanks used it during the war.'

'Dartmoor was used a lot for training the Army, wasn't it?'

'Always 'as been. An' still is. So don't you go wandering too far the other side of the road there. Come onto the firing range if you does. Marked on the map, if you've got one.'

'Yes, I have,' I assured him.

'Well, I'm going this way to check on our sheep. You take care, now.'

'I will! And I'll see you soon!'

He turned back to wave as he strode up over the moor with remarkable agility, and I made my way back to the cottage. I felt so reassured, knowing there were such good people living a stone's throw away.

A little later on, I set out for Princetown. I followed along the track in the opposite direction from the farm towards the railway halt, and another magnificent vista opened up before me. The land dipped away on the far side of the railway whose single track looped about on itself below me. My eyes swooped along the horizon and caught sunlight shimmering on the distant sea, or perhaps it was the river estuary. As I turned slowly on my heel, the endless moor cut a wild, dark slash against the open sky through all three hundred and sixty degrees. Not far away, a group of wild ponies were standing like hairy statues, long, tangled manes and flowing tails drifting in the light breeze. I was enchanted and watched as they settled to cropping the grass. I could hear the soft tug and munch of their teeth as they grazed unperturbed not ten yards away.

And that was how I suddenly felt. Free and untroubled, as if the grief was trickling from my heart. It didn't matter that Sidney was going to give me a tough time. I would need infinite patience, but I would eventually talk to him about the family I had never known. In the meantime, I would allow this sense of calm and belonging to heal me. Was that what Artie Mayhew had meant when he said the moor was alive? I was beginning to understand.

I had no idea if there was a train due that would take me into Princetown, so I decided that I would attempt to follow alongside the railway line which, from the map, seemed the most direct route. It was a splendid walk, relatively flat and with constant, far-reaching views, so that I seemed to cover the two miles in next to no time. I called in at the station to get a timetable, and then went on into the centre. I knew, again from studying my map, that the prison was just outside the main settlement, so I wasn't surprised that it wasn't visible from where I was. I found not only the shops that Sidney had described but a Post Office, a Town Hall advertising various functions, several cafés and no less than three pubs.

Amazingly, I found a pitcher and bowl set quite easily in the shop called Bolts, and when the lady learnt where I lived, she said her husband would deliver it as it would be heavy to carry, which I thought was very kind. I purchased that much-needed pair of Wellingtons from her, too, but decided there would be a wider choice of shoes in Tavistock. I also bought some Camp coffee and registered for the few items that were still on ration, including meat in one of two butchers, but it seemed that the rules were adhered to less strictly than in London! It meant I had to introduce myself, but that was no bad thing. I gained the impression that Sidney Latham wasn't particularly liked. *Miserable old bugger*, someone said. When I briefly explained my situation, rather than being eyed suspiciously as a *fureigner*, I was pitied for having to live with him.

I did mention in several places that I was looking for a job, but no one had anything to offer me, so Sidney had been right that I would probably have to work in Tavistock. I made enquiries into the bus service, but it only ran three days a week and at such unsuitable times that it wouldn't be much use. But with the train having a good connection to the mainline at Yelverton, the journey should take about three quarters of an hour, so much longer than I was used to, but it would give me my independence again.

As I sauntered back to Foggintor wearing my new wellies and carrying my shoes, I sang softly to myself, realising it was the first time I had felt like singing since Ellen had died. When I arrived home, I went in search of the old earth privies, cautiously peering into each cubicle in the little row. Oddly enough, they didn't smell at all, but they were draped with cobwebs like something out of a horror film. They were cold and draughty, and from then on, the pot in my room seemed infinitely preferable, even if it meant slopping out each morning!

I shut the last rotting door with a shudder, and decided to walk along the great mound of discarded, inferior stone on which the closets stood. Big Tip was two hundred yards long and perhaps forty foot high, and when I came to the end, I imagined I was standing in the prow of a great ship, steaming across the ocean of the moor. Sidney was a difficult man and was going to make the voyage stormy, but as I watched the sun sink, painting the sky with apricot and topaz and draping the hills in an indigo haze, I made up my mind. I was courageous – or foolhardy – enough to want to set sail.

'Did you have a good day?' I asked with a jaunty smile when Sidney arrived home not long afterwards.

He scowled. 'It was work. What do you expect?'

'I've made you a cup of tea,' I answered undaunted. 'And dinner won't be long. I got us some chops with my rations, and I'm doing potatoes and carrots and onion gravy.'

Sidney grunted with no hint of gratitude as I poured his tea. I had opened up the vents on the range and brought it up to full heat, adding a little coal when necessary. I already felt like an old hand with an acute sense of satisfaction that I had mastered it so quickly. I ignored Sidney's black humour and, as I cooked, bombarded him with a cheery relation of my day. It was like talking to a stone, but I was happy and expectant, and he was bound to come round. 'Oh, and tomorrow I'm going to Tavistock to look for a job,' I concluded.

'About time, too,' was the response.

I wanted to catch the first train of the day which passed King Tor Halt soon after half past seven. So I had to get ready at the same time as Sidney which meant washing in my freezing cold bedroom using the new china set that had been delivered as promised. But hurrying along the track soon warmed me up again. The moor was fresh and smelt of damp peat following overnight rain. After an evening incarcerated with Sidney, the invigorating sense of freedom was more than welcome!

'Hello again, maid! How you be?' my guard of the Dartmoor pixies greeted me with a broad smile as I went to purchase my ticket from him. 'Staying long?'

'For good, I hope. I'm going job-hunting in Tavistock.'

'I hopes you find summat, then. Now move along, you girls and boys!' he ordered, opening the door to a third class compartment. After all, I didn't have money to waste! 'This be... Sorry, miss, I doesn't know your name.'

'Lily Hayes.'

'Right everyone. This is Lily Hayes an' she's come to live here, so you be nice to her, or else.' He jabbed his head sternly at half a dozen school children and then winked furtively at me as he held open the door.

'Yes, Mr Renwood,' they chorused obediently as they made room for me. It was somewhat unnerving being in a compartment full of strangers who must know each other intimately, but I knew I would have to make the first move.

'You all off to school?' I asked. 'I thought there was a school in Princetown?'

'We go to the *grammar* in Tavvy,' a girl of about my age answered, smiling proudly. 'Where you from, then?'

'London,' I replied, relieved that she seemed quite friendly.

'London? What's that like?' a tubby boy of about twelve asked. 'Better 'an yere, I bet.'

'Oh, I don't know about that. The moor's beautiful.'

'Yes, it is,' the girl nodded. 'But it makes things

hard livin' at Princetown. Sally and me are in the Fifth Form doin' our O-levels. First year of them, so we're guinea pigs, really. We have so much studyin' to do, we could do without this long journey each day. And this is Pete, doin' A-levels. I'm Kate, by the way. So how old are you, Lily?'

'Fifteen. But I left school in the summer. My mum wanted me to stay on, but she's just died anyway—'

'Oh, you poor thing!'

'Thank you. So I've come to live with my estranged father at Foggintor.'

'What! Not old Long Face Latham?'

I had to chuckle. 'I'm afraid so. But...' I hesitated slightly, but decided to throw caution to the wind. 'Perhaps you can tell me something about him? I'd not met him before, and he's pretty hard to talk to.'

The boy called Pete lifted his head from the textbook he was reading. 'Don't suppose any of us can tell you much. Keeps himself to himself. Comes to chapel every Sunday. Scarcely says a word. Except to pray, of course.'

It was disappointing that none of them could tell me anything, but they were really chatty, and I arranged to meet up in Princetown with Kate and Sally the following afternoon which was Saturday. The journey down to Yelverton seemed to take no time at all, and we all changed onto the main line for Tavistock. I walked down into the town centre with them, admiring the wide square with its magnificent Town Hall on one side and the beautiful old church on the other. While they went off in one direction, they pointed me the opposite way. After elbowing through London's crowded, fume-filled streets, Tavistock was relatively quiet, yet it was still full of life with people going about their daily business. I, too, was there for a purpose. To find a job.

I turned a corner into a pleasant street lined with shops. Almost at once, I saw a branch of Boots, and then my heart gladdened as I spied a familiar shop front with large gold lettering on a red background. Woolworths. I swallowed down my sudden nerves and, shoulders back, marched straight in and asked to speak to the supervisor.

'I'm Mrs Kershaw, the manageress,' a bustling woman smiled at me as I was shown into a small office. 'I understand you're looking for work.'

She was so much more pleasant than our strait-laced manager in London had been, and I immediately felt at ease. 'Yes, I am. I've been working at the Lavender Hill branch at Clapham Common since August, but my mother's just died and I've had to come to live here with my father.'

'Oh, dear, I'm sorry to hear that. But I am actually looking for experienced extra staff for the Christmas period, and I have someone leaving in the New Year, so if you prove good enough... Tell me, what were you doing before that?'

'I was at school. My teachers wanted me to stay on, but I needed to help my mother out financially.'

It was only a partial fib, and it sounded good. Money *had* been tight, and I had enjoyed treating my mum to a little luxury each week. I had been secretly saving to buy her a television, but she had never known. I wished now I had told her.

'Ah. And what counter did you serve on?'

'I moved around. But cosmetics was my favourite.'

'Really? That's what I had in mind. Now, if you'd like to wait outside, I'll just ring through to your old branch for a reference, and if it's good, you can start on Monday.'

So, by ten o'clock, my mission was accomplished and I had the whole day free to explore the town. I was looking in the window of a shoe shop displaying the sort of stout footwear I would need to walk between the cottage and the railway halt each day, when I caught the reflection of movement from across the road. A little boy in a double-fronted coat with a velvet-trimmed collar was merrily waving a balloon attached to a string. I turned round to watch, his total absorption in his own small world bringing a smile to my lips. I was just about to return to my study of the shoe display when the string must have slipped from his hold and a gust of wind blew the balloon towards me. The child's mother was talking to another woman and was clearly taken entirely unawares when her son tugged his hand free from hers and plunged across the road after his plaything.

Whether it was sheer luck or intuition, I shall never know, but I sensed rather than saw the car that was moving down the street. It was only going slowly but the boy shot out like a bullet from a gun. I didn't stop to think. My body hurled itself in front of the car, scooping the boy into my arms. I heard the screech of brakes, felt the bumper glance off my thigh and throw me into the gutter with the child safely in my arms. And then I lay, motionless with shock while my heart thudded in my chest.

The silence lasted but a few seconds before there were people all around, kind and concerned. I handed up the boy to his hysterical mother while passers-by helped me to my feet.

'Oh, my God, are you all right?'

I was being supported upright now, and stared into the anguished face of the driver who had sprung from his car in an agony of horror. I blinked at him in a daze and nodded my head, he looked so appalled and mortified. He was young, with a mop of unruly, sandy curls and lovely, green-blue eyes that were staring at me with deep anxiety. I'm not sure who was more embarrassed, him or me.

'I'm fine,' I assured him with a smile. 'At least I think so. Just a bit bruised probably.'

'Oh, I'm so sorry—'

'No, it wasn't your fault, honestly. The little boy just—'

'Is he all right?' he gulped now, turning to the mother who was cradling her son who seemed utterly oblivious to the near accident he had caused. 'Let me look. I'm a medical student. Oh, God, I can't believe this has happened.'

''Tweren't your fault, son. We all seed it. An' the little boy's proper clever. Not a scratch.'

'Are you sure? Oh, but the young lady. Can we take her into a shop for a few minutes? You're shaking. Oh, that was so brave of you.'

'Thank you so much,' the mother was saying to me now. 'Little devil just got away from me.'

'I'm just glad I happened to see him. Really, I'm not hurt.'

'Well, if you're sure. I could take you to the hospital.'

'Please don't worry. And really, you weren't to blame. Please, go on your way.'

'If you're sure.'

'Yes, perfectly, thank you.'

The crowd had dispersed, and the young man

climbed back into his car, his brow ruched with concern. At the last second, I nearly changed my mind. Not that I was injured at all, but because he was so attractive and a real young gentleman. But he was driving slowly away, probably more shocked than I was.

After that, it was hard to concentrate on my shopping. But I eventually chose some shoes and a pair of warm slacks, and bought some thick socks and a good torch. I would need a thicker coat than my old school gabardine, but that could wait.

By three o'clock, I was ready to leave, but the next train to leave Yelverton for Princetown wasn't until ten to five. Being Friday, however, a bus was about to leave Bedford Square for the moorland village, so I caught that instead. The bus laboured steeply uphill for the entire journey, taking a far more direct route than the train. The driver promised to put me off as near to the track to Yellowmeade Farm as he could, and I settled down in the seat behind him. We hadn't gone far when a tall, slender woman in her forties climbed onto the bus, and although there weren't that many passengers, she sat down next to me, despite all my shopping.

'Hello,' she greeted me, eyeing my purchases. 'You look as if you've had a busy day. Stranger round here, aren't you?'

I should have preferred to look out of the window

at the views and contemplate the events of the day –
especially the incident with the little boy and the car
and the handsome driver thereof – but the woman
was friendly enough and I sensed her conversation
would be lively. She was smartly dressed in a thick
winter coat with a good tweed skirt showing below
and heavy brogues on her feet. Her hair was short and
permed in a modern style, and she wore lipstick and
dainty earrings. Altogether she gave the impression of
sophistication, and although there was a Devonshire
lilt to her voice, she didn't sound anything like the
other local people I had spoken to.

'Yes, I am,' I answered politely. 'I've come to live
with my father here on the moor.'

'Oh, really?' She tipped her head at me and smiled.
'Where are you from, if you don't mind my asking?'

'London.'

'Goodness me, you'll find life here very different,
I'm sure. I've been to London once. Couldn't get
back here quickly enough.'

We chatted pleasantly, and she was as eager to
point out places on the moor as I was to learn about
them. 'Have you seen any of the ancient remains
yet?' she asked.

'No, I haven't. I've seen stone rows and circles
marked on the map, though. Is that what you mean?'

She nodded with marked enthusiasm. 'That's
right. Shows people have lived and worshipped on the

moor since, well, who knows? Pre-history. And it's a very special place, don't you think? Full of mystery and so close to nature. You can understand why they worshipped gods of the earth and the sky, can't you?'

I was somewhat surprised by the unexpected question. 'Yes, I suppose the elements would seem quite mystical to people of ancient cults,' I agreed.

'And not just ancient.'

I was slightly bemused by her comment and was about to ask what she meant when the driver announced over his shoulder that we had reached the point where I should get off and he brought the bus to a halt. 'That there track leads to Yellowmeade,' he told me.

'Oh, thank you,' I answered, gathering up my purchases.

The smart woman stood up to let me out of the seat. 'Good luck, dear,' she said as I squeezed past. 'Perhaps we'll meet again.'

I watched the bus trundle off up the hill, a little nonplussed. Had the woman been about to tell me that strange things happened on the moor even now, or merely that she found the moor an amazingly inspirational place? I wondered what my Ellen would have made of what the woman had said? Stuff and nonsense, probably. And as I crossed the road to the track, I smiled to myself as I heard her voice in my head.

Chapter Four

I kept my promise. On Saturday morning, I washed some smalls – wondering how on earth we managed towels and sheets – and then walked into Princetown. I found Kate's house in Hessary Terrace easily enough. When she opened the door, Sally was at her shoulder and as I stepped inside, I was nearly knocked over by two little boys roaring past me as they pretended to be air-raid bombers.

'Ooops, sorry!' Kate laughed. 'I did warn you! Eldest of eight, me.'

'Golly, how do you manage?' I was amazed. There seemed to be children everywhere, but unlike Jeannie's crowded home in London, all was neat and tidy.

'Oh, Dad has us all regimented to do our own jobs. That's what comes of havin' a prison officer for a father.' She gave a mock salute, and grinned.

'Hey, Mum, this is Lily, the new girl I told you about on the train.'

A voluminous woman with frizzy permed hair welcomed me with a broad smile from the open door to the kitchen. 'Why don't you go up to the bedroom and play some music? I'll bring you up some sandwiches. That all right, Lily?'

'Yes, that would be lovely, thank you.'

I followed Kate and Sally up the stairs. I knew at once this was a happy household, just what I needed to lift my spirits. There were bunks and a narrow single bed with another younger girl lying on it on her front, reading a magazine.

'Budge up!' Kate commanded. 'Lily, this is my sister, Doreen. Dor, wind up the gramophone, will you? What shall we listen to? Sorry it's a bit cramped, Lily. Only we don't have a sittin' room. Mum and Dad have to use it as a bedroom.'

There was only one way to describe Kate's home, and that was relaxed and noisy. 'How do you manage to do your homework?' I marvelled, remembering how I always liked total silence to do mine.

'Easy,' Sally shrugged. 'We go to my house. Like a morgue, that is. But I am an only child. My dad's a prison officer, too, only he usually works nights so we have to be like mice during the day while he's asleep. We did half our homework there this morning. Now, what'll it be? Old Blue Eyes?' she asked, shuffling through half a dozen seventy-eights on a shelf.

My heart really felt light and I enjoyed myself so much, chatting, dancing in the few feet of available space and not thinking at all about Sidney, that I was quite shocked when I looked at my watch. 'Oh, goodness, I must go! I've got to do the shopping and catch the four o'clock train back to the halt.'

'Oh, what a shame! But you will come again next week?'

'I'll be working on Saturdays from now on,' I answered, genuinely disappointed. 'But I'll see you on the train each morning.'

'Tell you what, there's a pre-Christmas dance at the Town Hall the Saturday after next. Why don't you come? It'll be fun!'

'That sounds great!' But then my heart sank again. 'I can't, though, can I? I wouldn't be able to get home afterwards. I don't fancy walking across the moor at night.'

Kate pulled a long face. 'Can't stay here, I'm afraid. No room. And my Dad doesn't have a car so he can't drop you home.'

'Mine neither,' Sally put in. 'He'd be on duty, anyway, and Mum doesn't like people coming to stay.'

'Oh, well, never mind. I'll see you both on Monday morning, anyway.'

I tried not to think about it as I did the shopping, but I did feel frustrated. Those few hours spent with

Kate and Sally had made me feel *normal* again, but it wasn't going to last. And before I knew it, I was letting myself into the cottage and back into Sidney's dour company.

'Oh, there you are,' he greeted me as I struggled in with the shopping. 'You've saved me some time, so I've got everything ready for the bath, instead of doing it later.'

I dumped the basket and three string-bags on the table, and felt the knot of apprehension as I took in the tin bath he must have dragged in from one of the outhouses. Every available pot and pan was squeezed onto the range which I could feel by the warmth in the kitchen had been stoked up as hot as it would go.

'You can go first.'

I thought I detected a begrudging tone in his voice, but assuming we had to share the water, I was grateful for small mercies. As I unpacked the shopping, I could see Sidney pouring steaming water from the pans into the bath, refilling them from a line of buckets and replacing them on the range.

'Right, I'll be upstairs. Shout when you've finished.'

I stood for a few seconds and stared. This was hardly what I was used to, but there was nothing for it. I drew the curtains. It was almost dark outside, and Sidney had already lit one of the oil-lamps. I took a deep breath, and began to strip off. Then I realised there was no lock on the door, and uneasiness churned in my stomach. I took one of the chairs and jammed the back under the door handle. It was the best I could do.

There was barely three inches of near-boiling water in the bottom of the rough, galvanised tub, hardly enough to get myself wet in, and the tin bath itself looked decidedly uninviting. I added a little cold from one of the buckets and stepped in, cautiously, shuddering, feeling utterly degraded. I sat down, noticing the odd spot of rust and wondering if I wouldn't get out dirtier than I got in. There would be no lying back comfortably, wallowing in bath-cube scented ripples and turning on the gas wall-heater tap to top it up. I quickly lathered myself all over and scooped up water to rinse off the soap. Exposed to the air, my wet skin went straight into goose-pimples and I abandoned any thought of washing my hair. The water was already only lukewarm and I got straight out, shivering with cold and revulsion. The whole experience had brought tears to my eyes. I wanted to go home. But someone else was moving into our old house that very day. And anyway, Mum wasn't there. She was lying in a hole in the ground.

'You're not coming to chapel in those!' Sidney thrust his head towards my new trousers on Sunday morning.

I met his glare with a challenging lift of my chin. 'Chapel?'

'Of course,' he snapped. 'Your grandfather was a preacher and he'd turn in his grave if—'

'Was he?' My eyebrows lifted with genuine interest. Was this an opportunity to find out something about my family? My heart began to race. 'I assume you mean *your* father?'

'Yes, of course I do, you stupid child.'

'And was he very strict?'

'He'd certainly make you go to chapel decently dressed.'

'I don't think he would, make me go to chapel, I mean.'

'I suppose that woman brought you up as a heathen, then, did she?'

I was seething. If he might have been able to persuade me to go with him, I certainly wasn't going now! Not after hearing him speak of my mother like that. Again! 'No, she didn't. She was Chapel, just like you. Only she didn't ram her religion down my throat.'

'So you're not coming, then?'

'No.'

We stared at each other, horns locked, for all of ten seconds before Sidney went out, slamming the door behind him, and I breathed a sigh of relief. So his father had been a Methodist preacher. Well, that perhaps explained Sidney's religious verve. I wondered what his mother had been like. A mouse, dominated by her husband, or – dare I say it – more like me?

I had bought a cheap hand and spring joint with our coupons and it would take all morning to roast. I actually found keeping an eye on the range quite satisfying. Not only had I mastered the thing when Sidney had doubted I could, but there was a strange sense that I was living as the occupants of the cottage had done a hundred years before. As Artie Mayhew's mother would have done. I wondered if I would ever see him again.

Sidney returned in a better mood and actually commented on the delicious meal, which was encouraging. By the time we had finished and cleared away, it was so late that if I'd walked into Princetown to see my new friends, I'd just about have time to say hello before I'd have to set out for home if I was to get back before dark. And then I remembered my odd encounter on the bus, and decided to go and take a quick look at the Merrivale stone row which should be easy to find being not so far from the main road.

The sky was low with a canopy of dense, white cloud, and as I stood on that wild, exposed spot on that first Sunday afternoon just into December, I could understand why ancient man could find some sacred significance in such surroundings. I could somehow imagine some strange ritual being conducted there by a mythical figure in a long robe with a grizzled, ancient face and grey hair blowing in the wind.

I shook my head, mystified by the fanciful vision that had drawn itself in my brain. I stayed there for a few minutes, allowing the atmosphere to soak into my soul, and it made me feel close to Ellen, as if her shadow had brushed against my shoulder. Then I shivered, and as I turned for home, the first snowflakes began to fall.

I reckon it must have snowed all night. When I drew my curtains at half past six the next morning, whiteness glowed at me through the darkness and heavy flakes were driving against the window pane. I shivered. Just what I needed on my first morning at work! I prayed the snow wouldn't make me arrive late.

I decided to pull my new thick socks on over my nylons, wear my Wellingtons and carry my shoes. Thank goodness I did. The snow was so deep as I battled my way through a near blizzard that it came over the top of my boots several times as I trudged through the white sea no one else had trod before. It was only just light, and with icy needles lashing into my face, I was worried I wouldn't find my way in the unfamiliar landscape. But there was the faithful little train chugging through the pearly blanket that covered the moor, and as it reached the halt, Kate opened the door to wave to me.

My cheeks puffed out with a ponderous sigh as I sank onto the seat next to her. 'Oh, gosh, I didn't know if I'd make it! The snow's so deep.'

Sally grinned back. 'Oh, you'll get used to it. We have snow every winter. This is nothing. I remember that winter, forty-six to seven, wasn't it? We had drifts as high as houses. The train really got stuck then, and they had to call in the Navy from Plymouth to dig it out.'

'Oh, yes, I remember that winter,' I chimed in. It was good to have my new friends to chat with as it stopped me from thinking about my new job. I wasn't exactly nervous, but I wondered what the people would be like that I'd be working with. 'I must have been nine,' I went on. 'London ground to a halt and we didn't have to go to school for—' I broke off as we juddered to a halt, and I glanced fearfully at my new friends as Kate stuck her head out of the window.

'Oh, just a drift,' she announced cheerfully. 'Mr Gough will get us through.'

The train reversed. Oh, no, we weren't going back to the station? But then we suddenly raced forward again at full pelt, faltered slightly and then ploughed onward with snow spraying up past the windows.

'There we are. Told you so. Nothing to worry about. Train always gets through. Not like on the roads. Dangerous, they'll be.'

I could well imagine! And I was so grateful for the little moorland railway that was going to play such a part in my life. As I chatted to Kate and Sally, and their friend Peter who for once didn't have his nose in a book, and thought of my new future here on Dartmoor, I wondered what Jeannie would think if she could see me.

30th March, 1953

Dear Jeannie,

I haven't heard from you since Christmas, so I hope you are all right. I know you're not a great writer, but I'd love to hear from you. I think of you such a lot. I imagined the jolly Christmas you'd have had with your family. Mine was so dull.

Huh! That was a bit of an understatement! The highlight had been going to chapel with Sidney on Christmas morning. I'd quite enjoyed it, actually, singing carols and with everyone in happy mood. I'd even seen Kate to wave to. But back at the cottage, the mood had been sombre. We had a normal dinner, nothing special at all, no crackers, no jokes or silly hats. I wanted to cry as I recalled the happy day I should have been spending with my mum. But

I forced the memories aside. That was then, and this was now. Surely I should take advantage of it somehow. Our daily life was normally so busy that I had never felt the atmosphere was right to approach Sidney with the questions I was burning to ask. But when darkness closed in at five o'clock on Christmas Day, and with nothing else to distract us, I dared to consider the time had come.

We had been sitting in silence reading. I was delving into Rumer Godden's *Black Narcissus*, one of my favourite books that transported me to the exotic climes of the Himalayas. At least, it did usually, but now I found it difficult to concentrate as I summoned up my courage. A hot slick of sweat broke over my skin as I ventured, 'You... you never speak about my mother. What was she like?'

The room sizzled with tension. Sidney lifted his head, his eyes scorching into me so that I recoiled against the back of the chair. I'd clearly made a mistake.

'I don't want to talk about her,' my father barked, dropping his gaze back to his Bible. That was it. Subject dismissed.

I sucked in my lips. I felt half scared of him, but why should I be? My heart was pumping as I faltered, 'I know it must be painful for you, but don't you think I have a right? I don't know anything about her.'

His roar broke the general quiet so suddenly that

I jerked on my seat. 'Your mother was a conniving strumpet. Now is that good enough for you?'

Ice ran through my veins, freezing solid somewhere below my ribs. I must have heard wrong. But I hadn't. I was shocked to the core. I had imagined all along that Sidney had never mentioned my mother out of grief, not anger, and now... It was unbearable. My bottom lip was quivering. I felt let down, enraged, bitter, but above all *deprived*. Would I ever dare to ask him again? It had been Christmas Day, and yet I was in a pit of despair. Tears misted my vision, blurring the words as I had tried in vain to return to my book. I had felt lost. Ashamed almost, so that I couldn't even tell Jeannie about it, so I continued the letter on an entirely different tack.

The people I work with are all very nice, but we don't have the fun you and I did. I get on very well with our supervisor, too. I have Wednesday afternoons off, of course, and sometimes I go to the pictures in Tavistock. I saw Cry the Beloved Country *and* Rebecca *recently. Have you seen them? Then I catch the same train home as my friends at the school. The weather here's been quite spring-like the last few days, so at lunchtimes, I've had my sandwiches sitting by the old canal in the park and feeding the ducks. I keep hoping I'll meet that handsome young man who nearly knocked me down in his car. I'm sure you remember me telling you about it. Wasn't* his fault, and he was gorgeous, but I haven't seen him since.

The other thing that's happened with the better weather is a tradition on the train. I wondered what was going on! As I got on at the halt the other day, a couple of the schoolboys got off and began to run down a grassy track. Apparently they race the train! The railway has to make a great loop around King Tor because of the gradient and then comes right the way back on itself, nearly two miles altogether, whereas the grassy track that cuts across is only about a quarter of a mile. If the train wins, Mr Gough, the driver, waits for them to catch up! I was a bit late getting to the halt one morning and I was worried because there's no other way to get to work, but bless Mr Gough, the train was waiting for me! Imagine that in London?

And I must tell you this. The other day, Mr Gough was leaning out of the cab window as the driver does, and he had such a huge sneeze that his false teeth flew out of his mouth and landed somewhere in the grass. Well, he stopped the train and we all got out to look for them. It was just so funny! And then someone found them and gave them back to Mr Gough and off we went again!

I paused, giggling at the memory and imagining Jeannie laughing as she read the letter. Oh, how I'd love Jeannie to be here to share all these new experiences with me. I liked Kate and Sally, but it wasn't quite the same. My heart clenched with regret, but there was something I could do about it.

Oh, Jeannie, I'd love you to see all this, and the moor. You can't imagine how wild and enormous it is. I go exploring whenever I can. Wouldn't you like to come and stay with me for a week in the summer? We'd have such a laugh! Do write soon and say yes! And tell me all about what's going on in London.

With lots of love,

Lily.

I read through the letter before I folded it and put it into the envelope. It made me sound so happy, which in some ways I was. But I couldn't tell Jeannie how my father remained like a closed book, and that I had discovered nothing from him about my family. My brothers had been called Eric and David was all I had dragged out of him. When he had told me, I could see the pain on his face. I hadn't intruded further.

Chapter Five

Apart from Sundays when I tried to spend a few hours with Kate and Sally, my favourite time was Wednesday afternoon, the one day in the week I arrived home before Sidney rather than after half past seven. As the evenings lengthened, I used that extra daylight to explore, mainly the quarry whose colossal dimensions never ceased to enthral me. Wednesday was also the only occasion when I was the first to see any post, which, as with many outlying addresses, was delivered later in the day, the isolated cottage being more easily reached on horseback.

It was on one such afternoon in mid-April that I eagerly picked up a letter from the mat, hoping it might be a reply from Jeannie. It wasn't. Instead, I found a brown, official-looking envelope, addressed to my father. I frowned. I had noticed that he had received several such letters of late, but to my knowledge, they had ended up in the range firebox. I was beginning to wonder what it was all about, and a niggling doubt took seed in my mind. My eyes kept being drawn back to the envelope as it sat on the table, as if it was one of those giant house-spiders. I expected it at any moment to raise itself up on eight hairy legs and scamper across towards me. It was somehow equally as menacing, and I eyed it warily.

Up until then, it had been too cold to be in my room for very long, but that afternoon I went upstairs to listen to some music to keep my mind off the letter.

'Would you mind if I got a gramophone?' I had dared to ask one evening, trying to sound light-hearted about it. 'I'd only play it in my room, of course, and not loudly.'

Sidney glared at me, his eyes like flaming coals. 'Ungodly, sinful things!' he snarled. 'So, no, you may not have one.'

The hope plummeted to my feet, but surely it was a reasonable request. 'Oh, please!' I cajoled. 'What harm is there in enjoying a little music? You sing hymns, don't you? I promise I wouldn't play anything noisy. Except the 'Eighteen Twelve Overture', perhaps. You know. Tchaikovsky. With the canons.'

I could see the incomprehension on his face. I had learnt that he liked to think he was better educated than he was, and refused to admit to ignorance in any way. I thought everyone knew the 'Eighteen Twelve', but I supposed many people of my father's generation had probably never had access to such things. Knowing what pleasure recorded music had always brought me, I felt a twinge of pity.

'You'd probably like it,' I said quickly, taking advantage of his momentary retreat before he came back to snap at me again. 'I like classical music best, with nice melodies. I promise I wouldn't play anything you disapproved of.'

I didn't add that there were some modern records I liked, such as Frankie Laine singing 'I Believe', but even that was a ballad. I waited, holding my breath. Sidney raised his chin, inhaling deeply through his nostrils to emphasise that he was in charge.

'All right. But I don't expect to hear it playing every hour of the day and night.'

'You won't, I promise. And thank you.'

And so, on that afternoon when the letter lurked on the kitchen table, I wound up the gramophone handle and let my mind drift away with the few seventy-eights I possessed. I gazed out of the window, the dulcet tones of some philharmonic orchestra or other enhancing the spectacular views over the moor. Then I lay on my sagging bed with my eyes closed as I contemplated my life as it now was. I wished things weren't as they were with Sidney. Nothing would have pleased me more than to talk to him about the family I had never known, but whenever I broached the subject, I was vehemently rebuffed. But I lived in hope that one day, he would open up.

When it was time he was due home, I went downstairs to have a cup of tea waiting for him. For dinner, we were just having spam fritters with leftovers made into bubble and squeak, so there wasn't much preparation to do. I had some ironing, though, which I always put off as long as possible. Using a flat iron heated on the range was the one thing I struggled with.

'There's a letter for you,' I announced, nodding my head towards the table, and for some reason, my heart began to beat nervously.

Sidney put on his spectacles and his eyes narrowed as he tore open the envelope. I pretended to busy myself at the range but I was watching him furtively. I was appalled as his face turned the colour of ripe mulberries, his cheeks bloating so that he resembled some unnatural gargoyle. For a few seconds, I was frightened as he looked as if he was about to have a fit and, indeed, he staggered sideways. But then he pushed past me, crumpling the letter into a ball and throwing it into the range firebox before storming outside.

Quick as a flash, I grabbed the oven-gloves to turn the handle. The paper was just beginning to catch and I hooked it out, stamping the tiny flames with the back of the gloves until they were extinguished. The edges were curled and scorched, but the main text was still readable. And although I think it was the only really dishonest thing I had done in my life, I somehow felt compelled to read someone else's correspondence. As it happened, I would have found out sooner or later, so I suppose it didn't matter.

At the time, though, I was so shocked that my heart flipped over in my chest. Sidney had, apparently, been ignoring letters to quit the property. The cottages had been condemned as unfit for habitation and demolition was due to start at the beginning of next month.

It was my turn to feel weak at the knees and I lowered myself unsteadily into a chair. I had been flabbergasted at the lack of facilities at the cottage when I had arrived, but life there had provided a challenge and had been quite an adventure. But it had never really struck me that my new home could have been deemed uninhabitable. I had seen people struggling in appalling, overcrowded conditions in London as a result of the Blitz destroying so many thousands of homes, and our cottage seemed somewhat peaceful after that. Quarrymen and their families had lived at Foggintor for a hundred years, and it struck me like a flash of lightning that I had *enjoyed* living here. And now it was to end. From the letter, Sidney had first

been told about it six months before, so why had he
ignored the eviction notices? Not for my sake, I was
sure. But whatever the truth of the matter, it seemed I
was now to be homeless again.

The peace of the moor, feeling part of it with all
my new friends in my daily life, had been healing my
grief over Ellen, but now all the suppressed emotion
flooded back. I knew that I had coped with my loss
by convincing myself that Ellen's death was merely
part of the eternal plan of timelessness that Dartmoor
inspired in me. But knowing that, once again, I had
nowhere to live, brought the misery crashing down
around me.

I took a deep, calming breath and shook my head
as I threw out the self-pity. This really wouldn't do.
Ellen had coped with the tragic death of her daughter
and two grandchildren and, in later years, her dear
husband. And here was I, crying because I could no
longer live in a damp, crumbling, condemned hovel
in the middle of nowhere.

I got to my feet, pursing my lips defiantly as I
prepared myself to face Sidney and marched outside
to the garden. My heart was battering against my
ribs as I waved the letter in the air and strode up to
Sidney, planting myself before him.

'Why have you been ignoring these letters?' I
demanded, bracing my shoulders.

Sidney stopped what he was doing and thrust the

garden spade hard into the earth. He glared at me, his face wild with anger, and I reared up my head to challenge his gaze.

'How dare you read my post!' he yelled. I'm sure they must have heard him down in Tavistock.

'Just as well I did!' I retorted. 'When were you going to tell me? When the bulldozers move in?'

'Don't you be so cheeky!'

'Well, what are you going to do about it? We've only got a few weeks to find a new home!'

'And where do you suggest we go to live?' he barked at me. 'It suits me living here, with no one to interfere in my life. I can forget about the past and keep myself to myself. At least I could until *you* came along. And how am I supposed to get to work from anywhere else? Answer me that, clever brain! Living here, I can just walk to the quarry.'

'Get a car and drive, like other people do,' I sighed with exasperation.

'Drive?' His eyes suddenly bulged out like a frog's. It was so frightening that I had already taken a step backwards when he bawled, 'No! I'll never drive, not *ever*!'

His voice crackled viciously, sending an icy shiver through my limbs. I couldn't understand the fury in his reply, and I wasn't going to wait for an explanation. I spun on my heel and fled out of the walled garden. I was confused and torn, my anxiety turning to bitterness as I ran down the track, driving my anger into the ground beneath my feet.

'Where you'm going in such a hurry, maid?'

I almost collided with Barry Coleman as he dropped down onto the track near the farm. He must have been out on the moor checking livestock as he had the two dogs with him. Seeing him at once calmed my irritation with my insufferable father.

'Oh, nowhere in particular,' I answered, coming to an abrupt halt.

'You wants to come in? And, oh, look! We've a visitor. That's Artie's car.'

Oh, yes! Artie Mayhew, my phantom of the mist. I hadn't seen him since my very first day at the cottage. 'Oh, it'll be lovely to meet him again,' I said enthusiastically, so glad of something to divert my thoughts.

I followed Barry into the now familiar kitchen, and sure enough, sitting at the table with Nora was the elderly man I had met before. He recognised me straight away.

'Hello, there. Nice to see you again,' he smiled. 'How you getting on?'

'Fine, thank you. I've settled in well. And I've got a job in Tavistock. In Woolworths. This is my afternoon off.'

'Ah, I see,' he said pleasantly. 'But you haven't looked up my brother and his family at all?'

'Well, no,' I admitted. 'To be honest, I've been pretty busy. I have lots of new friends here, so I don't actually find I have that much time.'

'That's good, then!' Artie beamed. 'And everything's all right with you, like?'

'Well, yes, except that I've just learnt they're going to be pulling down the cottages, so we'll have to find somewhere else to live.'

I wished I hadn't blurted it out as Artie's face paled before he gave a forlorn smile. 'Well, I suppose it had to happen some day. Life moves on, doesn't it?'

No one knew that better than I did myself, but talking to Artie Mayhew and my good friends, the Colemans, had soothed my agitation. As I walked back to the cottage, I reflected on what Artie had said. Life moves on. Certainly I felt as if I had begun to step out of my grief over Ellen. The peace of the moor had been my salvation, and I didn't want to go backwards. Sidney, too, had said that he wanted to forget the past. But forget what exactly? That my mother and brothers had been killed over twelve years ago? Surely that was time enough? Not to forget, because you could never do that. But enough to be able to talk to me about them? At least about my brothers. But why he had spoken so bitterly about my mother, I had yet to discover. Now clearly wasn't the time to press him.

* * *

'Right,' I announced when Sidney arrived home the following Wednesday evening. 'We're moving on Saturday. To Albert Terrace in Princetown. I arranged it all this afternoon.'

'You've done *what*? What the devil do you think—'

'Mr Cribbett, you know, the coalman—'

'Yes, I know perfectly well who he is.'

'He's kindly agreed to bring his lorry at two o'clock on Saturday. I'll be at work, of course, but you won't. And you can see I had some empty boxes delivered from Bolts, so we can start packing. You can sign the lease on Saturday afternoon when you get there.'

'Oh, I can, can I?'

Not only had I been practising my opening speech and had spilt it out quite rehearsed, but I was also ready for Sidney's tirade. I hadn't lived with him for four and a half months without learning how stubborn and unreasonable he could be wherever I was concerned.

'Well, one of us had to do something,' I replied sharply. 'If we'd waited until we were thrown out, we might not have been able to find anywhere to live. As it is, I've found us a nice little terraced house with electric light and running water—'

'And how do you expect me to afford that?'

I clenched my jaw for a moment, and at my sides,

my hands balled into fists as I struggled to contain my resentment. After all the trouble I had been to, I felt galled at Sidney's ingratitude. 'I'm sure we can manage,' I succeeded in saying in a level tone. 'Other workmen do, and most of them have wives and a clutch of children to support. I don't know what you do with your wages,' and indeed I often wondered, 'but I'm sure you can afford it. I'll contribute what I can, you know that. Anyway, I don't see that we've much choice, unless you've a better idea.'

His eyes had been flaming into mine, but now I saw the muscles about his mouth slacken in defeat. I almost felt sorry for him as relief overtook my own determination.

'For what it's worth,' I admitted in a sympathetic whisper, 'I've really enjoyed living here, too. The peace and quiet have brought me some kind of comfort. Helped me accept my grandmother's death. And that I had another mother and brothers I never knew about before.'

I saw his eyes flash. It had been a mistake to mention them, and I cursed myself. I must swing the conversation around before he jumped down my throat again, but at the same time, I felt a pang of compassion. 'Look, we're in this together. You might even enjoy having people around, and you don't have to live out of your neighbours' pockets. I've even spoken to the wife of one of your workmates,

Mr Mead, and she says she's sure he'll give you a lift into work each day.'

I stopped, waiting for his reaction. It wouldn't have surprised me if he had come back with some cutting response, but he merely raised an eyebrow.

'You've got it all worked out then,' he observed.

'It seemed the best thing to do. It'll be heartbreaking to see this place pulled down, mind. I'll miss it.'

'Not as much as I will,' he moaned.

I'm sure it was true. Though it clawed at my soul to see the humble stone dwellings being turned into uninhabitable shells, it must have been far more hurtful to people like my father and especially Artie Mayhew who had known them as a thriving community. The cottages weren't totally demolished at first, but were stripped of their roofs and all internal timbers. The granite stones and sections of wall that collapsed in the process were left where they fell, a soulful remnant of the bustling quarrymen's hamlet.

Though I missed drawing my curtains each morning to the spectacular and treasured views of the moor, life in Princetown had its compensations. As far as the house itself was concerned, although there was no mains gas and I still had to cook on a range, we at least had electric light and an outside flushing lavatory. Once again, we had a parlour that was never used or heated, but the whole house seemed that much warmer. And, of course, the shops were on our doorstep so I didn't have to lug heavy bags home any more as Sidney always left the purchasing of provisions to me nowadays.

I had just popped into Bolts for some cocoa powder on my first Wednesday afternoon. I had only seen our neighbours on one side, and so when I saw the back of a smartly dressed lady struggling to open the gate on the other side, I was grateful for the opportunity to introduce myself.

'Oh, let me help you,' I said, leaping forward eagerly. 'I'm your new neighbour.'

I dutifully opened the gate, but when the woman turned to thank me, the smile froze on my face. Good Lord, it was the mysterious woman I had met on the bus. I had gone to all those lengths to move next door to her!

'Oh, hello, my dear,' she smiled back. 'How are you? What a lovely surprise!'

'Er, yes, isn't it?' I stammered.

'Would you like to come in for a coffee?' she went on. 'Don't drink tea, do you?'

How on earth did she know that? To my dismay, she must have seen my frown. 'I overheard you in the shop one day some time ago,' she laughed. 'I don't think you saw me.'

She was looking at me with her head on one side,

and I couldn't help but smile back, even though I still wasn't sure quite what to make of her.

'Oh, I see,' I answered. 'Thank you for the offer, but I won't come in. I've got to get the dinner ready.'

'All right, then. But another time. We must be friends.'

Friends? Well, I wasn't too sure about that!

'Oh, it's super havin' you here in the village!'

Kate waltzed me down the narrow hallway of her house. It was Saturday evening and I'd just got off the train from work. There was a dance at the Town Hall, and I had gone straight to Kate's house to get ready, having left my change of clothes there the night before. Sidney had complained, but Kate's mother had convinced him that I wasn't about to launch myself into a den of iniquity. It wasn't just a dance for youngsters. People of all ages went to these affairs. When you lived in such an isolated community, this sort of entertainment was seen as a family event, attended by everyone.

'Look, I got some new lipstick today,' I said, delving into my bag. 'What do you think? It's deep pink rather than red. More subtle, I thought.'

'Oh, yes, that's nice! Suits your colourin'. Have all the boys after you!' Kate teased, grinning broadly.

I shrugged. 'I'm not interested in boys. I just

want to have a good time. Let my hair down, as they say.'

Kate threw me a sideways glance. 'Oh, come on! We're all on the lookout for a boy! You can't tell me you're any different!'

'Well, I suppose if the right one came along. But quite honestly, I just want to enjoy myself. My father's so solemn, it's just good to get out of the house.'

'Well, we'll have to make sure you have a great time tonight, then, won't we?'

She winked at me, and I gave a wide smile. I was really looking forward to the evening, rather than sitting at home with Sidney. But it was true I wasn't out to find a boyfriend. I still had a picture in my mind of the young man with the car in Tavistock. Although I had told Jeannie about him, I somehow felt I couldn't confess my silly daydream to Kate. It was special, and I wasn't ready to share such things with her.

We had a super time at the dance, though, and I met some of Kate and Sally's other friends from Princetown. We jitterbugged, hokey-cokeyed and conga-ed to a local band, laughing outrageously. I had a quickstep with Peter, but while he danced the last waltz with Sally, Kate and I partnered each other. I thoroughly enjoyed myself, forgetting for a few hours the stiff and starchy atmosphere in our house in Albert Terrace.

They showed films at the Town Hall as well, twice a week, so I started going there of an evening, either alone or with Kate or Sally, if their homework schedule allowed. So on Wednesday afternoons, instead of going to the cinema in Tavistock, I came straight home and went for a walk on the moor. I always had a particular aim in mind, a tor, a waterfall, or a stone row or circle. I imagined strange, ancient people worshipping the sun that gave them life and the moon that gave them the seasons. Could it possibly be that *my neighbour* still came out to these places to perform intriguing rituals? I wasn't sure if I was fascinated or scared. She still seemed so *pleasant*, and I couldn't help but like her. She greeted me cheerily whenever I saw her, but I knew little more about her apart from her name, Gloria Luckett, and that she lived alone with – guess what – a black cat!

The second of June that year was, of course, the coronation of Queen Elizabeth the Second, and I was really looking forward to the celebrations Princetown had been planning for months. It wasn't easy, what with sugar, dairy products and meat still on ration. Sally's mother had been on the committee, and so for weeks we had heard titbits of tantalising information. When the big day came, though, it was cold and miserable, more like winter than the beginning of summer.

As usual, Sidney was up at the crack of dawn. When I came down, he was reading as he consumed a breakfast of tea and toast, and he looked up at me over his spectacles. No doubt he took a dim view of me coming down late and wearing my dressing-gown, but I wasn't going to let him spoil my anticipation of a wonderful day.

'Good morning!' I smiled, and to my surprise he smiled back. 'What a pity it's such a rotten day,' I said, encouraged. 'You are coming to the public tea this afternoon, aren't you?'

'I think I'll give it a miss. But you go.'

I wasn't sure if I was pleased or disappointed. I wouldn't want to sit with him instead of my friends, but by the same token, it might bring him out of himself if he had people all around. I just couldn't understand why he seemed to shun company so much.

'You sure you won't come? And this morning I've been invited to Sally's house to watch the ceremony on television. They've bought one especially. The reception's terrible here, though, all fuzzy.'

'Unnatural, that's why.'

'Well, yes, maybe. I certainly don't understand how it works.' I had been making myself some coffee and now I sat down at the table to drink it. My father seemed in a good mood and I immediately began to wonder if I couldn't take advantage of it. For six months now I had been biding my time, yearning to find out about my lost family. Well, my brothers, anyway. I'd long given up expecting Sidney to talk about my mother.

'I was looking at the photographs of Eric and David last night,' I began tentatively, feeling sweat oozing from my skin. I saw him glance at me daggers and my heart bounced in my chest, but he slowly put down his book. Every nerve in my body stretched.

'You're not going to be satisfied until I tell you about them, are you?'

I somehow managed to hold his withering stare, and yet my heart leapt with expectancy. 'I know it must be painful for you,' I said with compassion I truly felt, 'but they were my brothers and it would be nice to know just a little bit about them.'

'Not much to say, really, when you're only four and six when you're killed,' he answered, bitterness harsh on his tongue. 'Eric was more serious and very bright, and David was a scamp. They were two lovely little boys, and God took them from me and just left you. Now if you're satisfied, just leave me alone, will you?'

I lowered my eyes. What had I expected? At least he hadn't bitten my head off.

'Yes, I'm sorry,' I murmured, feeling the heat in my cheeks. 'Thank you.'

Later, I went off to Sally's house, trying to hide the

hurt inside me. As we watched the black and white images, I gradually began to feel better, marvelling that we could see what was going on nearly three hundred miles away, even if it did look as if it was snowing!

'Bit like a weddin', isn't it?' Kate said dreamily.

'Yes, I suppose it is,' I agreed. 'But then she's being married to her role as monarch, I suppose.'

'Like nuns get married to the church?'

'Exactly so,' Sally's father nodded gravely. 'Now then, who's for some lemonade to drink Her Majesty's health?'

It was the start of more jollifications, and as we all trooped off to the tea later that afternoon, it seemed that everyone from Princetown – except my father – was out to enjoy themselves. We sat at long trestle tables and gorged ourselves on spam and egg sandwiches, jam tarts and fairy cakes that had been cooked by an army of willing helpers.

'Proper good spread, that!' Kate declared, smacking her lips. 'Now, you comin' back to my house till the bonfire, Lily?'

'Oh, yes, please! I don't fancy going back to my father just yet.' I didn't add that, although we hadn't had words that morning, there had been that unwelcome tension. At long last, I'd learnt just a little about my brothers. I had the feeling I'd never know any more. Had the time come for me to hand in my notice and return to London? No. With Kate and Sally, and all the other friends I had made, I felt this was now my home.

As on hills and high places throughout the country, the inhabitants of Princetown had built a gigantic bonfire that was lit as dusk melted into darkness. People spilt out of every door, cramming the roads, and I was amazed at how many faces I knew, shopkeepers, the men from the railway, prison workers and others who were employed by the Duchy of Cornwall Estates. I spotted Barry Coleman with Mark and Nora and their children and I called across, but they couldn't hear me above the clamour of hundreds of happy voices. The bonfire crackled and blazed, sending tangerine and russet sparks to snuff themselves out in the sable dome of the sky, all quite magical in the chill June night.

'When's they fireworks startin'?' Kate asked impatiently as she was jostled against me. 'Cold, innit? Wish we could get nearer that fire, instead of havin' that silly cordon.'

'That's to keep you safe,' Sally told her, rubbing her hands together. 'Wish I'd brought some gloves, mind.'

'Certainly wouldn't think it was June,' I agreed. 'Oh, look!'

The first rocket spiralled into the darkness with a whooshing shriek and exploded in a vault of gold and silver stars that glittered like diamonds as they floated earthwards. The crowd gasped and clapped, all heads turned towards the sky. Another rocket followed, and another, all the colours of the rainbow, emerald, crimson, turquoise and gold, shimmering in the blackness and filling the air with sulphurous smoke. I was sandwiched between my two friends, and the excitement glowing on their faces was reflected in my own heart. I felt happier than at any time since Ellen had died. Nothing could bring her back, but I knew now I could find contentment again.

After the rockets came a display of fireworks on a specially constructed gantry, Catherine wheels spinning crazily in mesmerising swirls and dripping sparkling shards onto the grass below, and golden fountains and pyramids of twinkling spangles blossoming like flaming bushes.

'Hello, girls! Enjoying it?'

'Hello, Pete! Yes, good, isn't it? Gosh, look at—'

I didn't get any further. We all suddenly realised that anxious voices were shouting aloud, telling us all to run. We exchanged glances, not sure what on earth was going on as the crowd began to move backwards. We moved with them, and I for one was gripped in fear. A resonant bang cracked through the night air, followed by a series of smaller explosions like gunfire. I ducked. I was in the air-raid shelter again, crouching with Ellen, praying as the bombs dropped all around me.

'Hey, it's all right, Lily!' Kate was shouting in my ear and I realised I was clutching onto her arm, my eyes tightly shut. 'Look, it's stopped now. I reckon as the rest of the fireworks somehow got set off together!'

I opened my eyes. Everyone was muttering as it seemed the display had indeed ended prematurely, and the crowd was dispersing.

'Oh, what a pity! Still, no one was hurt.'

'And *I've* got a bottle of beer,' Peter smirked proudly. 'You girls want a drop?'

'Oh, Pete!' Kate giggled. 'D'you think we should?'

'Coronations don't happen every day.'

'Oh, all right, then!' She snatched the bottle and took a long swig.

'Hey, not too much! What about you, Lily?'

I hesitated. Ellen always kept a bottle of sherry for special occasions and I'd had a little sip once or twice. The little accident with the fireworks had upset me, and perhaps a mouthful of beer would settle my nerves. It tasted foul, like bitter washing-up water. I pulled a face as I handed it to Sally who was eager to try it, but ended up spluttering it down her front, much to Kate's amusement.

'Sh! Look, everyone's gone home!' I warned. 'I really think we should, too.'

'Yes, you're right. Goodnight, all! See you on the train in the morning.'

I crept indoors, trying to be quiet as I expected Sidney to have gone to bed. He hadn't. He was waiting for me in the kitchen.

'Had a good time, then?' he asked, surprisingly pleasantly.

'Yes, lovely, thank you.'

He suddenly frowned, and before I knew it, he grasped my arm and pulled me towards him. Fear gripped me in a vice as his eyes narrowed to frosty slits.

'By God, you've been drinking! I can smell it on your breath!'

'Oh!' I all but squealed from terror rather than pain as his fingers dug into my arm. 'Yes, I had one little sip of beer, that's all! And it was horrible! One sip, that's all!'

'One sip is all it needs!' he bellowed at me, spittle spraying from his lips. 'The devil's brew is drink! I might have known you'd start on it one day! But then you always were trouble, even before you were born. Now get yourself off to bed, and don't you *ever* take the devil's drink again!'

He let go of me with a violent thrust and I fell back against the wall. The wonderful day had been ruined, and I felt as if my courage had been torn into shreds. Hot tears sprang to my eyes and I fled up the stairs and threw myself on the bed.

What the hell had he meant, trouble before I was born? It just wasn't fair! He always seemed to be blaming me, as if there was some secret I still didn't know about myself. And just as I was beginning to think my life was improving, Sidney had shattered my contentment yet again.

The next morning, it was as if nothing had happened, and I almost began to wonder if I hadn't imagined his outburst. But, no. His words kept coming back to haunt me.

Chapter Six

'You're not happy, are you, Lily dear? Would you like to come inside and talk about it? A trouble shared is a trouble halved, you know.'

I blinked into the concerned face of Gloria Luckett, a little startled since I had been somewhat lost in my own thoughts. She had never been anything other than kind and friendly towards me, and other than her enthusiasm for the moor's ancient sites that she had revealed to me on our first meeting, I had no reason to suspect that she was involved in anything untoward. And now she was the only person among my acquaintances who seemed sensitive to the turmoil I was indeed trying to keep concealed. I was secretly so distraught that I was ready to lean on someone, and all at once, Gloria seemed to be that person.

'Well, yes, if it wouldn't be too much trouble,' I faltered, still somewhat hesitant.

'Come along in, then,' she smiled invitingly.

I followed her indoors. I always found it odd going into a strange house for the first time. You never knew what you'd find. Everybody's house seems to smell different, and Gloria's was no exception. I couldn't put my finger on it. But there was nothing odd about her house. In fact, it was just a mirror image of ours, only much more cosy and inviting.

'Take a seat,' Gloria smiled, and I obeyed, sitting down at an old pine table not dissimilar to our own. 'Drink this,' she said kindly, placing a small glass of amber liquid in front of me.

'Oh.' I looked up at her apologetically, Sidney's outburst on the evening of the coronation still fresh in my mind. 'I'm afraid I'm not allowed to drink alcohol.'

'And I wouldn't offer it to you. This is just a little herbal decoction to relax you. It's all natural, I promise.' Then she smiled reassuringly. 'Didn't I tell you, I dabble in herbs? Only simple remedies anyone can make, but I help a few people here and there.'

She gestured to a set of shelves crammed with bottles and jars, and it was then that I noticed bunches of greenery hanging from the drying rack above my head. So that's what I could smell! It all fell into place, and I felt ready to trust her. Whatever was in the remedy, it tasted quite pleasant and within a few minutes, I was feeling more at ease. When

Gloria refilled my glass, I was happy to accept it, and I noted that she poured some out for herself.

'Now then, tell me all about it,' she said persuasively. 'And take your time.'

I lowered my eyes, not quite sure where to start, so I told her about my mum first, Grandma Ellen that is, and the letter. And then all about Sidney, his strict, religious attitude to life and his strange reaction to various things that had happened since I had come to live with him. And as I spoke, it dawned on me that I had never told anyone all these details, not even Jeannie in my letters. I somehow felt ashamed, as if it was all partly my fault, but confessing everything to Gloria was definitely a release. She was patient, not interrupting but listening intently until I came to the end of my story. Then she sat back in her chair, tapping her joined fingertips against her lips.

'Your father's a very unhappy man,' she pronounced simply.

'Yes, I rather think he is,' I agreed. 'I feel sorry for him really, but I just wish he wouldn't take it out on me.'

Gloria nodded. 'It does seem unfair. But you have a big heart, Lily, and I sense a strength in you, and I'm rarely wrong. In fact, I think you're stronger than your father. I'm certain it'll all work out in the end. I can feel it in my bones.'

She said it with such conviction, but I raised my

eyebrows sceptically. 'I wish I could be so sure.'

'You just believe in yourself, and have patience. But to help matters along, did your grandmother have any friends in London she might have confided in?'

I shook my head. 'No. I asked at the funeral, but everyone was as astounded as I was to learn she wasn't my real mother, so I drew a blank there.'

'Oh, well, something will turn up. I know in my bones it will. Trust me, Lily.'

I really hoped she was right.

Oddly enough, I felt far more at ease after my conversation with Gloria. So much so that I didn't even consider pressing Sidney about my past. Or perhaps because I was subconsciously putting it off. For the next few weeks, I simply enjoyed the better weather that followed the coronation and the opportunity it gave to explore the moor further. Kate and Sally weren't great walkers but they were happy to come with me on Sunday afternoons provided I didn't plan too long a ramble!

The warm, humid weather suddenly broke one morning in a violent thunderstorm. I was at work and even in the shop we were aware of the torrential rain that bucketed down incessantly. It was just after lunch that the lights flickered and went out seconds before a tremendous crash resounded overhead and we were plunged into gloom.

'Goodness!'

The young lady who was choosing some nail varnish at my counter opened her lovely eyes wide. Their wonderful green-blue colour seemed familiar, but I had served her on several occasions, so perhaps that was why. We both glanced up as another crack of thunder exploded outside and the building shook.

'Oh, dear, I was hoping it would stop,' the girl complained. 'I'm already soaked through and I'm going to be late back to work as it is.'

'I think it's coming down worse, actually,' I sympathised. 'Have you got far to go?'

'Only to Plymouth Road.'

'That's far enough in this. I don't think I've ever known such a storm.'

'Oh, we get them over Dartmoor. It's the warm, moist air from the Atlantic rising up high over the moor, or something like that.' She shrugged her shoulders carelessly. 'Never was a great one for geography. You're not local are you?'

I didn't get a chance to reply as a piercing shriek from the front of the shop silenced all other conversation. My customer forgot all about her nail varnish, turning to look, and I stood up on tiptoe while Mrs Kershaw rushed out of her office.

'Whatever's going on?' she called.

'Oh, Mrs Kershaw, there's water comin' in the doors!' came the hysterical reply.

It seemed we all moved forward, drawn by the catastrophe. There were audible gasps as puddles an inch deep were seeping under the doors, spreading and growing deeper by the second. When I glanced out through the glass, water was streaming down the road and the few pedestrians braving the downpour had been caught in the deluge and were running and splashing in a veritable flood.

'Oh, Good Lord above!' my customer cried, putting her hand to her head in a dramatic gesture while I gazed in dumbstruck horror beside her.

'Quick, everyone! The brooms in the cleaning cupboard!' Mrs Kershaw commanded. 'We must brush it back!'

For the next few minutes, all was pandemonium. It was so dark with the lights gone out, the sky evidently black outside, and as we all worked furiously, I was reminded of my childhood days in London when people emerged from their shelters after a raid to inspect a familiar scene the bombs had rendered unrecognisable.

'Mrs Kershaw, this is hopeless!' I exclaimed, suddenly prompted by the memories. 'But haven't I seen some sandbags out the back? We could—'

'Oh, clever girl, Lily! Come on! You two keep brushing and the rest of us can bring them in!'

'I'll help!' my young lady offered enthusiastically. And then, winking at me, she added under her breath, 'Quite exciting, really. And a good excuse to be late back to work!'

Exciting it may have been, but it was more like hard labour as we struggled through the shop with the heavy sacks while Mrs Kershaw evacuated the few other customers out the back way. But I was really glad of my new friend's help and when, working as a team, we all stood back with fingers crossed to see if our makeshift dam would hold, there was a strong sense of combined achievement.

'Oh, well *done*, everyone!' Mrs Kershaw sighed with relief. 'And especially you, Lily! And thank you, too, dear,' she nodded at my customer. 'Now I must make some calls to get this mess sorted out!'

'Well, I suppose I ought to see if I can get back to the office without drowning,' the girl said with a grimace. 'The rain's easing off now the damage is done.'

'I'll take you out the back way,' I offered. 'It's strange. You'd think the back would be flooded with the river being there.'

'Ah, well, the front isn't called Brook Street for nothing. An old stream runs underneath and I suppose it hasn't got so much room to expand as the river, so it floods more easily.'

'That would make sense,' I agreed. 'And thank you so much for your help.'

'Oh, I enjoyed it! I like a bit of fun!' And she waved cheerily as she stepped across the yard.

The next momentous occasion in my life was a month later, my sixteenth birthday on the twenty-eighth of July. Or at least it *should* have been momentous. I'd always thought of sixteen as being a milestone. You could get married. Not that I would want to. I hadn't met anyone that special yet. Actually, that wasn't strictly true. I still had the joyous memory of my fleeting acquaintance with the young doctor in the car. But I was beginning to give up hope of ever seeing him again.

Sidney never even wished me happy birthday, let alone produced a card or gift. He just turned a frosty stare on me as I opened the envelope that had arrived the previous morning. I recognised the writing so I knew it was from Jeannie. I read it eagerly as I hadn't heard from her since May. Her cousin's family had moved out, having at long last been offered a flat in a new high-rise block in Chiswick, so the house was less crowded now. Jeannie asked if I was sure I didn't want to come and live there now. I seriously wondered if I shouldn't take up the offer. But then I would never have the chance of extricating any more information about my family from Sidney, and that remained all important to me. In the meantime, Jeannie didn't fancy a week's holiday in the back of beyond, thank you all the same. I was disappointed, but at least she had sent a card, and in the evening I had been invited round to Kate's house for a special tea.

The schools, though, had broken up for the summer and so my friends weren't on the train in the morning. Instead, I bought myself a newspaper to read on the journey. *It's Over*, the headline read. After all the bumbling negotiations that seemed to have been going on for months in Korea, a treaty had finally been signed the previous day and the war was over. It was just a case of bringing our lads home. The lucky ones who had survived.

I recalled the celebrations back in 1945. I had been seven, nearly eight years old. London had gone mad, and rightly so. There were street parties everywhere, despite rationing. It was over and we had won. No more fear. Just a flood of weary men in demob suits coming home to wives who thought they would never see them alive again, and children they scarcely knew. And others who watched with wistful, unshed tears because their menfolk would never be coming home or were still fighting in the far east. I doubted the ending of the Korean War would be celebrated in anything like the same manner, but I felt deeply happy that it was over.

Later that morning, Mrs Kershaw invited me into her office. 'You've been an exceptional worker from the start,' she smiled at me, 'but you saved the store a great deal of damage with your quick thinking. Now, I've asked head office if I can have an assistant supervisor, and, though you're a bit young, the job is yours. You'll start on the first of August. That's if you'll accept the promotion?'

Accept? Does the world turn once a day? Of course I'd accept. Another step towards the independence I craved. The grin was still splitting my face as I skipped back to my counter. And who should be there choosing the nail varnish she had forgotten a month before on the day of the storm than my young lady with the lovely eyes!

'Oh, hello!' I beamed at her. 'How are you?'

'I'm very well, thank you! Sorry I haven't been in, but I've been so busy. My brother's coming home from London for a few weeks. And our elder sister's getting married to an American, so there's heaps to do. I'm chief bridesmaid and the dresses are blue, so what colour varnish should I have, do you think?'

'Oh, I'd have thought clear or at least very pale. How about this one?'

'That looks excellent! Yes, thank you, I'll have that one.' She took out her purse and paid me while I found a small paper bag to put it in. 'Tell you what,' she said brightly, 'when it's all over, why don't you and I get together?'

'Oh, yes, I'd like that!' I returned her broad smile.

I somehow knew instantly that we were going to be friends, although I was sure she was a few years older than me.

'Great! Won't be till the end of August, mind. I'll come in and find you! I'm Wendy, by the way. Wendy Franfield.'

'Franfield?' I cried quite incredulously.

'Yes, my father's a doctor, a GP. You've probably heard of him.'

'No, it isn't that! I know someone who must be your uncle. Artie Mayhew.'

'Uncle Artie? Good Lord!'

'Yes, we met up at Foggintor. We live at Princetown now but my father and I were the last people living up at the quarry.'

'Well, I never! Uncle Artie did mention you! But, oh, look at the time! I simply must go! But I'll see you in a few weeks! We can have a good old chat!'

'I'll look forward to it! Hope the wedding goes well!'

She turned to wave as she left the shop, and I felt that I was having a good birthday after all. If only Sidney would tell me a bit more about my family, it would have been perfect, but I instinctively knew he wouldn't.

Chapter Seven

I first saw him at the Princetown Carnival towards the end of August. This was apparently an annual event that everyone was looking forward to tremendously. Although I was thriving on my new position at work, I booked the day off as I hadn't had any holiday at all yet. There would be all sorts of activities, but the main events would be the crowning of the carnival and fairy queens and the fancy dress parade down the streets.

'Come on, Lily!' Kate cried at me. 'Try and catch some!'

She was jostling along the crowded pavement, trying to keep pace with Mr Cribbett's lorry that had been cleaned of coal-dust for the occasion. The lady from Bolts and another woman I didn't recognise were standing in the back and throwing sweets and packets of crisps to the spectators as the procession moved slowly through the village.

'Oh, look at those little ones! Aren't they cute?' Sally chuckled beside me.

'Oh, yes, and look at that little boy!' I smiled back. 'The one dressed as Robin Hood! Isn't his costume good?'

'I wonder where his mum got the material from.'

'Dyed an old sheet green, I should think, and made it. She must be pretty clever with a needle. I wonder if she made Maid Marian's as well.'

'We'd better catch Kate up before she takes all the sweets and crisps,' Sally laughed. 'Collects them for her little brothers and sisters, she does.'

I followed in her wake as she elbowed her way through the crowds that lined the streets. I lost her for a moment, and it was then that I almost collided with the tall figure skulking against the wall of the building behind as if wanting to witness the festivities and yet remain invisible at the same time. It was difficult, though, with him being so tall, a good six foot, I reckoned. He bore a severe crew-cut, and though his face was deeply tanned, it was cadaverous, almost like a living skeleton. His gaze shifted furtively as our eyes met briefly, as if he wanted to avoid any contact with those around him.

I wondered if he was up to no good, and hastily

moved on to find Kate and Sally. Spirits were high, and I soon forgot the forbidding stranger. People were waving those tiny Union Jacks on lollipop sticks, calling and laughing as the parade passed by. When it was over, we went back to the field where the crowning had taken place. There were various stalls, a coconut shy and a raffle. I treated my friends to a sausage roll and a glass of lemonade, and we sat down on the grass to consume them.

'When do you go back to school?' I asked through a mouthful of pastry.

'Week after next, on the Tuesday,' Kate groaned. 'Not sure I want to, mind. I did all right with my O-levels – not as well as old clever clogs Sally here—' She broke off as Sally dug her playfully in the ribs and she shoved her back with a grin before going on, 'But I'm not really sure I want to do A-levels. Old Pete had to work *so* hard. Wonder how he's getting on with his National Service? At least there's no Korea for him to be sent to any more.'

'Yes, but there's still Malaya, and what about this trouble with the Mau Mau in Kenya? I wonder what will happen there. Sounds pretty frightening to me.' I saw them exchange mystified glances but I didn't want to spoil the day with a serious conversation about what was going on in the big wide world, so I went on instead, 'But look, I've got a week off starting next Saturday. Perhaps we could do something on the days before you go back to school.'

'As long as it doesn't involve traipsing across the moor!' Sally grinned back.

I was so pleased I had taken a day's leave. That night I went to bed, flushed and elated. Even Sidney had not been able to disapprove of the innocent celebrations, and I had almost begun to think his abrasiveness might be softening. How wrong I was.

Kate, Sally and I took a trip into Plymouth on the Saturday, but with no trains on Sundays, a walk on the moor was the only option! On the Monday, my two friends were busy getting everything ready for the new term, so I had the rest of the week to myself. I had wondered about buying a train ticket to London to stay with Jeannie for a few days. I dreamt about Battersea Park, of larking around and collapsing in hysterical laughter as we used to. But I knew I had changed. Grown up. Matured. I had the feeling I wouldn't find Jeannie as funny any more. With the savage beauty of Dartmoor all around me, London had definitely lost its appeal. And if I went back to our street, it would only open up the wounds to see someone else living in the house I had shared with Ellen for as far back as I could remember, cradled in the belief that nothing would ever change.

So I walked for miles on end, sometimes using the railway halts at the start or end of my day. Once Mr Gough stopped the train for me to get off along the route! I explored in every direction with the help of my trusty map and my compass, following rivers and streams, paths and bridleways. The weather, though not blessed with blue skies and sunshine, was at least dry and clear with good visibility and no threat of the disorientating, swirling mists that could descend in minutes. I had learnt to read the signs and only ever ventured where I believed it was safe. And I always told Sidney where I was going just in case some mishap might befall me.

'I'm not sure where I'll go today,' I frowned as I stood by the range at breakfast towards the end of the week. 'Should I go out to the stone row at Drizzlecombe, do you think? It's got one of the largest menhirs on the moor. Or I could leave the track near Nun's Cross and cut across to Down Tor stone row. Then I could go down to the reservoir and catch the train back from Burrator Halt.'

'Huh! I don't know what your fascination is with these places of heathen ritual.' Sidney suddenly attacked me with such venom that I shrank back. 'That grandmother of yours really did bring you up in an ungodly fashion. But then she wouldn't have stood much chance against a little Satan like you!'

I felt as though I had been doused in icy water that soaked through to my bones and numbed the very core of me. A little Satan! What had I ever done to deserve that? And Ellen had brought me up with good Christian values even if she hadn't forced her religion on me. To hear her name reviled by Sidney for the hundredth time was just too much, and as the sense returned to my brain, the rage boiled up inside me and overflowed like lava erupting from a volcano in a spitting, unstoppable river.

'I'm just about sick and tired of you running my grandmother down!' I raged, restraint flung to the four winds and my eyes sparking with all the festering resentment of the last nine months. 'You're a real hypocrite, you know. You pretend to be holier than thou, but underneath you're just a mean, bitter old man! It's no wonder nobody likes you. If I'd known what you were like, I'd never have come here.'

'Then go back to London. I won't stop you.'

'Oh, believe me, I would if I had much choice in the matter and I didn't love the moor so much! I don't know why you agreed to have me in the first place, unless it was for some perverse pleasure in punishing me for something I've never done! I don't know why you hate me so much!'

I sucked the breath in hard through my bared teeth, fury blazing in my eyes. We glared at each other across the room, neither of us moving as the hatred froze solid. But I wasn't expecting what came next.

'Well, I'll tell you, you little bitch,' Sidney snarled, his voice sizzling. 'Despite what your birth certificate says, you're not my daughter. Your mother was having an affair and you were the result.'

My body, my entire being, turned to water. The blood drained from my head and I staggered, my hands blindly seeking the back of the chair for support. I was like a proud stalk of wheat that had been felled by the farmer's scythe and was now lying, crushed and helpless, on the ground. It seemed that Sidney had been saving his trump card to slay me when I was getting above myself. He had certainly succeeded.

'I...I...' I stammered, my mouth wanting to retaliate but unable to formulate any words.

'So you see, madam,' Sidney gloated, his eyes glinting with malevolence, 'that makes you a bastard and not the self-righteous prig you think you are.'

The withering, deprecating way he was looking at me finally galvanised my tongue into action. I might be smarting under the degradation he had heaped on me, but I wasn't going to take it lying down.

'If what you say is true,' I hissed through my clenched jaw, 'it makes me no more or less of a person than I ever was. And quite frankly, if my mother was having an affair, I don't think I could blame her. I expect she rued the day she married you. Oh, that's right, hit me,' I leered as I saw him go to raise his hand. 'It's what I'd expect from you. But why you should have let me come to live with you, I'll never know.'

'Huh, I'm beginning to wonder myself! So if you pack your bags and are gone when I get back from work, it'll suit me down to the ground. I can't stand the sight of you.' And with that, he got to his feet, grasping his jacket and his packed lunch – which I had prepared for him as usual – and marched out of the kitchen.

The front door slammed behind him, reverberating through the house, then leaving a shattering silence in its wake. I lowered myself into the tatty armchair like a rag doll, my heart still hammering nervously. I couldn't believe it and yet it made sense. I sat for half an hour, waiting for the fog of shock to clear and to untangle the twisted mesh of emotions that heaved in my breast. I felt choked. Stifled. I didn't know who I was any more. I had always believed I was Lily Hayes, daughter of John and Ellen. Nine months ago, I had learnt that I was actually Lily Latham, third child of Sidney and Cynthia, and that the mother I couldn't remember and my brothers were dead. I had come to terms with that. But now I was neither of these people. A lost soul, with a father about whom I would clearly never learn a solitary fact.

Had Ellen known? She had gone to her grave unable to leave me in ignorance of my true parentage.

She had never liked Sidney, she had said in her letter, so if she had known, why would she not have told me the whole truth? Perhaps to save me the shame of knowing I was illegitimate, or whatever the term would be for a married woman having a baby by another man. Love child, maybe. But Ellen would know that however I was conceived, I wouldn't consider it my fault. She had brought me up to be more sensible than that. But why would she have led me to believe that a man like Sidney Latham was my father? Make of this what you want, she had written, as if she had predicted that I would want to contact him. No. The more I thought about it, I was convinced Ellen hadn't known about her daughter's affair. Perhaps it was better that way.

I finally dragged myself from the chair and made a mug of coffee. I sipped at it, unnerved. Would I ever feel the same again? I looked at myself in the mirror. Who was I? Did my silvery blue eyes and my strawberry blond hair come from my father? What had he been like? He must have been special to make my mother sin, for Ellen would have brought her up as a good Christian. Or was she driven by Sidney's puritanical ways to the first person who showed her some affection? I preferred to think that they were passionately, hopelessly, in love. In the same way that I hoped to be one day. But if that was how love could destroy people's lives – *my* life

– perhaps it would be best never to love at all.

I was feeling calmer, my hands no longer shaking. But I was still too numbed to make any decisions about my future. Why should something that had happened to other people seventeen years ago change my destiny? I wouldn't let it until I'd had time to think. And there was no better place to do so than out on the moor where the wind would drive the doubts out of my head and settle my heart.

As I strode out along the ancient track towards Nun's Cross, anger stealthily ousted my distress. Sidney hated me. Blamed me. The injustice of it flared inside me like a torch of flame. I could understand the jealousy gnawing away at him over the years, but he shouldn't lay the fault at my door. It wasn't fair. He expected me to leave, and it was my initial reaction to do so. But deep down, I really didn't want to go. I loved my new life. I loved Dartmoor and the sense of freedom it evoked in me. Just now, its gentle balm was mending my aching heart and reviving my spirit, allowing me to think more clearly.

What were my options? My recent promotion had brought with it a pay rise. Would it be enough for me to rent a little house or a flat in Tavistock if I didn't have the fare from Princetown each day? It was doubtful, and anyway I wasn't allowed to live alone, however ridiculous that seemed to me. The local welfare people had been contacted by the

London authorities and were *keeping an eye* on me, as they put it. Fortunately, they hadn't visited me at the cottage or I might have been taken into care there and then! But an official had inspected and approved of our new home in Albert Terrace and Sidney had greeted her with a degree of civility. So, to live alone was not a possibility. Not until I was eighteen, which seemed an awfully long way off. At least I had a room of my own in our house in Albert Terrace. My private territory where I could lose myself in a good book or play my growing record collection – very quietly, if Sidney was in the house. So perhaps, for the time being, I would stay and see what happened.

I stopped at Nun's Cross and, consulting my map, took a careful compass bearing towards the stone row. Once or twice before, I had explored the valley of the little stream from there and the intriguing evidence of former tin extraction, but now I needed to strike out across the moor where there was no path to follow. The ground was undulating so that I didn't have a clear view ahead. I had to hold the compass in my hand, constantly checking my direction and watching the uneven, tussocky ground under my feet. It was tough going, my entire concentration needed so that all considerations as to my future were temporarily banished. But at last I reached a point where that part of the moor opened up before me, bleak and barren, and there, way in the distance, I spied the avenue of tall standing stones, possibly a quarter of a mile long, sweeping down a shallow dip and way up on the far side. They looked like dots from where I stood, but distinct enough for me to be able to abandon the compass and wend my way towards them unaided.

Why had those ancient people chosen that particular spot, I mused as I trod forward over the wild, rough grass. Had they approached it from the same angle as I was now, in full daylight or by the pewter gleam from the moon, at certain times in nature's mysterious cycle? Did they come to worship or to bury their dead, only interring their priests or other dignitaries, since the circle at the far end was believed to be a tomb? I had certainly come to bury *my* dead. Since Sidney had reawakened my grief over my grandmother, I had come to bury Ellen's memory once more. But more than that, I had come to bury Lily Hayes. Lily Hayes, as she had always been, no longer existed. Now, it seemed, she was alone in the world, with no family and no identity. From now on, Lily Hayes's life would be whatever she made of it.

I halted as I reached the first of the upright stones, breathing in the silence, letting the mystery spin its web about me. A religious site, a burial ground of whatever creed, deserved respect. I bowed my head as I glided along the row, the sense of timelessness echoing in my heart. I was one small speck in the universe, insignificant. My own distress was immense to me, but in the scheme of things, it meant nothing.

I was caught up in the thread of my own thoughts, confused and uncertain, so that when I reached the far end and the burial mound with its surrounding ring of stones, I didn't spot it at once. My eyes and my mind were dulled to anything except my own emptiness. I turned my gaze skyward, spinning in a slow circle so that my pleas for some security in my life would spiral upwards to whatever deity would take pity on me. When I looked down and saw the dead sheep spread-eagled on the central stone at my feet and the dried pool of its blood, horror slashed at my throat. I was aware of the tiny, anguished squeal that escaped from my lips, and I staggered backwards in an explosion of rage and disgust, blundering and sickened, so that I tripped blindly over the stone behind me. I felt myself falling, but there was nothing I could do to save myself as I landed hard on the ground.

I think I must have let out a short, high scream as a sharp pain shot through my ankle and seared up my leg. I lay for a moment, winded and shocked, a little faint even, which annoyed me. I was Lily Hayes and I could take care of myself. My vision had clouded with black spots, but as they faded away and I came properly to my senses, the agony in my ankle intensified. I drew in a deep breath, waiting for it to subside, but the moment I tried to move it again, I yelped in pain.

Fear crackled down my spine. Oh, dear Lord, what was I to do? I hadn't noticed any ramblers on that part of the moor, and Sidney didn't know where I had gone, and even if he did, would he care if I didn't return? I exhaled sharply. Pull yourself together. Just wait ten minutes, half an hour, and I would probably be able to hobble homewards.

The beautiful wilderness of the moor began to seem savage and hostile, my stomach tightening with nervousness. I kept my eyes averted from the horrible spectacle of the sacrificed sheep. Did such things still go on? Apparently they did. But it was vile and cruel, and I had to get away. I hauled myself upwards and tried to put my weight on my foot. At once, my ankle stung with pain and I thumped down again on my bottom, my eyes filling now with tears of desperation.

'Hey! Are you all right?'

The disembodied voice coming out of nowhere at first startled me, but then my heart spilt over with relief as a tall figure suddenly appeared from behind me. But I was filled with dismay as I recognised the suspicious stranger from the carnival. Here was I, in the middle of nowhere, with an ankle at best badly sprained, and the only person around was some furtive character who for all I knew might be driven by ill-intent! My brain numbed with terror, but I forced myself to think. I mustn't let him know I was afraid.

'I think so,' I said coolly with a stubborn lift of my chin. 'Just twisted my ankle a bit. I saw *that*,' and I jabbed my head at the dead sheep, 'and it gave me such a fright, I tripped over.'

I saw the fellow look towards where I had indicated and he jerked back with a sharp intake of breath. He had stiffened, and I was curious as his tanned face seemed to drain of its colour. *Jesus*, I was sure he muttered under his breath, and then he turned to me, his eyes, an amazing violet-blue, narrowed accusingly.

'You out here all on your own?'

My heart beat even more furiously, but it was obvious there was no one else around, and it would have made my terror more evident if I had denied it. 'Yes,' I answered boldly. 'But my father knows where I am.'

Father? Huh! Sidney. But none of that mattered now. Sidney had never *frightened* me, but just now, I was staring up at this tall, broad-shouldered young man absolutely petrified. His face didn't look quite as gaunt as it had when I had noticed him a few weeks previously, and his shorn hair had grown a little, but he was still painfully thin, so I wondered optimistically if he wasn't as strong as he looked.

'Well, that's not much help, is it? Bloody stupid to come right out here all alone.'

His scornful, abrasive attitude drove away my fear and an acid disdain took its place. '*You* have!' I snapped back.

He glared down at me, his wide mouth in a hard line. 'But I'm not a girl, and I know this part of the moor like the back of my hand. And I'm wearing proper walking boots, which if you had any sense, you'd be wearing, too. You should at least keep to the proper tracks if you're going to wear those things.'

Indignation rumbled deep inside me. My stout lace-ups had served me well enough up until now. I was about to tell him so when he dropped down on his haunches and, without a by-your-leave, pushed up my trouser-leg and turned the top of my sock down as far as it would go over my shoe. His long fingers closed around my ankle and he frowned as his hand moved firmly over my skin. I scowled back, but as he was looking down, concentrating on my foot, I couldn't help noticing the incredibly long, dark lashes fanning out from his eyelids.

'I wouldn't have thought it was broken,' he pronounced at length.

'How can you tell?' I quizzed him warily.

He flashed a look of contempt at me. 'Let's just say I've had some experience. What you need is to get some ice on it. Where have you come from?'

'Princetown,' I told him apprehensively.

He shrugged his eyebrows. 'At least that's nearer than Tavvy. But my house is nearer than that. Come back with me and I'll drive you back to Princetown. Here. I'll help you up.'

He grasped my hand with one of his and placed the other underneath my upper arm. To my surprise, he didn't yank me upwards but supported me firmly as I levered myself into a standing position. I mumbled my thanks and the hint of a smile flitted over my face. He didn't return it, his expression set and those striking eyes looking at me darkly.

'Right. Try walking on it,' he ordered.

I did. Nothing would have given me greater pleasure than to be able to walk away from this curt devil, but I winced aloud and found myself grasping at him for support. As I glanced at him, there was no sympathy sketched on his features. If anything, his scowl deepened.

'This is going to be fun,' he grunted sardonically.

He put his arm across my back, his hand gripping about my waist. With the greatest reluctance, I laced my own arm around him so that our two flanks were pressed close together. His body was warm and

I could feel the hardness of his muscles through his thin shirt. He was bony with not an ounce of flesh, and I wondered vaguely if he'd been ill. Not that I really cared. I might have done if he'd been more amenable.

'Come on, then,' he grumbled. And then jerking his head over his shoulder at the dead sheep, he murmured, 'I'll see to that later.'

His strong jaw was clenched as I hobbled slowly forward, half hopping and clinging to him tightly. 'Was it…was it some sort of sacrifice?' I dared to ask. Despite my abhorrence, I was inquisitive, and it was something to fill the awkward silence. I wished I hadn't bothered.

'Of course,' he barked back. 'What else do you think it was?'

My self-control was fraying and it was all I could do to stop myself telling him not to be so surly. But he *had* rescued me, and without him, I'd have been up the creek without a paddle, so to speak, so I decided to bite my tongue.

'I didn't think that sort of thing still went on,' I said instead, thinking of Gloria's strange words on the day I had met her.

'It doesn't. At least, to my knowledge, it hasn't for donkey's years. I mean, there are still people playing around. Harmless enough. But sacrifices, well, I thought they'd died out centuries ago. But who knows? It's supposed to be some sort of fertility rite, or so I believe. And you use dried blood as a garden fertiliser, so it makes sense.'

'Oh, well, yes, I suppose so,' I mumbled, not quite sure what he was intimating. But I needed all my wits to limp forward over the uneven terrain – and to check where he was taking me! But he seemed to be leading me in the direction of the main track across the southern moor, which was something. It was late in the season but there could well be holidaymakers walking there and I would feel safer.

We carried on in silence. Progress was frustratingly slow, and I could hardly put my foot to the ground, my other leg aching as it took the strain.

'I'm sorry, but I need to stop,' I announced after a while.

He glared down at me, his lips pursed. 'Look, we're never going to get anywhere at this rate. It'll be easier if I give you a piggyback. Come on. Climb aboard.'

He squatted down in front of me and my heart bucked in my chest. This was even more intimate, but what choice did I have? He sidestepped, slightly unbalanced, as he straightened up with my weight on his back, linking his arms through my knees, and I clasped my arms around his neck, trying not to strangle him.

He walked steadily. I could feel the strength of

him beneath me, the steel in his arms. So that if he tried anything funny, God knew it would have been impossible to fight back. But though his muscles were like iron, his stamina didn't match. A damp patch soon appeared on the back of his shirt and he was breathing hard. Several times he had to stop to rest. He stared ahead as he sat on the grass, as if his own thoughts were far away. I didn't interrupt them. I had enough of my own.

We crossed over the track when we came to it and continued on to the tarmac road that ran from Princetown out to the old mine at Whiteworks and the notorious Foxtor Mire. I had walked out that way before, passing the few isolated buildings that made up Peat Cott clustered in a depression to the eastern side of the road. Further along, I had seen an old high wall, unusual for the area being built of brick rather than stone, but I hadn't really taken much notice. Rusted wrought-iron gates, once elegant, were wedged open into a weed-encroached gravel drive, and looked as if they hadn't been moved for decades. Not much was visible from the gates because the drive curved sharply, but from what I could see of the garden, it was overgrown and neglected. A row of dense pine trees, their lower branches dark and intertwining, obliterated the view up the driveway to whatever edifice might be lurking around the corner, and the whole place was grimly forbidding. My heart sank when my taciturn saviour turned in at the gates and came to a halt.

'You'll have to hop or whatever from here,' he said gruffly as he lowered me back onto my feet. 'I'm sorry. I just can't carry you another step.'

There was a catch in his voice and he shook his head as if ashamed. But although I didn't relish his company, I was grateful for what he had done for me.

'I'm not surprised,' I told him. 'I don't know what I'd have done without you. Thank you so much.'

'Let's get you to the front door. Wait there and I'll let you in. Save you walking round to the back. I never use the front, so I haven't got the key with me.'

I nodded, holding onto his arm as we crunched up the gravel. My ankle was feeling a touch easier, but there was no way I could walk on it properly. I stopped in amazement, snatching in my breath, when the house came into view. It was huge and imposing, built in a grand style from dressed stone with a pillared portico over the entrance. I waited while the young man disappeared round the back, and my gaze wandered over the peeling paint on the large casement windows. The place had clearly seen better days.

I heard movement on the inside of the massive double front door, and one side creaked open. The fellow was waiting for me to hop inside and my heart thudded against my ribs. I was in this isolated, apparently empty, house with this tall, strong stranger and no one on earth had a clue where I was.

'Come into the kitchen and we'll put some ice on your ankle.'

He held out his hand, his face still stern, and I took it cautiously. We crossed a light, spacious hallway with a beautiful, curved staircase sweeping to the upper floor and a galleried landing. Lovely old wooden doors led to several different rooms and I glanced into a fine dining room with a long, highly polished Regency table. The house echoed eerily with the spirits of the past, I fancied, and I felt happier when I was led into the cosy atmosphere of the kitchen, even though it was a large, cool room with a quarry-tiled floor and white-tiled walls. The biggest range I had ever seen took up the entire end wall, evidence that this household must once have employed servants. Now it seemed to have but one occupant who abandoned me by the enormous old table in the centre of the room and went to open a tall refrigerator next to a double butler sink with long wooden draining-boards. If I hadn't been so acutely aware of my own vulnerable situation, I would have been intrigued.

I was made to sit down with my bare foot propped up on another kitchen chair while the owner of the house folded a towel around a mound of ice-cubes and packed it around my ankle. At least, I assumed he was the owner, although he seemed somewhat young to possess such a home. I judged him to be in his mid-twenties, although premature lines radiated from the outer corners of his eyes as if he had been squinting into the sun too much. But then he was deeply tanned even if it had faded slightly from when I had first seen him at the carnival, so he must have been staying in warmer climes of late. A man of mystery.

He disappeared into the hall, allowing the door to close behind him. He must have made a phone call as I could hear him talking, quietly at first and then raising his voice in agitation. I couldn't hear what he was saying, but his face was like thunder when he strode back into the kitchen.

'Nothing they can do, apparently, the police,' he sighed in exasperation, and then flung himself down into one of the other chairs, long legs stretched out before him. 'Oh, I suppose they're right. They can't be everywhere all the time. And it's the first report they've had of anything like this. And the last, I hope. I'll go out there tomorrow and check the ear-markings. I should be able to work out who the farmer is. Whoever it is won't be too pleased, I'm sure.' He ran his hand hard over his mouth and leapt to his feet. 'I'll make us a cup of tea, Carrot Top, and then I'll run you back to Princetown.'

If I was beginning to feel less anxious, my hackles bristled at the derogatory term which he used so casually, as if I should accept it quite without question. I sucked in my cheeks, my eyes hardening, as I fought to control my temper. I wanted to give him the length of my tongue, but on reflection, I was in no position to do so. Instead, I tersely refused his offer of a drink and asked to be taken home at once.

'OK,' he shrugged. 'I'll strap your ankle for you first, though. Must be some bandages upstairs somewhere.'

I was left alone again as I heard him take the stairs two at a time. He hadn't given me a chance to protest and I couldn't wait to get away from him, but I sensed he was genuine enough. It was just that his manner was so abrupt, and after my almighty row with Sidney and the stunning revelation, well, it was the last thing I needed. And I could never forgive anyone for calling me carrot top or copper knob or any other jibe at my hair.

He was back in minutes, kneeling at my feet without a word. I must say he made an expert job and my ankle felt much better for the support. I thanked him politely but he merely grunted in response.

I tottered on his arm back out through the hallway and was left to wait on the drive while he went back into the house. It was an attractive building, I reflected as I stood there alone, and I reckoned the inside had been beautiful once. It was in a sad state of repair now, though, and I really thought the chap should get off his backside and do something about it.

The vehicle that trundled out from somewhere behind the house was a battered old Army jeep, splattered in mud, canvas roof in place, but with the sides rolled up. It was like something out of a war film set in the desert. I guessed they must have been sold off in their thousands for next to nothing after the war. He drew the jeep up beside me, but didn't get out to help me in. The image of the young gentleman driving the gleaming car in Tavistock flashed across my brain. Now *he* would have helped me, I was certain! As it happened, since there was no door, I was able to slide in without too much difficulty and we sat in tense silence while we bumped along the road and back into Princetown. It was draughty and uncomfortable, and as far as I was concerned, we couldn't arrive quickly enough.

'Where do you live, then, or are you on holiday?' came the blunt demand.

'I live here,' I answered just as testily. 'Drop me in the centre and I can manage from there.'

I somehow didn't want him to see where I lived, and I think he realised. He brought the jeep to a stop but kept the engine running, as if he couldn't wait for me to get out.

'As you wish. And remember, Carrots, next time you venture out on the moor, wear some decent footwear.'

I slid out of the seat, barely containing my resentment, and hopped round on the pavement. 'Don't you dare call me that!' I called, wishing there was a door for me to slam.

I saw him blink at me in surprise and then, as he put the vehicle into gear, his eyes lit up roguishly and he laughed before turning his head away to concentrate on the road. A surge of anger darkened my spirit and I clenched my jaw in annoyance. He was mocking me, taking the mickey, and there was nothing more humiliating. I watched, fuming, as he turned the jeep around and drove off without a glance in my direction. I felt like running after him, dragging him out and punching him on the nose.

Although my ankle was throbbing, the whole incident had put me just in the right mood to confront Sidney!

Chapter Eight

'You're still here, then.'

It was a statement, ground from between clenched teeth, and not a rhetorical question. Sidney was glowering at me, his face stiff and accusing, but I wasn't going to cow down before him. I'd had the remainder of the afternoon to calm down, nursing my ankle with cold compresses made from wringing my flannel in water since we had no fridge with readymade ice. I'd had time to reflect on my loss of identity, and had emerged on the other side of an empty void ready to defend myself. And remembering Gloria's words that I could be stronger than Sidney, I was determined to reason with him rather than be forced to do battle.

'Unfortunately I don't have much choice,' I answered steadily. 'I went for a walk and sprained my ankle quite badly. But even if I hadn't, I'd still be here. I've at last got some stability back in my life, and I'm not going to give it up so easily.'

Sidney had been staring at me, opening and shutting his mouth several times like a goldfish, but I wasn't going to let him interrupt. It seemed now, though, that I had taken the wind out of his sails and he appeared lost for words.

'I don't see why I should be made to suffer for something my mother did,' I went on in a pleading tone now that I appeared to have won the first hurdle. And then I added more softly, 'You are *sure* I'm not yours?'

I arched my eyebrows sympathetically and waited. He met my steady gaze.

'Oh, yes,' he grated with a bitter shake of his head. And for a few seconds, he looked as lost as I had felt earlier.

'Well, I'm sorry for that,' I said gently, and was surprised by the genuine compassion that tugged at my heart. 'I can understand that I must be a constant reminder. But can't you see that you shouldn't blame me for the past? Whatever my mother did wasn't *my* fault. Can't you just look upon me as some sort of lodger? I'm actually quite a nice person if you'd give me a chance to show it.' And here I smiled in what I hoped was a winning manner. 'I know I'm not really a churchgoer and I do like to enjoy myself, but I have good morals, just the same. So,' I said expectantly, seeing the effect my reasoning had produced on his expression, 'can't we start again? Be friends? *Please*?'

I felt I had said enough and gazed at him, my heart thrumming with anticipation, as he considered my words. I prayed I wouldn't have to argue my case further. It had hit me like a thunderbolt that I would be devastated if I was forced to leave my Dartmoor home and all my new friends. Strangely enough, that included Sidney. I had grown used to his gruff ways, and I still lived in hope of persuading him to reveal more of my unknown past – now more than ever.

I waited, hardly daring to breathe.

'Does this mean I've got to cook the dinner, then?' his response came at last.

Something inside me heaved with relief, and for some reason I couldn't quite fathom, I wanted to cry. I suppose the tensions of the day – my earlier row with Sidney and the shocking revelation, my throbbing ankle and the sullen individual who had rescued me – had broken over a crest and were now draining out of me. A reaction to it all now the crisis was over.

'Oh, no,' I assured him, swallowing the sudden ache in my throat. 'I managed to make toad-in-the-hole. It's already in the oven. And I've chopped up some cabbage to go with it.'

'That's all right then. But I'll do the washing-up

afterwards. Have I got time to do some digging in the garden?'

'About half an hour.' And then, feeling encouraged, I ventured, 'The soil's much better here, isn't it?'

He paused as he made for the back door, cocking an eyebrow. 'Yes, it is, as it happens,' he conceded.

And I found myself smiling as I heard him go out.

I dreamt about my saviour that night. He was a dark, oppressive hulk bearing down on me, his face distorted and his mouth laughing cruelly. I tried to run from him, but my ankle was burning in pain and I was fettered by my own leaden legs. He twisted his head to glare at me with a malevolent sneer, and as his black cloak swished open, I saw him withdraw a bloodied dagger from a white, woolly sheep.

I screamed and woke up in a bath of hot sweat. I had turned awkwardly in the bed and my ankle really was protesting. I shifted until it was comfortable again and settled down to go back to sleep. It took me some time to drift off. The nightmare had unnerved me and I kept thinking of the ungracious stranger. In its unravelling of the previous day, my mind had muddled everything together. The fellow had been as appalled by the sacrifice as I had been – unless he was an extremely accomplished actor! But although he had shown me grudging kindness, his attitude had been insufferable. And he had committed the ultimate sin of teasing me about my hair as if I was some sort of alien creature with no feelings of my own. I vowed never to walk in that part of the moor again. Hopefully our paths would never cross, for if I didn't see him again, it would be too soon. Why I should feel so adamant about it, I couldn't think, especially in the middle of the night. But having decided that there were plenty of other places to walk, and anyway, I didn't want to come across the horrendous sight of a sacrificed sheep again, I felt more relaxed and was able at last to slip back over the brink into a deep and peaceful slumber.

'Hello, Lily, dear! What on earth have you been up to?'

The next morning I was hanging out some washing, limping on my bandaged ankle, when Gloria's concerned head appeared over the garden fence.

'Oh, I fell over yesterday out on the moor,' I answered, shaking my head. 'Silly, really. Should have been looking where I was going.'

'Oh, I'm sorry to hear that. Anything I can do?'

'No, not really, thank you.' And then I hesitated. Perhaps Gloria was just the person... 'Actually...' I hopped up to the fence. 'I came across what looked like a sacrificed sheep at Down Tor row. It was horrible. But,' and I felt the colour flood into my cheeks, 'you're interested in things ancient, aren't you, so I just wondered if you'd know—'

'Sheep sacrifice, you say?' Gloria frowned darkly, her lips knotted in caution. 'No, I wouldn't know anything about that, but I'd keep away for the time being if I were you.'

'I certainly will,' I told her with a shiver. 'I don't think I'm going to be doing much walking for a while anyway.'

'Well, you look after yourself!' she commanded, raising her eyebrows at me. 'And how are things progressing between you and your father?'

I caught my bottom lip between my teeth. I should have liked to tell her what had happened the previous day, but I didn't think Sidney would have approved. 'Oh, I think things will be better between us now,' I answered enigmatically.

Gloria nodded her head at me with a knowing smile.

'Oh, there you are! I came in last week looking for you, but someone else was on your counter.'

I turned my head and looked into the radiant face of Wendy Franfield as I hobbled across to the plants counter, concentrating on the stock list in my hand. A wave of pleasure washed through me at the sight of the pretty girl I had thought of several times over the last few weeks.

'Oh, hello!' I beamed back at her. 'How are you? How did the wedding go?'

'It was wonderful! But my sister's gone to live in America now, and we *really* miss her. You know, she met Wayne at the very end of the war when he was stationed here. She was only fourteen then, but they kept in contact all that time! Frightfully romantic, don't you think? But where have you been?' she asked brightly, swiftly changing the subject.

'I've been promoted!' I preened. 'To assistant supervisor. So I'm in the office a lot of the time. And I was on holiday last week. I spent half of it walking on the moor and the other half with my foot up on a cushion! Sprained my ankle,' I grimaced.

'Oh, dear! Yes, I saw you limping a bit. Has anyone looked at it?'

'Well, we have two visiting doctors in Princetown, but I didn't bother. It seems to be getting better on its own.'

'Oh, I insist my dad has a look!' Wendy said determinedly. 'When's your lunchtime?'

I consulted my watch. 'In about five minutes, actually.'

'I'll wait for you, then.' She crossed her arms purposefully. 'Dad should be at home, unless there's been an emergency at the hospital.'

'I really don't want to bother him—'

'Nonsense! What are friends for? Anyway,

we can have lunch there! And you can meet my parents. Dad's Uncle Artie's younger half-brother,' she added, frowning in concentration, 'but I think you know that. Mum's from Plymouth. She was a nursing sister. That's how she and Dad met. Now she's Practice Nurse and Secretary rolled into one. Oh, come on, that five minutes must be up by now! And they should be lenient with you, coming into work when you could be off sick.'

I couldn't help but chuckle. Wendy was so lively that she reminded me of Jeannie, but in a much more sophisticated way. I felt in my bones that we were going to become firm friends.

A few minutes later, Wendy was insisting on propping me up as we walked through the town centre and soon we were turning into one of the grand Victorian villas in Plymouth Road. There was a sign by the gate to the long front garden, saying *Doctor's Surgery*, and as we approached the front door through a wide conservatory, I noticed a brass plate on the wall. Wendy let herself in, and waving her hand at a room on the right of the spacious hallway, made for a door at the back of a lovely staircase.

'That's Dad's surgery,' she informed me flippantly. 'Mum sits at that desk in the hall and patients wait in the conservatory. Mum and Dad will be down in the kitchen. Oh, do you think you can manage the stairs all right?'

'Oh, yes, thank you. My ankle's not that bad.'

I could see that the house was as elegant inside as it was out, with large windows that let in plenty of light, but I followed Wendy down a servants' staircase to a huge kitchen in the semi-basement. Her parents were sitting at the table, a couple in their early fifties I would have thought. Mrs Franfield was a little on the plump side, but with a pretty face and a surprised, welcoming smile, while her husband was tall and athletic with those lovely green-blue eyes Wendy had inherited.

'This is Lily!' she announced without preamble. 'Remember I told you about her? She was the person Uncle Artie met up at the quarry. Only take a look at her ankle, would you, Dad? She sprained it last week and, very naughtily, hasn't seen anyone about it.'

'Hello, dear,' Mrs Franfield beamed as the doctor got to his feet, swallowing a mouthful of his lunch and holding out his hand.

'Mmm, yes, just a minute. Of course I'll take a look.'

'You will join us for lunch, won't you, Lily?'

'I've actually got my sandwiches,' I answered, overwhelmed by their hospitality. 'But thank you all the same.'

'Cup of tea or coffee, then? Or something cold?'

It was as if we had all known each other for years, and I instantly felt at ease. It struck me that the atmosphere in the Franfield household was the nearest I had come across to my home back in London, happy and animated and yet secure at the same time. Wendy's father examined my ankle and strapped it firmly while Mrs Franfield chatted merrily to me. I could see exactly where Wendy got her talkative disposition from!

'I'm Deborah, by the way,' she smiled at me. 'And my husband's William.'

'After my father's mentor, Dr William Greenwood of Tavistock,' he explained, pulling on his suit jacket. 'Well, I'm off to the hospital. Don't you be late back to work, Wendy.'

'And I've got some paperwork to do, if you'll excuse me.'

'Yes, of course. And thank you both so much.'

'You wouldn't mind if Lily stayed over any time, would you? She could have Joanna's room.'

'No, of course not. See you later.'

I glanced at the large kitchen clock on the wall. Wendy and I had ten minutes before we had to leave.

'Your parents are really nice,' I said with envious enthusiasm. 'I wish my father was like that.' I hesitated as I wondered if I should confide in my new friend about Sidney turning out not to be my father after all, but perhaps it was too soon. 'He's, well, odd to say the least. I do like your house, though,'

I went on to change the subject. 'It reminds me of my home in London. Someone else lived in the semi-basement. She had the original kitchen and a bedsit, a bit like this but much smaller. We had our own little kitchen on the ground floor.'

'Yes, Mum wishes we had a kitchen upstairs instead of down here. The other room down here's the surgery office. And the surgery takes up the dining room, and there's a patients' cloakroom squeezed in under the stairs. But it's more than my Grandfather Elliott had to start with. His first practice was in a cottage in the little street at the back of here. He was there for years before he was able to buy this house. It was all private medicine back then, of course, long before the Health Service. Dad says he used to charge his patients what they could afford, which often wasn't much. Eventually he inherited his parents' house up in Watts Road, but it wasn't practical to have a surgery so far from the town centre and up such a steep hill, so he sold it and bought this instead.'

I nodded, her words conjuring up a vision of the caring physician her grandfather must have been, a trait evidently carried down into the family. I was curious. 'You didn't want to follow in the family tradition, then?'

Wendy shook her head, horrified. 'Good Lord, no! Bedpans and vomit? No thank you! Being secretary to a solicitor's suits me much better! My younger sister, though, Celia, she's doing her nurse's training here at Tavistock Hospital, but she lives at the Nurses' Home. More convenient for night duty and a lot more fun, apparently! And my brother, Edwin, he's in London, training to be a doctor at Guy's. You'd like him. He was here for the wedding, but he took most of his holiday then. Heaven knows when he'll be able to come down again. Come upstairs to the lounge and I'll show you a photo.'

The lounge went the full depth of the house but was homely, despite its size. Though furnished with taste, it very much had a lived-in feel. Wendy went over to a sideboard which boasted a collection of freestanding photographs in an array of frames. She picked one up and handed it to me.

'This was the wedding,' she announced proudly. 'You can see Joanna's the only one of us who looks like Mum. That's Celia, and that's Edwin.'

My eyes followed her finger over the image behind the glass, and my heart vaulted into my throat. And I knew exactly why Wendy had always seemed oddly familiar to me. Although in black and white, the same smiling eyes looked at me from the handsome face of a young man with light curls. I recognised him instantly as the driver of the car that had nearly knocked me down in Duke Street when the little boy had dashed into its path.

My pulse began to pound furiously. So often I had dreamt of the polite, thoroughly apologetic gentleman who was so concerned and seemed to blame himself for something that wasn't his fault. And it turned out he was the brother of my new friend! I felt myself blush to the roots of my hair.

'I think I might actually have met your brother,' I murmured.

'Really?' Wendy was evidently burning with curiosity.

'Well, it *looks* a bit like him,' I answered evasively in an effort to conceal my feelings. 'Did he ever mention a little boy running out in front of his car? Here in Tavistock? It would have been shortly before Christmas.'

Wendy scratched her head quizzically. 'Well, come to think of it, yes, he did. He was here for a few days shortly before Christmas. He was quite badly shaken by it, as I remember. He said a young girl snatched the boy out of the way and he nearly ran her down as well. Oh, Lily! That wasn't *you*, was it?' she gasped delightedly.

I felt utterly mortified. 'Oh, you wouldn't say anything, would you?' I begged. 'It would be so embarrassing if we ever met!' Which I was, of course, secretly hoping that we would. 'I mean, it wasn't his fault at all. Not a bit of it. He was driving really carefully, but the little boy—'

'Gosh, how brave of you! What a heroine! But of course I wouldn't mention it to him. Not if you didn't want me to. But do I detect a touch of admiration there?' she chirped, cocking a pert eyebrow. 'He's frightfully handsome is Edwin.'

I lowered my eyes. 'He was very kind to me that day,' I mumbled, and then gasped in gratitude as my eye caught the ornate clock on the mantelpiece. 'Oh, no! I'm going to be late! Come on, Wendy!'

'Oh, yes, you're right!' But then she grinned irrepressibly. 'Come on, Hoppalong! I'll help you!' And we hastily made for the door.

Chapter Nine

My life really settled into a happy routine after that day. I was still friends with Kate and Sally, travelling into Tavistock with them each morning, but their studies left them with less and less time for socialising. I spent virtually every lunchtime with Wendy, cementing our relationship which was proving every bit as strong as my long friendship with Jeannie had been. Several times, we had gone to the pictures or to a public dance in Tavistock on a Saturday evening, and I had stayed overnight, sleeping in the room *next to Edwin's*! I still couldn't believe it! The only thing was that he was unlikely to be able to come home for months. But on the other hand, I was so nervous about meeting him again because if he didn't show any particular liking for me, I knew I would be devastated.

It didn't spoil my present contentment, though. I

woke up each morning, looking forward to the day ahead. As far as Sidney was concerned, since that awful day at the beginning of September when his bitterness had erupted and overflowed, we appeared to have cleared the air and had been getting on so much better ever since. Although the outside world still believed us to be father and daughter, at home we weren't pretending any more. It felt as if the barrier between us had been broken down. Sidney seemed to be accepting me as a person in my own right rather than the enemy, and as such we were getting on as friends.

'Neither Ellen nor John had any family,' he told me out of the blue one evening. 'They were both only children and both had lost their parents before I met Cynthia.'

I looked up sharply and with no little surprise. I had been quietly studying the blurred photograph of my mother hidden between the pages of the book I was reading, and Sidney must have noticed. It was the first time he had ever volunteered any information without being prompted, and I held my breath.

'There might have been distant cousins through your great grandparents, but I don't remember anyone like that ever being mentioned,' he went on, scrutinising my face. 'John came from the Midlands and Ellen from somewhere in Essex. I never knew her maiden name, I'm afraid, so that's all I can tell you.'

I nodded. 'Yes, she told me she was from Essex. It was where she got her sense of humour from, she always said. But she never told me any more.'

'And I can't help you, either.'

I sucked in my cheeks. It was a start, even if I hadn't learnt anything new. Perhaps, some time in the future, he might speak more of my mother. I could hardly expect him to talk about the man she'd had the affair with, but I realised the little he had said had cost him a deal of courage.

'Thank you,' I said, and I kissed him good-night.

It was nearing the end of October. British Summer Time was over, the evenings drawing in, and we had the long and difficult winter in our exposed moorland home to look forward to. But I was facing life with renewed spirit. The whole area, though, was reeling under the tragic death of the Twelfth Duke of Bedford a couple of weeks earlier. Shot himself in the most dreadful freak accident, and him such a lovely man, respected by all, as were his ancestors, for his generosity and care for the local people. He was deeply mourned, especially in Tavistock, where his death was seen as the end of an era. Times were changing, I mused, although for me it would seem for the better.

It was Wednesday and my afternoon off. I had just got off the train in Princetown and had decided to call in at Bolts for some bread. They baked it themselves, and especially now that the *white loaf* was back, it was mouth-wateringly delicious.

'Oh, come on, the team *needs* you!' I heard the exhortation as I shut the door. 'You were a star player as a lad. We've lost every match this season against the Rangers *and* the Prison Officers' Club. We need someone like you—'

'I told you, I don't play football any more!'

Somewhere at the back of my mind I recognised the irate voice. Sure enough, as I turned round into the shop, I almost collided with the tall, thin figure of my rescuer as he made a dash for the door. It was as if he was so desperate to escape that he was blind to anything in his path, including me. He seemed startled, pulling back sharply when he noticed me. I was ready to tell him to mind where he was going, but something in his expression stopped me. His skin was still tanned as if he spent much time outdoors, but somehow, beneath it, he looked ashen. His penetrating, violet-blue eyes were savage, trapped. I read recognition in them as he stared at me, and for a moment, they softened. But then they were sharp again, and defensive.

'Oh, if it isn't my little miss Carrot Top!' The anger had gone out of him now, as if his jeer had put him in control again. It spurred my contempt that he was humiliating me for his own needs, and to add insult to injury, he half smiled as if I should be friends with him. 'I take it your ankle is mended?'

'Yes, thank you,' I answered coldly. I gazed at him, keeping my eyes steady, determined not to back down. I noticed that although still lean, he had gained a little flesh and looked better for it. His hair was growing and was thick and dark, and as the hint of a smile persisted, his wide mouth and strong, white teeth made him strikingly handsome. It made me instantly rebel, and I wished I could think of some belittling response. I couldn't, and instead I said cuttingly, 'If you'll excuse me, I have shopping to do.'

He blinked at me, one eyebrow lifting, and stood aside with a mocking half bow. 'Please forgive me, miss.' And as he made for the door, he threw up his head with a light, teasing laugh.

I watched him leave, furious at myself for being unable to think of any way to return his ridicule. I groaned in frustrated anger as, a few seconds later, I saw the jeep, canvas sides down this time, turn up the narrow road onto the lonely moor.

'Rotten devil,' the shopkeeper sighed as I came up to the counter. 'Now what can I do for you?'

For a few seconds, I was still so incensed that I couldn't recall what it was I had come to buy. 'Oh, er, I'll have a large split tin, please. Who was that, then?' I enquired, jerking my head towards the door.

I don't really know why I asked. I didn't care who he was, as long as I didn't bump into him again.

'Used to be our best player. Lives up on the moor. Disappeared for a few years, and now he's come back a proper temperamental customer. Now, anything else you'd like?'

I hoped my meeting with the loathsome stranger would be a chance encounter, but he was bound to shop quite regularly at Bolts which was almost opposite Albert Terrace. As time went by, on the odd occasion I did spy him, I always crossed over the road to avoid him. And if I spotted the jeep, I would wait indoors until it had gone. Its driver was never long. He appeared to be as much of a recluse as Sidney had been when I had first arrived. Sidney and I were beginning to make something of our relationship, and I certainly didn't want another battle on my hands!

'Have a lovely Christmas, Wendy!'

'Yes, you, too, Lily! I'll miss not seeing you, though. And it's going to be a bit quiet without Joanna *and* Edwin. He simply couldn't get any time off. But Uncle Artie's coming to stay, and so are my grandparents. And Auntie Mary and Uncle Michael are coming on Christmas Day, so I suppose it won't be so bad!'

'It'll be a bit livelier than my Christmas will be!' I

assured her with a mock grimace. 'You should think yourself lucky!'

'Oh, I do! Actually, I might call in to see you and brighten up your day! It'll be Boxing Day, mind. Edwin has a friend living up on the moor your way, and as he can't get back to see him, Mum and Dad said they might pop up, so I could cadge a lift. Wouldn't want to go myself. Right old kill-joy is Daniel.'

I'd heard her mention the name before and I was going to ask where he lived, purely out of politeness rather than any real interest, when the train lurched and began to move forward. I was leaning out of the window, breathing in the smell of coal smoke in the frosty evening air, as Wendy hurried alongside on the platform.

'Bye, then! Love to all! And Merry Christmas!' I called as the engine gathered speed and Wendy became a small, wildly waving figure in the distance.

I settled down in the carriage, relaxing after the hectic time I'd had at work and thinking how much better Christmas was likely to be this year. Indeed, the following morning, I beamed across at Sidney as I served out the Christmas Day breakfast I had cooked for us both. As usual, we were up at the crack of dawn, but I didn't mind. Sidney had mellowed so much recently that I was actually growing quite fond of him. I even went to chapel with him sometimes. As it was virtually next door, it was hardly inconvenient! I took an interest in the garden which was his other love. In the autumn, I'd presented him with a huge bag of mixed spring bulbs that I bought at work, and had spent some hours burying them deep in the borders. Sidney, too, seemed much happier for our improved relationship. I had even persuaded him to listen to some classical music which he had begun to enjoy. The gramophone now lived downstairs with us, and sometimes we would listen to a record or two of an evening as we sipped cocoa before bedtime.

We had a little artificial tree decorated with *lametta* and garish glass baubles, all obtained from Woolworths. We'd had nothing at all the previous year, so it was all a step in the right direction. Sidney had cast a deprecating eye at it, but had indulged me, and the previous evening, a couple of packages had miraculously appeared beneath the green paper pines. I eyed them excitedly as I finished washing up the breakfast things and preparing the chicken the Colemans had kindly given us. Meat was still on ration, so I considered ourselves fortunate to live somewhere that managed to bypass the rules somewhat.

'Have we got time to open our presents before we go to chapel?' I asked eagerly.

Sidney's brow furrowed and then he actually chuckled. I think it was the first time I had ever seen him being guilty of merriment.

'Go on, then. I can tell you can't wait.'

'Thank you!' I cried, and rummaging under the tree, produced the packages I had hidden there myself. 'And these are for you.'

He looked at them, and his frown deepened as he took them from me. 'You first,' he insisted, and then I noticed the corners of his mouth curve upwards.

I returned his tentative smile and nodded. The last time I had been given a present had been eighteen months ago for my fifteenth birthday. Ellen had bestowed on me her double row of pearls, which I treasured. Looking back, I expect she had done so because she knew her days were numbered. Now, I opened the packets carefully to preserve the paper for next year. Wrapping had been like gold dust during the war, and old habits die hard.

The telltale shape hardly disguised the two seventy-eights. One was Richard Addinsell's 'Warsaw Concerto' from the war film, *Dangerous Moonlight*, and the other was Hubert Bath's 'Cornish Rhapsody' from *Love Story*. They were both old films, but both had been shown again recently at Princetown's Town Hall. I had actually enticed Sidney to come with me once or twice if the subject matter wasn't too frivolous, and he had admitted to having enjoyed himself. Now he was smiling broadly at me, taking me totally by surprise.

'I thought you'd like those. At least, I asked other

people, what with your love of films and classical music.'

'Oh, yes! Thank you so much!'

'And the book's *Rebecca*,' he added, using his head to indicate the remaining present. 'I know you liked the film, but I didn't know if you'd read the book.'

'No, I haven't. Oh, you couldn't have chosen better!'

I felt a gentle contentment swell up inside me. Yes, I was delighted with Sidney's choice, but more than that it was an indication that we could live peaceably, even happily, together. The future no longer stared bleakly at me, and a bud of hope unfurled in my breast, driving me to place a swift kiss on his cheek. I stood back, coloured with embarrassment.

'Go on, open yours,' I urged him in order to conceal it.

I'd bought him a tie, not too colourful but less austere than the grey one he sported perpetually, and two books, one the memories of a missionary in Africa, and the other one Thor Heyerdahl's *Kontiki Expedition*. My heart was in my mouth as he turned them over.

'Thank you,' he mumbled at last, and then I believe I noticed his eyes glisten as he whispered, 'It's a long time since anyone gave me a present. Before the war.'

His lips pressed together, and I drew in an elated breath and held it as I grinned at him. 'Come on, we'd better go or we *will* be late.'

The service was bright and happy, as it had been the previous year. But this time, a deep pleasure lulled my heart. So much had happened in the last twelve months. No longer at loggerheads, Sidney and I had become friends. Of an odd sort, perhaps, and I thanked God I had found the courage to stand up to him. We had brought the truth out into the open, and Sidney had begun to divulge snippets of information. But then I have always believed that problems should not be left to fester in the shadows. They should be brought out of the darkness and into the sunlight where they will shrivel and die.

I couldn't wait to listen to the records and played them while I put the finishing touches to our dinner. We pulled crackers, laughed over the silly jokes and wore the paper hats. Afterwards, we went for a walk until a miserable drizzle drove us home. A couple of rounds of that new game, Scrabble, then, both of which Sidney won, but I was eager to listen to my new records again. Sidney offered to light the fire in the parlour, a huge concession for him, but we were so cosy in the kitchen, we decided to stay put. We both read our new books, and later I made some chicken sandwiches. I devoured Jeannie's Christmas letter yet again, only two pages but long for her.

Full of amusement. She had a boyfriend now, and intimated at what they got up to in the back row of the cinema.

'You're right, Lily,' Sidney said as I bade him goodnight. 'You *are* a good girl.' And then he stunned me by adding, 'Your mother was, too. Lively, bright and caring. Until... She broke my heart, you know, and I could never forgive her. And when she was killed, I wished I had. And I blamed your grandmother as well, because she never liked me. But she was just as innocent as you were. I'm really sorry for the way I treated you, Lily. You didn't deserve it.'

Not a muscle in my body moved for a full thirty seconds as a warm serenity rippled out from the very core of me. I knew what the words had cost him, and I said with conviction quavering in my voice, 'That's all in the past. Let's forget about it and just be friends, now, eh?'

'Yes. Thank you, Lily.' And he got to his feet and hugged me.

Five minutes later, I snuggled down in bed, feeling happier than I had done since my peaceful life in London had been so cruelly shattered. It made me think of Jeannie, and I tried to imagine this boyfriend of hers. He didn't sound my cup of tea, unlike my sensitive, caring Edwin who I prayed would still be unattached when I met him again and fulfil my heady, glorious dream.

But when I finally fell asleep, I dreamt of
Manderley, just like the nameless heroine of
Rebecca. Except that the iron gates weren't chained
and padlocked. They were lodged wide open and
had been for years, and I crunched between them as
I limped up the sweeping gravel drive towards the
great house with the pillared portico and the stone-
mullioned windows.

'Hello! Happy Boxing Day!'

Wendy stood on the doorstep, muffled up to
her ears against the cold, even though she had only
just got out of the car. Above her brightly coloured
scarf, though, I could see her eyes were shining and
I hugged her tightly.

'Come in, come in!' I cried euphorically. 'Did you
have a lovely time yesterday?'

I stood back to let her in and waved to her parents
as William turned the car round and, to my surprise,
turned up Tor Royal Lane which of course led up
onto one of the most isolated parts of the moor. I
frowned, as there were few houses along the way.

'Yes, super, thank you! Edwin rang which was
great.' She unwound the scarf and threw it over the
end of the banisters. 'Mum and Dad are just going
to visit Daniel. His parents couldn't come down
from London because his mum's got the flu, so he's
been on his own. Don't suppose they'll be long,

though, so we'd best make the most of it.'

'Where does this Daniel live, then?' I asked, my curiosity roused.

'Oh, it's a great big house,' she gestured theatrically. 'You can't see it that well from the road 'cause it's behind a high brick wall and some tall pine trees. It's way out on the moor the other side of Peat Cott.'

I shivered as a coldness crept through my flesh. It had to be. There certainly weren't two such houses along the lonely road. This Daniel, who was a close friend of Edwin's and who the family obviously cared deeply about, could be none other than the surly ogre who had rescued me when I had injured my ankle!

'Oh,' I said, wishing my dismay hadn't been so audible. 'I think I've met him. Drives an old Army jeep?'

'Yes, that's right. Small world, isn't it?' Wendy grinned. 'But he's a moody old so-and-so, and I don't want to waste time talking about him!'

No, nor did I! 'Come and meet my dad!' I said instead.

Chapter Ten

February became known as the *Big Freeze*. January
had been cold enough, with ice causing problems
on the roads and, yet again, I was thankful that
I journeyed to work on the train. The rails might
be frozen but, with a little sand, the wheels always
gripped and delays were minimal. It was far more
difficult for Sidney to get to the quarry although it
was so much nearer. Mr Mead's old army Humber
staff car, one of thousands sold off cheaply after the
war like the jeeps, slithered along the moorland road
and ended up in a ditch. It had to be ignominiously
dragged out by a tractor, its wing and Mr Mead's
dignity slightly dented. No one was hurt, but after
that, he and Sidney and the other man he gave a lift
to made the long walk to work each day. Water froze
in pipes and even the milk left for collection at the
dairy farms down in the valleys towards Cornwall

became solid with pearly white ice crystals. A convict was mad enough to escape, but was recaptured nine miles away. It wouldn't surprise me if he hadn't given himself up because of the weather. It truly was like Siberia, with the howling wind racing uninterrupted across the moor and wailing like some mythical hound from hell.

I got out of the warm railway carriage at Princetown Station and the night air at once trapped me in a freezing vice. It blew up inside the sensible serge skirt I wore to work, seeking out the bare skin between the tops of my stockings and my knickers. I shivered, pulling up the hood of the duffel coat I'd bought in the sales at the end of the previous winter, and crossing my arms tightly over my waist. I tried to hurry but it was too slippery underfoot and I had to pick my way carefully. I thought of how lovely and warm the kitchen would be since Sidney would have got a good fire going in the range as he got home from work so much earlier than I did, and I couldn't wait to hurry into the centre of Princetown and our snug little house in Albert Terrace. Sidney and his workmates must have been frozen at the quarry, and I pitied them and anyone else who had to be out on the exposed, windswept moor in this weather.

I always prepared the dinner the night before so that we didn't eat too late. We were having a rich, nourishing stew made of scrag end of lamb and vegetables from the garden which Sidney admitted was far more productive than his plot at Foggintor had been. The warmth as I put my key in the door and came into the hall made my skin tingle and I sniffed for the enticing aroma of the meal which I expected Sidney to have heated through as he would with something like this that wouldn't spoil. But the distinctive smell of lamb wasn't there and my lips pouted. I was starving, and the hot, steaming meal that could so easily have been waiting for me obviously wasn't. Oh, damn you, Sidney, I cursed in my head. Probably had his nose stuck in his Bible and forgot the time.

It was as I came to the kitchen door that I noticed the strange odour. It was like burning, as if someone had overdone some pork chops. But we weren't having chops. The hairs on the back of my neck stood on end and my stomach started to churn with apprehension. I knew instinctively that something was wrong and, as I threw open the door, my heart leapt into my throat.

Why is it that, at moments of sheer horror, time seems to stand still? There's an instant when your brain absorbs what it has seen or heard, followed by calm acceptance, a voice that says *this has happened* so you must get on and deal with it. You feel strange, unreal, as if you're not actually there but are watching someone else. Like a film. It's only very slowly that feeling dribbles back into your soul. You move as if in a dream, waiting to wake up, and it isn't until hours, days, have passed that you realise you're not going to. Because you already are awake, and this is really happening.

Sidney was stretched out on the floor, straddling the space between the table and the range. He was lying on his front, one leg bent beneath him but the other foot still trapped under the edge of the rug he had evidently tripped on. One arm was outstretched as if he had tried to break his fall. His neck was twisted unnaturally, his head almost turned backwards as if he was looking over his shoulder. A dark red liquid had seeped out from beneath his temple and dried into a sticky puddle on the stone hearth.

I stood rigid as the shock pulsed through me. I knew before I sank on my knees beside him that he was dead. Stone, cold dead. Apart from his face. The range firebox was open and Sidney must have built up a roaring blaze just before he fell. And as he lay unconscious or instantly dead, the heat had scorched the skin of his face so that it had puckered into raw, oozing blisters, and it smelt of burnt flesh. One eye was open and staring, the other, which had been far more exposed to the heat, a horrible, viscid, unrecognisable pulp. The fire had died down to nothing, a layer of flaky grey ash over vacillating, glowing embers.

Oh, no. The sigh spiralled up from deep inside me, soundless, a whisper. Emptiness. Silence. Stillness. There was no need to hurry. I knew there was nothing that could be done. I should call someone, but my muscles refused to move, and my mind somehow couldn't make them.

I don't know how long it was before I was able to stagger to my feet and totter on wobbling legs to Gloria's door. When she opened it a few moments later, I peered at her through a veil of shock and made a small, squealing sound at the back of my throat. 'My...my father.' I wrung the words from somewhere in my chest. 'He's had an accident. He's...he's dead.'

I saw the shock register on her face and then, very slowly, she nodded. And then time seemed to accelerate. Gloria sat me down by her blazing fire and gave me some of that amber liquid again. I was shivering so violently that it hurt and she wrapped a blanket around me before she disappeared for a few minutes. I had left our front door ajar and I guessed she must have gone in to make sure. Then I heard her voice on the telephone, and she was back in the room, crooning to me. Making me feel safe.

It was all a blur, but soon afterwards there were voices and movement, and Gloria left me again briefly. I had hoped they might send William, but because of the dangerous travelling conditions, the

MO from the prison came instead and had the body taken away to the morgue. He confirmed that Sidney had been dead for at least a couple of hours, and that the fatal blow to his head had been from the fall onto the stone hearth which had also probably broken his neck. Then the doctor gave me a sleeping draft and said Gloria should put me to bed before I dropped off in the chair.

'Shouldn't we scrub the bloodstain while it's still fresh?' was all I could ask as she tucked me up in one of her spare rooms. The sheets smelt clean and fresh, and Gloria had put two hot water bottles in the bed.

'Don't you worry about that,' she soothed me. 'You just sleep. It won't seem so bad in the morning.'

The medicine didn't work straight away, morose thoughts chasing each other round in my head. My life had once seemed so ordered, but since Ellen's death, it had been turned upside down. I had fought back all the way, slowly winning, and with so many new friends now, I was looking forward to a brighter future. I had begun to hope that Sidney would eventually tell me more about my lost family. Now he never would, and I felt all alone in the world once again.

Had I made Sidney happier in the last few months of his life? I should like to think so. He had been so

hurt by my mother's infidelity, and as well as losing
the woman he loved, he had lost his two small sons.
It must be the worst thing imaginable to lose a child,
and my sorrow over Sidney's grief far outweighed
my own as I lay in the shadows of the strange room.
Outside I caught the screech of a hunting barn owl
followed by the gentle hoot of a tawny. A little
way off, a fox barked. Sounds of the night that
had become familiar to me since coming to live on
the moor. Dartmoor that had come to soothe and
comfort me...

'Is there anyone I can call for you? Any family?'
Gloria asked kindly the next morning.

My head ached and I felt awful, my eyes heavy as
if I had been awake all night, which I hadn't. Gloria
had made me some coffee, and I was sipping at it,
huddled in a dressing gown that was far too big for
me and waiting for my thoughts to clear.

'Yes, please,' I nodded wearily. 'But if you
wouldn't mind me using your phone, I think I'd
rather ring myself.'

'Of course, my dear. Anything you wish.'

I rang Mrs Kershaw first as it was just gone nine
o'clock and she would be wondering why I hadn't
turned up for work. She was very kind and just asked
me to keep in touch. Then I rang the Franfield's
private number as I knew both telephones were on

the desk in the hallway. Deborah answered, calm and efficient as I knew she would be.

'Oh, I'm so sorry, my dear. How dreadful,' she said at once, her voice ringing with sympathy. 'You must come and stay with us, but I'm afraid surgery's in full swing now, but as soon as it's over, I'll drive up and collect you.'

'Oh, no, you mustn't do that. The roads are treacherous up here. I'll come down on the train later on. I'll need to pack a few things, and there are a few people I must tell.'

'Whatever you want, dear. I'll be in all day. Oh, I feel awful about this, but I must go. I'm needed.'

'Yes, of course I understand. I'll see you later. Thank you so much.'

It was a day for saying thank you. Gloria was kindness itself, but she understood that Wendy had become my best friend. I called in at Kate's house on my way to the station and told her mum who was horrified and gave me a crushing hug. But there was no room for me to stay there and I wouldn't have wanted to stay at Sally's. And so I was soon gazing out of the carriage window at my beloved Dartmoor. I barely saw it, my mind filled with an image of Sidney lying across the kitchen floor.

Deborah opened the front door and took me straight into the lounge. 'You warm yourself by the fire and I'll bring up some of the soup I've just made.

I thought it would be just right for you.'

'Oh, that's very kind,' I answered, a little absently I'm ashamed to say. I still felt numbed and truncated from the world around me, and went to stand in front of the roaring blaze in the grate as if in a stupor. The fire reminded me for a moment of Sidney's blackened face, and I shuddered. But the bitter weather had chilled me to the bone on the walk from Tavistock Station, and I put the horrific vision to one side as I pulled off my gloves and held my hands out to the heat.

'There.'

Deborah smiled compassionately at me as she came into the room carrying a tray with two steaming mugs and some buttered rolls. I took one of the mugs, but I knew a roll would only stick in my throat. The hot soup, though, began to warm me through as I sipped at it.

'How dreadfully sad for you, especially after what you've already been through.'

Her friendly face was creased with compassion, and I felt the anguish begin to drain out of me. But before I had a chance to answer, I heard voices in the hall and a moment later, Wendy and her father came into the room. William's expression was solemn and Wendy dashed over and folded me into her arms.

'Oh, Lily, how awful!'

She held me for several seconds before sitting

down beside me with one arm still around my shoulders. I felt humbled to be in their caring company, especially when I had never told them the entire truth. I took a deep, shuddering breath.

'The worst of it is that, well, about six months ago, he told me that I'm not actually his daughter,' I confessed somewhat shamefaced. 'Apparently, my mother had an affair and I'm this other man's child. And I feel so awful that I've never told you when you've always been so kind, but I didn't want anyone to know in case they tried to take me away and put me in a children's home. I'm so sorry, really I am.'

I glanced across at Deborah and William's astonished faces, not sure what to expect from them. But I felt Wendy squeeze me even tighter.

'We won't let them put you in a home, will we? I couldn't bear that!'

I think I released a ponderous sigh as I turned to her. 'But they could,' I groaned despondently. 'Until I'm eighteen.'

'That's preposterous!' Wendy remonstrated. 'Is that right, Dad?'

'Unfortunately, it is. There were so many children living in odd circumstances because of the war that the government wanted to protect them. I'm sorry. That isn't what you wanted to hear, is it, Lily?' William drew in a deep breath and pursed his lips thoughtfully. 'I can have a word with the local welfare people, mind, and see if I can pull some strings. You have a reasonably paid job and you're a very capable young lady. But I can't promise anything.'

'Oh, that's very kind,' I sighed with relief.

'And in the meantime, you must stay with us, of course.'

'Really? Are you sure you don't mind?'

'It'll be lovely to have you!' Wendy cried beside me.

'It's the least we can do. And we'll help you to arrange the funeral and everything else that'll need sorting. Can't expect someone of your age to do all that.'

It was then that I burst into tears.

I was surprised how many people came to the funeral. Sidney's workmates, of course, the Colemans and Gloria, but everyone I knew well from Princetown as well as my own particular friends. I was really touched. And then it dawned on me that they hadn't so much come to mourn Sidney as to support me. It made the constriction in my throat squeeze even more tightly. I would miss everyone so much while I stayed with Wendy, not to mention the moor itself. To me, it was a living thing that had given strength and purpose to my life when it had been at such a low ebb. But at least I wouldn't be far away.

The morning of the funeral had dawned crisp

and bitterly cold, the sun shining brightly from a colourless disc in the sky which made the whole affair a little less daunting. Sidney's hadn't been a happy life and I felt sorry for that, forgiving him the way he had treated me. It was all too soon after Ellen's funeral and I wanted to cry. Yet again, I found myself biting the inside of my bottom lip to hold back the tears, but once it was all over, I was aware of a sense of release.

Wendy and Deborah had come up by train to be with me, as William needed the car for his rounds. They had taken a boot full of my belongings back with them the previous day, so I only had a small bag to take with me on the train. I would be back, of course. I would have to go through Sidney's personal belongings, but hadn't yet found the courage. For who knew what I might find among them. I could be disappointed, or I could discover something that could set me on the trail to my lost identity. But for now it would have to wait.

'Fancy going to the pictures tonight?' Wendy asked on the Friday morning as we parted company outside the solicitors' offices where she worked.

I had been back at work since Wednesday and already my life had become so wonderfully normal again. It felt so secure and comforting, living in the bosom of a family that was so sensible and yet so lively. Wendy in particular was determined that I wouldn't feel sad. Of course, I had stayed there on several occasions before and easily fell into a relaxed routine. The only thing I found hard to get used to was that once she had cleaned the surgery at seven o'clock each weekday morning, the 'daily', Mrs Salmon, then turned her attentions to the rest of the house until lunchtime!

'Oh, yes, that would be lovely!'

'Celia might come as well. I think she said she's got Friday evening off. You know she's not as keen on films as we are, but she'll probably come. And tomorrow night there's another public dance at the Town Hall.' Her sparkling eyes clouded, then, as she asked, 'Unless you feel it's too soon after, well, you know, your father. Or rather, Sidney.'

I shook my head with a reassuring smile. 'No, not at all. In fact, I think it's just what I need!'

'That's settled then,' she grinned. 'See you at lunchtime!' And in she went, pulling off her gloves and stuffing them into her handbag while I cut across Bedford Square towards Woolworths.

I had a great weekend, almost forgetting that Sidney had died in a horrible accident less than a fortnight before. I thought about him a lot but as a living person, remembering little details. But I didn't feel so sad any more. Deborah and William had made me so welcome, and Wendy and Celia really felt like sisters, linking arms with me between them as we walked back from the cinema on that frosty Friday night. But I was still fraught with anxiety as to my future. William had been in contact with the welfare authorities, but no decision had yet been made. The prospect of a children's home was looming menacingly nearer. Then something happened to change everything.

The telephone rang one evening while we were all chuckling over *What's My Line* on the television. Deborah went out into the hall to answer it. She was quite some time and we heard her laughing so it obviously wasn't an emergency call. When she came back into the room, her excitement was palpable.

'That was Edwin,' she breathed with bubbling anticipation. 'He's managed to get the whole of Easter off and he's coming down to stay!'

'Oh, that's top hole!' William cried, his oft serious face lighting up like a beacon. 'He certainly won't be able to next year. He'll be coming up to his finals then.'

'Trust you to think of that, Dad!' Wendy grinned, and leaping up from the sofa, dragged me to my feet and jumped up and down with glee. 'Edwin's coming home, Edwin's coming home!' she chanted, and began to waltz me round the room.

'We can have a birthday party for him!' Deborah announced joyfully. 'After all, one's quarter century is a special one, isn't it? Just a small family celebration. We must make sure Celia's off duty. Edwin's friends are all in London nowadays, of course. Unless…you don't think we could persuade Daniel to come, do you?'

At the mention of Daniel, my own heart clenched, and I noticed that the lovely sparkle suddenly went out of Deborah's eyes and a doubtful frown took its place. The smile left William's face, too, and he raised his eyebrows ruefully.

'We could try, but I doubt he'd accept, not even for Edwin. You know what he was like when we went to see him at Christmas.'

'That's very true.' Deborah puffed out her cheeks and dropped back into her chair, quite deflated. 'Such a pity Sheila had the flu so he was on his own for Christmas.'

'He could have gone up to them if he'd wanted to,' William observed. 'But he chose not to. Peace and quiet is what he craves, not the hustle and bustle of London.'

'Oh, I do worry about that boy.' Deborah shook her head, all her earlier elation fled.

'Well, don't.' William fixed his wife with steady eyes in a way I hadn't seen in him before. Professional, I suppose. 'It's not surprising after what the poor lad's been through. But he's a lot stronger than you think. Always had a will of iron. He'll get over it. He just needs time.'

'I don't want that old grumpy guts to spoil our party anyway!' Wendy's ecstasy broke through the sober conversation, banishing the downcast interlude. 'We'll have a much better time without him! Now, we will make Edwin a big birthday cake, won't we, Mum? So lovely that sugar's off ration at last, and we can pool our butter rations, can't we?'

I was so relieved that the decision seemed to have been made to leave Daniel out of the party. I really didn't want to meet up with him again and have him ruin any time I might have to get to know Edwin better. My heart was already fluttering at the thought that Edwin, the young man whose handsome, anxious face had remained in my dreams for over a year, was coming home to his family, the very same I was staying in with!

'Yes, of course we can. Seems quite ridiculous to me that butter and cheese are still on ration, mind, after all these years. And meat, too.'

'Hopefully for not much longer, dear.'

'Well, I'm sure we can have a super party!' Wendy was beaming again. 'Oh, I can't wait to see Edwin again, and he must be dying to meet you, Lily! You did tell Edwin about Lily, didn't you, Mum?'

A warm tide of expectancy rippled through me, but at the same time I was trembling. Would Edwin have thought of me again as I had him? Would he remember me *at all*? And would he light the same fire inside me as he had on that distant day when the wind had snatched the balloon string from the child's grip?

'I hope you've never told him I was the person he nearly ran over!' I cried in horror, imagining all my hopes being shattered. 'It could be awfully embarrassing for both of us.'

William pulled in his chin. 'Well, he might prefer not to be reminded of the incident. But I suppose he's bound to remember when he sees you again.'

'Well, we'll keep it as a surprise for him, won't we? A birthday surprise!' Wendy chortled as she danced around the room.

Chapter Eleven

'Edwin, this is Lily.'

Wendy stood back, her eyes dancing above her mouth which was sealed into an excited, impish grin. I waited in the lounge doorway and suddenly my heart was pounding. I had been telling myself at work all day that it was childish to feel nervous about meeting again with the stranger I had been acquainted with for all of five minutes such a long time ago, and I had managed to keep the butterflies at bay. But now the moment had come, my stomach was turning cartwheels.

He had his back to me, tall and slender of build, just as I remembered him. He was wearing a brown knitted jumper, his fair hair cut short this time so that it didn't reach the collar of his beige checked shirt. He turned round, putting down the glass he had been drinking from, and came forward, smiling, his hand outstretched. I was sure my heart stood still as I looked into those green-blue eyes.

'Hello, Edwin, I'm very pleased to meet you,' I said, my lips moving of their own accord. 'Did you have a good journey?'

'Yes, thank you.' But his words sounded distant as he shook my hand, his head tipped to one side. 'Have…have we met somewhere before? You seem familiar somehow.'

He was staring at me, his smooth brow corrugated with a questioning frown, and I gazed back into the clear depths of his eyes. A fizzing euphoria foamed inside me as if this was a very special moment in my life. One I would savour for ever.

'Ha, ha, you remember her, then?' Wendy chortled, bounding across the room to hop at her brother's back. For a second, I hardly noticed her, as if Edwin and I were sharing a dreaming sleep.

'Oh, goodness me.' Edwin put his hand over his mouth, and the spell was broken. Reality, but a good, happy reality, took its place as those captivating eyes stretched wide and he smiled broadly again. 'It was you I nearly ran over! When the little boy…'

He broke off, his expression incredulous as he laughed softly. The apprehension flooded out of me and I grinned back.

'That's right! What an amazing coincidence, isn't it?'

I waited, judging his reaction. He shook his head with a grunt of pleasurable disbelief.

'Well, I never did. And how are you, anyway? Is my sister here looking after you properly?'

'Oh, absolutely. And your parents, they've been so kind. But I've been here a month now, and I'm sure I've outstayed my welcome.'

'No, not a bit of it!' Wendy cried. 'We love having you.'

'Oh, you mustn't feel like that. Mum and Dad are enjoying your stay. They were just saying before they opened up evening surgery what a great person you are to have around.' The steady smile reached his eyes and I felt the scarlet in my cheeks as I realised he was paying me a compliment. I think he must have appreciated my embarrassment as he said with a flick of his head, 'Oh, I'm sorry. You haven't even got your coat off yet. You go and, well, do whatever you do when you come home from work, and I'll pour you a drink. Oh, wait a minute. I suppose, strictly speaking, you shouldn't. But a little sherry wouldn't hurt. I think Mum's got a drop left.'

'Oh, no, don't do that,' I answered pleasantly. 'I'll make myself a coffee.'

'I'll make it for you. Do you have it black or white?'

I hurried up to my bedroom, my heart soaring. Edwin seemed to like me! I was bursting with joy as

I quickly changed out of my sensible work clothes and put on my favourite twin-set. It was a strong aquamarine which went well with my hair which I let down from its French roll. It hung around my shoulders in a mass of sleek, golden waves, and I fastened Ellen's pearls around my neck. Then I put on my full, floral skirt and the soft shade of lipstick I had bought from the cosmetics counter last week. I glanced in the mirror. That looked much more appealing, and I had to put a curb on my tingling excitement as I trotted down both sets of stairs to the kitchen.

Edwin was just pouring out the coffee, and Wendy was tackling a pile of late sprouts for dinner. A cabbage was also waiting to be chopped.

'Let me help you with that,' I offered jauntily.

'No, you sit there and have your coffee. I'll help Wendy. I can handle a knife, you know.' Edwin was grinning cheekily as he picked up another vegetable knife. 'Right. First incision so.' And he carefully scored down one side of the cabbage. 'Then we cut deeper, being careful to avoid the arteries and main nerves. Protractors, please. Well, hold it open with your hands, Nurse Lily. Now, through the peritoneum and now…yes, there's the offending appendix!' He poked the blade into the heart of the cabbage and twisted it round. 'Now, let's get the little devil out and…there! Suture it up and we're all done!'

I had been giggling at his antics, but Wendy was laughing aloud. It was infectious, and soon we were falling about helplessly as Edwin performed another operation on the hapless cabbage. Tears of mirth were pouring down our cheeks when William and Deborah appeared in the doorway, chuckling at us in amusement.

'Well, you young people are having fun! But, oh, Edwin! Just look at my cabbage!'

'Sorry, Mum. But you can still eat it. The pieces will just be funny shapes!' Edwin spluttered.

'I think you lot had better take yourselves into the lounge while your father and I finish off the dinner.'

'No, I'll stay,' Wendy insisted, tipping her head pertly at me. 'You take your coffee up to the lounge and you've got your whisky in there, Ed.'

'Yes, go on, you two.' Deborah flapped her hand at Edwin and me. 'Go on. Shoo!'

'Oh, well, if you insist, Mum!'

'You've come home for a rest,' she beamed indulgently.

We sat for half an hour on our own, Edwin and I, chatting easily. I felt relaxed and yet animated, kicking off my shoes and curling up in a chair opposite him while he sipped at his whisky.

'So you were living up at Foggintor where Uncle Artie was born? Amazing.'

'That's right. All through the winter. It was quite

cosy inside once I got used to it. Not having running water was a bit of a shock, mind. But then we moved up to Princetown. But I always came into work on the train every day.'

'Oh yes, it's a fantastic journey, isn't it? A wonderful sight, the old steam engine chugging across the moor!'

'And when it looms out of the mist, it's like some sort of mythical dragon breathing fire and flame, and then it disappears into thin air again!'

Edwin threw up his head with a chuckle. 'Yes, I suppose it does. Were you good at English at school? You seem to have a good imagination.'

'Yes, I was quite,' I admitted a little bashfully at what appeared to be another compliment. 'My grandmother wanted me to stay on at school, but I wanted to go out to work. But when she died and I came to live here, I'd probably have had to go out to work anyway. I've got a reasonable job now, though. But I can't see that I'll ever get promoted further.'

'You could always go to evening classes.'

I raised an eyebrow. 'Yes, I suppose I could. I hadn't thought of that. But only if I end up living in Tavistock permanently, and at the moment, I'm not sure what's going to happen to me.'

'Dinner's ready!' Wendy called from the door and skipped away again.

Edwin unfolded himself from his chair and getting

to his feet, offered me his arm. 'Shall we?' he said politely. 'And by the way, you look very fetching,' he added, his voice low and breathless as I linked my hand through his elbow.

My fingers tingled at the feel of his arm through the sleeve of his jumper, and my heart winged me to paradise as we went down to the kitchen.

The intense cold of February had long passed and there was a hint of spring in the air with early daffodils waving their vibrant yellow heads in the long front gardens of Plymouth Road. The weather on Good Friday was pleasant enough for a stroll in the park alongside the disused canal, and we even sat on one of the benches and fed the ducks. Deborah was obviously overjoyed at having her son back home if only for a few days, and was content to sit and listen to him chatting to myself and Wendy. She flitted about the house, clearly spoiling him which he openly acknowledged, returning her affection quite demonstrably.

After lunch, Edwin went with William to the hospital to visit his in-patients, and when they returned, they shut themselves in the consulting room for a couple of hours discussing medical matters. But over dinner and throughout the evening, the conversation was light and full of banter, and Edwin seemed to pay me a great deal of attention. I was sure he wasn't just being nice because I was his parents' house-guest!

It rained on Saturday, but I was at work anyway. I couldn't wait to get back and kept looking at my watch all afternoon. I was met by shrieks of hilarity coming up from the kitchen. There was Edwin, his face aglow with merriment as he chased Wendy around the table with Deborah's wooden spoon covered in cake mixture that he was endeavouring to flick at his sister. I burst out laughing as I was drawn to the doorway.

'Really, you two!' Deborah was attempting to reprimand them through her own guffaws. 'Don't you waste any! We all gave up our margarine rations for that cake, including poor Lily!'

Edwin stopped in his tracks, his face split in a grin as he saw me. 'Did you really, Lily? Oh, that was kind! Thank you!' He bent down and deposited a fat kiss on my cheek before dancing back to the table and replacing the spoon in the mixing bowl. 'Come on, Lily! Have a stir and make a wish! Isn't that what you do with cakes?'

'That's Christmas puddings, isn't it?' I grinned back.

His face fell and he looked so crestfallen that I couldn't help but chuckle. 'Oh, well, never mind. Do it anyway!' he instructed.

I did. And two guesses what I wished for!

* * *

The rain didn't let up all night. I heard it battering against the window as I turned over in bed and went back to dreaming about Edwin, my young heart running over with the new and elated emotion of my first real love. And the joy of it was that Edwin appeared to be returning my feelings. I kept patting my cheek where he had kissed me.

His youngest sister, Celia, arrived from the hospital early on Sunday morning, her umbrella dripping all over the tiles in the conservatory. She ran into the hall like a whirlwind and hugged Edwin tightly. She had only seen him fleetingly at the hospital, she declared, and could hardly demonstrate her sibling affection in the middle of the ward, could she? Especially when she was carrying a used bedpan! Deborah's parents, whom I'd met once before, arrived next from their little cottage at Newton Ferrers, and, not unexpectedly, sat down to a long and lively chat with their grandson who they hadn't seen since the previous summer.

The evening before, Edwin had drawn me aside, his jovial smile fading to the serious expression he had borne when I had first met him. In a way, I was glad. It was great to know how to let one's hair down, but life is a serious business. No one knew that more than I did, so it was gratifying to see that side of Edwin's character again. A perfect balance, and I loved him even more for it.

'You know Uncle Artie's bringing my Auntie Mary tomorrow?' he began gravely. 'She's Dad's proper sister, not half like Uncle Artie.'

I nodded. 'Yes. Your mum told me. She said her husband – your Uncle Michael, I think she said – is a captain in the Merchant Navy and he's away at sea, so he can't come.'

'That's right. He'll be retiring soon, though. But,' Edwin paused, his eyes solemn so that I could see the professional doctor in him, 'did Mum tell you about their sons?'

I instinctively knew he was going to impart something sad to me and I felt cold inside. 'No, she didn't. I think she was about to, but the phone rang.'

'Ah, well. Anyway,' he said, dropping his voice further, 'my cousin Dick was in the Royal Navy and was killed in forty-three.'

A barb of sorrow pierced somewhere around my heart and I felt that little knot in my throat. 'How dreadful,' I croaked. It really was horrible and brought the anguish home to me yet again. The darkness of war. So close. Once it had only been the loss of my father – or grandfather John as I now knew him to be – that had broken my child's heart. How Ellen had been so strong, I would never know, especially when before that she had kept hidden her grief over my mother and brothers, and nearly myself, for heaven's sake. The boy, then, whose bed I had slept in when I had lived with Sidney. And now it was Edwin's cousin. Another young life wasted.

'Yes, it was.' Edwin frowned and I saw the hurt in his eyes. 'They only live in Plymouth, so Dick and I saw a lot of each other as children and really got on well, although he was that much older than me. And Neil, too.'

I shuddered. 'The other brother? He wasn't...as well?'

The idea filled me with horror, but to my utter relief, Edwin shook his head. 'No. But he was in the Navy, too. In the far east. He met an Australian girl out there and now they live in Sydney. A bit like Joanna, only Australia's further away than America. So, anyway, we don't talk about the boys unless Auntie Mary does. Just thought I'd warn you.'

'Oh, yes. I'm glad you did.'

Edwin smiled appreciatively. 'I knew you'd understand.'

Our eyes met and I had that exquisite feeling of a moment shared, even if it hadn't been a happy one. 'Appalling, isn't it?' I almost whispered. 'There are people like you and your father dedicating your lives to saving people when the rest of the world has spent six years trying to kill each other. Thank God it's over.'

'Well, let's hope it stays that way. We've already

had Korea since. Talking of which—'

But he never got any further as Wendy burst into the room asking something about fish paste sandwiches and cream crackers.

'It's good to see you again, little maid!' Artie greeted me when he arrived with Auntie Mary the following morning. 'But I were sorry to hear about your father. But,' he paused, his face brightening, 'we're here to celebrate young Edwin's birthday. How are you, lad? Good to see you! And I hear you two are getting on well together?'

I wasn't sure if he meant Edwin and me or Wendy and me. In my mind, I was convinced it was Edwin, and my cheeks flushed hotly. But everyone was nattering away nineteen to the dozen. A hubbub of conversation filled every corner of the room, and I was drawn hither and thither as if the party was as much in my honour as Edwin's.

Later on, we pushed back the chairs and played frivolous games such as charades and passing a balloon from between each others' knees. Everyone enjoyed the jollifications, even Auntie Mary without her husband and surviving son. William had a gramophone in the lounge, larger and with a better sound than mine. The men rolled back the carpet and we cavorted up and down as we danced the *Gay Gordons* and the *Lambeth Walk*. Edwin and

Wendy had us all in fits with an impromptu and melodramatic version of the tango, and Deborah's mother surprised everyone by performing the *Charleston* with amazing energy. When William put on a waltz and Edwin took my hand, my pulse missed a beat. He held me close, and I melted against him. Edwin's eyes were deep and intent when he smiled down at me, his mouth in a soft curve, before he whisked me round in a magical, dreamlike spin. I wished it would go on for ever.

Chapter Twelve

'Could I possibly borrow the car this afternoon, please, Dad?' Edwin asked at lunch the following day, Easter Monday. 'The weather's so much nicer today and I'd love to go up on the moor before I go back to London. Uncle Artie was talking yesterday about Foggintor, and I'd like to see it again. Haven't been there for years.'

'Yes, of course.' William nodded as he swallowed a mouthful of the party leftovers. 'Drop me off at the hospital on the way, though, would you? I need to check on some patients. No peace for the wicked, eh?'

'Thanks, Dad. Anybody else like to come?' Edwin enquired expectantly glancing round the table. 'Mum?'

Deborah released a weighty sigh. 'To be honest, I'm a bit jaded after yesterday. I think I'd rather put my feet up and read a book. But take Lily. You miss the moor, don't you, Lily dear?'

Mention of the moor reminded me of the question of my future, and doubt swooped like a raven across the sunshine that had blazed inside me ever since Edwin's arrival. 'Yes, I do. But not so much living here, though, as I will if they make me go to a children's home in Plymouth.'

'Actually, Lily,' William said, his eyes twinkling, 'we've been talking about it, and we'd like you to stay with us permanently. We love having you, and you fit in so perfectly. So?' He leant forward in his chair. 'What do you say?'

For a few seconds, I didn't say anything! I was dumbfounded. My brain attempted vainly to formulate some words, but any sound I made stuck in my throat. My wide eyes moved around the four faces that were staring at me in anticipation.

'Oh. Well. Yes!' The answer finally stumbled out of my mouth. 'That would be…wonderful!'

'Jolly good. That's settled then. Now, is there any more trifle left, Deborah?'

My stunned mind was beginning to work again. 'Are you sure? I mean…it's an awful imposition.'

'Not at all. We've asked you. And it would satisfy the welfare people. So now everyone's happier. Particularly Wendy.'

'Oh, I can't thank you enough!'

It was as if a sudden light had shone its way into the dark uncertainty of my future, illuminating every deep, worrying crevice. The Franfields were already like family, and what was more, I would see Edwin whenever he came home! The stars were certainly shining down on me that day!

'You going to come with us this afternoon, Sis? We can have a nice long walk if the weather holds.'

Beside me, Wendy pulled a face. 'You know me and walking. We don't really mix. No. You take Lily. I'm sure she'll enjoy it far more than me.'

My heart gave a bound. Edwin and I, walking on the moor together. Just the two of us. Oh, it would be heaven!

Joy flowed through my veins as Edwin parked the car just off the road by the track that leads past Yellowmeade Farm to Foggintor. I was effervescent, almost foolish in my euphoria at being not just up on my beloved moor again but alone with Edwin. Though the air had been still down in Tavistock, here it was, inevitably, rushing round us the instant we got out of the car, pulling at my hair and whipping it about my face. Edwin laughed at my futile efforts to tie on a headscarf to keep it in place, and I wished I'd brought a rubber band with me to put it in a ponytail. Edwin's own fair curls were being buffeted into his eyes, for though his hair was cut militarily short at the back, it was long and Brylcreemed down at the front. But the Dartmoor wind was having none of that! I took off my shoes and put on my Wellingtons, tucking my trousers inside them. I had deliberately never acquired a pair of proper walking boots as my blunt saviour I now knew to be Edwin's friend, Daniel, had advised. It seemed a way of snubbing him and paying him back for his rudeness. Not that he ever knew. So I fastened the toggles of my duffel coat and off we went.

I realised then how I had missed the pure, clean feel of the wind, the familiar scent of peat in my nostrils, and the immense panoramas down over the moor to the indistinct shadow of the Cornish hills. We walked along the track past the ruins of other quarrymen's dwellings that had been known as Red Cottages. But there was no sadness in my heart as there sometimes was when I imagined what life must have been like in that remote community in the past. Today I felt I could fly! Barry Coleman and his son-in-law were working on their tractor when we passed, and we stopped to chat. They vaguely knew Edwin through Artie, of course, but hadn't clapped eyes on him for years.

'You was a mere little tacker last time I saw you!' Barry proclaimed with a grin. 'And now look at you! And as for you, young maid, I be proper pleased for you.'

'Thank you. But you were always so kind to me,

and I do miss living on the moor, I have to say.'

'Well, you knows where we are, like!'

We bade them farewell and waved back as we walked further along the track. It would have been perfect if Edwin had taken my hand. He didn't. But I suppose that would have been too much to expect. All I knew was that Edwin liked me, and I was rocked in a comforting cradle. There was plenty of time, and I was sure that a deep and lasting love would develop between us. For now, I was supremely happy.

My insides, though, lurched when we came up to the dismal sight of the derelict cottages where I had lived with Sidney. Edwin, too, stopped in his tracks and shook his head.

'Golly, it all looks so different. Not that I've been up here since I was a kid. Look, that's the cottage where Uncle Artie was born. Or what's left of it. Which one was yours?'

'This one.' I pointed to the separate row to one side. 'Can you imagine waking up to this view every day? And waving to the train?'

Edwin made a sucking noise between his teeth. 'Unbelievable. And here, on the end, this was a little chapel. Once upon a time, it used to double up as a school. My grandmother used to teach there.'

'Really? I didn't know that.'

'Oh, yes. Up until Uncle Artie was born. Then there wasn't a teacher here for some time. They used the Mission Hall for a bit, and then they built the proper school.'

'And now that's disused. And some of those children will have fought and died in the war.'

'Sadly, yes, they probably did. That's history for you. But let's not be morose. It's my last day.' He took my hand, and the sensation sparkled up my arm. 'We'll cross the railway line and walk over the top to Swell Tor. Don't fall into the quarry, mind. I'm not sure my medical skills are up to that yet!'

I giggled as I skipped along beside him. We came to the railway halt and paused for a minute or two to absorb the glorious, familiar view. It all seemed so different from that long ago night when I had first alighted from the train and all was dark and menacing. Now it was friendly and beckoning. I felt vital and alive as we made our way up to Swell Tor quarry and the great gash in the earth that it formed, so different in shape and character from the double amphitheatre at Foggintor. But here, too, I fancied I could hear the calls of the workmen, long since gone, echo in the wind.

We clambered down to the old siding where the gnarled wooden sleepers still lay half-buried in the grass that had grown up between them. Beside them was the row of massive, half finished bridge corbels. They made a convenient seat for us to take a rest and breathe in our dramatic surroundings.

'Meant for London Bridge, weren't they, when it was being widened?' Edwin asked lazily, running his hand along the smooth, dressed surface he was perched on.

I nodded. 'That's right. The story goes that someone measured them too short and only realised after they'd done all this work.'

'Whoops! Someone must have been in trouble!' Edwin pulled a long face and then grinned. 'Still, London's loss is our gain. Given us something to sit on. The grass would be soaking after all the rain.' He tipped his head enquiringly at me, and I shivered with excitement. 'Do you miss London?'

I shrugged my shoulders. 'No, not really. I thought I would. But I fell in love with Dartmoor straight away. It may sound silly but it has a sort of healing effect on me.'

I had coloured with embarrassment so I was relieved when Edwin nodded. 'Yes, I know what you mean. Peaceful.' He paused, and I saw his eyes follow the course of the railway line as it coiled its way across the dip below us. 'Do you think you'll go back?' he asked, meeting my gaze again. 'To London, I mean?'

I considered his question before I replied. Was he thinking of the future? *Our* future, perhaps? Something plunged into the pit of my belly. 'I don't know,' I answered cautiously. 'I suppose I would if

I had good reason to. But I'd rather stay here. I've thought of going back to visit my friend, Jeannie. We still keep in touch. Sort of. I write to her but she takes for ever to reply. Usually waits until Christmas or my birthday.'

Edwin gave a rueful smile. 'That's what happens. People move on. Which is what we should do if we're not going to freeze solid.'

'Oh, yes.' I shivered. 'I've suddenly come over cold.'

I went to wriggle from my seat, but Edwin jumped down in front to help me. The feel of his hands about my waist, even through my duffel coat, was enthralling. We struck out homeward, exhilarated, and in my case, not only by the exertion of the walk! But as we trudged back along the lengthy track from Foggintor to the main road, the wind was driving directly into our faces. It was unpleasant and made me breathless, and I was glad to get back in the car.

'Actually, Lily,' Edwin questioned me as he reversed round to face the road, 'as we're up on the moor, would you mind very much if we called in to see Daniel? It's taking a chance that he'll be in, but I would like to see how he's getting on.'

Dismay suddenly dampened my euphoric mood. I really didn't want to meet Daniel again!

'Tell you what,' I answered instead, 'you can drop

me in Princetown and I can call in to see my friends. I haven't seen them for ages.'

'Oh.' Edwin sounded disappointed. 'I rather thought Danny might like to see you again. After the way he rescued you. Wendy told me about it.'

I drew in a deep breath. It was the last thing I wanted, but I didn't want to upset Edwin when we were getting on so well. 'Oh, all right, then,' I agreed, wishing I could have thought of a way to get out of it. 'I can see my friends another time.'

'Thanks, that's great,' Edwin nodded at me. 'We're all actually very distantly related to Daniel, you know, but only by marriage, not blood. It's very complicated.'

'Really?' Now this was something I didn't know.

'Yes,' Edwin began, changing gear. 'I'll try and explain. My grandmother – the one who lived at Foggintor – she was a protegée of Mrs Warrington, and *she* was Daniel's great-grandmother. Then *her* daughter, that is to say Daniel's grandmother, married a Pencarrow, and that's what Daniel is. A Pencarrow. Their family still farm over at Peter Tavy.'

'Oh, I've seen that on the map. On the moor north of Tavistock, isn't it?' I said, trying to sound interested. 'But I don't see how that makes you and Daniel related.'

'That's because it's only half the story. You know my Auntie Mary is married to Uncle Michael?'

'The captain in the Merchant Navy who's about to retire?'

'That's right. His surname is Bradley, but his mother was a Pencarrow. They all knew each other because my grandmother from Foggintor stayed friends with old Mrs Warrington until she died, and the Warringtons, the Pencarrows and the Bradleys were all friends for generations.'

'Oh, I see,' I frowned. 'Or at least, I think I do.'

Edwin chuckled as we drove past the daunting edifice of the prison. 'I told you the connection was pretty tenuous! We're three generations of doctors in our family, and they were three generations of sea captains in the Bradleys. Would have been four if my cousin hadn't been killed in the war. He'd have stayed on in the Navy afterwards and was sure to have made captain in the end. Unlike his brother, the one in Australia who couldn't wait to be demobbed.'

I shook my head as I gazed out of the window. 'So sad for your aunt. No wonder she can't wait for your uncle to retire.'

We had come into Princetown and Edwin turned up Tor Royal Lane onto the lonely road that ran out across the moor. I must have gone quiet as anything I might have said died in my throat. I was hardly breathing, causing my heart to pound in my chest. I just couldn't believe how Edwin could possibly be friends with the gruff so-and-so who had behaved

so ungraciously towards me when I had injured my
ankle.

We turned in at the gates and I tried to stop my
mouth from pouting sourly. The place seemed less
dark and formidable than I remembered, the pine
trees having been lopped back from the drive and
the overgrown garden now cleared to reveal neat
flowerbeds among the grass opposite the house. I
noticed that the windows that had been in a sorry
state of repair had received some attention as if
someone had been preparing them for repainting.

'Right. Here we are, then,' Edwin announced,
turning off the engine. 'Let's see if he's at home.'

I hoped to God he wasn't! But then I reprimanded
myself. That was unkind. But I wasn't looking
forward to it one little bit!

I followed Edwin across the gravel in front of the
old, rambling house. When Edwin knocked loudly
on the front door, I heard what sounded like a young
dog barking from somewhere inside. I waited with
baited breath. Nothing more. Oh, thank goodness.
And just as Edwin was about to turn away, there
came the rasp of a stiff bolt, the turning of a key, and
one side of the double door opened.

I hadn't seen Daniel close up for some months and
he looked different, probably because his hair had
grown considerably and was now almost overlong,
curling over his collar and falling in dark waves

across his broad forehead. He obviously hadn't shaved for a day or two, and beneath the stubble, his jaw was still lean, but he had lost some of the haggard look I had seen before. If those troubled eyes hadn't been set in a scowl, he would have been strikingly handsome. I hurled the thought aside with acid resentment. But then as he stared, immobile, at Edwin for some seconds, his expression changed and his face crumpled.

The two men locked in an embrace, hardly moving except to tighten their hold. Daniel Pencarrow's head was buried in his friend's shoulder, and for a full minute it was as if time stood still. When they finally drew apart, Daniel took a step backwards and pushed the back of his hand over his mouth and nose, his glistening eyes narrowed.

'Jesus, Danny, I'd have come before if I'd known I'd get such a reception.'

They were still gazing at each other, and then Daniel jerked his head as he noticed me for the first time. Edwin turned towards me and raised his hand.

'Daniel, do you remember—'

'Yes, I do. My little Carrot Top.' He sniffed, and his face moved from the lost expression of a moment earlier to a hard mask. Indignation exploded inside me and I fought to tamp it down. And then to my dismay, Daniel stepped forward and held out his hand to me. I had no choice but to shake it, though I did so as briefly as possible.

'Nice to see you again,' he said impassively and then turning to Edwin with far more enthusiasm, he went on, 'Do come in. You know the way. So how do you two know each other?' His eyes shifted swiftly in my direction with a flash of mockery that only I could see. I was seething, but I couldn't retaliate. Not in front of Edwin.

I hung back, a reluctant intruder at this reunion of two life-long friends. As we crossed the grand hallway, I noticed the smell of fresh paint. At least something was being done to restore the place to its former glory! But then my attention was caught by a snuffling that whimpered from beneath the kitchen door. When Daniel opened it, a wriggling bundle of black and white fluff hurtled out and bounced joyously about Edwin's and my knees. I was as pleased to see the young dog as it was to see me!

'Trojan, down!' Daniel's voice was firm but not raised. The dog at once lay down on its belly, but its tail still wiped the floor in vigorous sweeps and its head was held high, eyes alert and expectant.

'Where did he come from?' Edwin bent down and ruffled the thick fur.

'A present from Great Uncle Joshua. He thought he'd be a good companion for me.'

'You've got him well trained,' Edwin observed.

'Well, you have to start them young.'

'How old is he?' I finally found my tongue as the conversation seemed to have found a more normal level.

Daniel raised his eyebrows at me, almost as if he'd forgotten I was there. 'Eight months,' he replied dismissively, and then turned his attention back to Edwin. 'I'll make some tea. Or perhaps the occasion calls for something stronger?'

'No, tea will be fine, thanks.'

'Coffee for me, please,' I put in more assertively. 'Tea makes me sick.'

Daniel shot me a glance that seemed to question my presence, never mind my request. 'I've only got Camp, not the real thing,' he growled.

Camp was the only coffee I knew. It was all Deborah kept in the cupboard, too. I had no idea what the *real thing* was, but I wasn't going to reveal my ignorance and provide more ammunition for him to ridicule me with. 'That's fine. Thank you,' I added as an afterthought, feeling humiliated just the same as he turned away.

I sat down at the table on the first chair I came to, while Edwin followed Daniel across to the range where he put the kettle on the hotplate to boil. I was glad when the dog trotted up to me and I could entertain myself by stroking his beautifully domed, silky head. He was a border collie with lovely,

intelligent eyes and his rough, pink tongue tickled as
he licked my hands.

'I was sorry to hear about what happened with
Susan,' I heard Edwin say in a low voice. 'Jolly bad
luck.'

'Blessing in disguise,' came the grunted reply.
'Wouldn't have made a very good marriage, would
it, if she couldn't wait to see if I'd survive before
she went off with her fancy man? She couldn't really
have thought that much of me, could she?'

'Some didn't. Survive, I mean.'

'You don't need to tell me that. I was there,
remember.' The words were ground out with such
bitterness that my curiosity was aroused. I felt I was
eavesdropping and tried to pretend I couldn't hear
as I concentrated on playing with Trojan. He rolled
on his back and I rubbed his warm hairy chest, but
keeping an ear on the conversation at the far end of
the room. So, it would seem Daniel had been engaged
but his fiancée had broken it off. Very wise of her if
you asked my opinion! But they were referring to
something else that didn't quite make sense.

'And to lose Great Aunt Marianne as well. I know
how close you two were. It must have been a terrible
shock for you.'

'It was. Thinking of her, of coming back to this
place, was what kept me alive, you know. So many
just gave up. We even called it *give-up-itis*. It finished

you off. But I had *here* to cling to. And then to find she'd died and I hadn't even known she was ill…' His voice was so vehement, so broken, that I lifted my head before I realised it and was gazing across the room. Daniel's shoulders were slumped, and Edwin put out a hand to comfort him, both seemingly oblivious to my presence.

'I'm so sorry, old chap. Sixty-two was far too young to die. Dad did the best he could for her. Got her the best treatment available. But some cancers are so virulent…'

'Yes.' Daniel spoke on an intake of breath, held it for a moment and then even from the other end of the huge room, I heard him sigh. 'I know. But I still felt so…so angry about it. As if I blamed your father for not being able to save her. I'm afraid I behaved abominably towards your parents when they came to see me at Christmas.'

Yes, I could imagine! William and Deborah were kindness itself, and Daniel Pencarrow was the most obnoxious, galling brute I had ever come across! But I suppose he must have loved this great aunt of his very much, and I still hadn't worked out the circumstances…

'Oh, sorry, Lily!' Edwin suddenly turned to me. 'This isn't fair on you, we two talking away.' I felt relieved, but noticed Daniel appeared to have deliberately turned his back as he made the drinks, leaving Edwin as a sort of go-between. 'Lily's living with my parents now. In Tavistock.'

'Really?' Daniel handed Edwin a mug and then carrying one in each hand, walked down the length of the table. He put one of the drinks in front of me and, to my displeasure, sat down opposite me. 'Well, that's good then. Means you won't be walking out on the moor all on your own again.'

I felt the flush of anger at the memory of that day, and this time, despite Edwin's presence, I couldn't help answering back. 'I told you then I was perfectly all right.'

'Oh, come on, Carrots, you'd have been stuck if I hadn't come along when I did.'

His face was perfectly straight, but I could see his eyes were glinting with mischief. Jeering at me. I tell you, if the width of the table hadn't put him out of my reach, I'd have slapped his face! As it was, I had to content myself with a fierce riposte.

'I'd have managed somehow. I'm not helpless. And will you stop calling me that!'

My voice had vibrated with fury and I saw that Edwin was taken aback. Daniel, too, blinked at me in surprise, but a second later, he threw his head back with a bellow of laughter.

'Oh, you really are wonderful when you're angry!' He was grinning at me now, his wide mouth and strong teeth making him look so damnably handsome I could have punched him on the nose. Then he shook his head, eyes shut and the merriment gone. 'I'm sorry. Please forgive me.'

I doubted his sincerity and merely glowered back at him. It was Edwin who came to the rescue, and I was so grateful to him.

'I hear you found a sacrificed sheep at Down Tor row?'

'That's right. It was a pretty gruesome sight. It's not surprising Lily was upset.' Daniel threw me a sideways glance which I couldn't quite fathom, but at least he was being serious now. 'I didn't exactly welcome it myself.'

There was a short silence and I noticed Edwin fix his eyes on Daniel's face. 'And how are *you*, Danny? In yourself?'

Daniel looked up sharply before lowering his eyes, his mouth set. 'Trying to forget,' he murmured. Then he gave a wry smile. 'But all the better for seeing you. Both of you. But when do you go back to London, Ed?'

'Tomorrow, I'm afraid. And I'm afraid Lily and I must be going or we'll be late for dinner.'

Oh, thank goodness for that! I had felt totally humiliated and was brimming over with relief as Edwin drove back across the moor. And what had irked me most was Daniel's comment that he had been pleased to see me!

'Poor sod,' Edwin sighed as we took the sharp bend near Tor Royal again.

There was nothing poor about Daniel Pencarrow as far as I could see! But he was Edwin's friend so I bit my tongue. I couldn't think of a more appropriate answer, so I asked somewhat disinterestedly, 'What was it that happened to him?'

'Oh, God's teeth, Lily, hasn't anyone told you?' Edwin replied, vibrant with self-recrimination. 'He was a POW in Korea for over two years. Must have had a hell of a time. He was really lucky to survive.'

Chapter Thirteen

A spasm of shame tweaked at my conscience, but it didn't alter my opinion of Daniel Pencarrow. To be captured and held prisoner in Korea must have been horrific, but it was no reason to take it out on good people like William and Deborah, or innocent strangers such as myself. I simply couldn't forgive him for his ungracious behaviour towards me.

'Now that his Great Aunt Marianne has died, I don't suppose anyone knows Daniel better than I do,' Edwin said almost apologetically. A group of Dartmoor ponies had congregated in the centre of Princetown, drawn by Easter visitors who were feeding them titbits, and Edwin had been obliged to stop the car until they ambled off again. 'We've been friends since we were toddlers, even if Daniel was brought up in London.'

'London?' I was genuinely surprised. 'But I thought—'

'Oh, Fencott Place has been the Warrington family home since the eighteen seventies.'

'Fencott Place? Is that what the house is called?'

'Yes. Not that I ever remember there being a nameplate up anywhere. The Warringtons were pretty wealthy at one time. Made their money from worldwide investments, but particularly from the South African diamond fields. Ah, we can go now.' Edwin put the car into first and we moved smoothly through the village and back past the prison. 'But they lost a lot of money because of the Great War,' he continued, 'and soon afterwards, the old couple both died, not that either of them were that old. There was a son, but he was killed at the Somme. So that just left the two daughters. They were both eccentric, real characters. Marianne lived with her crippled husband at Fencott, but remember I told you Daniel's grandmother married a Pencarrow? Well, *he* was more interested in business affairs than farming, so he left the family farm in his brother's hands – that's Great Uncle Joshua who gave Daniel the puppy – and took his wife and children to London to salvage what he could of the Warrington fortune.'

'And that's how Daniel came to be born in London?'

'That's right. But the family always came back to Fencott Place or the farm at Peter Tavy for long holidays, especially in the summer. And through my grandmother, we always saw a lot of them, too. And Daniel and I being more or less the same age, we became pretty close.'

Edwin paused as he brought the car to a halt at the junction with the main road, and I shook my head. 'I'm a bit confused with all these different people. You'll have to draw me a family tree.'

He chuckled as we pulled onto the main road and headed for home. 'Yes, it is quite complicated. But you get the general picture?'

'Yes, I think so. But what's Daniel doing here now?' I asked as the story had aroused my interest. Not so much in Daniel, but because it seemed to involve Edwin and I wanted to know everything about him.

'Recuperating basically. Physically and mentally. Fencott's more his home than London, even if his family's still there. You see, he and I were ten years old when war broke out again, and it seemed logical for him to be evacuated here to live with his great aunt who he absolutely adored. They were like soulmates. Daniel and I were at school together in Tavistock all through the war, but at weekends and during the holidays, Great Aunt Marianne just let him run wild on the moor. And more often than not, I was with him. Fencott was my second home. I spent more time studying, though, than Daniel. He was always one of those infuriating people who did very little work and yet always got top marks in exams.'

Oh, well, yes, that would be typical, I thought begrudgingly, but I didn't want Edwin to know how I felt, so I asked, 'So what happened after the war?'

'Well, Daniel refused to go back to his parents in London. Dartmoor was his home. He even played for the local football team. A damned fine player he was, too.'

The scene in Bolts back in the autumn flashed across my memory. It fitted with what Edwin was saying. I wondered why Daniel no longer played, but the discourteous way he had refused remained fresh in my mind.

'He got his way by agreeing to work harder at school,' Edwin went on as we cruised down Pork Hill. 'Got into Oxford and got a first in English. Said he wanted to do his degree while he still felt fresh, so he deferred his National Service. If he hadn't, he wouldn't have been caught up in Korea.'

'What about you?' I asked, filled with sudden apprehension. 'Did you defer yours?'

'Oh, yes. It takes years to qualify in medicine. I'll have to do it at some time, unless it's phased out, of course. As a medic, I can defer it until I'm as old as thirty. And then I can go in on a short service commission so I get better pay and probably married quarters. Assuming I've tied the knot with some lovely lady by then.'

He took his eyes off the road for a second to turn to me and smile.

I missed Edwin dreadfully. I cried myself to sleep the following night, keeping my face buried in the pillow to muffle my sobs. I think Wendy had guessed, but I didn't want anyone else to know how Edwin had captured my heart. I had to persuade myself that he was safe in London which wasn't so far away, unlike during the war when thousands had said goodbye to their sweethearts, not knowing if they would ever see them alive again.

I imagined going with Edwin to some British Forces posting as his wife, and a little knot tightened deliciously inside me. Perhaps to somewhere exotic like Egypt. I had an image of living in an Army garrison, sipping gin and tonic with the other officers' wives. Not that I had ever tasted gin. What else did they do, I wondered. I wouldn't want to be bored, and I'd prefer to have a useful role of some sort. But as long as I was with Edwin, I'd be happy.

I had plenty to do, though, during those first few weeks of his absence. I sifted through all Sidney's personal effects, hoping they would reveal some more clues about my past, but there was little to go on. I found a box of wage envelopes going back years, so he had evidently been paid in cash, but there was no trace of a bank or Post Office account. So what had he done with all his money, as I was sure he hadn't spent all his salary on living expenses? Not that I wanted anything for myself, but I was curious. He had shown me a couple of photographs of my half-brothers as babies, and I came across one of my mother as a bride that I hadn't seen before.

There was nothing else except a bound notebook I had found in a small bureau that had stood in the parlour at both our homes. The book appeared to be a diary with a few newspaper cuttings between the leaves. At first, I couldn't bring myself to read it. It seemed too personal. And then one day I summoned up the courage. It fell open at the entry for the day I had left London and travelled down to my new home. *The brat arrived today*, I read. My stomach corkscrewed in agony and I slammed the book shut. I was devastated. Was that how Sidney had thought of me? And was that why he had been so furious when I had dusted the parlour, in case I had found the diary? It somehow destroyed the relationship we had finally built up and I didn't want to ruin my happier memories of him. So I put everything back in the box, and asked William to put it in the loft for me where it remained, forlorn and soon forgotten.

There was never a dull moment in the Franfield

household, and Wendy and I grew even closer. It was like having Jeannie back again. The firm of solicitors she worked for had just interviewed a young man who was about to graduate in law, and she had already earmarked him as her future boyfriend.

'And then you and Edwin can come out with us in a foursome!' she declared, her eyes rakishly teasing.

I was sure I turned a shade of beetroot. 'If you think Edwin would want to,' I said casually, 'that would be very nice.'

'Of course Edwin would want to!' Wendy retorted. 'He really likes you, Lily.'

'How do you know?' I quizzed her. 'Has he said so?'

'He doesn't need to.'

'Anyway, he's not here,' I observed a little truculently.

'But he will be soon. For two weeks in August!'

I couldn't wait. May brought clouds of bluebells nodding among red and white campion in the hedgerows. On the open moor, splashes of vivid gorse filled our nostrils with sweet scent and mingled with spikes of freshly blooming heather, while swathes of verdant ferns uncurled as the new season progressed. June became July, and the simmering excitement I kept locked inside began to froth and foam. I treated myself to a new summer dress with a belted waist and a full, flaring skirt to accentuate my slim figure. I hoped Edwin would notice.

'Happy Birthday, Lily!' everyone chorused on the twenty-eighth. I was bursting with happiness as the Franfields regaled me with cards and presents and a special supper. But most wonderful of all was a card from Edwin. Signed *with love*.

'And this is our main present to you,' William winked as he handed me an envelope. 'A course of driving lessons. I hope you get on better than Wendy did. Deborah finds it so useful.'

'I gave up,' Wendy grimaced with such a long face that it made me smile and brought me back to my senses. I had been dumbstruck. Learn to drive? Cars were still a largely male domain. Growing numbers of tourists were coming up onto the moor in their little Morris Minors and Austin Sevens, but the thought of being behind the wheel myself had sent me into a state of stupefaction.

'Thank you *so* much!' I cried as the shrill tones of the telephone out in the hall burst through my awestruck daze.

'For you, Lily,' Wendy announced through the open door. 'Edwin.'

Edwin? For *me*? My heart leapfrogged into my throat as I tottered out on wobbly legs. I picked up the receiver in a hand that was beginning to ooze sweat.

'Hello, Edwin. Lily here.'

'Happy Birthday! You having a good time?'

His voice at the other end of the line was so natural and familiar that I no longer felt nervous. It was just so wonderful to hear him, as if he hadn't been away all that time.

'Oh, yes! Everyone's been so kind. And thank you so much for your card.'

'My pleasure. I thought I'd bring your present rather than post it. It's less than a fortnight before I come home.'

'Yes, I know. I'm *really* looking forward to it!'

'Are you?' He sounded pleasantly surprised, and I shivered with elation. 'Can you put Mum on the line now, Lily?'

'Yes, of course. See you soon, then. Hope you have a good journey down.'

'Thanks. I'm sure I will. See you then, Lily, love.'

Lily love. I hugged the words to my heart, repeating them in my head whenever I turned over in bed at night. Wendy was right. Edwin really did like me!

'The National Trust certainly know how to pick their places, don't they? Thrilling, isn't it?'

'Absolutely!'

The five of us, William and Deborah, Wendy, Edwin and me had gone to Lydford Gorge. We had followed the zigzagging path down through the wooded ravine to the White Lady waterfall and now we were clambering alongside the river on uneven, slippery rock. I took Edwin's hand whenever he offered it to me whether I needed his help or not. The water was so clear over the gravel bed that we could see trout lying in wait for a passing snack.

The rush of swirling cascades gradually became deafening as the sky narrowed to a slit above us. We stole beneath vertical overhanging rocks glistening with water that dripped between a camouflage of emerald moss, lichen, harts tongue and springing ferns, the smell of dank earth and vegetation overpowering. And then we saw the river thundering through the crevasse, sweeping in a maddened vortex inside the cauldrons it had gouged out of the rock over millions of years.

I was enthralled, not least because I was with Edwin in this romantic, magical place. We were standing side by side, our faces so close as Edwin studied the wonderment on my face that I was convinced that, had we been alone, he would have kissed me.

It had been the same a few days previously. William had been needed at the hospital but Edwin had driven the rest of us to his grandparents' home in the picturesque riverside village of Newton Ferrers. It was a lovely ride but, sitting in the back, I spent much of the time studying Edwin's profile as he turned his head to watch for traffic, his bare forearm flexing as he changed gear. Once he caught my eye in the rear-view mirror and smiled at me.

His grandparents lived in a delightful cottage fronting directly onto the river. A narrow lane ran past the front door and on the other side, their garden dropped straight down to the water. We sat on the terrace admiring the quaint village of Noss Mayo across the broad, muddy estuary and watching the tide coming in. The river grew more lovely with every minute, and I felt at peace with the world. I could never bring Ellen back, but now I had a safe and secure future to anticipate, and at the heart of it would be the handsome, intelligent, caring young man who now lounged on the grass beside me.

'Would you mind if we took the boat out, Gramps, now the tide's coming in?' Edwin asked, his face aflame with boyish enthusiasm.

'Not at all. I'll help you get it in the water.'

Five minutes later, Edwin took my hand to help me into the little rowing boat. Fortunately, I was wearing shorts which allowed me the freedom to clamber aboard, and I flushed with excitement as I sat down on the wooden seat opposite Edwin as my bare legs would be under his nose. They were shapely and sun-tanned and surely he couldn't help but notice them as he rowed us right out across the river. Certainly I watched his hair blowing in the wind and the exposed V at the open neck of his shirt as he leant towards me with each stroke.

'Want a go?' he enquired. 'Pity Daniel's not here. He's a stronger rower than I am.'

Personally I was glad Daniel Pencarrow wasn't with us! He'd have ruined a perfect day.

'Yes, I'll row for a bit. I've done it before, on the boating lake in Battersea Park.'

The boat rocked as we swapped places, and I instinctively grabbed onto Edwin. His shoulder was bony through his shirt, and I relished the feel of him beneath my hand. My cheek was next to his and our eyes met. If Wendy hadn't been watching from the bow, who knows what might have happened next! I was determined to row well and could have died when after a while, my arms were tiring and instead of sliding beneath the water, one oar skimmed a glittering arc into the air and all over Edwin.

'Oh, please don't drown me!' he begged with mock pleading, and with a roar of laughter, scooped a handful of water over me in return. I dropped one of the oars to splash him back, and it slipped out of its rowlock and into the water, and I nearly fell overboard getting it back. It was a glorious day, and it wasn't until after our visit to Lydford Gorge that I was reminded of Edwin's mention of Daniel.

'I'm going to give Daniel a ring,' he announced

one evening. 'I must spend some time with him before I go back. You girls will come, won't you? I know he'd love to see you both.'

Oh, he would, would he? But what could I say to Edwin? On the spur of the moment, I couldn't think of a valid excuse, particularly when Wendy protested and Edwin mildly reprimanded her. The following afternoon, Wendy dived into the back seat so that I could sit in the front with Edwin. She seemed secretly as determined for us to be together as I was! But the plan backfired slightly.

'Why don't you drive, Lily?' Edwin suggested.

I broke out in a sudden sweat. Drive? With Edwin?

'I don't think I'm up to driving on the moor yet,' I objected warily.

'Dad's taken you out in the Rover nearly every day. He says you're really good. How many lessons have you had?'

'Four,' I mumbled.

'Well, have a go, and if you don't feel happy, I'll take over.'

I was more nervous than ever, my pulse racing like a traction engine, and not helped by the prospect of seeing Daniel at the end of it. I navigated the streets of Tavistock with no problem, but stalled turning up the steep hill of Mount Tavy. I felt sick, but Edwin calmly talked me through it and soon we were climbing steadily onto the moor. By the time we reached Princetown and turned up Tor Royal Lane, I was feeling more confident. As I brought the car to a smooth halt on the gravel outside Fencott Place, Edwin turned to me with a proud smile. I had barely turned off the engine, when the tall figure of Daniel Pencarrow appeared, and we all tumbled out of the car. I couldn't help but feel embarrassed as I went to hand Edwin the keys.

'Lily drove all the way!' were Edwin's first words to his friend. 'Didn't she do well? She's only been learning three weeks.'

Daniel dipped his head towards the Rover. 'It's a big car for a little thing like you,' he said without expression. 'You'd find the jeep easier.' Then he turned away to greet Edwin and Wendy properly and the three of them ambled off around the side of the house, leaving me standing there like a lemon.

I felt peeved. An outsider. And what the hell had Daniel meant by his deadpan words? I stomped after them, irritated that Edwin had put his precious friend first and dropped his gentlemanly attitude to me if only for a moment. I was glad when I followed through a side gate and Trojan bounded up to me in a flurry of welcome. He seemed more of a young dog than the puppy-like bundle of last time, but he still jumped up at me like a jack-in-the-box.

'Trojan, sit,' Daniel commanded and the dog

immediately obeyed, his tail still swishing. 'Good dog! Trojan, come.' Once again, the young collie did as he was told, and to my surprise, Daniel squatted down to reward him with a generous hug. 'He must learn not to jump up,' Daniel explained, looking up at me quite affably. 'Some people don't like it, and he could knock a child over. Oh, shut the gate, would you, Lily? I don't want him sneaking out alone.' And then he went to catch up with the others.

I suppose that was civil enough, but I still felt left out. I hadn't seen the back of the house before, though, and I was curious. I had vaguely noticed that the front gardens were now immaculate and the windows had been repainted, and now it seemed that the rear of the property was receiving similar attention. A wide flag-stoned terrace ran the full length of the back wall with wide steps leading down to an extensive lawn with one or two trees and several flower beds. It was still partially overgrown as if it had been neglected for years, but the rest was well tended. Someone – Daniel I supposed – had a mammoth task on their hands, and when I glanced back at the house, a ladder was propped up at one of the windows and various tins of paint were neatly stacked against the wall.

I turned my back on the superb view over the moor and followed the others through the second of two sets of French doors. I found myself in a huge room with a magnificent fireplace but a threadbare carpet and sofas and armchairs in dire need of re-covering. The floorboards, though, were polished to a high lustre and the wooden furniture gleamed. Someone had been hard at work!

'You girls make yourselves at home, and Edwin and I'll make some coffee. My family's coming down next week so I've been stocking up and I've got the real stuff now. Especially for you, Carrots,' he added with a sly wink at me and then disappeared out of the door before I had a chance to react.

I ground my teeth as I glared after him, and Wendy spun round to face me. 'Did he call you *Carrots*? Oh, how rude! How dare he? Your hair's gorgeous, Lily. Like gold. Edwin said so the other day!'

'Did he?' My heart stopped beating and I almost swooned. I felt instantly so much better! Blow Daniel! I shouldn't let him upset me, but the remnants of my agitation kept me on my feet and I wandered about the room, inspecting all I found. I guessed everything had belonged to the Great Aunt Marianne who Daniel had apparently worshipped. Next to the door hung a Victorian portrait of a stunningly beautiful woman. A thick ringlet of glossy, raven hair coiled down one shoulder, giving a devil-may-care character to the otherwise formal pose. Yet the facial expression was so full of vitality, so alive, I thought the lips were about to move and speak to me. She seemed familiar, and then I recognised the violet-blue eyes that were staring at me from the canvas.

'That's Daniel's great grandmother,' Wendy informed me. 'Isn't she glorious? An amazing person, they say. Never afraid to speak her mind, but so big-hearted. Daniel looks like her, don't you think?'

'Yes, I do,' I mumbled. And then, throwing caution to the wind since I was aware of Wendy's reluctance to visit Daniel, I commented tartly, 'Pity he didn't inherit her big-heartedness.'

'Oh, Danny didn't used to be like this. It was what happened to him in Korea that changed him. And losing Great Aunt Marianne and then his fiancée going off with someone else. Before all that, we used to have a lot of fun together.'

She stopped abruptly as Edwin and Daniel came back into the room with the coffee. I don't think they'd heard her, but to cover up, she said with an exaggerated sniff of the air, 'Mmm, real coffee!'

'My grandmother likes it,' Daniel answered shortly, 'so I thought I ought to get some. Don't know what they'll make of my cooking, though.'

'Pity Lily's got a full-time job, or she'd come and cook for you, wouldn't you, Lily?' Edwin beamed at me. 'She's a super cook is Lily.'

Cook for Daniel? You must be joking! 'I'm not *that* good,' I answered, hoping my voice didn't show my contempt.

'Must be better than what I survived on in Korea,' Daniel murmured under his breath. I wasn't sure if we were meant to hear, but Edwin cleared his throat and neatly changed the subject.

'Let's go for a walk when we've had this. Pity to waste such a lovely day.'

'Do we have to?' Wendy complained over the rim of her cup.

'You don't get enough exercise, Sis. And I know Lily would love to have a walk on the moor. Danny?'

He shrugged. 'Fine by me. I see the girls haven't got the best footwear but it's relatively dry underfoot and we can always rescue you if need be.' He shot a glance at me and I glared back. He wasn't going to let me forget the incident when we had met, was he, particularly as he added, 'We could go out to the Drizzlecombe stone rows. Don't expect we'll find any sacrifices, though.'

I struggled to control my fury, but I had to admit that a ramble out to one of the loneliest places on the moor would be wonderful. My curiosity over its ancient cults was rekindled, and even if we did happen on anything untoward, being in Edwin's company would make it more bearable.

It lifted my heart to feel the vast emptiness of the moor again and to allow its intense harmony to sink into my spirit. It smoothed away the antipathy I felt towards Daniel, even though he and Edwin were striding away in front of Wendy and me as if we didn't exist, Trojan running circles around us as he tried to herd us together. Every so often, he would scamper too far and Daniel would call him back. I marvelled, quite reluctantly, that Daniel had trained him so well.

Daniel led us past the remains of Eylesbarrow Mine and across the moor to the three stone rows at Drizzlecombe, scattered unevenly and incomprehensibly, and with one of the tallest menhirs or standing stones on Dartmoor. I laughed as Edwin stood with his back against it, arms outstretched, so that we could get the full idea of its size as it towered above him. What had it meant to the men who had put it there at such huge effort so many thousands of years ago? Perhaps Gloria would know.

'I'll take you back a different way,' Daniel announced. 'Along this stream – it's the source of the Plym by the way – and then up through Evil Combe. Could be a bit boggy along here, but we'll help you.'

He seemed casual, more relaxed, the shadow of a smile pulling at his mouth. But was he amusing himself at my expense? I scowled back.

'I'm sure we can manage it if you can,' I told him frostily, and he shrugged in that annoying gesture he seemed to have as he turned to lead the way.

'Look at that rabbit!' Wendy cried as we at last scrambled away from the stream up through the gullies of Evil Combe. 'It's not running away from us at all. Must be very brave.'

We all stopped to look. I'd seen many a rabbit when I lived at Foggintor. Hundreds of them colonised Big Tip, but they disappeared if you went anywhere near.

'Oh, my God,' I suddenly heard Daniel mutter, and then he shouted as Trojan went to pounce forward. 'Trojan, no!' It wasn't his usual calm command, and I caught the agitation in his voice. Trojan reluctantly slunk back to his master's side and Daniel clipped on the lead.

'Hold him, would you, Lily?' he asked swiftly, passing it to me. I knew something was wrong and I forgot my feelings of rancour as the boys crept stealthily forward towards the rabbit that was crouching, immobile, in the long grass.

'It's myxomatosis, isn't it, Ed?'

I felt cold, as if there was ice in my veins. I'd heard about this dreadful disease that had somehow entered Britain the previous year. There was speculation that some unscrupulous farmers had been encouraging it in order to keep down numbers of their considered enemy, the rabbit. They no longer had any need to do so. It was spreading like wild fire, and now it had reached Dartmoor.

I came slowly forward. The sight of the poor, trembling creature, its nose running and its eyes gummed up with matter, tore at my heart. I gulped hard, feeling so helpless. 'Is there anything we can do?' I whispered.

I don't know why, but I looked to Daniel for an answer. Perhaps because he knew the moor better than any of us. But he shook his head, his face twitching.

'No. Nothing. Just keep Trojan away. In fact, you and Wendy go on ahead. Keep going straight up and you'll come to the track. We'll catch you up.'

I frowned questioningly, but I was glad to get away. I glanced at Edwin, and he nodded as well. The horrendous discovery had ruined what had been a lovely walk, my dislike of Daniel aside, and sadness weighed down on us like a cloud. Wendy and I obediently walked on, neither of us speaking. We knew what the boys were doing. When they caught us up, they were both very quiet and pale. I noticed there was a splatter of blood on Daniel's shirt.

I tried not to let the memory of the incident spoil the last few days of Edwin's holiday, but all too soon, it was time for him to go. I was the only one free to go to the railway station with him, and though my heart was heavy, it felt amazing to be alone with him. Would he kiss me at last, like in the films? When the moment came, I lifted my head, and when his mouth brushed against my cheek, I was disappointed. But Edwin was a gentleman, and I knew he wouldn't rush things. Instead, he waved vigorously out of the window as the train bore him away.

I waited until he was out of sight, a desolate fist tightening in my chest. God knew when I would see him again. But while he was away, I would better myself. Prove I was worthy of his love. I would go to evening classes, get a couple of those O-levels and learn shorthand and typing. In the meantime, I would thank my lucky stars that I was firmly accepted into the bosom of Edwin's wonderful family.

Jeannie had just sent a belated card for my birthday with no note. Too occupied with her boyfriend, I supposed. So I wrote to her, telling her all about Edwin. I imagined her teasing reply.

I never received one. London became a veiled, murky fog to me now. My new life was here on Dartmoor. And somehow it felt as if it always had been.

Chapter Fourteen

'Hello, Lily.'

The familiar voice brought me up short, and I bristled with irritation. It was my lunch hour and I had just met Kate off the train. Unlike Sally, who was devoted to her studies, Kate was struggling in her second year of A-levels and had finally made the decision to leave school and find a job. She had asked me to have a word with Mrs Kershaw and now I was taking her for an interview, for while she was bubbling and confident in the world she had grown up in, she was nervous about spreading her wings and wanted to work with me. I thought it was a shame that she had given up her studies at that late stage, but perhaps she didn't have what it takes, and who was I to talk when I hadn't even stayed on long enough to do my O-levels? The resemblance to my own situation when Ellen had wanted me to stay on at school made me feel somewhat guilty, so to have the unwelcome presence cut through my despondent mood was more than riling.

'Daniel,' I answered flatly, turning on my heel.

He blinked those penetrating, violet-blue eyes at me as if I should be the one to open up the conversation. I met his gaze stubbornly, refusing to think of anything to say. For once, I appeared to make *him* feel awkward, which pleased me no end.

'How are you?' he finally enquired, and I noticed he ignored Kate totally despite the fact that she was gazing at him, goggle-eyed, beside me.

'I'm well, thank you,' I replied tersely. 'What are you doing here?' Although why I asked, I really didn't know.

'Ordering some building materials and things I can't get in Princetown. And I thought I'd call in to see William and Deborah. I haven't seen them since Christmas and I owe them an apology.'

I couldn't suppress a scornful snort. 'A bit belated, wouldn't you say? It is the end of October.'

Daniel flashed a dark look at me. 'You're quite right, of course. It's taken me this long to pluck up the courage. Are they in, do you know? Edwin tells me you're still living there.'

I felt myself soften at the mention of my dear Edwin. So he had been talking to Daniel about me on the telephone from London, had he? It must be a good sign and my heart gave a little bound.

'William might still be in if you're quick, but I think Deborah will be there all afternoon,' I told him, feeling less annoyed.

'Oh, good. Thank you.' He half smiled, hesitating as if he wanted to detain me but couldn't quite think how. 'And how's the driving going?'

I was surprised, not only by his interest but by his pleasant tone. Was he mellowing? Or perhaps he was trying to make up for his former mocking abrasiveness in the same way as he was about to apologise to William and Deborah eight months too late! Well, it wasn't going to wash with *me*!

'I passed my test,' I said cautiously.

'Oh, well done!' His generous mouth broke into a grin, revealing those sickeningly straight, white teeth. 'In that case, why don't you see if you can borrow William's car one day – unless you have your own, of course – and drive up to me? I could see how you love the open moor, and I could take you for a walk somewhere. Or I could come and pick you up in the jeep.'

His eyebrows had arched expectantly, his head tilted to one side, while I seethed. Why on earth should he think I would want to go for a walk with *him*? So that he could poke fun at me again?

'I'm afraid I really don't have the time,' I answered tartly. 'Some of us have a proper full-time job, and I'm doing several courses at evening classes—'

'Really?' His eyebrows reached up further in genuine surprise, it seemed, as he ignored my scathing remark – which peeved me somewhat. 'What are you doing?'

'Shorthand and typing, and O-levels in English and English Lit,' I informed him shortly in an effort to brush him off. 'Look, I must go. Kate here's got an interview.'

'Oh, I'm sorry. You should have said. Good luck,' he added, jabbing his head at Kate. And as we hurried away, he called to me, 'If you need any help with the literature, let me know!'

I didn't reply as I increased my pace across Bedford Square, Kate trotting along beside me.

'Why on earth did you turn him down, Lily, you lummox?' she gabbled, dancing sideways to look at me, her nerves about the interview apparently dispelled. 'He's gorgeous! I've seen him up at Princetown. Wish he'd asked *me* out!'

'You're welcome to him, Kate. Personally I wouldn't touch him with a barge-pole. He must be one of the rudest, most bad-tempered brutes I've ever come across. Now, come on, or you'll be late.' And as we turned into Duke Street, I wondered quite why I felt so piqued.

* * *

It was absolutely true that I didn't have a moment to spare. I worked five and a half days, attended evening classes three nights a week and spent all my spare time studying or practising my new secretarial skills. Wendy was a brick, helping me with little tips and reading out shorthand dictations for me to transcribe. We always went out together on Saturday nights, though, to one of Tavistock's two cinemas or to a dance whenever there was one. She was very friendly with the new junior partner at the solicitors and he often came along, too, usually with a friend in tow for me. I had the feeling Wendy was delaying cementing their relationship for my sake, guessing that I was secretly waiting for Edwin. When I hinted at it, she merely shrugged and said she and Ian were just good friends, but I was sure her feelings ran much deeper.

It all helped to keep my mind off being separated from Edwin, and I felt that while I was bettering myself for him, I was also sharing his dedication to study. He rang home once a week and I always spoke to him for a few minutes. Just chit-chat, but it was marvellous to hear his voice. He never mentioned a girlfriend, so I kept my fingers crossed it would stay that way. I just prayed that, after his finals, we would be able to see more of each other and bring our feelings into the open.

He wasn't able to come home at all, and we all

missed him over Christmas. I couldn't help thinking how last year Sidney and I had spent the holiday contentedly together, not knowing what lay around the corner. I had been convinced that, in time, he would have told me more about my mother or indeed about himself. It was too late now. There was the box with the diary in the attic, of course. Should I swallow my pride and look at it again? My heart lurched every time I thought about it, bringing me out in a cold sweat and trapping me in a tangled coil of conflict. In the end, I always came to the same spiritless conclusion, that it was better to bury the past. And that, in itself, made me feel ashamed.

There was only one person who would truly understand how I felt. Gloria. It was February and the first anniversary of Sidney's death. I had some flowers to put on his grave in Princetown's churchyard and took the train up on my afternoon off. I hadn't ridden on its glorious, winding route for a year, and it filled my heart with wistful memories. The moor had been blanketed in deep snow since New Year and looked quite magical from the warmth of the carriage. Outside, though, it was freezing. I went straight to the grave and stood there for a few minutes as the Dartmoor wind turned the tears on my cheeks to icicles. Then I shivered my way to Albert Terrace, reminded of how much colder it was on the moor than down in sheltered Tavistock.

I had rung Gloria the previous evening so that she would be expecting me. As I crossed the road that had been partially cleared of snow, I noticed Daniel's jeep parked outside Bolts. He must be doing some shopping so I dived up Gloria's front garden before he could come out and see me.

Gloria opened the door with her usual welcoming smile and she smelt of expensive perfume when we hugged.

'Come in, my dear. How lovely to see you!' she sang as I followed her into the back kitchen. 'I've got another visitor. Someone you know, I believe.'

My heart sank like a stone as I entered the room. Daniel got to his feet, his hand outstretched. I had no choice but to let him shake mine. His grip was warm and firm.

'I'm sorry. I had no idea you were coming. I should go,' he said evasively.

'No, no, lad, you stay,' Gloria insisted. 'We haven't finished talking. You two sit there and I'll make some coffee.'

Daniel's forehead dipped as he looked at me apologetically and resumed his seat. Was my message getting through to him at last? I reluctantly sat down opposite him.

'You didn't come up with William and Deborah at Christmas,' he observed without expression. 'Pity. You could have met my parents. And my grandmother. She's not Great Aunt Marianne, but she's still quite a character.'

'I'm afraid Wendy and I had other things to do.' I had nearly said *better* things, but that would have been churlish and Daniel *was* being polite for once. 'So how do you know Gloria?' I asked, my curiosity getting the better of me.

'My great aunt was a friend of hers.'

'Dear Marianne,' Gloria sighed as she set three cups of coffee on the table. 'She talked of Daniel here so much when she was dying. She was so worried about you, you know. Word had got through that you'd been taken prisoner, but then there was nothing. No one knew if you were dead or alive. Why didn't you write?'

Daniel shot me a dark glance with those brooding eyes. 'I did,' he answered, his words directed as much to me as to Gloria. 'On the rare occasion we were allowed. It wasn't my fault they didn't get through. I never received any either, though I know Edwin wrote to me several times and my parents wrote every week.'

'Well, you're home and safe now. And looking so much better, I have to say. I didn't recognise you for some time, you looked so dreadful. But then, I hadn't seen you since you went to university, which was when?'

'1947.'

'There you are, then. It was only last spring I realised who you were, and then it was really because of Marianne's old jeep. But it was only just now, when you were saying about this sheep sacrifice and mentioned the earlier one that Lily had told me about, that I learnt about you two meeting.'

I glanced from one to the other in appalled horror, and I saw Daniel lower his eyes.

'I'm afraid I told Gloria how I met this young girl who'd twisted her ankle out at Down Tor, and she put two and two together.'

'You mean there's been another sacrifice?' I faltered.

'Yes, there has. But there doesn't seem much the police can do,' Daniel said, swallowing down his coffee. 'Well, I'll leave you ladies to it. Thanks for the drink. 'Bye, Lily. See you soon.'

I nodded, and waited for Gloria to show him out. 'Well, then,' she smiled, coming back into the room. 'Fancy you knowing Daniel. Poor troubled lad.' She seemed distant for an instant, and then shook her head and beamed at me. 'Now, what was it you wanted to talk about?'

I gazed at her for some seconds, slack-jawed. Poor troubled lad? Well, I suppose Daniel was troubled in some ways. He certainly troubled *me*! I always seemed to be thrown into unwanted confusion whenever I met him.

'Oh, just a social call,' I smiled. 'And to ask your opinion on something. Do you think I should read my father's diary, even if I might find something hurtful in it? Or should I let sleeping dogs lie?'

Somehow, in Gloria's company, it seemed so simple. She didn't know, of course, that Sidney wasn't my real father. One day, I would probably tell her, but just now, I thought it would complicate things. She tipped her head to one side and breathed in deeply. 'If you're asking my opinion, it means the time isn't right yet. But one day you'll really feel you want to read it, and *then* the time will be right.' Then her expression lifted again. 'I've got some chocolate biscuits. Quite a treat. Shall we open them?'

And suddenly Daniel, Sidney and my real father, whoever he might have been, were pushed to the back of my mind.

'Well, that's settled then!'

William's face was positively glowing as he came back into the lounge. It was early May and I was enjoying after-dinner coffee with the rest of the family before I shut myself away in my room to study. My exams weren't far off and I was determined to do well so that Edwin would be proud of me. William had been having another lengthy telephone conversation with him and now Deborah looked up, beaming with satisfaction.

'Go on, dear, tell them,' she encouraged him.

'Yes, of course,' William grinned, inhaling with proud excitement. 'Edwin's going to join me in the practice when he qualifies in the summer. George, Dr Simmonds that is, wants to retire, so Edwin and I will take on most of his patients, and Edwin will rent George's surgery from him. It's all settled bar all the legalities and red tape, of course.'

'Oh, that's fantastic!' Wendy cried, jumping to her feet with glee. 'Oh, but what about his National Service?'

'We'll cross that bridge when we come to it. Hopefully it won't be for a while and we can establish a firm joint practice – the first in Tavistock – before he goes, and maybe I'll get a long-term locum.'

'Oh, right. Oh, this is marvellous, isn't it, Lily?'

Wendy turned to me, her eyes shining knowingly. I hadn't said anything simply because I couldn't find the words to express the rapture that whipped through my heart. Edwin was coming to live here permanently. In the same house. I could have keeled over with happiness.

'Oh, yes! That's terrific news!' I found my tongue at last. 'How lovely for you to have him back! I know how you've all missed him!'

A broad smile split my face. None of them could have missed Edwin as much as I had! He was everything to me. And now I could see a golden future unfurling before us, filling every minute of my life with joy. It didn't matter any more that I knew nothing of my real father and very little of my mother. As Edwin's wife, I would know exactly who I was. And I would never want to be anyone else.

He came home towards the end of July, just a few days before my birthday. My heart was dancing a jig in my chest as I stood back, allowing the family to greet him first, although Celia couldn't be there as she was doing her nursing rotation at Plymouth's Greenbank Hospital. My fingertips were tingling with excitement as I waited, and then Wendy stood aside and I faced the man I loved across the small space that separated us. He hadn't changed one little bit and his eyes lit up with mischief when he saw me.

'Lily! It's good to see you!' He held me at arms' length, looking me up and down, and I held my breath, praying he'd approve. 'Well, I can't say you've grown,' he laughed, 'but you do look very well and very pretty.' He hugged me then, just for a moment, and I was in heaven.

'Did you have a good journey?' I asked breathlessly when he released me.

'Yes, I did, thanks. But I can't say that I'll be sorry not to have to spend so long on a train again. The first thing I'll need will be a car of my own. Something much smaller than the Rover. You did really well to pass your test so quickly, by the way, Lily.'

I knew that I blushed, not so much at his praise but because it had come from *him*. 'Thank you,' I mumbled as joy nevertheless exploded inside me.

'And what about your exams? Any news yet?'

'Oh, I got all my RSAs, but the O-level results won't be out for another few weeks.'

'Well, I'm sure you'll have done well. It was a very brave thing to have done, gone back to studying *and* with a full-time job as well.'

'Oh, that reminds me,' William chimed in, 'one of the clerks at the hospital gave in her notice today, so there'll be a vacancy coming up. I wondered if you might be interested, Lily? I could maybe pull a few strings. It would be a bit of a challenge for you, but you're so bright, you'd pick up the medical side easily and Ed and I could help you. You'd be in the office and dealing with both patients and the medical staff. I think you'd be ideal.'

I took a sharp, snatched breath. That, on top of everything else, was the crowning glory. Yes, I had started to look around for a new job where I could use my recently acquired skills. But being assistant supervisor to Mrs Kershaw for the last two years had been extremely interesting. I didn't want to go from that to sitting behind a typewriter all day. I was looking for a responsible position where I could use my initiative and feel really useful. Through William and Deborah, I already knew most of the doctors and some of the nurses. They were a super crowd and I couldn't think of another job that would appeal to me more. Especially as it would mean that not only would I be living in the same house as Edwin, but I would see him quite often at work as well!

'Oh, yes, I'd be really interested!' I replied, burning with enthusiasm. 'Do you think I'd stand a chance?'

'An excellent one, I'd have thought. Wouldn't you say so, Edwin?'

'Yes, Dad, I'm sure she would.'

Edwin turned on me a smile that reached his eyes, making the skin crinkle at the corners, and hope blossomed inside me. Everything was perfect. I didn't even mind that Daniel had been invited to the party William and Deborah had planned. It was supposed to be jointly for my birthday and Edwin's final qualification, but Deborah especially could always find an excuse for a get-together. It was to take place the following Sunday afternoon, in the garden if the weather was kind. In the meantime, I had booked a week's holiday so that I could be with Edwin while he took a break before he began working with his father.

'What do you think, Lily?' Edwin grinned as he ran his hand proudly along the gleaming wing of the

Austin Healey a few days later. 'I was really lucky to find her. There's not many around. She's two years old, but I never expected to spot anything like this in a garage in Tavistock. Not sure Dad entirely approves, mind. Fancy going for a spin?'

'Oh, yes!' I answered, my heart flying to the stars. And I couldn't help thinking that the little sports car was far superior to someone's battered old jeep I'd ridden in once before.

'Tell you what, why don't we drive across the moor to Widecombe and have a pub lunch? There's a superb little place just outside the village called the Rugglestone Inn. Do you know it?'

I shook my head, hugging to myself the dream of being alone with Edwin again. 'I've never been over the other side of the moor.' I didn't remind him that I had only turned eighteen the previous day and so had never been inside a pub before. The doubt cast a shadow over my joy, but to my relief, Edwin didn't appear to notice.

'I haven't been there myself for years. You'll love it. It's really old and quaint, and the bar's just the little front room of the original farmhouse. And there's a stream that runs across the front. It's really romantic.'

Romantic? Oh, it sounded perfect! I sat next to Edwin, feeling as if I could fly as we climbed up onto the moor. It was a beautiful day, the rugged scenery bathed in a clear, golden light that accentuated every wild contour of the land and glistened on the meandering ribbons of Dartmoor's many rivers and streams. The furthest I had ever been was to Dartmeet where the curling road plunged down to the old narrow bridge over the river. Edwin grinned at me as the car took the steep hill on the far side with ease and we gathered speed as we headed east. I was all eyes to take in the softer character of that side of the moor. The little village of Widecombe was busy with holiday-makers, but we left them behind as we turned up a side lane and, within a few hundred yards, arrived at our destination.

Edwin was right. It was like stepping back in time. We managed to get a sandwich and a packet of crisps, and Edwin bought me half a pint of lemonade shandy. As I untwisted the little blue packet of salt and sprinkled it over the crisps, I couldn't have been happier. A tidal wave of elation was sweeping me along to the heaven I had dreamt of for so long.

'Are you nervous about the interview?' Edwin asked, putting his tankard of bitter on the table.

I swallowed the crisps in my mouth. 'Yes, I am a bit. But only because I'd really love the job.'

'And I really hope you get it.'

He leant across the table and squeezed my hand, his lovely green-blue eyes looking deep into mine. A thrill of ecstasy tumbled down my spine as if Edwin was trying to tell me something. I knew in my heart what it was, but such matters should not be rushed. What mattered was the here and now, and I was with Edwin. I was content.

I was so awash with a deep sense of euphoria that I didn't even mind when Daniel came up to me at the party. I had to admit he was looking as disgustingly handsome as ever, a white shirt enhancing his tanned skin and dark, glossy hair that always seemed in need of a cut. I could understand why Kate fancied him. Deborah had asked me to invite my friends, so Kate, who had been working at Woolworths since the autumn, and Sally, who was awaiting her A-level results to get into university, were both there, looking a little shy among all these strangers. I was determined to look after them.

'Excuse me, Daniel,' I said with a smile, but he caught my arm as I turned away.

'Hang on a minute, Lily. I want to give you your present.'

'Present?' I was so surprised that I forgot to be abrupt with him.

'It *is* your birthday.'

'Yes, but I don't expect—'

'Go on, open it,' he urged, his expression set as he held out a small box.

I took it warily. Knowing Daniel, it would be

something to ridicule me with and his straight face would deepen his mockery. So I was doubly shocked when I opened the box to find a silver filigree pendant necklace set with a large amethyst. It looked Victorian and was somehow familiar.

I gazed at it in wonder for several seconds while my heart began to pound. 'Daniel, it's beautiful,' I scarcely managed to mumble.

'It was my great aunt's. She left it to me in her will. It was my great-grandmother's before that.'

His voice was low, quavering slightly. I realised that he was perfectly serious, and that the necklace really meant something to him. It was then that I remembered where I had seen it before. It adorned the swanlike neck of the stunning woman in the portrait at Fencott Place.

I snapped the box shut. Daniel had been playing with me after all. I was fuming, but I couldn't retaliate in front of all these people.

'Thank you, but I can't possibly accept it,' I said tersely.

He gave a sardonic grunt. 'Well, *I'm* never going to wear it, am I?'

'Save it for the future, then. For whoever becomes your wife.'

I saw his face turn to a mask of stone. I had said it in all innocence, forgetting for a moment the fact that he had been jilted while he was being held prisoner in Korea. I immediately felt guilty, but it was too late.

'Who's ever going to want to marry *me*?' he muttered under his breath, and then he glared almost accusingly at me. 'I want you to have it, Lily. If nothing else as an apology. And I promise never to call you my little Carrot Top ever again.'

A teasing sparkle had suddenly come into his eyes again and he failed to prevent his lips from curving into a jibing smile. Fury erupted inside me. I wanted to slap his face but instead I thrust the box against his chest and spinning on my heel, hurried across the lawn to Kate and Sally, forcing a carefree grin to my face.

Whether Daniel caught the box or whether it fell to the ground, I didn't see and I didn't care. I just wished Daniel hadn't accepted the invitation to the party, but it wasn't long before I noticed him shaking Edwin's hand. After that, I didn't see him again, so I assumed he must have left. And good riddance, too. How dare he try to humiliate me again at my own party? What would he have done if I had accepted his gift? Snatched it back with a derisive laugh and sneered at me for thinking he would actually have given me a family heirloom that was worth a small fortune? Thank goodness I had been one step ahead of him!

I joined back into the party, but I still felt ill at

ease. How was it that Daniel always managed to unnerve me and leave me feeling guilty? Yes, I felt sympathy for all he had been through, but he had this uncanny knack of upsetting me. I had thought just now that he was being sincere and wanted to be friends. If only he had offered me something like a box of chocolates, but the necklace had made me distrust him once again.

I felt sorry, though, for the ungracious way I had rebuffed him, and wished I had found some subtler words to reject the gift. I was torn with shame and wished he hadn't left so that I could have spoken to him again and put things right between us. But then Edwin came and rested his hand on my shoulder as I was talking to Kate and Sally, and the memory of Daniel and the necklace melted away. I had Edwin and nothing else mattered.

Chapter Fifteen

Dr Higgins grunted and glared at me over the rim of his spectacles as he handed the pile of signed correspondence back to me. I was quaking in my shoes. I had been lucky enough to get the job and it was only my third day working at the hospital, but I had already learnt that Dr Higgins was the one to watch out for. I had been told that he frequently returned his letters criss-crossed with red pen, ranting and raving at the smallest mistake and hissing that we couldn't even *bloody* spell. I was appalled. I had never heard William or Edwin swear, and certainly such language had never passed Sidney's lips. The only person I had known to use that same word once or twice was Daniel, which wasn't surprising. And, of course, Jeannie, but swearing was part of the culture she had been raised in, and any of the more uncouth oaths had been forbidden to her. But

Jeannie, who I hadn't heard from for over a year, was a fading memory.

So, I had taken extra care when I had been summoned to take some dictation from the known tyrant and had perhaps spent longer than I should have done over typing up the letters, double-checking the spelling of any medical terms in the special dictionary. There were three of us working in the hospital's clerical office, one plain clerk and two with secretarial skills. Mrs Elderman had been elsewise occupied when Dr Higgins had appeared so it had been left to me to bear his boorishness which made Daniel's usual ill-humour look like a ray of sunshine!

'Well done!' Mrs Elderman, who was back in the office now, grinned at me as Dr Higgins shut the door after him. 'A baptism of fire if ever there was! Now, put on the stamps and you can post them on your way out as it's lunchtime now. And don't forget to write it all down in the stamp book and file away the copies.'

I had learnt that there was a book for everything in which meticulous details were recorded, orders and expenditures as well as admissions, discharges and outpatient clinics. Absolutely everything went through the office and it amazed me that only three people ran the whole affair. It meant that we were incredibly busy and there was an awful lot to learn, but it was varied and interesting and I knew was going to give me a deep sense of satisfaction. Apart from Dr Higgins, all the staff I had met were friendly and helpful. Matron, although a stickler for discipline and able herself to do everything better than any of her nursing staff, had the reputation of a mother hen who would fiercely defend her chicks. If you had a problem of any sort, she was the one to turn to.

I could have had lunch in the Nurses' Dining Room, the cost of which would have been deducted from my wages, but I preferred the short walk home down the hill, knowing that Edwin was likely to be there. So at one o'clock, I trotted down the main stairs and along the side corridor to the outside world as the main door was virtually never used. I popped the letters in the postbox by the hospital gates, feeling immensely proud that I had passed muster with Dr Higgins, and hurried down to Plymouth Road in the warm September sunshine. I was so happy, I was bursting with joy.

'Hello! How did you get on this morning?'

William, Deborah, Edwin and Wendy had already started lunch around the kitchen table as we were all on a tight schedule. I washed my hands and sat down to join them, explaining about my success as I did so.

'Ho, ho, you did well, then!' William chuckled. 'Bit of a task-master is David!'

'Well, yes, he seemed irritated that I'd been a bit slow,' I admitted, 'but then I had checked some of the medical words so that I got it right first time.'

'Very wise,' Edwin nodded. 'I'm a bit scared of him myself, I have to say. I'm glad it's orthopaedics I'm specialising in and not his field.'

'It was his chest clinic today, and he does ENT on Saturday mornings, doesn't he?'

'That's right,' William confirmed. 'He's a brilliant doctor, mind. Very rarely needs to call in a consultant from Greenbank. And he's nowhere near as gruff with his patients.'

I should hope he wasn't, but I was glad for the women who had to come to the Gynae clinic that it was William with his gentle, understanding manner who would deal with their sensitive problems. Nothing was set in stone, though. The hospital was run by the half dozen local general practitioners, and each had his own speciality. But rather than refer a routine case to a colleague, they would usually treat the patient themselves using the superior facilities at the hospital, including performing operations. Visiting consultants attended certain clinics on a rota system which made it all very complicated, and one of our responsibilities in the office was to make sure everyone knew exactly who was doing what and when, so that patients were booked in to see the right doctor at the right time!

'I'll walk back with you, Lily,' Edwin suggested, helping himself to an apple. 'I've got an ulcer patient I want to check on.'

'All right. I've nearly finished,' I replied, gulping down my drink. I didn't want to miss an opportunity of being with Edwin, did I?

'See if you can be the clerk for my Ortho clinic on Friday,' he said as we started on the steep climb up Spring Hill. 'It'll be my first entirely on my own, so we can muddle through together. Mr Nunn, the consultant, he helped me with the first two, but normally he only comes once a month unless he's asked for specifically. It was so lucky that George's speciality was orthopaedics when it's my particular interest. If it hadn't been, I'm not sure I'd have come to work with Dad.'

A kernel of uncertainty unfurled in my breast. I had hoped that *my* being there had been part of Edwin's decision. But then I tossed the thought aside. It wouldn't have made any difference. If Edwin had gone to work elsewhere, it would have forced our relationship onwards, but as it was, it allowed him to take his time. Such as now. The brand new clerk arriving at the hospital in the company of the handsome young doctor. It sent a thrill rushing through my body.

'Right, Lily, might as well throw you in at the deep end,' Mrs Elderman smiled that afternoon.

'We've half a dozen specimens to be packaged up and posted to the Path Lab in Plymouth. They're on the table there. Now, you need to go down to the cellar and find some suitable boxes and some straw.'

I dreaded going down to the cellar, the only part of the job I didn't love. The original part of the hospital had been built back in the 1890s and despite the addition of electric light, deep shadows enshrouded the unimaginable plethora of items stored down in the cellar. I expected to encounter the ghost of some long-dead patient lurking in the darkness. Once I did and my heart stabbed in terror. But it turned out to be a porter hunting for something in the gloom. I always ran up the steps and escaped as quickly as I possibly could.

There were three blood samples, two of urine, one faeces and one unrecognisable lump that from the label was a piece of a tumour that had been removed in an operation that morning. I began to box them up carefully, but one of the urine bottles was leaking.

'Go to one of the wards and ask Sister for some brown cotton wool to plug it,' Mrs Elderman advised.

I did. But first of all I went to wash my hands! Then I popped into the Duty Room which was almost next to our office to see if one of the sisters was taking her break there to ask permission to go to her ward. If I didn't recognise their faces, they were distinguished by their starched veil caps and dark blue uniforms. I was out of luck, but a homely, mature nurse, the sort of rotund figure you felt you could trust, did the honours for me, and soon I was on my way to the Post Office with my precious cargo.

It was one of the great things about the job, being so varied. On Friday morning, we did the wages which I had assisted with at Woolworths so I knew all about working out tax and national insurance. Then I was entrusted with going to the bank to collect the cash. Mrs Elderman had already rung ahead so that it would all be waiting for me, and had also explained that someone new was coming with the authorisation note. So off I went, feeling somewhat nervous and hoping no one would try to steal the money from me on my return walk!

As I opened the door to the bank, a man was coming out and stood back to hold it open for me. I looked up to thank him and caught a sharp intake of breath.

'Daniel!'

'Lily.'

He had seemed momentarily startled but then his voice had been flat, a mere acknowledgement of my presence. The instant I crossed the threshold, he slipped past me and went to stride away. Remorse welled up inside me, and I sprang after him, leaving the door to close on its own.

'Daniel, wait. I want to apologise,' I blurted out. 'About the necklace—'

He turned round, shaking his head so that he didn't meet my gaze. 'No, I'm the one who should be sorry. I understand why you couldn't accept it. It was stupid and thoughtless of me to have put you in such an embarrassing position.'

He glanced at me, his forehead swooped in that habitual frown, but at least his words had filled me with relief.

'Then we're both sorry,' I smiled back.

'Yes,' he answered with a wry grunt, and then one eyebrow lifted. 'Friends?'

'Of course.'

His eyes softened to a shade of lavender, pricking somewhere inside me. Just as I was feeling more relaxed in his company, he had done it again. Unsettling me and putting my nerves on edge. But at least I had made my peace and now my conscience was clear.

'How's the new job?' he asked, but more out of politeness than interest I felt.

'I'm enjoying it. I'm on an errand for the office now.'

'Then I mustn't detain you.'

His formal choice of words and the little bow

of his head as he turned away made me feel as if I had been dismissed. I went back into the bank, totally nonplussed. But the chance meeting was soon forgotten. That afternoon, I was to assist Edwin with his clinic.

The waiting room was hopelessly small, no more than eight feet wide and not much more in length. The tiny receptionist's table, where I sat feeling very proud in my white coat, was crammed with admission cards and papers, with scarcely any room to write. I had already become used to seeing patients sitting along the corridor on hard, uncomfortable chairs and benches because the waiting room was overflowing! And being the orthopaedic clinic made it even more chaotic with people on crutches or with limbs in plaster trying to negotiate the ridiculously restricted space!

It all made for a jolly atmosphere, though, especially as, being such a small town, everyone seemed to know everybody else and chatted away as if they were at a party rather than a hospital. So different from when Ellen had collapsed on that dreadful night nearly three years ago now and had been spirited away in an ambulance. I had been left to wait in a silent, empty corridor that echoed with gloom.

The memory flashed across my mind like an

arrow. How that evening had changed my life! But there was no room for such contemplation now. I was living with a professional family, I was a hospital clerk-cum-secretary and I was in charge of my very first clinic.

'Farmer Giles reportin', young maid,' a voice above me boomed.

I had been busy writing and, as I glanced up, the first thing I noticed were the biggest pair of hands I had ever seen. They were huge and would have covered the entire table if the fingertips hadn't been merely resting on the very edge. My eyes moved upwards to the giant of a man towering over me. Daniel was tall, a touch over six foot and with broad shoulders, but this chap would have made him look like an elf! His tweed jacket must have been specially made for him, and he had evidently hung onto it for years as it was in holes in several places and covered in bits of straw and animal hair.

'Yes, sir?' I gulped, putting an innocent expression on my face. I was glad I had met him in a crowded hospital room and not up a dark alleyway at night! 'Name, please?'

'Like I said, Farmer Giles.' He smiled down at me from a ruddy, weather-crinkled face and nodded vigorously. 'Not pullin' your leg. Really am, like. John Giles, farmer. Doctor 'Iggins sent us ter see this Doctor Franfield. I 'opes 'er can do summat. It's my shoulder, see. Cas'n move it. No good fer a farmer.'

'Well, no, I'm sure it isn't,' I sympathised. 'You're a new patient so I'll have to fill out a form for you. Now I've got your name and you say Dr Higgins is your GP, so address, please?'

'Meadcliffe Farm. Comes under Moorshop, like.'

'And your date of birth?'

'Ah, well, I'm not sure 'bout that. 'Ow old d'you think I am, maid?'

I glanced up, my eyes stretched wide in a mixture of surprise and horror as I realised the waiting room had suddenly gone quiet and every gaze was riveted on me. I shut my mouth and swallowed hard as colour flooded into my cheeks.

'Oh, er…' I stammered. I was thinking on my feet, trying to compare the fellow's seamed and wrinkled face with other older people I knew. The skin was brown and leathery, more so than Barry Coleman's who had told me he was some years older than Uncle Artie who I knew to be sixty-two. So, I took a deep breath and croaked, 'Nearly seventy?'

A deathly hush settled on the waiting room and I could hear my pulse crashing at my temples. John Giles's animated face had become stilled.

'I be fifty-three,' he said quietly.

I wanted the ground to open up and swallow me. I felt as if my face was on fire, but then a deep, rumbling belly laugh exploded like a bomb in the confined space. I dared to look up at the said gentleman who was crying with mirth as he wobbled like a jelly.

'I be sorry, young cheel!' he spluttered. 'But you'm so serious fer a littl'un, I couldn't resist! Eleventh of April 1902 I were born.'

'Oh, thank you,' I mumbled, writing it on the form in my neatest hand to a chorus of laughter. I hoped to goodness that Matron couldn't hear the frivolity, and I vowed never, *ever* to be taken in again like that!

'Well, you seem to have cheered everyone up!'

My heart filled with relief as Edwin appeared in the doorway, a bright and sunny grin lighting his face as he came towards me. And suddenly everything was all right again.

'Lily, would you arrange for Mrs Stupples to have an X-ray, please?'

I nodded efficiently. 'Of course, Doctor.'

Edwin's eyes smiled into mine and he winked mischievously.

The weeks flew by and I hardly noticed the late summer turn into autumn. Edwin took his turn as the duty doctor for the month and was once called out in the early hours to remain at the hospital for the remainder of the night. Occasionally an emergency would keep him away, but basically he was there when I went to bed at night and when I woke up in the morning, and I saw him on and off throughout the day as well. I was in my seventh heaven. But even if Edwin hadn't been part of it, I should have loved my job. It was so varied, the people were wonderful and I really felt as if I was playing a useful role in life.

We celebrated Wendy's twenty-first birthday in November with an even bigger party than usual. Uncle Michael had finally retired from the sea and I met him for the first time, a tall, slight man, nothing like I imagined. Ian was now officially Wendy's boyfriend, and a couple of her work colleagues came to the party as well. Daniel had rung at the last minute to decline his invitation with the excuse that the generator at Fencott Place had broken down and he was still in the middle of repairing it. I had never considered before how the isolated house was supplied with electricity, and the thought fleetingly crossed my mind that, as well as being gifted academically, Daniel seemed able to turn his hand to all manner of practical matters. But I for one wasn't going to miss him at Wendy's party.

'May I, Miss Hayes?'

Edwin gave a mock bow, eyes twinkling merrily, and I responded with a sham curtsey. The lounge was bursting with so many people and there was little room to dance properly. So it was slow numbers only, and Edwin held me very close. My heart thrilled with rapture and, as the evening wore on, a few glasses of cider gave me the courage to rest my head against his shoulder as we danced. He didn't seem to object, and when the music came to an end, he dropped a kiss on my forehead. The breath caught in my throat, and as the guests eventually left, Edwin had one arm around me as we said goodnight to them. I really felt the evening had brought us that much closer, and I was so happy, I could have burst!

Then it was all down to preparations for Christmas both at home and at the hospital. Naturally, every effort was made to discharge patients for home wherever possible, but the wards were still half full and a couple of elderly people, both of whom lived alone, were looking forward to the company. One old lady who had been admitted in such a filthy, flea-ridden state that we'd had to burn all her clothes, later squeezed my hand and told me with tears in her eyes that it was the best Christmas she'd ever had.

On Christmas Eve, William dressed as Santa Claus and paid a visit to every single patient, hiding behind a false white beard and bushy, stick-on eyebrows borrowed annually from the local amateur dramatic society. My favourite event, though, was the carol service in the evening. It began with the nurses, dressed in their cloaks, forming a candle-lit procession, with other staff walking in pairs behind them. I paired up with Edwin and gazed up at his smiling face bathed in the warm glow from the candles. It was all quite magical, and I could understand why the little children stared at us in utter wonderment as we sang 'Away in the Manger' and 'Oh, little town of Bethlehem' as we glided serenely through the ward. Then we floated through the two women's wards which were also on the first floor, and the doors to the private and amenity rooms had also been left open so that the patients there could watch us, too. When we came to the ward for the terminally ill, my throat choked and I couldn't sing. And then my dear, sensitive Edwin took my hand and smiled down at me, and I found my voice again. When we went downstairs to the two men's wards, I was feeling relaxed and happy again, even when Edwin left me to have a welcoming word with the young staff nurse who had just started at the hospital. And then we walked home together through the frosty streets of Tavistock.

Christmas in the Franfield household was yet another jolly family event with visitors coming and going, and Deborah in her element. I was thankful, though, that Daniel had gone up to London to stay with his parents and grandmother, so that I could enjoy the holiday to the full without fear of seeing him. There should be no animosity between us now, but he still had that ability to make me feel uncomfortable.

A few days later, we three clerks were invited to the nursing staff's Christmas dinner which was presided over by the ward charge nurse and Dr Wilkins. I sat next to the new staff nurse, Sadie Jessop, and tried to make her feel at home.

'It's my first time at one of these dinners, too,' I told her with a smile. 'I only started here in September.'

'Really? What were you doing before?'

'I was assistant supervisor at Woolworths. What about you?'

'I trained at Truro, and then I was working at Greenbank, but I fancied a change. Somewhere smaller, just like this. And I can still get back easily to Truro to see my family.'

'Ah, I thought I detected a Cornish accent there! But if you worked at Greenbank, you might know Celia Franfield. She did part of her nursing rotation there.'

Sadie Jessop shook her head. 'No, I don't think so. But it's a big hospital as I'm sure you know. But *Franfield*? That nice young doctor's Franfield, isn't he?'

I nodded with a grin, my heart warming as it always did when I thought of Edwin. 'Yes. Celia's his sister. And there's a Dr Franfield senior as well.

He was the one dressed as Father Christmas. I live with them all.'

'Oh! You know, I thought you seemed rather friendly with each other.'

I'm sure I must have blushed. It was somewhat more than friendly, but I couldn't say so to anyone yet. So I just explained what had happened when Sidney had died.

'Oh, how sad.' Sadie appeared genuinely moved, a concerned expression on her pretty face, and I really rather liked her.

'Yes, it was. But the Franfields are a wonderful family. Mrs Franfield's a nurse, too, but for the general practice. She's ever so nice. Are you coming to the January Ball? You'd meet her there.'

'Yes, I am. I thought it'd be a good way of getting to know everyone better. It's held in the Town Hall, isn't it?'

'That's right. Third Friday in January each year. I've not been to that before, either. Everyone really lets their hair down, so I'm told.'

'Then that'll be a first for both of us, too!' Sadie beamed back at me with a smile that showed to perfection her beautiful mouth and flawless skin that made me feel humbled.

I had been making myself a gown in a scarlet taffeta that strangely enough complemented my hair, accentuating its golden rather than its ginger

hues. I had never had it cut or permed, and planned
to let it swing naturally in its waving curls around
my shoulders. The dress was tight-waisted and the
bodice was topped with a broad, off-the-shoulder
yoke. All I needed was a necklace. The one Daniel
had wanted to give me would have been perfect.
Instead I wore Ellen's pearls. I wished she had been
there to see me off. *Cinderella shall go to the ball*. I
felt that tonight Edwin would declare his love to the
urchin his family had taken in off the streets.

I heard him stifle a little gasp when he saw me and
my stomach tightened deliciously. Oh, yes! Tonight I
would reach the stars! Edwin, looking as handsome
as ever in a new suit, helped me into my best coat
and offered me his arm.

'Oh, you look lovely, Lily!' Wendy exclaimed,
winking at me on the sly. 'Wish I was on the staff
and could go. Have a wonderful time, won't you!'

The four of us hurried along Plymouth Road as it
was so near that it wasn't worth taking the car. It was
a lovely winter's night, crisp and clear, but very cold
so that we were glad to arrive at the Town Hall and
climb the stairs to the beautiful function room on
the first floor. It was set out for the formal dinner for
the local doctors and visiting consultants and their
respective wives, silver cutlery and crystal glasses
sparkling in the electric light. There was some mild
joking as it was explained to those who didn't know

me who I was and why I was partnering Edwin.

'I feel a bit of a fraud,' I laughed as I spoke to Mr Nunn, the orthopaedic consultant who helped with Edwin's more complicated cases. 'But I'd be coming to the ball afterwards, so it made sense.' And by next year, I might be by Edwin's side officially. As his wife, I thought dreamily.

He was the perfect, attentive gentleman during the meal, and my heart overflowed. I loved Edwin with a passion that overwhelmed me, and I stared into the clear brilliance of his green-blue eyes as he smiled at me, passing the salt or the butter. I was on top of the world and couldn't wait for the dancing and all the other frivolities I had heard about to begin. After the meal, the rest of the staff who weren't on duty that night started to arrive. Everyone was greeted by Matron who appeared a different person in a ball-gown, gaily showing the human side of her nature more than ever. The band struck up and I was tingling with excitement as I danced the first two quicksteps with Edwin.

'I think I'll ask the new staff nurse for the next one,' he smiled down at me. 'Don't want her feeling left out. You'll be all right on your own for a few minutes, won't you?'

'Of course!' I replied with a light toss of my head. It was typical of Edwin to be so considerate. I was so proud of him and went to sit with William and

Deborah who were chatting with Dr Wilkins and his wife. I watched Edwin foxtrotting with Sadie. She looked even lovelier than ever in an evening gown, and was talking easily as Edwin whisked her around the dance floor.

'Come on, Lily. Let's show them how to do it properly!' William crowed, pulling me to my feet. A good dancer, was William, and I followed his lead, my mouth in a wide smile as our feet rose and fell in time to the music.

'That was great, Lily!' William grinned as we clapped at the end of the second tune. 'But I'd better have a dance with Deborah before I get too worn out!'

He led me back to my seat and he and Deborah left me talking to Mrs Wilkins who suffered somewhat from verbal diarrhoea and engaged me in conversation until long after William and Deborah came back, flushed and breathless. I nodded politely, trying to search the hall without appearing rude. When I was finally rescued by Dr Wilkins asking his wife to dance, I was able to glance across the floor.

Edwin was still dancing with Sadie but just at that moment, they decided to stop. He took her arm and gently guided her to where she had been sitting at the far end of the hall. Then he left her to go to the bar and returning with a tankard of beer and a smaller glass of something else, sat down next to her. They were immediately deep in animated conversation punctuated with hand gestures, smiles and laughter. Edwin's gaze left her face for just a second, and when he caught my eye, he gave me that mischievous wink and openly waved his fingers before turning his full attention back to Sadie.

I froze, the breath raw and stinging in my throat. Edwin's smile as he chuckled at something Sadie had said was rapturous, bursting with life and slicing at my heart. I had never seen him so elated. Among all the noise and gaiety that surrounded me, I was suddenly lost and alone, the muscles of my chest contracting in pain.

Edwin didn't love me.

No. It couldn't be true. He was simply being kind and courteous to Sadie. But as I stared across at him, I knew I was only fooling myself. A tiny, strangled sound died on my lips as I tried to deny once again what I could see before my very eyes.

Everything, every moment I had spent with Edwin over the past two years raced through my head. He had always been affable and chivalrous. Full of fun. But had he ever shown me anything more than brotherly affection? As my heart turned to a solid block in my chest, I realised what a blithering idiot I had been. Edwin saw me as a little sister, a child. And I wanted to die.

My senses reeled away as the music ceased

and I was only vaguely aware of the band leader announcing that we should form teams for the traditional party games. Edwin had never loved me. He was fond of me as the orphan his parents had taken into the bosom of their family. But he had never loved me, not with the fathomless passion I had always felt for him. And now his interest had been drawn by Sadie Jessop, who was bright and intelligent and more of his age. And beautiful.

I sat immobile. Glued to the chair. Stunned. Stupid. And feeling as if I was falling into a deep, dark abyss of despair. And then Edwin was pulling my hand, laughing and grinning, dragging me up to join him and Sadie in the chaotic line. Spearing the agony deeper and deeper somewhere beneath my ribs.

Somehow I fixed a stiff smile on my face. Did whatever it was I was supposed to do with a balloon and a beanbag, moving like a clockwork doll. One of the ward sisters kicked off her shoes to move more freely, and beside me, Sadie did the same. Even her feet were pretty. She made me feel like a wilting daisy next to her blooming rose. I didn't stand a chance.

I dragged myself desolately through the rest of the evening, struggling to hold my shattered soul together and hide my anguish from everyone around me. When it came to the last waltz, Edwin danced it, not with me but with Sadie. Other nurses partnered each other, but I sat, alone and bleeding.

'May I have the pleasure, Miss Hayes?'

I scraped my gaze upwards to Dr Higgins. It was the first time I had ever seen him smile. He was a confirmed bachelor, and everyone said he attended the ball on sufferance. Perhaps he felt as I did now. Isolated and left out. Two lost souls together.

We moved slowly around the dance floor, both rigid and silent. I bit back my tears. At the end, I clapped mechanically and Dr Higgins gave a polite bow.

'You know, you've done very well,' he growled. 'You've got the makings of a good secretary.'

'Thank you,' I answered through bloodless lips.

'Goodnight then, Miss Hayes.'

I stood, alone for a moment as the dance floor emptied. I wanted to sink on my knees and howl with misery.

'Tell Mum and Dad I'm just walking Sadie back to the Nurses' Home, would you, Lily?'

Edwin didn't give me a chance to reply as he made for the door, his arm protectively around Sadie's shoulder. Just as he had done so often with me.

I walked back, almost blundering along Plymouth Road and shivering with shock. William and Deborah, a pace ahead of me, were arm in arm, romantic and happy. I went straight to bed, thankful that Wendy hadn't waited up, bubbling and expecting to hear all about it. I curled up beneath the blankets, numbed and disbelieving, all my hopes and dreams dashed to smithereens. Then I heard Edwin come in, whistling softly, and retire to his room next to mine. Some time later, the house was in stillness, and only then did I weep until I thought my heart would break.

Chapter Sixteen

The next morning, I had to haul myself out of bed as I had to be at work by eight-thirty. I hadn't slept a wink and now I felt like death warmed up. My whole world lay in splinters at my feet like broken glass. Edwin didn't love me. The belief that he did had held my life together so that now it hung in tatters all around me. The dream had been dissipated like spray in the wind, leaving behind nothing but emptiness.

All the old doubts flooded into the void, filling my aching head until it was ready to explode. Who really was I? Why had my mother had an affair? What had she been like? Who was my real father, and was he alive or dead, killed in the war, perhaps? Why had Sidney suffered that freak fatal accident before he had told me more, as I had been sure he eventually would? Most of all, why had Ellen died before I had reached the magical age of eighteen? If I had been but three years older, I could have stayed in London living independently, and none of this would have happened. And I would still have had my dear friend Jeannie to make me laugh at every twist and turn. That night I vowed to write to her again, telling her everything and inviting myself to go and stay with her.

I washed and dressed with lightning speed. I was overseeing Dr Higgins's ENT clinic and mustn't be late. He always performed four operations beforehand, mainly tonsillectomies, and I would have to see to the paperwork for him.

My heart was too sickened for me to be able to eat anything, so I was just swallowing a coffee when Edwin stumbled into the kitchen in his pyjamas, bleary-eyed and yawning.

'Morning, Lily. Great evening, wasn't it?'

I nodded, unable to speak, pretending I had a mouthful of drink. And then Deborah wandered in looking as pretty as I had ever seen her, despite her years, and smiling serenely.

Edwin immediately came to life. 'Hey, Mum, would it be all right if Sadie comes to tea tomorrow? She's off duty and that only happens once a month on a Sunday.'

'Of course, dear. You two looked as if you were getting friendly last night.'

That was it. I wanted to scream and my stomach rebelled. I made a dash upstairs to the toilet, but I wasn't sick. I just felt a cloud of misery bearing down on me.

I made my first error in one of Dr Higgins's post-operative reports. Despite our last waltz the night before, he yelled at me and I burst into tears. He mumbled something about blubbing children. A child. That was how everyone saw me. Especially Edwin. I was eighteen to his twenty-six, nearly twenty-seven, years. Sadie must be twenty-three or four, much more his age.

'I think Ed's a pig!' Wendy scowled that afternoon.

I was lying on my bed pretending to read, but in truth the words were marching through my head without any meaning. I had wanted to be left alone and wished Wendy hadn't come to plonk herself, uninvited, on my bed at my feet. I sat up, organising my face into a carefree expression.

'You won't say anything, will you, Wendy?' I said, trying not to sound too desperate. 'I don't think anyone else realised how I felt about him.'

'Felt?' Wendy's eyebrows shot up.

I shrugged as casually as I could. 'Well, nothing was ever said between us. About love, I mean. And he's obviously smitten with Sadie, and I wouldn't want to spoil it for him by being silly about it. And

Sadie's very nice. And there'll be plenty more fish in the sea for me. There was Ian's friend, Rob, for a start. I rather liked him.'

'Really? Oh, I'll see if he's still unattached, then.' And with that, she jumped up quite satisfied, leaving me to drown in my own wretchedness.

'Could I possibly borrow the car for a couple of hours after lunch, please?' I asked William, trying to sound relaxed and contented the next day. 'I'd like to visit Kate. I haven't seen her for ages except in the shop.'

'Yes, that's fine,' William smiled back. 'Good to keep your hand in at the wheel. Just be careful if it's at all icy.'

'Don't forget Sadie's coming to tea, though, will you?' Edwin put in, his eyes shining. 'She said she likes you and wants to get to know you better, too.'

My heart shrivelled. 'No, I won't be very long,' I lied, since it was my intention to stay away as long as possible.

As it happened, I wasn't that long after all. Kate's mum opened the door to me with her usual welcoming grin.

'I'm afraid Kate's not here. You know Pete's been back from his National Service for a bit? Well, they've gotten pretty friendly, like.' She paused to wink knowingly at me. 'Don't know where they've gone, I'm afraid.'

I felt my shoulders sag. 'Oh, never mind. Tell her I've called.'

'Of course, dear.'

I stood on the pavement, totally deflated, and glanced towards the jail. The prisoners were on the inside and I was on the outside, but I felt equally as trapped – in my own despair. Sally had gone back to university and the only other person I could talk to was Gloria. But when I knocked on her door, there was total silence.

I went back to the car and sat inside for a few minutes, drumming my fingers on the steering wheel. I even felt tempted to drive out to Fencott Place. I hadn't seen Daniel for months, not since we had met in the bank. Edwin sometimes went to see him, but I never went with him. But how would seeing Daniel help except to give me someone to vent my frustrations on? Even Daniel didn't deserve that.

So I set off home and then, at the last minute, I turned off to the little car park by the track to Yellowmeade Farm and my old home at Fogginter. I wouldn't risk the Rover's suspension on the old stone setts of the original horse-drawn tramway, so I walked along the uneven way even though I wasn't really wearing the right shoes for it. The wild Dartmoor wind pulled at my hair, whipping it across my face and in some ways driving away the demons. But then I remembered the happy time when Edwin and I had walked there together, and I wanted to cry again.

I felt even worse when I glanced along to where the cottages had stood. They had been totally demolished the previous summer. The stone had been used to face the buildings at the new television transmission station at the foot of the towering mast on North Hessary Tor just outside Princetown, which was due to start broadcasting in a few months' time. All that remained of the cottages were the foundations of the walls, pathetic mounds that the grass was gradually reclaiming. Only the back wall of our block had been left to brave the elements, a sorry reminder of my time there with Sidney. So I hastily turned away and, knocking at the backdoor of Yellowmeade Farm, let myself in.

Barry Coleman, Nora and Mark were sitting at the kitchen table, unusually in sombre mood. But they looked up in unison as I came in.

'Hello there, young maid,' Barry smiled, his craggy face brightening. 'Us 'asn't seen you in a while.'

'Is there anything wrong?' I asked, the irony that they might have been asking me the very same question pricking my conscience.

'Two of our sheep 'as bin killed over at Merrivale stone rows,' Barry moaned. 'And not by dogs or ort like that. But by 'uman 'and. Sacrificed and... Well, you doesn't want to know the details.'

'Oh, no!' I was genuinely shocked and shuddered with revulsion as I recalled the horrific sight that had led to my first encounter with Daniel.

'And us 'asn't bin the first,' Barry sighed. 'If I catches they buggers, I'll kill them.'

'If I doesn't get them first,' Mark added, speaking quite forcibly for once. 'What with that and all they dead rabbits from that myxo whatever it is. Must be putting the old warreners out of business. At least *that* don't seem to affect our livestock, mind.'

I nodded. When I had come to live on the moor, I had been surprised to learn that there were still isolated rabbit farms where these cute wild animals were encouraged to breed in man-assisted warrens later to be culled for their meat and fur. I wasn't sure I approved, but I supposed it was no different from any other sort of farming.

'I'm really sorry about the sheep,' I said instead. 'Have you contacted the police?'

'Oh, yes. Us 'as to for the insurance. Valuable ewes, they was, not young wethers that'll go to slaughter afore too long. The insurance people wasn't too 'appy 'bout it, neither.'

'And the police?'

'Making enquiries, but they needs to catch they devils red-'anded and with three hundred and sixty odd square miles of moor to patrol, it won't be easy.

Can't watch every ancient site twenty-four hours a day, as one officer put it.'

That was exactly what Daniel had said, nearly a year ago now when we had met at Gloria's. It wasn't a particularly pleasant subject to discuss, but at least it gave me something else to think about. But the black depression gradually settled over me again as I drove home, knowing that Sadie and Edwin would be there together. I couldn't help liking her, mind, as she chatted in an open and friendly way, totally oblivious to the fact that she was ripping my soul to shreds. Once or twice, Wendy caught my eye and threw a disgruntled glance at Edwin as if *she* should be the one who was so distraught.

I had decided that to show my feelings would simply be childish, and Edwin wouldn't thank me for that. My only chance to win him back was to be pleasant and mature. This thing with Sadie might just be a flash in the pan, and if I could hold on, waiting in the wings, Edwin might turn to me for comfort if they broke up. I would be more than happy to step into the breach.

It didn't happen. As the weeks passed, my only escape was to get up on the moor and wander alone for hours. William and Deborah weren't at all happy about it and limited my use of the car as there was no other way of getting there with no suitable connections on Saturday afternoons and no trains at all on Sundays. There was time, though, after I finished work at Saturday lunchtime, to catch a train to Whitchurch Down, the village of Horrabridge with its access to Knowle Down, or to Yelverton and the popular open area of Roborough Down and the obsolete wartime airfield there. William and Deborah felt that these places were safer, but it wasn't the same for me. They couldn't understand my sudden need to roam and I couldn't tell them the truth. But I did decide to buy myself a car so that I could go anywhere I pleased. I paid for my keep, of course, but had saved enough to purchase something fairly small. Before I did, however, something else happened that weighed heavily on my heart.

It was announced that the little moorland train that had played such an important and happy part in my life was to close. Why was it, I despaired, that fate seemed to be bringing the past back to haunt me, reviving all the soul-searching that had torn me apart? My thoughts kept returning to the box up in the loft. Gloria had said I would know instinctively when the time was right, but I was still hesitating, so perhaps I should wait a little longer.

The news about the closure drew hundreds of people to travel on the line that last week. If only they had used it more regularly it would never have closed. Instead of the engine and one carriage that the service had been reduced to even in my time, three coaches had been required for each trip. I couldn't go until Saturday afternoon, the very last day. The third of March 1956. I would always remember it.

The Princetown Railway had meant little to the rest of the family. Only Edwin shared my sense of bereavement as he had used it frequently to get to Fencott Place, particularly during the war when William had only been allowed sufficient petrol to visit his outlying patients. Sadie was on duty and so Edwin and I were to ride on the train together for the very last time, but at the last minute, he was called to an emergency. So I set out alone.

When I arrived at Yelverton Station, all was chaos. I had never in all the time I had used the moorland train, seen it like this. There were even policemen controlling the queues. Many of the people milling around me were in jovial mood, perhaps never having ridden on the line before and so enjoying a day out. But others stood quietly, their expressions fixed. People to whom, like me, the Princetown train had been a life-saver. Not only had it taken me to work and back each day, but through it I had made the new friends who had rebuilt my existence. The moor would still be there in all its beauty, but the railway had been the link between man and his struggle to survive on this savage wilderness. It was like burying a friend and I felt bereft.

I couldn't believe my eyes. Six carriages were

waiting at the platform, needing two of the sturdy engines to pull them up the steep, twisting incline. I was lucky enough to claim a seat by the window, and I wouldn't give it up for anything. I was saying goodbye to part of my life. I had said so many goodbyes in the last few years. Even my letter to Jeannie had been returned with *not known at this address* scrawled on it. So she had moved away and was lost to me for ever.

Morose thought jangled in my head as the engines strained uphill with their heavy burden. We stopped at Burrator Halt high above the dark sheen of the reservoir, but nobody got off to walk around this glorious man-made lake, one of the many jewels in Dartmoor's granite setting, as I had often done. We wound on, high on the embankment, through the dark woods and crossing the main road, came out onto the magnificent open moor. So many landmarks passed my tear-misted vision, and when we slowed to navigate the sharp bend around King Tor and the ruins of Foggintor came into view, my heart finally broke. Everything I held so dear was falling apart. Gone. Lost. Once again, I was forlorn and alone in a big empty world.

I kept my head turned firmly to the window so that my fellow passengers wouldn't see the tears rolling down my cheeks. And then shortly before we came into the station, the train bore me past a solitary figure standing erect and respectful as if at a funeral, with a black and white collie sitting obediently at his feet. He was near enough for me to see the set expression on his face.

I was shocked as we came into Princetown Station. Already the buildings wore a derelict look, windows boarded up and most of the equipment removed. I got off, not knowing quite what I would do next. Kate, who would now have to travel to work on the extended bus service that was, ironically, to replace the train, would be at work, and besides, just now, I felt I wanted to deal with my grief alone.

'Dreadful, isn't it? The end of an era.'

I was outside the station now. Daniel had evidently walked up briskly, Trojan at his heels. I felt embarrassed rather than annoyed as I was sure it must be obvious I had been crying. But he shook his head sadly.

'You know, I can't help thinking that if I'd used the train more often instead of the jeep, I could have saved it.'

I looked up at him, surprised. His voice had trembled slightly. So we shared this sense of deep loss.

'I don't think one person would have made that much difference,' I answered gently.

He lowered his eyes. 'All the same,' he muttered, and then looked up at me with a half smile. 'It's good to see you again, though. Do you fancy afternoon tea – or coffee,' he corrected himself, 'at the café?'

I blinked at him, considering for a moment. A familiar face, even one I was uncertain about, was perhaps just what I needed.

'Why not?' I replied.

I had a job to keep up with his long stride. He tied Trojan up outside and we entered the café which had never done such brisk business. We were shown to a small table tucked away in a corner. The atmosphere was hot and steamy, and my cheeks flushed to the realisation that I had actually accepted Daniel's invitation.

'You know, the train was our lifeline during the war,' he said when we had ordered. 'With no petrol, everyone relied on it. It brought in the provisions we all survived on. I mean, it still does, but then it was the *only* way. For me as a boy, it was magical. Oh, and the coal! Seeing if I could creep up and steal a lump without being caught.'

Normally I would have been horrified, but Daniel had bowed his head sheepishly in a suppressed smile and I couldn't help but see the amusing side of it.

'And did you? Get caught?'

'Oh, every time,' he admitted buoyantly. 'Except once. And then I got caught putting it back. Still got a clip round the ear. But it was all only a game.' The smile slid from his face. 'And tomorrow it'll all be gone.'

'Coffee for you, madam, and tea for you, sir?'

'Yes, thank you,' we answered in chorus, and we both smiled as our eyes met.

'So how's the job going? Still liking it?' Daniel resumed when the young girl moved away.

'Yes, very much.' I didn't know what to say after that. My job meant the hospital, and the hospital meant Edwin and Sadie. I didn't want to talk about it, so I was pleased when I thought of a way to change the subject. 'Trojan's come on well.'

Daniel's eyes lit up. 'Yes, he's a good dog. Never chases after sheep at all, but he will try to herd them if I don't stop him first.'

'Talking of sheep,' I told him as I sipped at the hot liquid, 'my friends at Yellowmeade Farm had a couple of sheep killed in a ritualistic sort of way a few weeks ago. They were so upset.'

'Well, you would be. It's horrible what's been happening. I saw a chap trying to drag a sheep away a while ago. I don't know if he was anything to do with it. Maybe he was sheep rustling or perhaps it was all totally innocent, but he ran off pretty quickly when I shouted at him.'

'Well, that sounds a bit suspicious, doesn't it? And you didn't recognise him at all?' I felt deeply involved, the incident with Barry and his family bringing it even closer, and I'd have loved to see the culprit get caught. But Daniel shook his head.

'No, unfortunately. He was too far off for me to see him clearly, and there was no point in running after him. I'd never have caught him up at that distance.'

'Pity.'

We both fell silent for a few minutes as we finished our drinks and then Daniel looked at me questioningly. 'Are you going back on the train?'

I gave a ponderous sigh. 'Yes, I am. But I don't want to wait for the last one. That would just be too sad. I want to watch it steam out of Yelverton just once more and imagine it puffing its way across the moor for ever.'

Daniel gave a wry smile. 'Yes. I know exactly what you mean. But I'll walk back to the station with you if you don't mind. I want to watch it leaving one more time, too. And then Trojan and I had better walk home before it gets too dark to see. I didn't expect to be so long, so I didn't bring a torch and it doesn't look like there'll be any moon this evening.'

He paid the bill and we walked slowly back through the centre of Princetown. As we approached the station, the next train coasted in and passengers spilt out of the carriages. We had to push our way onto the platform and I was glad of Daniel's assistance. As we jostled past one of the engines, Mr Gough was standing on the running board, wistfully surveying the scene.

'Hello, Lily!' he called when he saw me. 'Haven't seen you in a while.'

'No, but I had to come. A sad day. What are you going to do now?'

'Been given a job working out of Laira Junction, so we've got to find a new house there. Twenty-one years I've worked this line. I'll miss it.'

'We all will.'

'That's a fact.' Mr Gough bounced his head up and down, and then frowned intently at Daniel. 'I seem to recognise your young man here.'

My eyes opened wide at the idea of Daniel being my *young man*, but before I could put Mr Gough right, Daniel said half under his breath, 'Try *bloody little tyke*.'

Mr Gough's face was a picture of surprise. 'My God! Young Danny! Naughtiest little monkey I ever had the pleasure of coming across!' he grinned. 'Haven't seen you in years. Where've you been?'

Daniel shrugged carelessly. 'Here and there. I've been back on the moor for some time, though, but I'm afraid I've never used the train. Wish I had now.'

'Oh, well, life moves on. And I've got to get this train moving in a minute. Take care of yourselves, both of you.'

'And good luck to you, too, Mr Gough!' I managed to croak. 'And thanks for everything!'

Daniel ushered me along the platform and saw me into a carriage. I managed to get another seat by the window and sat looking down at Daniel through the glass, wondering at how unruffled Trojan seemed to be by all the noise and the crowds.

The train lurched gently and we began to move down the track. I waved back at Daniel as we chugged out of the station, and soon he was lost in the gathering dusk. My very last ride on the moorland railway that meant so much to me, and I watched the dramatic scenery melt into the gloom. It really was the end of another chapter in my life, and I felt the lump rising in my throat again. Mr Gough, the fireman, the gangers and the station staff, I would never see them again. And my hopes, my belief in the idyllic future I had envisaged for myself with Edwin, were fading into the twilight.

Chapter Seventeen

I kept hoping. Every time Edwin and Sadie went out somewhere together, I looked for signs of a row. I knew it was unkind as both of them would be terribly upset, but I couldn't help myself. And I would be there to comfort Edwin until he could see how deep my own feelings for him went. But there was no such chink appearing in their relationship. If anything, it seemed to go from strength to strength.

'Ian and I are going to the coast tomorrow,' Wendy announced gleefully one Saturday late in May. 'Do you want to come with us, Lily? We could ask Rob and make a foursome.'

'Oh, yes, that would be lovely!' I answered, lending a sparkle to my voice I didn't feel inside. 'Thank you!'

In the event, Rob declined the invitation. He was pleasant enough but there was no chemistry between us and I think he felt the same. I seemed to have convinced Wendy, though, that I was over Edwin, but each time I saw him and Sadie together, it was a dagger in my side. So I went with Wendy and Ian, sitting alone in the back of Ian's car like a wallflower. We crossed the old bridge at Gunnislake and so into Cornwall, and headed for the Rame Peninsula. It was a glorious day for so early in the year and as we lay on the beach, I dozed off and dreamt of Edwin. When I woke up, the sun had gone behind building clouds and we had to make a dash back to the car.

As we drove home through the rain, I felt cold and miserable. In my dream, I had been talking with Edwin and he had been smiling down as he held me in his arms. But it was all in my mind. I had merely been talking to myself. And yet I still clung to the belief that one day he would be mine.

But that day motivated me to go and buy the car I had been thinking about for so long. No longer would I sit in the back feeling like an intruder, however much Wendy, bless her, tried to include me in the conversation. William came with me as the garage owner was a patient, and negotiated a good deal for me on a Ford Popular. So now I could be independent and explore wherever I fancied. With the light evenings, I sometimes drove somewhere after dinner, often with Wendy if she wasn't seeing Ian, and sometimes with Celia who was back at Tavistock

Hospital. She wasn't as lively and exaggerated as her sister, but she was good, steady company.

As yet, though, I hadn't been back up on the moor. I somehow couldn't bear to see it without the railway and the little train puffing its way up the steep incline. When I thought back to that last day of service, I was glad I had met Daniel there for without him I would have felt unbearably sad. Despite our former differences, we had shared the same feelings of bereavement, and that had helped me to withstand it.

I didn't even mind that he was coming to the birthday party that Deborah and William were, inevitably, throwing for me. I could have done without it, but everyone's special day was celebrated in style, a good excuse to get all the family together. All I wanted for a present was for Edwin and Sadie to split up, but amicably so that neither of them would be too hurt. I would be so kind to Edwin until, one day, he would realise he had transferred his feelings to me. I wondered if I should have my hair cut short like Sadie's.

'What a pity it's raining so hard, like,' Kate moaned as she and Pete hurried through the front door and into the lounge which was already crowded with the Franfield family members. 'It were lovely out in the garden last year.'

'Yes, it is a shame,' I agreed. 'Lucky it's a big

house. And Deborah *loves* giving parties. And I'm so glad you could come. So what are you doing now, Pete?'

'Going to study engineering. I got into it during my National Service.'

'You enjoyed your service, then?'

'Very much. Helped me make up my mind what I wanted to do with my life.'

'So he's going off to college in September and leaving me,' Kate grimaced.

'Only to Plymouth, girl! Think it was the end of the earth!'

'Well, it seems like it!'

I couldn't help notice, though, that she glanced across at Daniel more than once during the evening. I had to admit he was terribly handsome, even more so than Edwin, tall, lean and his broad shoulders finely muscled. And with his brooding good looks and mop of dark hair that curled over his collar and had a habit of flopping over his forehead, he gave the impression of some sort of bohemian gipsy. To complete the picture, he was the only male not wearing a tie, but still managed to look smart in a crisp, open-necked shirt and grey flannels that clung around his slim hips with the aid of a narrow belt. If only his character wasn't so unpredictable, he might make someone a good catch.

'I hope you'll accept my present this year,' he said

when he caught me in a quiet corner out of earshot of anyone else. 'It's a little less stupid this time.'

His eyebrows were raised in a tentatively teasing arch as he handed me a small package, and I couldn't help myself smiling back at him. We seemed to have reached a somewhat odd understanding and were friends of a strange sort.

'Oh, thank you, Daniel, it's beautiful,' I answered as I unwrapped a silky scarf in a lovely shade of turquoise.

'I thought it would go nicely with your hair.'

I glanced up at him sharply, not quite sure how to take the comment. His mouth twitched as if he was trying desperately to keep a straight face, and then he finally broke out in a grin. 'Carrots,' he murmured under his breath as if he really couldn't resist it.

I glared at him and my lungs filled with annoyance. I could have thrown the scarf in his face, but he ducked away, laughing sheepishly. I could see it wasn't meant nastily, and an instant later his expression was full of remorse as he took my arm.

'Lily, please, I'm sorry, really I am. And I really did choose it to go with your hair. And that's meant as a compliment, however much I might tease you about it.'

I frowned. But I supposed in his own odd way, Daniel was genuinely being nice to me and I shouldn't be so sensitive.

I nodded in acceptance of his apology. 'Yes, it really is very pretty. The scarf, I mean.' I felt a little awkward and to make it worse, Daniel gave me a quizzical, sideways look that I couldn't quite fathom. So I was relieved that I managed to think of another topic of conversation. 'I invited Gloria to the party,' I informed him, 'but she declined. I don't think she's one for social gatherings. A pity. I haven't seen her for a while.'

'Have you not? I've seen her once or twice recently. We discussed... Well, there's been...' He hesitated and then shook his head. 'I suppose I shouldn't be telling you on your birthday, but there's been several, well, pretty horrible sacrifices up on the moor. All in our sort of area. I found two, both at Down Tor again, but there's been others as well. You can imagine the farmers are up in arms over it, and the police are taking it seriously now. I went to see them myself. You know I spend a lot of time out on the moor and a couple of times I've chased off the same fellow I saw before. At least I'm pretty sure it's the same chap. Trying to take a sheep. You remember I told you?'

I pursed my lips. No, it wasn't a pleasant thing to hear at my birthday party, and it was worrying in the extreme. 'Daniel, you should be careful,' I said automatically.

He held my gaze for a moment and then shrugged

carelessly. 'Well, so far I've not got near enough to give the police much of a description, let alone put myself in any danger. Anyway, he was an older man so I reckon I could hold my own against him. And who knows, he might not have anything to do with it. One man on his own doesn't seem right for ritual sacrifices. That's why I went to see Gloria. You know she's interested in ancient cults so I wondered if she had any ideas. She didn't, though. But I really don't want to spoil your party discussing such things.'

'No, I'm glad you told me—'

'Come on, Lily!' Wendy had appeared from nowhere and grabbing my arm, yanked me forward. 'We're doing the conga and, as it's your birthday, you've got to lead.'

'Oh, right,' I babbled. I glanced helplessly over my shoulder as Wendy pulled me to the head of the line, but Daniel just answered me with a shrug. From then on, I was swept up in the whirlwind of a typical Franfield party, dancing, playing games and generally having a whale of a time. There was beer and lemonade, bottled cider and sherry, and also some French wine that was becoming more available now and that I was developing a taste for. Everyone was in high spirits but sensible with it, though I noticed Kate had probably overdone the alcohol and was behaving a little on the silly side. I doubt if anyone else realised. It didn't seem to matter a jot that the party was confined to indoors. I just wished...

I tried not to think about it but I just wished that I was Edwin's girlfriend and not Sadie. It tore at my heart to see them dancing together, holding each other close and whispering happy secrets. I was the only person apart from Uncle Artie who didn't have a proper partner and I wished Sally had been able to come, but she had gone on holiday with her parents. Even Celia was walking out with the son of one of the nursing staff at the hospital and so had a partner. There was Daniel, of course, but he never joined in the dancing. And I don't think I'd have wanted to dance with him even if he'd asked me. So it was just as well he lounged back against the wall, often lost in his own thoughts, or so it would seem by the serious expression on his face.

And then my prayers were suddenly answered. I saw Edwin and Sadie talking in what appeared a somewhat heated way. Sadie, tall and willowy but with full curves in all the right places, suddenly pulled away from Edwin, her hand over her mouth and her eyes wide with shock. Edwin stepped towards her, taking her elbow in a pleading gesture, but she shook him off and, dropping his hand to his side, Edwin spoke another few words and allowed her to walk away.

I could feel my heart racing. Was this the moment

I had been patiently waiting for, that would lead to my dream coming true after all? I unconsciously held my breath. I must play this perfectly. Edwin would be hurting so deeply and I wanted to be there for him, to comfort and support him. God knows I didn't want either Edwin or Sadie to suffer and I had never done anything to drive a wedge between them. But if they were going to split up, I would show Edwin what a strong, loyal friend I could be, and his love for me would, I prayed, grow from that.

He turned his head as he followed Sadie's progress out of the room so that I could see his face clearly. He looked lost and my heart bled for him. Then he saw me watching and his bewildered expression moved into a wan smile as he came towards me.

'May I have the pleasure of this dance, Miss Hayes?'

I knew he was feigning lightheartedness so I went along with it and grinned up at him. 'I should be delighted!' I replied, which I was, except that I hated seeing Edwin like this. The gramophone was sending out the lilting notes of a waltz played to perfection by Mantovani and his orchestra. I relaxed against Edwin who wasn't afraid to hold me close as the dance required, but when I looked up at his face, he appeared distant, his eyes searching for Sadie's return. Poor Edwin. *But I am here waiting for you.*

When the music drew to a closing crescendo,

though, he swiftly left me and went in search of her. My heart sank like a stone, but I turned to the merrymakers who were, after all, celebrating *my* birthday, and arranged my face into a picture of enjoyment.

'Come on! Let's liven things up!' Wendy cried. 'Put on the hokey-cokey, would you, Dad?'

For the next few minutes, I was caught up in the jollifications, laughing as I put the wrong arm in and out of the circle, and performing an exaggerated knees-bend, arm-stretch, ra-ra-ra. When it was over, we all fell about in happy exhaustion, shaking our heads and catching our breath as the noise subsided.

It was then that Edwin came back into the lounge, holding up his arms, with Sadie standing coyly by his side. 'Can I have your attention, everyone, please!' he called, and there was a general shushing as the room fell silent. 'I have an announcement to make.' And here he glanced at Sadie, his face alight. 'Or rather, *we* have an announcement. I'm afraid I gave Sadie rather a shock just now when I asked her to be my wife. I know we haven't been together for very long but I knew the instant I met her that she was the one for me. And after a few minutes to recover from the shock, Sadie has accepted my proposal.'

The room erupted in a chorus of congratulations. I stood, motionless, unable to move or to fight against the band that closed around my neck, throttling the life from me. People jostled me as they went forward to shake Edwin's hand or kiss Sadie's cheek. I felt all alone, a stranger in a foreign land. Empty and afraid. I mustn't let my feelings, my own devastation, show. Somehow I must find the courage to bury my aching heart. To remain calm and dignified.

I took a deep breath, controlling the desire to run and flee my anguish as I stepped up to Edwin and hugged him.

'Congratulations!' I said fervently. 'He's a very lucky man!' I added, turning to Sadie. 'I hope you'll both be very happy!'

I pulled my mouth into a broad smile. The person on the outside, the joyful exterior, mustn't be the real me. Inside, I was bleeding. Dying. But no one must know my pain. I must melt into the sea of happy faces around me.

I managed to drag myself through several more records on the gramophone. William asked his future daughter-in-law to dance, and Edwin turned to me to partner him. He had no idea of his cruelty, that he was wringing my very existence from me. I felt faint, sick, but I concentrated on keeping the smile on my face while my feet moved mechanically through the familiar steps of the foxtrot.

A little later, all was merry and nobody was taking any notice of me. I slipped through the old servants' door in the hallway and down to the basement. A hubbub of joyful voices wafted down through the ceiling and I unlocked the back door and ran up the steps to the dark seclusion of the garden. I felt I would break and the only way to survive was to escape into the night. It was still raining, not hard but steadily. It was gone ten o'clock and dark, but the curtains at the back of the house hadn't been drawn, the light spilling onto the lawn in large squares. I kept to the shadows in case anyone happened to look out of the window and see me. I stood at the bottom of the garden, hiding behind a tall shrub, and finally allowed my misery full rein.

My soul had fragmented into tortured splinters and, try as I might, I couldn't piece them together again. Edwin and Sadie were to be married, and the agony of it pierced my heart like a shard of glass. I tipped my face skyward, letting the rain mingle with my tears, but it did nothing to wash away my pain. After all this time of longing and waiting, my dream had finally been crushed. I didn't know how I was going to cope, but I would have to. I had lost Ellen, Sidney, my home, my identity, and I had come through all that. Surely I could withstand this as well? But just now, everything had collapsed all around me, and I was drowning in the mire.

'Lily.'

The quiet, level voice behind me when I had heard

no footsteps startled me so much that my whole body jerked. So someone had noticed me leave and had the audacity to follow me. A fiery sword of resentment cut through my soul that someone had dared intrude upon my strangling grief.

'Daniel, go away,' I choked. '*Please.*'

I couldn't wring another sound from my throat, and in my head I begged him to leave me alone. I couldn't move a muscle and waited, praying. There was silence, just the patter of raindrops falling on the broad leaves of the shrub.

'Lily?' Daniel repeated at last, still low but this time in a questioning tone.

I gritted my teeth. 'Leave me alone, Daniel, please. I'm all right.'

I heard him draw in a long, slow breath. 'No, you're not,' he almost whispered. 'You're in love with Edwin. Always have been. I saw it in your eyes the first time you came to the house. And now he's to marry Sadie.'

My throat ached as I shook my head. 'No,' I mumbled torturously, still praying he would go back inside and leave me in peace.

'Turn round and tell me you don't love him.'

How dare he! I obediently turned, ready to give him the length of my tongue, but when I glared up at him, I could see even in the gloom that his face was still and concerned. I had the feeling that whatever I said, he wouldn't be satisfied. My fragile hold on my emotions suddenly snapped. I knew I couldn't fight Daniel's strong will and all I could do was to cover my face as I broke down in tears once again.

I wasn't aware at first of his arms around me, and when I did realise, I felt so wretched that I didn't really care. I needed someone to lean on and Daniel happened to be there. He held me gently, not saying a word as the misery emptied out of me.

I wasn't sure how long we stood there in silence in the rain. My head had drooped against his chest in exhaustion as I bit on my thumb in an effort to stop my tears. I was beginning to wonder how I could get out of this odd situation when Daniel finally spoke.

'Come on, Carrots, you're soaking my shirt,' he murmured, 'as if I'm not wet enough already.'

I at once threw up my head. 'You didn't have to follow me out here, and if you call me that one more time, I swear I'll—'

He interrupted me with a wry chuckle. 'That's more like the spirited Lily I know. Here. Dry your eyes and we'll go back inside before we have to swim for it.'

He handed me a clean, folded handkerchief, and I took it with a watery smile. Daniel might not be the refined, utter gentleman Edwin was, but he was being chivalrous in his own peculiar way. As we walked back up the garden path, I noticed his hand on my shoulder and I was happy for it to be there.

'We can't go back upstairs looking like this,' he said as I locked up again. 'Everyone will wonder what we've been up to and I assume you don't want that. We'd better try and dry off a bit first.'

'I hope no one comes down here,' I told him anxiously as we went into the kitchen. I took a couple of towels from the drawer, handing one to Daniel, and for a minute or so we both stood, rubbing our hair and clothes as best we could.

'We still look like drowned rats,' Daniel frowned. 'And you're shivering.'

'I'll put the kettle on then, and make some hot coffee. Deborah only keeps Camp though.'

'Just the thing,' he smiled enigmatically.

A few minutes later, we were sitting at the table, sipping scalding drinks in awkward silence.

'Great invention, the electric kettle,' Daniel observed and then he looked at me steadily from under swooped eyebrows. 'You know, sometimes we have to learn to deal with the hurt. To cry inside and somehow get on with life. And then one day the pain turns to bitterness and it's easier to lash out at bitterness.'

I blinked at him in surprise and studied his face. He had lowered his eyes and I realised he was talking about himself. Lashing out at bitterness. I supposed that was what Sidney had been doing, too, but it hadn't brought him peace.

'I don't think I could ever feel bitterness towards Edwin,' I confessed, not quite sure why I felt able to open my heart to Daniel of all people. 'I love him too much for that. And looking back, I realise now that he's never given any indication that he's been in love with me at all. Oh, yes, he's always been kind and affectionate, but only in a brotherly sort of way. *I'm* the one who's been misinterpreting our relationship. So forgiveness or feeling bitter doesn't even come into it.'

'Then…that's what makes you a far better person than me,' Daniel muttered. He slowly looked up and for several uncomfortable seconds, my gaze was held by those arresting, violet-blue eyes. Was he trying to tell me something about himself? Using the situation to make confessions of his own?

I shook my head in confusion. I could do without that, so I said instead, 'Well, now I feel pretty stupid as well as devastated.'

Daniel's mouth twisted slightly. 'That's all part of it.'

It occurred to me that he had actually been engaged and so had more reason than I did to feel bitter and far less to feel foolish, but I wasn't going to argue about it. The fact was that talking to Daniel had helped in some incomprehensible way.

'I suppose we should think about going back upstairs,' I sighed with reluctance. 'It is *my* birthday party, after all.'

'Yes, you're right. You still look a bit bedraggled, mind. But it suits you.'

He leant forward, a faint smile tugging at his lips as he ran his hand through my tousled hair and let it fall forward in a tangled cascade. I was astounded and bewildered, and remained seated while Daniel washed up the mugs in the sink.

'Shall we?' he asked, gesturing towards the door. 'Or would you prefer to go up separately?'

'Yes,' I gulped. 'You go first.'

I heard him spring up the stairs and then I waited for five minutes before following him. I felt strange, all at odds with myself, as if the half hour I had spent with Daniel was a dream that had never happened. I still felt nervous when I rejoined the party, but no one seemed to have noticed that either of us had been missing. Whether by accident or design, Daniel was chatting with Edwin and Sadie, laughing with them, his eyes bright. Yes. He had learnt to draw a shield of steel around himself, and I supposed I was going to have to do the same. When I caught his eye across the room and he smiled at me, I felt stronger.

Chapter Eighteen

It wasn't easy.

For the next few weeks, the house seemed full of Edwin and Sadie's engagement. With great difficulty they had persuaded Deborah that, as they had made the announcement at my party, there really was no need for further celebration. Cards and presents kept arriving, though, and Joanna wrote to ask when exactly the wedding would be as Wayne would need to book a long vacation to allow for the return voyage. To William and Deborah's delight, Joanna also announced that she was expecting at long last, and so would relish the opportunity to show off her first child to its grandparents back in quaint old England.

Edwin and Sadie seemed overwhelmed by their own whirlwind romance. They chose a beautiful diamond ring together and talked of where in Tavistock they could afford to live. They would perhaps start house-hunting in the spring as they thought August would be a good time for the wedding as Joanna's baby would be several months old and better able to travel. And while all these happy plans were discussed, I remained quietly in the background, smiling as if I shared everyone else's joy.

I sighed with relief when the happy couple managed to arrange a few days off duty together so that they could go to Truro to stay with Sadie's parents who Edwin hadn't yet met. I felt the pressure ease the moment they left the house and I began to think that it really was time I moved on. I had enjoyed the Franfield's hospitality for more than two years. I was nineteen, had my own car and a good job that would cover the cost of a little flat somewhere in the town. Above all, I would have the solitude to lick my wounds in private.

I understood now why Daniel had chosen the life of a recluse up on the moor, but unlike him, my feelings couldn't turn to bitterness. I loved Edwin too much for that. And so I was left floundering in the mud and the only way to be rescued was to make a new start. The only thing was that I knew Wendy would be upset. But maybe she'd like to strike out on her own as well and share a flat with me. We could have a lot of fun together, but I would have to break the idea to her gently.

I was thinking about it as I oversaw Edwin's orthopaedic clinic one hot and sticky afternoon towards the end of August. The trip to Sadie's parents had apparently been a complete success, and it brought it all back to me. I loved my job, but could I stand being in such close proximity to Edwin day in, day out, even if I moved into a home of my own? It might all depend on how much I could earn elsewhere, so I decided to buy a copy of the *Tavistock Gazette* after work and look in both the Positions Vacant and the To Let columns.

I suddenly realised that the subdued murmurings of the waiting room had been disturbed by a commotion out in the corridor. I hardly wanted a riot in *my* clinic and sprang to my feet just as the giant of a man appeared in the doorway and breathlessly lumbered across the short space that separated us.

'Hello, Mr Giles.' I smiled calmly at his unusually agitated manner. I wouldn't want to be on the wrong end of those huge hands, however gentle their owner might appear. 'You're not on the list today. I didn't think—'

'Get some 'elp, young maid!' he panted, gulping air into his lungs. 'I got this young lad in the back o' my lorry. Found 'en at the side o' the road up on the moor. Looks like 'is jeep 'ad turned over, like.'

I had turned on my collected, efficient face. We had no separate casualty department as at some of the larger hospitals and had to deal with emergencies whenever they occurred and carry on with any clinic that was in progress as best we could. But at the mention of a jeep, my blood ran cold and something deep inside me began to shake. I told myself that Daniel wasn't the only person on Dartmoor to drive a jeep, but I almost broke into a run – an unforgivable sin – as I swept down the corridor to the consulting room.

Three pairs of eyes turned on me as I went in without knocking.

'Lily!' Edwin reprimanded but I totally ignored him.

'Casualty. Car accident. Sounds serious,' I announced, my mouth moving of its own accord.

Edwin stood up calmly. 'Excuse me, Mr Jarvis,' he nodded at his patient. 'Hopefully I won't be long. Nurse will look after you.'

He strode briskly across the room and as we went out into the corridor, he hissed in my ear, 'Really, Lily, you should at least have knocked.'

Under any other circumstances I would have been mortified, but just now, I really didn't care. 'It was a jeep,' I gasped back. 'What...what if it's Daniel?'

Our eyes met. I saw his face blanch and then he, too, was half running to where Mr Giles was dancing in agitation, arms flapping helplessly at his sides like a gorilla. Edwin was out of the door without stopping and the huge man had to chase after him.

'My son's with 'en in the back o' the lorry. Us 'ad an old door and put 'en on that, like. Jonty said us must keep 'is 'ead and back as still as possible, so that's what us did.'

I followed them on wobbly legs out into the car park. Somehow Edwin sprang up into the back of the open lorry like a jack-in-the-box and as I stood on the tarmac gazing up at him, I saw him freeze.

'Jesus.'

The word barely breathed from his white lips. Oh, dear God. It *was* Daniel. My stomach corkscrewed as if it was being clamped down in a vice, and I thought I was going to be sick.

'Lily, get the porters. Tell them to bring a trolley and a collar. And then get Matron.'

Edwin's voice came to me as if from another planet. No. Oh, no. The words echoed tauntingly in my head. Daniel, who I had once intensely disliked, had become part of my life. I couldn't bear it if—

'Lily! Hurry, girl!'

My brain clicked back into gear. My legs found a fleetness they had never had before as I shot back inside, shouting for the porters. Then I flew upstairs to Matron's office, rapped on the door and went in without waiting for a reply. She looked up in severe disapproval but I didn't give her time to reprimand me.

'Sorry, Matron, but there's been a serious accident,' I panted. 'And it's a friend of ours. A very close friend.'

She nodded calmly as she rose to her feet. 'All right, Miss Hayes. Take some deep breaths or you'll be no use to anyone, especially your friend.'

I don't know how she did it but Matron always managed to glide everywhere without apparent haste and yet she arrived ahead of anyone else. I caught her up back in the car park where Daniel was being lowered with infinite care onto the waiting trolley, Edwin and the porters being assisted by John Giles and his son who was just as colossal as he was.

'Keeps passin' out, like,' he was telling Edwin. 'An' when he do come to, he don't make no sense. Keeps mutterin' summat about chinks an' sergeant, I thinks.'

I saw Edwin glance up darkly. 'He was in Korea. A POW.'

'Ah', father and son answered in unison.

Matron had disappeared and the men were guiding the trolley carefully across the car park. As I rushed ahead to hold open the doors, I caught a glimpse of Daniel and the cumbersome collar Edwin had fixed about his neck. My mouth was as dry as sand. I opened the doors to the examination room next, and then I leant back against the wall for support. What use was my white coat now?

Matron was back with two nurses while issuing instructions. One of them was cutting off Daniel's clothing, while the other was collecting equipment.

'Hello, old chap,' I heard Edwin say. 'Stay calm. We've got you now.'

I crept forward, wanting to assure myself that Daniel wasn't too badly hurt, despite the grim expression on Edwin's face. But when I saw him, I pulled back in appalled horror. His eyes were half open but glazed and wandering, his mouth drawn wide in a grimace of agony as he struggled to breathe. Every tiny, snatched intake of air seemed to increase his pain. I could see the panic in his eyes and his shoulders, one of which was covered in blood, were heaving rapidly as he fought for breath.

Edwin was tapping Daniel's chest, his own forehead pleated, and then was listening with his stethoscope while Matron studied the falling level in the sphygmomanometer as she released the inflated cuff around Daniel's left arm.

'BP sixty over forty and heart-rate a hundred and forty,' she reported, and my own heart buckled. I wasn't medically trained but I knew that was hellishly dangerous.

'Tension pneumothorax on the right side,' Edwin pronounced. 'Hang on in there, Danny. We'll get you relief in a minute. Lily, do you know how long ago it happened?'

His question took me by surprise but I only took an instant to collect my thoughts. 'Mr Giles said he found him up on the moor so it must have been some time ago.'

Edwin was standing by with a massive needle while Matron was swabbing the right side of Daniel's chest with antiseptic. 'Now, keep still, Danny, old boy. This is going to hurt a bit, but you'll feel better afterwards.'

Daniel's groan made me shudder and I instinctively took his left hand and squeezed it tightly. 'It's all right, Daniel,' I soothed, not knowing where my voice came from. 'It's me, Lily.'

'Carrots?' His eyes opened a little wider, searching, and I watched them focus on my face. I forced a reassuring smile.

'Yes. Carrots,' I answered, and he seemed to relax for a second but then he was back to battling for those ever shallower, agonising breaths. Out of the corner of my eye, I saw Edwin feeling his breastbone, measuring with his fingers, feeling again and then working his fingertips to about halfway across the right side of Daniel's chest. He seemed to find the spot he was searching for and went to insert the needle. And then he stopped, his right hand shaking so that the point was quivering in the air. In that moment, Edwin was suddenly no longer the knight in shining armour he had always been to me.

'Hurry, Dr Franfield,' Matron instructed, her voice for once taut with agitation. 'You must have done this before.'

'Yes, but he's my best friend,' Edwin mumbled.

'Then pull yourself together and do it. I've called in your father, but there's no time to wait for him. You know that.'

My own jaw was trembling so I knew exactly how Edwin felt. I saw him take a deep breath and guide the needle to where the first two fingers of his left hand were still firmly on the spot he had sought. I couldn't look.

'Come on, Daniel,' I crooned, as much for my own sake as his. 'It'll be all right.'

Daniel looked up at me and his eyes narrowed as Edwin inserted the needle. And then as he drove it in deep, Daniel screamed.

'There, got it!' Edwin cried in triumph, and I heard a soft hissing of air. 'Hang on there, Danny. Your breathing will be easier in a minute. Matron, can you draw me up some procaine now, and can I have a BP and pulse check, please.'

I squeezed Daniel's hand even more tightly. His face was creased with pain and he was trying to thrash his head from side to side, but it was being held steady by the collar.

'Stop it, you bastard,' he moaned. 'Leave him alone!'

I glanced up questioningly at Edwin and he dipped his head as he took the syringe from Matron and injected around where he had inserted the needle.

'Rambling again,' Edwin murmured back. 'It's the concussion. See the lump coming up on his forehead. Try talking to him again, Lily. It might help to calm him down.'

I don't know what I said, but I kept up some banal one-sided conversation, shuddering as Edwin made a small incision. Daniel didn't appear to react this time, so the local anaesthetic must have done its work, but I was still horrified when Edwin eased the sharp end of a metal rod through the incision and drove it deep into Daniel's chest. I watched in appalled fascination as the inner metal tube was removed from the shaft and this time a massive rush of air escaped from it. Almost instantly, Daniel's breathing was greatly eased. He seemed to gaze up at me, his eyes plunging into mine. The tight muscles of his face slackened, his shoulders relaxed and he drifted into unconsciousness again.

'Right, what've we got? Good God! It's Daniel!'

I turned my head with a thankful sigh as William strode in to join us in the examination room. I could clearly see the relief on Edwin's face as he glanced up from feeding a long rubber tube through the metal one into Daniel's chest.

'Tension pneumothorax,' he told William as he carefully withdrew the metal tube leaving the rubber one in its place.

'You seem to have dealt with it pretty well. Well done.'

'Yes, but I haven't had a chance to examine him for anything else yet. He's concussed, this shoulder's a mess and that shin doesn't look right. Fractured tib and fib, I expect. Suture, Staff, please.'

I stood back out of the way, feeling weak at the knees. Edwin was stitching the tube into place while at his feet the staff nurse was connecting the other end to an underwater seal apparatus of the sort I had seen before on the wards. Matron was doing her checks, announcing that Daniel's blood pressure was coming up and his pulse gradually slowing. William was looking in his ears and listened to his chest again, and when the other nurse finished cutting away his torn clothing, William and Edwin examined his entire body by feel.

I watched, stunned, feeling as if I was witnessing a film, not a real life drama. Daniel, who I had once detested as my reluctant saviour but with whom I had recently shared some deep, surprising emotion, was lying, unconscious and stripped naked, on a hospital trolley, his life in William and Edwin's hands. I didn't know why, but it made me feel guilty. And I wanted to cry.

'I'll take over now so you can get back to your clinic,' William was saying. 'I'll just get a line in and then we'll take him for a full set of X-rays to see what else we're dealing with.'

'Thanks, Dad. Come on, Lily. You were great, by the way. Really helped. It isn't always easy to think of what to say.'

We were out in the corridor now and I shot Edwin a sideways glance. There was a time when I would have basked in the approving smile he had turned on me, but now it meant nothing.

'W...will he be all right?' I stammered.

Edwin puffed out his cheeks. 'Should be. It was touch and go for a minute there. It means he must have at least one broken rib that's punctured the lung.'

'Yes.' I nodded, trying to steady myself with some deep breaths. 'A pneumothorax is when air leaks from the lung into the pleural cavity where it's not supposed to be.'

I heard Edwin chuckle softly. 'Make a doctor of you yet.'

'I don't think so,' I grimaced. 'But the tension bit?'

'Ah.' He was immediately serious again. 'It means the hole must have a flap that's acting like a valve so that most of the air passing through gets trapped. The cavity gets blown up like a balloon making it more and more difficult to breathe and squeezing the heart and the main vessels to it. So you can see why it's a life-threatening emergency and why there was no time to put in some local anaesthetic. The quickest way to relieve some of the pressure is to stick in a needle and then do the proper chest drain afterwards. I'm just furious at myself for losing my nerve like that.'

'It's different when it's someone you know and care for,' I said, my brain working automatically like a machine. 'And we're all only human, after all.' Yes. Only human. Edwin wasn't the god I had worshipped. A young doctor. A very skilled and excellent one, but lacking the years of experience of his more mature colleagues. Admittedly, William wasn't as close to Daniel as Edwin was, but look how unruffled he had been in taking over the situation.

'True, but I'm still cross with myself. But let's get this clinic finished and by then, Dad'll have more details about Danny.'

I found it difficult to concentrate. Mr Giles and his son were still waiting and seemed suitably pleased when I told them they had saved Daniel's life by bringing him in when they did. The police arrived and, having interviewed John and Jonty Giles, they all went up onto the moor to investigate the scene and take the jeep away for examination. Apparently it had happened at a point a mile or so this side of

Merrivale where there was a drop at the side of the road. The jeep had turned over and Daniel had been thrown out, but why it had happened was, so far, a mystery and the police would be appealing for witnesses.

As I smiled at patients, took their details and generally oversaw the clinic, I felt unreal, as if I wasn't really there. My heart was thrumming away like a drum, my stomach turning sickening somersaults, and all I could see in my head was Daniel's broken body lying stretched out on the trolley. The minute the last patient left, Edwin and I went in search of William. We found him in the anaesthetic room, still keeping an eye on Daniel with the assistance of the staff nurse, and he smiled encouragingly as we came in.

'How is he?' we asked with one voice.

'He'll mend.' William bobbed his head reassuringly. 'Four broken ribs, one displaced that caused the pneumothorax. The X-ray showed you got the drain in perfectly, by the way, Ed. He's drifting in and out of consciousness, but it doesn't look like a bad concussion that's going to cause any permanent damage. Most importantly, there's no spinal injury, but we'll have to reduce the leg fracture.'

He picked up one of several X-ray films and held it up to the light, pointing something out to Edwin. 'See that? There's a pulse in his foot but it isn't great, so I don't want to wait, and his condition's stable enough now for a short general. Matron's preparing theatre. I'll do the anaesthetic and you can set the leg, Edwin. And while he's under, Matron's going to clean up his shoulder. It's a bit of a mess, but it'll heal on its own. Now, Lily,' he continued, turning to me. 'I suggest you get off home and bring Deborah up to date. She was going to cancel all but the essential appointments at this evening's surgery, and warn them they may have to wait. And she was going to ring Daniel's parents and give them the bad news. I expect they'll come down from London tomorrow.'

Another part of my brain absorbed William's words. All I was aware of thinking about was Daniel. I crept over to him, holding my breath. The rubber tube from the hole in his chest was sealed into the glass bottle fixed to the leg of the bed, and air was slowly bubbling through the water. A crisp white sheet was tucked over his bare chest, William had obviously put a temporary dressing on his shoulder and there was a drip into his left arm. He looked so helpless lying there so still, so different from the strong, forceful Daniel I knew.

'Daniel, it's me. Carrots,' I whispered.

His closed eyelids flickered but didn't open, though the shadow of a smile twitched at his mouth. 'Trojan,' he barely breathed at me, and I took his hand.

'Yes. We'll see to him. Mr Giles brought in your keys. They were still in the ignition.'

'Thank you,' he murmured. 'God, it hurts. There was a lorry, I think. I can't remember... When are those bloody reinforcements coming? Christ, Tommy...'

His voice trailed off into incomprehensible mutterings and William came up beside me. I bit my lip, glancing at him through tear-misted eyes, and turned my gaze back to Daniel's ashen face.

'He's still confused, but he'll be all right. It'll be a long road, but I see no reason why he shouldn't be as right as rain in a few months.'

'I hope so,' I choked, and I couldn't understand why I was so distraught when there had been a time when I had never wanted to see Daniel again.

Chapter Nineteen

A strange, hushed atmosphere settled on the house that evening, everyone treading around each other in stunned shock. Nobody wanted to eat much at dinner. Although William and Edwin were pleased with their reduction of Daniel's fractured leg, they both went back to the hospital later to check on him. Wendy and Ian were away on holiday together and Deborah wanted to stay by the telephone in case Daniel's parents rang back about any arrangements, so I drove up to Fencott Place on my own.

It was really peculiar letting myself into the huge, empty house. Trojan barked like mad and I was a little apprehensive, but fortunately he seemed to recognise me and licked me all over. I let him out into the garden and watched him chasing after the ball I threw for him. Little did he realise that his master had nearly died earlier that afternoon and that it would be several weeks before he would be back on his feet.

Dusk was drawing in, turning the still, oppressive evening to a misty purple. I reluctantly went back inside to feed Trojan and collected up some tins of dog food and some dog biscuits. A mournful silence echoed about the large rooms, and while Trojan wolfed down his dinner, I wandered into the drawing room. Yet again I found myself mesmerised by the portrait of Daniel's great-grandmother. She was amazingly beautiful, with those disconcerting violet-blue eyes he had inherited. There were other family photographs, too, dotted about the room, some of them very old. I found one of the same lady in her more mature years. She was still lovely, and the man beside her was equally as handsome in a reserved sort of way even though he must have been approaching sixty at the time, I should have thought. Daniel looked nothing like him.

Trojan's claws clicking on the polished wooden floorboards brought me from my study of Daniel's ancestors. Trojan would need his bed so I put the dog food and his two bowls in the basket, clipped on his lead and struggled out to the car, managing to lock the back door on the way. I hoped Trojan would behave himself on the journey as I'd never seen him in Daniel's jeep, but he jumped up eagerly into the passenger seat. I opened the window an inch or two and told him firmly to *stay*.

To my relief, other than a few whines of uncertainty at first, he was as good as gold. I made a conscious effort to drive smoothly so as not to throw him off balance, and he seemed quite happy with his snout stuck out of the window. As we came down off the moor in the gathering twilight, the boulders at the side of the road were illuminated eerily in the headlamps. On the way up, I knew I had driven past the spot where Daniel had gone off the road. I wasn't sure exactly where it was and had been on the opposite side, and the police had already taken the jeep away. But coming down, the headlights picked out skid-marks on the tarmac. They ended at a dislodged stone and gouged turf on the open verge where there was a drop of about eight feet onto the moor. I shuddered, my heart thumping in my chest. And then I realised there were actually *two* sets of tyre-marks on the road. The second, larger set swerved, converged with those of the jeep, but then continued on the road before petering out.

I gasped aloud. So there *had* been another vehicle involved. Daniel hadn't been driving recklessly or too fast. In his confused mutterings, he had mentioned a lorry, hadn't he? A lorry whose driver had caused him to crash and then had callously left him for dead at the side of the road.

I was incensed and ground my teeth in fury. If

Daniel hadn't received medical help when he had, he would have died. There hadn't even been time to administer a local anaesthetic, for heaven's sake! I allowed my thoughts to wander at will to give my rage the chance to subside. Edwin had undoubtedly saved Daniel's life, but that moment's hesitation had shown the less than perfect side to him that I had been blind to. I still loved Edwin, but that slight doubt seemed to have made the pain of his engagement to Sadie more bearable. Or was it that my head was so filled with my wrath for the driver of the other vehicle that I could think of little else? The accident had happened on one of the two main routes across the moor and Daniel would have been found before too long, but it could easily have been too late and I was ready to explode.

Trojan instantly made himself at home in the unfamiliar house, although we had to keep the door to William's consulting room firmly closed, of course. Edwin was still at Daniel's bedside, but William was happy enough with his condition.

'He's still pretty groggy after the anaesthetic, but that's no bad thing,' William updated us as we tried to relax over mugs of hot cocoa. 'Those ribs will be agony for some weeks. We'll keep him on morphine for a few days and then gradually reduce the painkillers, but the poor lad's going to be uncomfortable for some time. The police came back and wanted to interview him, but I told them they'd have to wait a few days.'

'Yes, I passed the spot,' I said at once. 'I saw the tyre-marks. There was definitely another vehicle involved.'

'That's what the police said. They've measured and recorded everything. Looks as if Daniel was forced off the road.'

'He mumbled something about a lorry.'

'Did he?' William looked up sharply.

'Yes, but he was a bit incoherent.'

'Nevertheless, I think I'll give the inspector a ring. It could be useful.'

'Inspector?'

'They're taking this very seriously,' William informed us as he got to his feet. 'Causing a near fatal accident and then driving off will certainly end in prosecution.'

'If they can find the culprit,' I muttered bitterly.

'Try not to get too angry, dear,' Deborah advised when we were alone. 'It won't help. The important thing is that we're all here to support Daniel through this.'

'His parents are coming down tomorrow, aren't they?'

'That's right. Sheila and Adam. And his grandmother, too. At least I was able to assure them that Daniel will make a full recovery. They're going to stay up at Fencott, of course. It belongs entirely to his grandmother since Great Aunt Marianne died. What an eccentric she was!'

'Daniel was very fond of her, wasn't he?' I asked, my curiosity, for some reason I couldn't explain, deeply aroused.

'Thick as thieves, I'd say. I think it rather upset Sheila.' Deborah sat forward confidentially. 'Adam was always out at business meetings when Daniel was small. Continuing his father's work of trying to restore some of the family's fortunes.'

'Yes, I remember Edwin explaining about it all.'

Deborah nodded. 'Well, Daniel was always a handful. He needed a man's influence but Adam was never there, and even when he was, he wasn't much of a disciplinarian. And when Daniel was evacuated down here, Marianne was no help at all. If anything she encouraged him to run wild.'

'Edwin said he was nearly always with him.'

'That's right. It used to worry me that he'd lead Edwin astray, but I think Edwin was always keeping *him* out of trouble. I mean, Daniel was never *bad*. He was just mischievous. Marianne had her husband to care for, which I suppose didn't help. He was still alive at the beginning of the war. He was an invalid, you see. She'd driven an ambulance in France in the First World War.'

'Really? Oh, gosh, how brave! Daniel said she was a character.'

'She was that! She rescued this young soldier, you see. He lost both his legs, but it didn't stop them falling in love and having a wonderful marriage. No children, mind. So I suppose Daniel was a sort of substitute.'

'Oh, I didn't know all that,' I answered, genuinely intrigued. I was about to ask more about this charismatic great aunt as it seemed a way of distracting me from the current situation, but just then William came back into the room.

'Well, they were pleased to have that piece of information,' he announced gravely. 'The jeep's a write-off and they can see the dents from the collision on the off-side. But unfortunately there was no paint to give them a clue as to colour. And the tyre-marks weren't clear enough for them to be able to identify the other vehicle, just that it had a wider axle. Could have been any number of possibilities, so they were glad to know it was a lorry. Not that what Daniel said can be entirely relied upon, what with the concussion and everything.' William paused, rubbing his hand over his eyes and yawning. 'Well, I'm shattered and I really think we should all get to bed. I hope Ed won't stay with him too late.'

I stood up, stretching, and realising how tired I suddenly felt. Trojan swivelled his eyes at me without lifting his nose from his front paws and his tail eagerly thumped the carpet.

'I suppose you should go outside for a few minutes,' I smiled down at him. 'Come on then.'

He scampered over to me, his young body twisting with excitement. I collected the dirty mugs and took them down to the kitchen and then Trojan and I went outside and up the few steps to the garden. He bounced about in the darkness, stopping here and there to sniff at unfamiliar scents. I watched his black and white shadow, remembering the night scarcely four weeks ago when I had stood out here, crying in Daniel's arms because Edwin was to marry Sadie. And now I was crying because Daniel was lying in a hospital bed and I was confused and angry.

I didn't sleep very well. Every time I closed my eyes, I saw the old jeep careering off the road and turning over, and Daniel being flung out and hurled over the boulders, breaking his leg, banging his skull and finally, we supposed, landing on his right side, cracking his ribs and scraping the skin off his shoulder in the process. I kept coming out in a hot sweat. Daniel might have upset me on several occasions, but now I knew him better, I realised it had never been intentional, and he didn't deserve this. Some lunatic who didn't respect the livestock on the open road had obviously overtaken him dangerously and pushed him over the bank. My heart was beating relentlessly hard and it was well into the early hours before I fell into a fitful doze.

Nevertheless, I was awake early and had time to take Trojan for a walk in the park opposite the house before I went to work. As soon as I arrived at the hospital, I went to the men's surgical ward to see Daniel. Even as clerical staff, we were supposed to ask the sister's permission to go on a ward, but that morning I really couldn't care about rules and regulations.

I stood at the foot of Daniel's bed. He was asleep, or had perhaps drifted into unconsciousness. Beneath his strong overnight stubble, his face was grey, long dark lashes fanned out on sunken sockets. A cage held the blankets off his legs and there seemed to be tubes everywhere. My heart burst in a squall of rage against the heartless coward who had done this.

'Have you got permission to be here, Miss Hayes?' Matron's stern voice cut through my silent contemplation.

'Sorry, Matron, no, I haven't.' But to be honest, I wasn't sorry at all.

'I'll forgive you this time, but out of visiting hours, please ask in future.' Then her voice softened. 'I take it you and Mr Pencarrow are—'

I felt myself flush. 'Oh, good Lord, no. He's just a friend. Through Dr Franfield.'

'But a friend you care deeply about.' She picked up the charts clipped to the bottom of the bed and her eyes quickly scanned the papers. 'Well, his Obs are improving and he's had a reasonable night, but then he is under sedation. We'll see how he is later on. I suggest you get back to your work now and come and see him during the proper hours. What he needs now is rest.'

'Yes, Matron.' I bowed my head in deference, but then met her gaze boldly as some force I didn't understand swept through me. 'You will look after him, won't you?'

She straightened her shoulders. 'I look after all my patients, Miss Hayes.' But then I thought I detected a slight curve of her lips.

'Oh, my poor boy, just lying there like that. And after all he's been through already,' Sheila Pencarrow moaned.

That evening, we were all sitting in the lounge after the meal Deborah and I had prepared for everyone. I had been at Daniel's bedside, just watching the bubbles in the jar, when his family had arrived in the middle of the afternoon. He was certainly a sorry sight, hardly moving and had a great, mottled blue lump on his forehead now. If he did mumble an odd word, it didn't make much sense.

'We'll bring him out of the sedation tomorrow,' William explained in that wonderfully comforting way of his, 'but don't expect him to be totally lucid for some time, not with that degree of concussion. And his ribs will be agony, so we'll keep him on morphine for a few days which will make him pretty groggy. But hopefully after that, we can get him on oral painkillers and he'll begin to be more himself.'

Sheila's face was nevertheless pulled into a desperate grimace and her husband leant across to pat her hand. He was a man of few words, but I could see his eyes – Daniel's eyes – taking everything in. There was a depth behind the quiet façade, and I could see where Daniel's brooding sullenness came from. But that other side, the teasing liveliness that only showed itself on occasion – usually when he was pulling my leg about my hair which I realised now was out of fondness and not malice – was his grandmother's. She had kept her figure well for a woman in her late sixties and, despite her grey-laced raven hair, was the image of her beautiful mother whose portrait hung in Fencott Place. The room, even the hospital ward, seemed to fill with rushing meteors the moment she walked in.

'Now, I know he's your son, Sheila dear,' she said briskly but with infinite compassion, 'but you must listen to what William says. Daniel is strong—'

'Strong? Look how he was when he came back from Korea!'

'Well, that was hardly surprising, was it, dear? And it was precisely because he is so strong that he survived all that. And it *was* three years ago now. He'll pull through this, won't he, William?'

'Absolutely no reason why not,' William nodded with confidence.

'There we are, then. Now then, young Lily, I understand you played a very important part in keeping Daniel calm when he was brought in.'

She turned those piercing, lavender eyes on me, and I felt I had been pricked with some sort of stimulant, or had received an electric shock. If Daniel reckoned his grandmother was a mere *character* beside her sister, I wondered quite what Great Aunt Marianne had been like!

'I did my best,' I replied, surprised by my own animated expression when I was feeling utterly drained after my near sleepless night. 'It was such a shock, but I naturally wanted to help.'

'Well, I'm sure you were wonderful. Daniel told us all about you when he stayed with us over Christmas.'

'Did he?' I answered in surprise.

Katherine Pencarrow's eyes twinkled brightly. 'Oh, yes. He's very fond of you, you know.'

I pressed my lips together. Yes. Fond. Like a little dog, perhaps. Or a child. I glanced across at Edwin who was, with William, trying to console Sheila and convince her that her son would recover. I didn't really care how Daniel thought of me. I knew already.

Carrots. A sort of teasing endearment, I supposed. One that, once he was better, he would continue to taunt me with. But Edwin. Fondness. That was all it would ever be. And I wondered if the wound would ever heal.

It was, nonetheless, such a happy relief when, a few days later, Daniel broke into a smile when he saw me coming down the ward. Even if it was, in truth, more of a wry grimace.

'You've caught me at a good time,' he announced, although I noticed that his words were a touch slurred and his eyes lacked their usual clarity. 'I'm due another shot of morphine soon which means the last lot has worn off and I'm apparently more lucid, as they put it. But as soon as they give me the next one, they make me do these deep-breathing and coughing exercises before the morphine makes me fall asleep again. Supposed to avoid pneumonia or something. But I tell you, it's bloody torture. Still,' he added, raising one eyebrow, 'at least it keeps my mind off everything else that hurts.'

I realised he was rambling slightly, but I couldn't help but smile. 'Oh, dear, you're not a very good patient, are you, Daniel? And don't let Matron hear you swearing. But Edwin tells me your X-ray this morning was good. The pneumothorax has nearly gone. And...' I stopped to glance down at the glass jar. 'There's hardly any air leaking out now, so the drain will be coming out soon.'

'Won't stop these bloody ribs hurting each time I take a breath.'

'Daniel!' I warned.

He threw me a dark look, but his pale cheeks coloured a little. 'Sorry.' He let out a sharp sigh but it made him wince and he tightened his arm across his chest. He really did look poorly, propped up wearily on a neat pile of pillows. I noticed that the dressing on his shoulder had been removed and a scab was trying to form over the extensive area of grazing, but it was deep and sloughing in places.

'That looks pretty sore, too,' I sympathised.

He turned his head slightly to look down at the wound. 'Edwin wanted the air to dry it out. Should get away without a skin graft, though, he reckons. But I'll be pleased when I can have a pyjama top on again. I don't feel right half naked.'

I actually thought he looked rather attractive with his broad shoulders and bare chest disappearing beneath the sheets, but perhaps that was what he meant. There were two young nurses on the ward seeing to his personal needs, and if even *I* could see how handsome Daniel was... 'You're not cold, are you?' I asked to disguise my own momentary embarrassment.

'No, no.' There was a second or two's silence

when Daniel lowered his eyes and then looked at me again sideways. 'Lily, do you know what happened? I can't remember a damn thing. All I remember is waking up here in this bed with my leg in plaster and a thumping headache. Not to mention the ribs, of course.'

I frowned. 'You don't remember going over the edge and being thrown out of the jeep?'

'No.' He shook his head. 'Not at all. Nothing.'

'Just as well. It must have been terrifying.'

'Yes, but I need to *know*, Lily.' He fixed me with those deep, arresting eyes, putting me on edge.

'It seems you were forced off the road,' I told him simply. 'It wasn't your fault.'

'That's something, I suppose,' he scorned with a hint of sarcasm.

'And you muttered something about a lorry.'

'Did I?'

'Yes. When you came in. We told the police, and they've been checking local lorries for damage, and they've asked all local garages to be on the lookout. But there's been no joy so far, and no witnesses.'

Daniel's eyes were trained intently on me, as if he was willing me to come up with an answer. When I didn't, he sank back onto the pillows. The slight movement obviously hurt him and he screwed his eyes shut, but he didn't complain. Instead, he lay utterly still as if I wasn't there. I stood looking down at him and I felt my heart lurch curiously. My eyes moved over his strong torso and I felt ashamed, as if I was taking advantage of his vulnerable situation. I wasn't, of course. I felt nothing but sympathy, and my brow furrowed as I noticed several small, round marks on his chest like faint scars. What on earth...?

'Right, Mr Pencarrow. Time for your morphine.'

Daniel's eyes flew open and he looked at me in desperate pleading. 'Oh, God, not again,' I heard him murmur under his breath. 'Those bloody exercises.'

'They're for your own good,' I said limply.

'Oh, don't *you* start.'

'Now then, Mr Pencarrow, it's in your own interests.'

'It's all right for *you* to say that. It's not your bloody ribs that hurt.'

'Mr Pen—'

'And all that morphine's making me feel so sick. In fact...oh, hell...'

His shoulders heaved and he let out a choked cry as he sat up abruptly, his hand reaching out and fumbling. In a trice, Sister swept the bowl from the bedside locker and held it under his chin, her other arm around his shoulders as he retched violently. I stood back, biting my lip. It must have been sheer agony, and when it was over and Sister helped him to lie back, I could see tears swimming in his eyes and his lips were curled back from his teeth.

'Poor chap,' Sister whispered, all her affronted efficiency fled.

Daniel groaned, his face savage with desperation. 'And now you're going to give me some more.'

Sister shook her head. 'No. The anti-emetics obviously aren't working. So I think we'll wait until Dr Franfield does his rounds, if you agree. He planned on taking you off the morphine tomorrow anyway and putting you on oral painkillers instead. They won't be so effective, but you should start to feel better in yourself.'

Daniel rolled his eyes. 'Can't win, can I?' he muttered.

I smiled encouragingly. 'But you're already improving. You seem over the worst of the concussion and your ribs will soon start to be less painful, won't they, Sister?'

'A little, yes. But it'll be slow progress. The one that punctured your lung was a nasty fracture. You know Dr Franfield told you it will probably take the full six weeks before you're totally pain free.'

'Great. Thanks for reminding me.'

'Well, never mind,' I put in hastily. 'Gloria's coming to see you this afternoon. Perhaps she'll have some herbal remedy you can take as well that might help.'

He gave a jeering grunt. 'You don't seriously

believe her potions work, do you?'

'Some of them do, yes!' I retorted, remembering the calming drink she had given me. And when a short, ironic laugh came from Daniel's mouth, I felt all the old animosities return. What was it about Daniel that always ended up riling me so? 'And if she could give you something to put you in a more civil frame of mind, I'm sure everyone would appreciate it!'

I knew my lips had firmed to a thin line and I met Sister's surprised gaze before I spun on my heel and marched back down the suddenly hushed ward.

'Lily, please! I'm sorry!' I heard Daniel call as the doors swung shut behind me.

Chapter Twenty

'For God's sake, get me out of this place, Ed. It's driving me mad. I want to go home.'

'Sorry, old chap. No can do. Absolutely not.'

I hadn't been cross with Daniel for long. After her visit, Gloria had reported that the *poor lad* was far from himself. She was such a kind and compassionate lady, and I had started thinking back on some of the things she had said. I would know when the time was right to search through the box in the attic. My life was changing again and somehow, I couldn't explain it, but since Daniel's accident, I was beginning to feel stronger.

And then a few days later, Edwin had said that Daniel was asking for me and I felt ashamed. I confessed to Edwin that the last time I had been to see Daniel, I had found him somewhat difficult. Edwin had explained that it was still the combined effect of the concussion and the drugs, and that we would all need to be patient with him. And he added with a whimsical lift of his eyebrows that Daniel had always been able to dig his heels in when he wanted to. I had nodded, sucking in my lips. But more because dear Edwin was being so kind and understanding. I knew that whatever happened in the future, part of me would always love him.

So I had gone back to see Daniel and he had greeted me with a sheepish smile.

'Thank you for coming, Lily,' he said at once. 'I just wanted to apologise. Apparently I've been abominably rude to everyone, yourself included. And Ed tells me you've been looking after Trojan for me, so I wanted to thank you for that.'

I frowned in bemusement. 'But we've talked about Trojan before. Several times.'

'Have we?'

'Well, yes. And Gloria said you—'

'Gloria?' His eyes widened incredulously. 'Gloria's been here?'

'Yes,' I answered guardedly.

Daniel rubbed his hand over his eyes and then winced slightly as his fingers touched the livid bruise on his forehead. 'God, I don't remember. I can remember yesterday quite clearly, but everything before that's a complete and utter haze.'

'We've had some quite lucid conversations,' I told him gently.

'So they tell me. And in which I've behaved unforgivably. So I just wanted to say sorry and...' He paused, and I noticed the rise and fall of his prominent Adam's apple as he swallowed hard. 'And I'll understand if you don't come again.'

He had turned his head away, averting those troubled eyes, and I had been engulfed in remorse. 'I'm sorry, too, Daniel,' I had said, glad that I could find the courage to match his. 'I was still upset, and I didn't realise... I thought you were being...' I had broken off abruptly, realising I was about to put my foot in it again.

'My usual belligerent self?' he had suggested with a half smile.

I grinned back. 'Yes. We always seem to rub each other up the wrong way, don't we?'

He chuckled, and instantly drew a pained breath through his teeth. His eyes screwed shut for a moment. When he opened them again, he was smiling. 'Will you come again, then? Only don't make me laugh. It hurts too much.'

'I promise. To come again, I mean. And I will *try* not to make you laugh, but don't be cross with me if I do.'

'I could never be cross with you, Lily.'

And I had felt his gaze following me as I left the ward.

* * *

And so I had gone to visit him every day, even if it had only been for a few minutes. He was improving but, as predicted, progress was slow. Without the morphine, he was in too much pain to sleep and dark smudges shadowed his eyes. But when Edwin and I called into the ward after the orthopaedic clinic exactly two weeks to the day since the accident, he was looking brighter, lying on top of the bed rather than between the sheets. His expression was so crestfallen, though, at Edwin's refusal to discharge him, that my own heart dropped like a lead weight.

'Oh, *please*, Ed,' he begged, his eyes doleful. A little like Trojan when he wanted a titbit from the table, I mused.

'No.' Edwin crossed his arms as if to emphasise his words. 'It's completely out of the question. Your family are going home on Sunday, so there'd be no one to look after you.'

'Are they?' I put in. 'I didn't realise.'

Daniel closed his eyes fleetingly as he sighed with dismay. 'Yes, they are. Dad feels he needs to get back to his investments, and Mum won't stay at Fencott without a man. An able-bodied one,' he added ruefully. 'Anyway, she fusses so much we'd end up having words. So that only leaves Gran. *She'd* stay up there alone, but she doesn't drive so that really isn't practical.'

'What about Great Uncle Joshua and your

relations at Peter Tavy?' Edwin suggested. 'Could you stay with them?'

Daniel puffed out his cheeks. 'That doesn't seem very fair on them, and they've got the farm to run.' He gazed down at his feet for a second before his mouth knotted mutinously and he flashed an angry scowl at Edwin. 'Damn it, Ed. I can take care of myself. Look, I've mastered the crutches—'

He swung his legs, plaster cast and all, over the side of the bed ready to demonstrate, but he must have moved too quickly and caught his ribs. His head fell back in a stifled cry, and then his shoulders dropped in exasperation.

'There, you see?' Edwin poked his face at his friend. 'You're not ready to be discharged yet. Crutches and broken ribs don't go together very well, you know.'

Daniel hung his head in dejection and then as he attempted valiantly but in vain to lift his plastered leg back onto the bed without hurting his ribs again, Edwin went to his rescue. I felt so sorry for him that the words tumbled out of my mouth before I knew it.

'I could come and look after you. I've got the week after next off, and I didn't have any plans for it.'

They both stared at me in astonishment, Daniel's jaw hanging open so that he looked quite comical.

It brought a smile to my face, and I found myself quite enamoured of the idea that had sprung to my mind of its own accord. It would be wonderful once again to open the curtains each morning to the wild beauty of the moor and, perhaps more importantly, I wouldn't be reminded of Edwin's engagement every hour of the day and night. The horror of Daniel's accident had put on hold the plan to move into a place of my own, but I had started to think about it again that very day. A week away from both the hospital and the Franfield home was just what I needed to allow my wounded heart to heal. And if I had to put up with Daniel's moods, at least it might stop me brooding over my loss of Edwin.

'Would you? Would you really?' Daniel's voice was low as his eyes bore intently into mine, unnerving me in that strange way he so often did.

'Well, yes. I'd be happy to,' I said, feeling more confident as I spoke. 'What do you think, Edwin? Would that fit in?'

'Yes, it would.' Edwin still looked surprised. 'I'd be happy to discharge you in a week with Lily to look after you. And after that, you should be all right on your own. And I think your parents are coming back down then as well. So.' He pulled in his chin. 'Can you behave yourself in here for one more week?'

'Oh, yes.' A soft light came into Daniel's eyes as they shifted in my direction. 'I think I can if you're dangling a *carrot* in front of me.'

His expression was so inscrutable that I wasn't sure if I wanted to slap his face or laugh.

'Could you...could you stop when we get to where it happened?' Daniel faltered, his voice like gravel. His joy at leaving the ward had been well evident, and even Sister had whispered in my ear that he was a *great lad when you got to know him*. But once we had reached the open moor, the car straining in second gear to take the steady incline, he had fallen silent. His eyes had been scanning the rugged landscape, relishing that sense of freedom and peace that always invaded my own soul. Or so I had thought. But as I glanced at him for a second, I saw that his face was set like the granite that surrounded us.

'It's hard to find from this side of the road,' I told him, 'but I'll try.'

My palms began to ooze sweat as I didn't know how he might react. That was the thing about Daniel, I supposed. He was so unpredictable, and I didn't want to start off on the wrong foot. When we came to the spot, I recognised it more easily than I had anticipated, and finding somewhere to pull off the road, I brought the car to a halt. Beside me, Daniel took as deep a breath as his ribs allowed, and his hand reached for the door handle.

'Oh, Daniel, I don't think you should. You'll have to walk on the road and—'

'I've got to, Lily,' was his grated reply.

I turned off the engine and hurried round to his side of the car to help him, knowing there would be no arguing with him. I made Trojan stay in the back of the car, and then hovered round Daniel as he made his slow and painful way back down the road on his crutches. I was cross with myself for giving in to him, but was more terrified that a car would come down the hill too fast and run him over. A couple of vehicles did approach but as soon as I saw them, I waved frantically and thankfully they slowed down to pass us in safety.

'Daniel?' I whispered anxiously, looking up at him as the rumble of the last vehicle died away, leaving the contemplative silence of the moor to encompass us.

Daniel was staring down the boulder-strewn bank at the patches of ploughed turf, the only evidence of the accident. His brow was creased in a deep frown, his mouth compressed into a thin line as without moving his head, his eyes swivelled to gaze at the road.

'Nothing,' he mumbled. 'Not a thing. It's a complete blank.'

I hesitated, not wanting to deepen his anguish. 'William said you might never remember. And...

does it really matter? We know it wasn't your fault, and you *survived*. That's the important thing.'

My voice had vibrated with a passion that astounded even myself. Daniel's eyebrows arched in surprise and he blinked his eyes wide at me. The pupils were dilated so that the violet-blue was darkened to indigo. Unsettling me again.

'Come on. Let's get you back to the car. I can hear Trojan barking.'

He moved more and more slowly as we climbed back up the road, and I was relieved when we reached the car. The short excursion had clearly exhausted him and he closed his eyes for the remainder of the journey, only opening them again as we turned in at Fencott Place and the gravel crunched beneath the tyres.

'Here we are, then,' I said somewhat inanely as I turned off the engine. 'Is it good to be home?'

He turned liquid eyes on me. 'You'll never know how grateful I am, Lily.'

His expression brought me up short and I felt the heat in my cheeks. 'I'll go through and open up the front so that you don't have to walk so far,' I suggested hastily to cover up my awkwardness. 'I'm a bit worried you've overdone it.'

He grunted. 'I hope you're not going to fuss over me.'

I felt the hairs at the back of my neck bristle. 'I'm

here to look after you, but I can assure you I've no intention of being your skivvy.'

'Good.'

An amused glint flashed in his eyes, leaving me swathed in uncertainty as I let myself in through the back of the house. Trojan trotted at my heels, wagging his tail and clearly as pleased as his master to be home. I had driven up the previous evening to collect a set of clothes for Daniel, carefully unpicking the right leg seam of a pair of trousers to fit over his cast. The house had echoed with silence and I was glad I wasn't going to be there alone. I wondered how Daniel could relish such solitude on a permanent basis.

He was waiting on the other side of the front door and I stood back to let him in.

'I'll just bring everything in from the car,' I said lightly. 'I did some food shopping after I finished work this morning, and I've got a case.'

Daniel cast down his eyes. 'I feel awful. I should be the one carrying the heavy things.'

'But then I wouldn't be here, would I? Come on, cheer up! You're home. I'll light the range when I come in. It'll be funny cooking on a range again. I'd got used to Deborah's gas cooker. It was like being back in London.'

I left him to hobble inside on his crutches while I went out to the car, but when I came back in, Daniel was standing by the drawing room door, balancing on his good leg and flicking the light switch.

'Damn it,' he grumbled. 'The generator's gone off.'

'Oh, no!' I felt my heart sink. 'Are you sure it's not just a bulb?'

'Unfortunately not. Everything's off.'

'So…what do we do?' I really was beginning to panic. Perhaps coming back here hadn't been such a good idea after all.

'Well, we could resign ourselves to groping around by candlelight this evening. It might be romantic, but that isn't exactly appropriate in our situation, is it? And it isn't very practical either, with my needing both hands free to get around.'

His tone had been stinging, sarcastic, and I lifted my chin to glare at him. But he had already turned away, swinging the crutches as he made for the back door. Feeling somewhat piqued, I followed him down the passageway in time to see him collect a bunch of keys from the small boot room. Outside on the terrace, it was typical September weather, overcast but the air warm and, thankfully, relatively still. The garden showed signs of its three weeks of neglect, but Daniel obviously kept it well in order and the views over the open moor were exhilarating.

He led the way through a gate in the high wall at the far end to an area I hadn't seen before. It had clearly once been the stable-yard with a row of wooden loose-boxes and what I imagined was a tack room at one end of the block. There was a huge barn with two sets of massive double doors sealed with giant padlocks, and several smaller outbuildings. The smell of fresh creosote was overwhelming, so I imagined that was what Daniel had been doing just before the accident.

The sight of him struggling to stand on his good leg, hang onto the crutches and unlock the door to the one brick-built shed brought me from my study of the yard. I hurried forward to take the keys from him. We didn't exchange a word, but he glanced at me in defiance, his cheeks sucked in obstinately.

'Daniel, you're going to have to swallow that masculine pride of yours and accept that you need help, or this isn't going to work you know!' I told him in no uncertain terms as I opened the door.

His lean jaw dropped slightly as he met my gaze. 'And you're going to become an engineer in the next few minutes, are you?'

'If need be!' I answered, my head held high.

He gave a short laugh. 'Well, let's hope for both our sakes it isn't necessary. The damned thing,' he said, jabbing his head at the oil-reeking contraption I assumed was the generator, 'is supposed to be self-starting. But it's a temperamental bugger. The times

I've had to strip it down. Keep your fingers crossed it just needs restarting.'

Behind my back, I did just that. And to my utter relief, God answered my prayers. Despite what I had said, I really didn't fancy wrestling with the oily monster under Daniel's supervision. He showed me what to do in case it happened again, and after a couple of attempts, it coughed and spluttered into life.

'Thank God,' Daniel muttered vehemently.

'Amen to that!'

'At least we agree on something.'

His face was taut and he was looking pale. Concern overtook my indignation and my heart softened.

'Come on. You look all in. You need to put your feet up and I'll make you a cup of tea.'

The hard lines about his mouth slackened. 'Yes, you're right. Thank you. And, Lily, I don't mean to fight.'

He smiled, his eyebrows arched as if asking my forgiveness and looking so handsome I would have melted if I hadn't known him better. He always seemed to present me with a challenge, as if he wanted to drive me away. I could do just that, I supposed, turn my back and leave him to it. But something inside me was perpetually ready to fight back.

I left him to struggle back indoors and went

ahead to light the range. I had prepared it the previous evening so it didn't take long to catch. I had discovered there were two fireboxes, but clearly Daniel only used one of them. It heated an oven, a small boiler to one side, and three hotplates which was sufficient for one person or a small family's needs. I let my imagination run riot, conjuring up visions of a time long past when the house had been full of people, Daniel's ancestors and their servants, and the entire range had been in full use.

I unpacked the shopping while I waited for the water to boil and took the opportunity to familiarise myself with the contents of the various cupboards and the pantry. When I was finally able to carry two hot drinks into the drawing room, Daniel was stretched out on one of the sofas. I thought he was asleep, but he opened his eyes when he heard me coming.

'Oh, you're an angel,' he said appreciatively, and tried to shift himself into a more upright position.

'Let me help you.'

'No, it's all right, thanks. I can...' But then his shoulders slumped. 'Well, no, I can't actually. Could you put some more cushions behind my back? I'm more comfortable propped up. And...could you get me some codeine, please?'

He lowered his eyes, almost as if he was ashamed. I had been there when Edwin had given him the painkillers to take home. He would probably need aspirin regularly for another week or two. The rib that had punctured his lung had been a bad break and the pain from it would last longer than a non-displaced fracture. It would heal crooked, but apparently that didn't matter. But the fact that Daniel was asking for the stronger codeine was an admission that the journey home and the sortie to the generator had considerably aggravated his discomfort. It dawned on me then that, since he had emerged from the influence of the concussion and the morphine, I hadn't heard him complain once about the pain from his injuries.

'Why don't you try and nod off?' I suggested sympathetically when I took the empty cup from him ten minutes later. 'You look as though you need it.'

'Are you sure you wouldn't mind? To be honest, I'm shattered.'

'Of course not. I'm here to look after you, remember?'

He smiled wryly. 'And I am grateful, Lily, even if I don't always show it. Why don't you explore the house? Choose yourself a bedroom.'

'Yes, I will. You have a good nap and don't worry about me.'

His eyelids were already drooping and I crept out of the room, clicking my tongue at Trojan who eagerly scrambled up, ready for an adventure. Well, it was for me anyway. I knew the kitchen, the drawing room and the dining room, and had used the lavatory, not original and so squeezed in under the stairs. On the ground floor, I discovered another huge reception room, closed off with all the furniture hidden beneath dustsheets, giving it a ghostly appearance as if stepping back into another age which, I supposed, it was!

The final room, and one which I had glimpsed before, was a substantial study with book-lined walls and solid wood filing cabinets. On the worn carpet stood a fine polished desk, an antique now but probably new in Daniel's great-grandmother's day, I imagined. The leather-inlaid top was strewn with papers, and a blank sheet had been inserted into an old typewriter. It struck me that the study was larger than the entire kitchen that Sidney and I had more or less lived in at the cottage, and that, at one time, the Warrington side of Daniel's family must have been very rich indeed.

I climbed the sweeping staircase, noticing that he kept the place clean and tidy. He had explained to me before which was his room so that I could fetch him some clothes, but now I explored them all, six altogether, each of a good size and the one at the end with a dressing room and a bathroom going off. There was another huge bathroom, which I guessed had originally been another bedroom. I wondered how the plumbing worked with no gas for hot water and only limited electricity, but there was obviously some sort of system in place.

I chose the room next to Daniel's as I thought I might feel nervous at night in this huge, isolated house on the moor. The views from the window were breathtaking, though, and a contented peace wafted about me as if I had come home. I found some sheets in a linen cupboard on the landing and made up the bed, but before I unpacked, my curiosity took me up a narrow staircase to the top floor, the servants' quarters in the attic space. And the nursery.

It was like entering a church, silent, dusty, sacred. There was a beautiful wooden crib, a larger cot, shelves of old toys, table and chairs and an old-fashioned highchair. Most wonderful of all was an exquisitely carved rocking horse the size of a small pony and almost as realistic. I pushed its nose and it swung smoothly. I wondered if it would take my weight. I would have to ask Daniel. I'd love to ride on it, and I wouldn't care if he laughed at me.

I stood for some minutes, allowing the ghosts of the past to sink into my soul. I knew that there had been a son killed somewhere in the Somme during the First World War. He would have been brought up in this room, a little boy playing on the rug or the rocking horse, not knowing in his innocence that his life would be cruelly cut short on the battlefield. Ah, the darkness of war. Pray God it would never happen again.

I suddenly had the most overwhelming desire to see the nursery full of children once more, to hear its walls echo with laughter. But with Daniel the last of the line and not expecting to marry, it probably never would, and it made me want to cry.

I carefully shut the door and left the room to its memories.

Chapter Twenty-One

The following morning, the sun decided to show itself and so we sat out on the south-facing terrace to enjoy the last vestiges of the summer. There were a couple of old deckchairs in the boot room, one of which had a foot-rest so that Daniel could put his leg up, as it was still inclined to ache. I got him comfortable and then went to make some fresh coffee as he had shown me how to use the filters the night before.

'Black, no sugar. That's right, isn't it?' I asked as I set the tray down on the folding table I had found with the deckchairs.

'It certainly is. Thank you.' Daniel took the mug, squinting up at me. 'Did you sleep all right, by the way? I forgot to ask.'

'Yes, I did.' I nodded as I added cream to my own coffee. 'How about you?'

He shrugged. 'I still can't get comfortable, and

my leg was itching. But it was good to be back in my own bed.'

'Nothing quite like it, is there?' I could hardly believe it. Daniel was being so pleasant that I was actually enjoying his company. It had been the same the previous evening when he had shown his appreciation over the simple meal I had cooked. I doubted it would last. Or perhaps I had always misjudged him. He certainly seemed a different person from the sullen brute who had rescued me three years ago. 'It really is lovely here,' I went on, feeling totally at ease. 'Looking over the moor like this gives me a sense of peace. And freedom.'

I noticed his eyes deepen to sapphire as they narrowed. 'That's right,' he muttered almost inaudibly. 'That's why I had to come back.'

I had the impression that he wasn't only referring to the present as I recalled his words to Edwin all that time ago. *It was thinking of this place that kept me alive*, or something like that. I didn't want him to change his mood, so I quickly commented, 'You keep the garden looking nice.'

He gave a sardonic snort. 'The grass needs cutting and there are weeds coming up everywhere. And I was trying to give the wooden outbuildings a coat of creosote while they were still dry. I'd been concentrating on the house and garden so I hadn't got round to it before. Now I mightn't get a chance until next summer.'

'I can do a bit of weeding for you. But is that what you do all the time, look after the place?' I asked lazily.

'It's my job.'

'Really? I often wondered.'

'Caretaker extraordinaire,' he replied dryly. 'Only I won't be doing much caretaking for a while, will I? Knowing Gran, she'll still pay me, mind.'

'Oh, it's a proper job, then?' I said, my curiosity genuinely aroused. 'I thought you were just... Well, I was never sure, to be honest.'

Daniel gave me a sideways glance. 'Oh, she doesn't pay me much. But what do I need money for? I've got the only roof over my head I've ever wanted, so it's a perfect arrangement. It might not be a *proper* job as I believe you once put it, but it suits me down to the ground.'

'Did I? Put it like that? Oh, I'm sorry. I'm sure I didn't mean—'

'Oh, I think you did at the time. But it doesn't matter. The fact is that Gran and my great aunt inherited the house jointly soon after the Great War. But Grandad took Gran up to London to try and salvage what was left of her family fortune, and they rather took to city life.'

'Yes, I vaguely remember Edwin saying something like that.'

'Oh, yes? Well, then, I expect you know that

Great Aunt Marianne's husband had lost both his legs in the war. That's actually how they met. She was driving the ambulance that rescued him. They lived here with the house only half belonging to her, but the only money they had to live on was a trust my grandfather set up for them. So they couldn't afford to have any work done and the place was left to fall into ruin for thirty years until...'

His voice ended in a thin trail and he stared out over the moor for some seconds as if he had forgotten I was there. But then he shook his head as if focusing his thoughts. 'So I've been renovating the house for a fraction of what it would have cost to pay someone properly. It's the only way Gran could afford it. We may not be poverty-stricken, but we're not that wealthy, either. Not after two world wars to ruin our investments. Most of our money's in bricks and mortar. The house in London. And yes, everyone shares the same one. And here. And this isn't worth as much as you might think,' he went on, raising his hand as if to emphasise the point. 'It's leasehold, you see, not freehold. And anyway, it would be hard to find a buyer, I reckon. I'd be devastated, mind, if Gran decided to try and sell it. I could never imagine myself following in my father's footsteps, checking his investments in the *Financial Times* every day, keeping his ear to the ground, attending shareholders' meetings almost daily. And I'd suffocate in London.'

He paused, chewing his bottom lip wistfully, and then surprised me by asking, 'What about you, Lily? Would you go back? I really know so little about you, but Ed told me you'd lived in London all your life before you came here.'

I had found myself intrigued and feeling privileged that Daniel was, I supposed, confiding in me. I was taken aback, though, by his question and hesitated, remembering how Edwin had once asked me the very same thing. But before I could answer, Trojan heaved himself reluctantly from the warm flagstones, growling softly and hackles raised.

'Oo-ee!' we heard faintly from the side of the house. And then more loudly, 'Oooo-eeee! Anyone there? It's me, Gloria! And Kate's with me!'

Daniel rolled his eyes. 'Damn it. I was really enjoying the peace and quiet. Now I suppose I'll have to be civil to them.'

'I'm sure they mean well,' I attempted to pacify him as I padded away. Trojan followed me, wagging his tail but moving guardedly, just the same. I held his collar as I let our visitors in the side-gate, and then he seemed quite happy when I greeted them as friends and not foes.

'We knocked at the front door but I don't suppose you could hear. Just wanted to see how you are!' Gloria announced as she strode to where Daniel was disguising his resigned expression with a smile.

'Glad to be home, and not in such discomfort as I was,' he replied amiably. 'Lily's looking after me a treat. Please forgive me if I don't get up. And take a seat.'

'Have mine, Gloria,' I offered, indicating the other deckchair. 'I'll get you both a drink. You must be gasping. I assume you walked all the way?'

'We certainly did. It's the only way as neither of us drive.'

'Thank you for coming to visit me in hospital,' Daniel said as Gloria sat down beside him. 'I don't remember, I'm afraid. The concussion, you see. But it was very good of you.'

'Don't mention it.'

'I'd have come, too,' Kate chipped in, 'but I wasn't sure if you'd be happy with that, bein' in bed, like.'

She was standing by his feet, gazing down at him with wide, starry eyes. She was still going out with Pete but here she was, almost fluttering her eyelids at Daniel, though I was sure she'd have been mortified to realise it was so obvious. I had to admit he was strikingly handsome and I supposed that being in a vulnerable situation would bring out the mothering instinct in any female. The accident had brought that haunted look back to his face and, in an odd way, it suited him. And I experienced a pang of, dear Lord, it wasn't *jealousy*, was it, as Kate eyed him coyly?

'Did it hurt very much?' she enquired now. 'You must've been mortal brave.'

'I don't know about that,' Daniel answered so sharply that I saw Kate recoil. 'You need to ask Lily. I believe I was quite obnoxious at times.'

'Oh, well,' I stammered. 'When you were still concussed, I don't think you knew what you were saying most of the time. But after that, yes. I think you were very brave indeed.'

He glanced up, his mouth in a firm line and his eyes boring into mine. I wasn't sure what was behind his expression and it unnerved me.

'I'll get that drink,' I said quickly, glad to escape. 'What would you like? Something hot, or there's some lemonade in the fridge.'

'Oh, lemonade, please.'

'Me, too. I'll come and help you.'

There was really no need, but Kate followed me anyway. The French doors to the drawing room were open, but I went in through the back door and along the passage to the kitchen. I noticed that Kate's eyes were everywhere.

'It's a grand house, isn't it? He must be very rich.'

'Oh, Daniel doesn't own it. He just looks after it for his grandmother.'

Kate shrugged. 'Same difference. Mind you, he might be good-looking, but does he always have such a short fuse?'

I glanced at her warily. 'No, not really. Not once you get to know him. He does keep things close to his chest, mind.'

'Well, I don't know how you stand him. I'd rather have my Pete any day.'

'Isn't he coming to see you with it being Sunday? It's been his first week away at college, hasn't it?'

'Exactly. He's got digs in Plymouth, but he says he'll come home most weekends. Only there's things on today so as they can get to know each other. So when I met Miss Luckett after chapel and she said she was comin' here, I thought I'd come, too. I'd love to see the house proper, like,' she hinted.

So I gave her a swift guided tour of the ground floor, not quite sure how Daniel would feel about my showing her upstairs. 'How's the job going?' I asked as she admired the drawing room.

'Oh, all right, I suppose. I'm still on the counters, though. You know I was hopin' for your job when you left, but maybe I'm not so bright as I thought I was.'

'Never mind,' I encouraged her. 'Perhaps you'll get something else one day. I'll just give Gloria her drink.' And so saying, I left Kate gazing at the mesmerising portrait of Daniel's great-grandmother.

'There have been more sacrificed sheep while you were in hospital, you know,' Gloria was saying as I handed her the glass of lemonade.

'Really? Well, I'm determined to get to the bottom of it once I'm able to get around again.'

'Oh, I do wish you wouldn't. I mean, it could be dangerous, and I wouldn't want to see you—'

I didn't hear the rest as I caught the shrill ring of the telephone from the hall. I hurried inside to answer it, thinking how odd it was that Gloria almost seemed to be trying to put Daniel off.

'Hello, Lily. It's Edwin,' the voice at the other end of the line announced when I picked up the phone. 'Just ringing to see how Daniel is. Behaving himself, I hope?'

'I think coming home yesterday was a bit much for him, but he's fine today,' I reported. 'Grumbling because he can't do anything, as you might imagine, but just now he's sitting on the terrace with his leg up.'

'Good to hear it! Would you like Sadie and me to come up? She's got a few hours off duty this afternoon.'

I felt my heart sink to my feet. My main reason for offering to look after Daniel had been to escape seeing Edwin and Sadie together, hadn't it?

'Oh, no. Really,' I replied adamantly. 'He's already had some visitors today, and I think he'd rather just be quiet, to be honest. And I'm sure you and Sadie would rather be on your own.'

'Well, if you're sure. Just give me a ring if he

becomes too hard to handle and I'll come and give him a lecture. Or if he has any problems at all.'

'Yes, I will. Thanks, Edwin. I'll tell him you rang.'

I replaced the receiver in its cradle with relief. I really did think Daniel would be better off with only myself for company, and I hoped I could think of a polite way to get Gloria and Kate to leave.

'I'll just get the roast in the oven and then I'll give you both a lift back, if you like,' I suggested with a smile as I went back outside where I found Kate perched on the stone balustrade to the terrace. 'I'm sure you don't want to walk all that way again.'

'Thank you, Lily. That would be very kind.'

And the grateful light in Daniel's eyes warmed my heart.

The weather broke the next day, plunging us into a typical Dartmoor autumn with a dense, impenetrable fog that blotted out the garden, let alone the moor beyond. We kept indoors, Trojan eyeing us both in turn and quite disgruntled that his only outing was to the garden. Daniel was concerned that either the dog or I would get lost on the moor, and I had to agree with him.

After a light lunch, we had both been reading in the drawing room when Daniel struggled to his feet – or rather to one foot and his crutches – and I heard the now familiar plonk, thud as he made his way out into the hall, presumably to use the lavatory. Indeed I heard it flush and a minute later, the plonk, thud again. But he must have gone into the study to get a different book from the shelves or maybe look at some accounts or bills, or some such. The dull tap on the typewriter reached my ears faintly. It was painfully slow, distracting my concentration from the bland novel Wendy had given me and which I didn't think much of. After half an hour, I couldn't stand it any longer and sauntered into the study to see if I could be of assistance.

Daniel lifted his gaze from beneath furrowed eyebrows. 'Help yourself,' he said, gesticulating towards the shelves. 'Sorry. Was I disturbing you? I'm a lousy typist, I'm afraid.'

'So I see,' I grinned. 'Can I help? Is it a letter or something that needs tabulating? I'll do it for you. Unless it's personal, of course,' I concluded in a fluster.

'Ah, well, it's rather longer than a letter. And it *is* somewhat personal. I'm writing, well, a book,' he confessed. 'I write it in longhand and then attempt to type it up.'

'A book?' I was genuinely surprised. But on swift reflection, I supposed I shouldn't have been. Daniel was highly intelligent, had a First from Oxford, and yet here he was, an odd-job man when all was said and done, even if he was excellent at it. 'How fascinating! What about?' I asked with intrigued eagerness.

To my dismay, he looked almost ashamed. 'It was Edwin's idea. He suggested that if I wrote down some of what happened in Korea, it would be a sort of release. I was pretty wound up when I came home, and then to find... Well, you know all that. I just...' He paused, spreading his hands. 'I just found myself taking it out on anyone and everyone. Including an innocent young girl who'd twisted her ankle out on the moor.' He looked up with a guilty half smile. 'Ed didn't like what he saw when we met up again, and he said so. That's a true friend for you. He rang me nearly every week from London, just to argue sometimes when I was being particularly awkward. I don't think I'd have got through it without him. There were times when I really did feel suicidal. But I kept bumping into...' He broke off abruptly. 'So you could say Ed saved my life on two occasions. I know how dreadfully he upset you, but—'

'Oh, no,' I interrupted. 'Edwin never did anything to upset me. Quite the opposite, really. It was all my own fault. I was infatuated by him. No, more than that. I truly loved him.'

'In...the past tense?' Daniel prompted gently.

I hung my head, wondering how I was opening my heart to Daniel when I hadn't been able to do so to anyone else, not even Wendy. But then, wasn't Daniel doing the same to me? 'I know I've got to get over him,' I answered determinedly. 'I took his friendship as far more than that. It was so silly of me. He's so much older and just sees me as a child.'

Daniel lifted his chin. 'He's exactly the same age as me. Twenty-seven. And I don't see you as a child. To me, you're more mature than Wendy, even though she's nearly three years older than you.'

Those incredible deep blue eyes met mine, throwing me off balance. Once again, I wasn't sure of Daniel's meaning. 'I'd be happy to do some typing for you, if you like,' I offered, pushing the uncertainty to the back of my mind.

Daniel shook his head. 'It's good of you to offer, but it... Well, it doesn't make very pleasant reading. The whole idea was to get it off my chest. All the horrible, sickening details.'

'I hope *you're* not treating me as a child now,' I retorted. 'Trying to protect me.'

'And would that be a bad thing? After all, the war was supposedly to stop the spread of communism. To protect the innocent. Make life better for all.'

'And has it, do you think?' I quizzed him.

He shrugged. 'Not for me personally. And not for the world in general, I don't think. That war was a shambles. I'm just writing my part in it. So people can know.'

'People? I thought it was personal?'

'It is. But I've got a publisher interested. I'll decide whether or not to contact them again if I ever finish it.'

'I'll read it when it's published, then,' I announced obstinately, though why I felt like that, I wasn't entirely sure.

'We'll see,' was Daniel's enigmatic reply.

Chapter Twenty-Two

I had left Daniel to his one-fingered typing, but it wasn't long before he plonk, thudded back into the drawing room as sitting at the desk wasn't too comfortable for him. He seemed to have forgotten our minor altercation, and I realised I shouldn't have pressed him. But I wanted to know about the war. Or more precisely what had happened that seemed to haunt him still. And why was I so interested? I shook my head in bewilderment.

I woke in the middle of the night, startled and with my heart thrumming nervously. For a second or two, I couldn't place where I was, and then I heard a man's voice. Surely we hadn't been broken into? And as it all clicked into place, I realised it was Daniel talking in his sleep in the next room. I turned over, relieved that we weren't being burgled and ready to go back to sleep. But Daniel's mutterings were growing louder and more agitated, and suddenly I was wide awake.

I sat up in the pitch dark, wondering what to do. If Daniel was having a nightmare, should I leave him to it? After all, he wasn't a child who might need comforting. But I was concerned and, I supposed, curious. The Daniel I had once resented and avoided like the plague had hidden depths that intrigued me.

I turned on the bedside lamp and waited. All went quiet and I was about to settle down when Daniel cried out in such anguish that I felt compelled to do something. So I left my door open so that there was enough light to see my way, and knocked lightly on Daniel's door.

'Daniel? Daniel, are you all right?' I whispered.

Silence. I was about to turn away when he answered.

'Yes. Yes, you can come in.'

I poked my head around the door. The room was in darkness but my vision was already adjusted to the gloom. Daniel's ribs still didn't allow him to lie flat and I could see his form as a shadow against the white of the pillows.

'Sorry. Did I wake you?' he mumbled apologetically. 'I think I was having another… I was dreaming.'

'You called out and I was worried,' I answered simply.

He rubbed his hand over his forehead and then dragged it down over his mouth and chin. 'Oh, I am sorry. Go back to bed. But thanks for coming in.'

'Oh, I feel wide awake now. Would you like a cup of tea or something?'

'Well, actually, if you're sure you wouldn't mind, I'd love a tea.'

I went downstairs, glad that the generator produced power for electric light. The spacious rooms seemed to echo even more dauntingly in the dead of night, and I was grateful when Trojan trotted up to me, tail swinging, ready for some nocturnal adventure. I wasn't going to stoke up the range in the middle of the night, so I turned on the electric kettle, praying it wouldn't fuse the lights. Daniel had told me to make sure as many lights as possible were off when using the kettle, so I groped my way around the kitchen by the light from the hall. But the water boiled without plunging the house into darkness, and I made a mug of tea for Daniel and one of cocoa for myself using dried milk instead of fresh. Trojan followed me upstairs and into Daniel's room, and Daniel took the mug from me with a grateful nod.

'My pleasure.' I tipped my head on one side, feeling my way cautiously. 'Your nightmare, was it...was it about Korea?'

He had turned on his own bedside lamp and I

saw him avert his eyes before he nodded, almost as if ashamed.

'Are you sure it's a good idea?' I ventured. 'I mean, doesn't writing it down make you relive it all?'

He shrugged slightly. 'Maybe. But I seem to relive it all the time anyway. And it is a sort of unravelling. I really do think it's helping me to come to terms with everything. It's almost as if I'm writing to Aunt Marianne. She was the one person I could really have talked to, having been in the thick of war herself. No one else in the family had, you see. Just like William, my father was too young for the First World War and too old for the Second. He did his bit, of course. Worked in an aviation factory, believe it or not. But without Marianne, there was nobody I felt I could really talk to.'

'You can talk to me. No one could have come closer to being killed in a war than I did.'

'*You*! Really? I had no idea. In fact, I know very little about you at all. So, what happened, if you don't mind my asking?'

I could see that his eyes had somehow mellowed and I sat down on the edge of the bed, carefully avoiding his plaster-cast. So there I was, sipping at my cocoa in the early hours and telling Daniel Pencarrow how as a toddler in the Blitz I had been the sole survivor in the house next door to a direct hit, dug out from beneath my mother's body buried in a pile of rubble. Daniel was a good listener, and I found myself relating my entire life story to him. I even confessed about Sidney not being my real father after all. So far, nobody outside the Franfield family knew, but seeing as Sidney had gone from this world leaving nothing but a diary and a few photographs to be inherited, there seemed no reason to keep it a secret any longer.

'You're so lucky knowing exactly who you are,' I concluded with a sigh. 'And you have that amazing portrait of your great-grandmother. You even have her eyes.'

Daniel gave a soft chuckle. 'Yes, I know. I might not have done, though. My great-grandfather had hazel eyes, and so did their son, the one who was killed at the Somme. But their daughters, Gran and Great Aunt Marianne, both inherited the blue. And on the Pencarrow side of the family, my Grandfather Philip was the only one of four children to have blue eyes. The others were all dark brown, so I could have looked very different. And I wonder if I'd have been a different sort of person as well?' he mused thoughtfully. 'So, yes, I suppose I *am* lucky to be able to trace my family right back. I'd never really thought about it. But you, my poor little Lily, I didn't realise what you'd been through. I knew from Edwin that you'd had to leave London when your mother died and you came here to live with your father. But all the rest, I didn't have a clue. And then I was so horrible to you on the very day you found out the truth. You must have hated me.'

'Yes, I think I did,' I admitted quite openly. 'But I don't any more. Otherwise, I wouldn't be here, would I?'

'No, I suppose not.' He paused for a moment before his eyes darted sideways at me. 'You could always look at those papers again. See if they give any clues.'

I felt my lips tighten. 'Yes, I could. But I'm afraid they'll only reveal some other horrible secret, and I've had enough of shocks.'

'But you wouldn't have to face things alone. I...I'd be there.'

His voice was low and steady. Strong. I had no doubt that the Daniel Pencarrow who had returned from captivity a wreck, but had dragged himself through it, would be willing to support me. In some odd way, we had come to help each other.

'I'll think about it,' I answered, suddenly aware how drained I felt. 'But it's starting to get light and I could do with some more sleep. But tomorrow it's your turn. If I'm going to do some typing for you, I want to hear the story from you first.'

Daniel pulled his head up sharply. 'I don't remember agreeing to that.'

'Oh, yes, you did.' I got to my feet, grinning down

at him. 'In exchange for the tea. If you've forgotten, I expect it was the concussion.'

'Oh, ha!' I heard him mutter as I closed the door.

'I really don't think this is a good idea.'

By the time we woke up again, a watery sun had risen above the remnants of yesterday's mist that hung over the moor in translucent white ribbons. It was a truly beautiful morning, the rays of sunlight beginning to burn away the pearly veil, though the air was sharp with the first tang of autumn. I took Trojan for a short walk, relishing that sense of liberty the moor always inspired in me, and then had set breakfast on the terrace. This was my holiday, after all, and although it was a bit chilly and we needed to wear thick jumpers, it was glorious to sit outside and enjoy such a wonderful atmosphere.

'For you or for me?' I replied as we lingered over coffee.

He arched an eyebrow. 'I meant for you, Carrots.'

He threw me an enigmatic frown and I knew he was trying to antagonise me. Put me off. Make me stomp away in a strop at being called what I supposed had become his nickname for me. But the fact was that I didn't mind being called it any more.

'Look, Daniel.' I could see by his expression that

I took him by surprise when my hand closed over his and jerked it forcefully. 'Sidney kept everything secret, and it made life hell for both of us. But once the truth came out and we understood each other, well, we became good friends. I mean, you and I are friends already, but I really want to know.'

I watched him draw in a deep breath and only wince slightly. His face was set, lean cheeks sucked in and his firm jaw rigid.

'All right,' he conceded after several seconds' consideration. 'But I don't think I can talk about the worst details. Not face to face. They're in the book, though, but you'll be prepared. If you still want to do some typing for me.'

I felt he was playing for time again, but I didn't mind. In a way, I was glad. I knew he would have some appalling tales to relate, but there shouldn't be any barriers between us. I wanted to understand the real Daniel beneath the gruff, irascible shell.

'I finished at Oxford at the same time the North Koreans invaded the South,' he began after I had cleared away the breakfast things and we were both seated in the deckchairs on the terrace which was now warm with the September sunshine. 'June 1950. I went back to my parents in London for a few weeks, but I felt so shut in that I was soon back here with my great aunt. My mother was fussing all the time that I'd be called up when there was a proper war to fight. As it happened, she was right.'

'You're her son, Daniel. Of course she'll worry about you.'

'Yes. You're absolutely right. And I'm sure I'd be the same if I ever had a child. But I found it pretty irritating so I came back here, doing odd jobs around the place and wondering what to do next. A First from Oxford might sound very grand, but English Lit isn't a very useful subject unless you want to be an academic, and I wasn't sure I did. And anyway, I was waiting to be called up. And of course, my fiancée was back in Oxford. I tried to see her as much as I could but it's a long way. She came down here once but she was a town girl and hated the moors, so looking back, I suppose our relationship was never as strong as it should have been. I was a fool, but it was one of the things I clung to when I was in the camp.'

He paused, lowering his eyes, and then took another deep breath before beginning afresh. 'Anyway, weeks passed and I didn't get my papers. The Americans had gone charging in expecting the North Koreans to run home at the very thought of American intervention. But the Yanks soon found themselves pinned down behind the Pusan Perimeter. That was when the UN forces joined in and Britain started sending out raw, virtually untrained conscripts. Thank God I wasn't among them. Thousands of them didn't make it. But then the tables turned and by the end of the September, the North Koreans were fleeing back home and it looked as though it was all over. My mother rejoiced and I was pretty relieved myself. I didn't fancy all that hand-to-hand fighting and sticking a knife or a bayonet into another human being, or having it done to me for that matter.' He paused again, shaking his head with bitter resignation. 'And then just as we were celebrating, that blessed General MacArthur decided that the North Korean Army should be totally crushed by a counter-invasion. And that was when I got my call-up papers.' He bit his lip, frowning as he turned to me. 'You don't knit, do you, Lily?'

'Knit?' My eyes opened wide with surprise. I thought we were discussing the Korean War, and now Daniel wanted to talk about knitting?

'My bloody leg's itching like crazy. I thought if you had a knitting needle—'

I tossed up my head with a laugh as the penny dropped. 'No, I don't. Besides, that can be dangerous. If you break the skin, you could set up an infection.'

'I'd be very careful,' he insisted glumly.

'I'm sure you would. But knitting was one thing I could never pick up. And even if I had, I'd hardly carry a pair of needles in my pocket, would I?'

'No, I guess not.'

He looked so crestfallen that I had to smile. 'Only another two and a half weeks and it'll be coming off,' I encouraged him. 'And anyway, you were about to tell me what happened when you were called up.'

'Ah.' His face hardened again and he shrugged his eyebrows. 'Well, at least by then they'd decided that we really should get some rudimentary training, so I had the benefit of two whole months of square-bashing and learning how to maintain guns – and how to shoot them, of course. The part I enjoyed – if I enjoyed any of it – was in the classroom, map-reading, tactics, that sort of thing. It was a complete mystery to a lot of them but to me it was like falling off a log, especially the map bit. And having spent most of my life out on the moor here, the endurance building was easy, too, even with a weighty back-pack. Some of the poor chaps really struggled, though, if they were unfit. And sometimes for those who weren't that tall, the packs could be bigger than they were. I made a good friend. Tommy.'

A wistful smile tugged at his mouth. Yes, I remembered him muttering about someone called Tommy when he was first brought in after the accident. It had sounded like some horrific memory and I mentally braced myself.

'Poor Tommy was so small you could hardly see him beneath his pack,' Daniel went on. 'I used to stuff whatever I could of his into mine. Highly illegal according to the military, but we were never caught.' He gave a wry chuckle and then his face stiffened again. 'A great kid was Tommy. Uneducated and with such a strong Geordie accent I could hardly understand a word he said at first. Just eighteen. He sort of slid under my wing somehow. And when we were only half-trained, we were suddenly told we were being shipped out because China had joined in the fight. Well, with that fool MacArthur blasting his way towards the Chinese border, what did he expect? An invitation to tea?'

His voice had vibrated with stinging sarcasm and I shuddered. Daniel could be very cutting and with his bitterness fuelled by such anger, I expected him to express himself in a fiery tirade. But I was beginning to understand how the pent-up emotions from his experiences had twisted the better side of his nature, and when he continued, I was surprised how calmly he spoke. So Edwin had been right. Writing and talking about it was definitely a release.

'By the time we arrived in mid-December, the Chinese had amassed a huge force on the border right under the Americans' noses and were hitting back hard. The Yanks simply hadn't been expecting it, and the Chinks were highly trained and experienced. But above all, they were fanatical. And they were driving southwards. They were used to hardship. I can't tell you how bloody cold it was. You couldn't think straight, and your jaw would freeze so that you couldn't speak. Our Army clothing simply wasn't up to it. Weapon-wise we were probably the best equipped of the British Forces, but the damned things jammed with the cold, and as for starting up an engine, well... The paddy fields, even the rivers, froze over. There were heavy snowstorms. It fell to thirty-six degrees below freezing at night. I was one of the few who didn't lose a toe or a finger to frostbite. It was too cold to sleep and our rations were so meagre, we were starving most of the time.'

I shivered at his description, the September sun suddenly seeming weak, and I pulled my cardigan more tightly about me. 'So you didn't see much fighting, then?'

'Oh, yes, we did,' he answered acidly, and I saw his mouth bunch into a contemptuous knot. 'The Chinese didn't have much in the way of big weapons, so they employed guerrilla tactics, set up ambushes. You lived on your nerves, never knowing when they might appear out of thin air. But there was fierce fighting as well, bigger battles like Happy Valley.' His shoulders sagged and he caught my gaze, his eyes dark and intense. 'And I killed right, left and centre. And, do you know what, I didn't care. None of us did, we were so numbed. It was kill or be killed. What was worse was that I'd been made second lieutenant, so I had to give orders. Make decisions over men's lives.'

He stopped, his face savage. I had no recollection of when I had so nearly been killed in the Blitz, but I remembered the air-raids later on. It had been terrifying, hearing, *feeling* the bombs exploding all around, knowing that any second could be our last. But we were innocent, our consciences clear, whereas thousands, millions of men had been forced into becoming murderers. Just like Daniel, out in a far-flung country that seemed to have nothing to do with life in good old Blighty.

I reached out and touched his hand. I could feel his fingers were tense. His eyes moved down, contemplating my small hand on his much larger one, and a faint smile flickered across his features. I'm sure my heart tore.

'You've heard of the Glorious Glosters?' he almost whispered.

My eyes stretched in amazement. Surely everyone knew about the Glosters as they had become known and the heroic stand they had made at the legendary Battle of Imjin in April 1951? 'You weren't one of them, were you?' I gasped.

'No. But I was at the Imjin. With the Northumberland Fusiliers.'

'Northumberland?'

'Yes. All that local pals stuff went out with the

First World War, although how I ended up with the Northumberlands, I don't quite know. But we were at Imjin, too. It's where I was captured.'

My heart was drumming nervously. There had been a slight tremor in Daniel's voice and he was staring out blindly across the moor. I held my tongue, not wanting to disturb his thoughts. I wasn't sure if he would go on, but after a short silence, he wet his lips and began again, his eyes still fixed on some point in the distance.

'We were stationed on four hills south of the Imjin, a couple of miles further east from where the Glosters were. We did a recce deep into no man's land and hardly met any resistance. And then just a few days later, another recce discovered that hoards of Chinese had crept up to the river. Twenty-seven sodding thousand of them apparently. Against seven hundred and fifty Glosters, a similar number of us, a Belgian battalion who held a tenuous position on the other side of the river, and some Royal Ulsters. That night, the Belgians were attacked and the Ulsters were sent to rescue them. It was a ferocious scramble with so many casualties… We could hear it and had been ordered to stand to, lying in silence in our slit trenches and gazing out into the dusk wondering what the hell was going on. And then we heard grenades and gunfire to the west, towards the Glosters' positions. And were ordered just to wait.

And then they started on us as well.'

He sucked in his cheeks, closing his eyes in despair. I didn't say anything. It was as if he was in his own world, relating each detail as he recalled it, and I thought it best not to interrupt.

'It was crazy. There was no way we could hold out against them. They just kept coming and coming, no matter how many of them we mowed down. All through the night. We were ordered to fall back, and even then, I lost half my men. By then, they *were* my men. Our lieutenant had been blown to pieces, bits of him scattered about... So as second lieutenant, I was in charge from then on. We fought every bit as bloody hard as the Glosters. Retreat was just as bad as fighting. It was utter carnage. We fought all through the next day and the second night. The Chinks were like ants, crawling up under heavy long-range fire and then jumping up, screaming and shouting at us as they attacked at close quarters. On the third day, we managed to hole up in new positions just listening to the Glosters' battle to the west. And there was nothing we could do to help. We kept being told that reinforcements were on their way. They weren't, of course. And we were almost out of ammo. Reduced to throwing rocks and bloody ration tins.'

He stopped again, breathing hard in his frustration, his jaw clenched. I couldn't think of anything to say, no comforting words, as I knew there weren't any. The horrors he had described had left me dumbstruck. It was unimaginable.

'It was the next day it happened.' His sharp tone after the short silence made me jump. 'Overnight the entire brigade had at long last received the order to withdraw. Too damned late, especially for the Glosters. A handful of them escaped but most of the survivors were taken prisoner. As for us, it was like one long bloody ambush, and after seventy-two hours of fighting, we could hardly walk let alone defend ourselves. Most of the Northumberlands got away, though. We reached the pass the Ulsters were holding, but Tommy and I stayed to help with the wounded. And then the Chinks were on us again. Tommy was hit in both legs. He lay there, screaming, while a Chink stood over him, pointing a pistol at his head. I shouted at the bastard and launched myself at him.'

He paused, and I glanced across at him, feeling sickened. There were tears running down his cheeks. I pretended not to see.

'Oh, I'm so sorry, Daniel,' I choked. 'I knew you'd been captured but I didn't realise you'd been through all that beforehand.'

'It was all one great bloody shambles,' he grated as if he hadn't heard me. 'But that was all I remembered. Tommy...I guess they shot him. When I came to, I had a shrapnel splinter in my leg and a thumping head from where I'd been knocked out. My hands were tied behind my back and there was a sharp pain when I tried to move them. *Barbed wire, mate*, a chap beside me said. The next thing, we were being herded forward. My leg was agony but I made myself walk. They didn't take non-walking wounded.'

He turned to me with such tortured ferocity in his eyes, the final tears trembling on his lashes. The meaning of his last words sank into my brain. I was stunned. I had lived through the terror of the Blitz, but I had never known anyone who had actually fought through the war. Except...Sidney. No wonder he had never wanted to talk about it. I felt churned up inside at what Daniel had told me, as if I shared his anger and resentment.

I was staring at him, mesmerised by his words, so that it scarcely registered with me when he suddenly reached for his crutches with desperate urgency.

'I can't do this, Lily,' he croaked as he stumbled to his feet. 'It's one thing writing it down, but quite another... I've never *told* anyone before. Not even Edwin. You're the only person I could... But if you want to know any more, you'll have to read the book. It doesn't get any better, mind. But...thank you for listening. And I'm sorry it was all... all...'

He didn't finish, but instead struggled to get his balance, adjusting his hold, clearly so upset he was unsteady. I rose up as if in a dream, planting myself in front of him, and lifting myself on tiptoe, brushed a gentle kiss on his wet cheek. I could taste the salt on my lips. He stared at me, his eyes the deepest purple I had ever seen, like glistening blackberries, and I watched as he angrily plonk, thudded away.

Chapter Twenty-Three

The sombre mood didn't last for long. I think we were both making an effort to be cheerful, and it was such a beautiful day with that clear golden light that can come over Dartmoor on occasion. That night I cooked a special meal that we ate by candlelight in the dining room. It was as if we were celebrating something, although neither of us knew what.

Daniel cracked open a bottle of wine that glowed ruby-red in the glasses. He seemed more relaxed than I had ever known him, as if talking to me about his experiences, however painful it had been, really had been a release for him. He almost seemed a different person, and certainly not a bit like the sullen ogre who had rescued me out on the moors. The handsome looks I had once scorned I realised with a start I was now finding deeply attractive. I could feel a tiny flame flickering inside me. I could scarcely believe it was there, and I wondered quite when it had begun. But it was definitely there, growing quietly and steadily like coals beginning to catch light in the grate.

But did Daniel feel anything similar? I doubted it. To him, I was just *Carrots*, and he had that way of drawing a defensive shield about himself so suddenly, I could never be sure of him. And I wasn't going to allow myself to be hurt again.

The week of my holiday passed so quickly, and I was enjoying it in a way I couldn't really explain. I spent a few hours each day typing up Daniel's book and finding myself increasingly drawn into it. He was writing it as a novel, reaching deep into the minds of the characters, and I had to steel myself against the brutal details he had left out when he had told me the bare facts that morning out on the terrace. I was fascinated by the way he described the anguished emotions of the hero, knowing it was really himself. It was as if he was secretly revealing his innermost self to me, craving my understanding, and I... Oh, yes, I was more than willing to listen. Sometimes I had to grit my teeth as I typed some of the horrific incidents, and often his appalling handwriting, which I was sometimes at a loss to decipher, was a welcome distraction.

Daniel's parents and his grandmother were coming down from London again on the Saturday, so on the Friday, our last evening alone, Daniel opened another bottle of wine and I cooked lamb chops in a tasty tomato and herb sauce from a recipe in an ancient handwritten book I found on the kitchen shelf. Daniel's Great Uncle Joshua from the farm at Peter Tavy had driven over one day bearing vegetables from his kitchen garden, and I cooked a selection with some Dauphinoise potatoes.

'This is delicious, Lily,' Daniel nodded appreciatively as he washed down a mouthful with some wine. 'I wouldn't have had anything like this in the hospital. I really am grateful to you, you know.'

He raised his glass to me, his mouth stretched in a broad smile. He looked so handsome in the candlelight, his hair falling waywardly over his forehead, and my heart turned over. It was all so romantic that if he had wanted to say anything more, surely now was the time? But he didn't, and I inwardly rebuked myself. Just as with Edwin, I was reading things that weren't there, and I wasn't going to make the same mistake twice. And anyway, how could I find myself falling for Daniel when I had resented him for so long? We had grown closer since his accident and would remain friends, but from now on I would concentrate on my independence, perhaps apply for the post of medical secretary I had seen advertised at Greenbank, Plymouth's big hospital, and then look for my flat.

'Oh, my darling boy, what a relief!' Sheila Pencarrow declared when the party arrived late on Saturday afternoon. 'You look so much better!'

'Son,' Adam nodded sombrely when Daniel was released from his mother's tight embrace.

'There you are, I told you he'd be fine.' Daniel's grandmother bustled through the front door, taking over the situation in her whirlwind manner. She kissed Daniel fleetingly on the cheek and then stopped to gaze about the spacious hall with a contented sigh. 'Oh, it's good to be back in the old place,' she muttered delightedly, and then suddenly catching sight of me, strode forward with her hand outstretched. 'And here's dear little Lily! Been looking after my grandson very well, I believe.'

One of her bright, lavender-blue eyes winked mischievously at me, and I felt myself colour. I had instantly warmed to her when I had met her before, but I prayed she wasn't going to make intimations at something that didn't exist between Daniel and me.

'I've done my best,' I smiled back. 'Did you have a good journey?'

'We certainly did, but it's a long one!' she replied, patting my hand which she linked through her arm as if I was a long-lost friend. 'We stopped at a lovely little pub for lunch—'

'You must be tired, Dad,' I heard Daniel say quietly as I was walked through to the kitchen. And for some reason, I was suddenly overwhelmed with envy, for I wanted to be able to say that to someone again. Dad.

'I'll put the kettle on,' I said to cover up. 'Tea or coffee, anyone?'

'Oh, coffee, dear, for me if you have the real thing. That instant stuff isn't bad, though, if it's all there is but I can't bear Camp.'

I had to smile to myself. Coffee in its various forms had once represented a bone of contention between Daniel and me. We had come a long way since then.

We sat around the kitchen table for a while sipping at our drinks, and then while Daniel's family went upstairs to unpack, I prepared the meal, a whole poached salmon I had driven into Tavistock to buy the previous day, followed by a lemon mousse. I noticed that Daniel's grandmother had changed into a somewhat old-fashioned evening dress when she came down, and I was reminded that she had been a child in this house in Victoria's reign when people in wealthy households changed for dinner. And her mother had been that glorious woman in the portrait.

'Let me help you wash up, Lily,' she said at the end of the meal, 'so that Daniel can have a nice long chat with his mum and dad.'

'No, it's all right, honestly. You might spoil your lovely dress.'

'This old thing? Oh, I can wear a pinny. Now you three go into the drawing room!' she ordered, ushering them through, and I saw Daniel cock a resigned eyebrow at me from the doorway.

'I see you use Quix,' Katherine Pencarrow observed five minutes later as I transported hot water in a jug from the range boiler to the sink. I had learnt that the hot water in the taps was supplied by lighting the separate stove in the boot room and that was only done when someone wanted a bath. 'Have you tried that new Squezy? I find it even better, and when you've cooked such a lovely meal, washing-up should be made as easy as possible. Where did you learn to cook so well?'

'Oh,' I shrugged as I lowered a pile of plates into the water, 'my mother taught me.'

'Ah.' She nodded, I guessed remembering that I had ended up living with William and Deborah because I had been orphaned. 'She taught you well, then.'

'Oh, I got those recipes out of an old notebook up on the shelf there.'

'Really?' Those amazing eyes opened wide and

she put down the tea-towel. 'You don't mean...?' She went across and picked up the book, handling it with loving reverence. 'Oh, my. Florrie Bennett's recipe book. I never imagined this would still be around! Florrie was my mother's nanny. She brought her up as my grandmother had died in childbirth. She was housekeeper, too, and eventually nanny to me and my brother and sister. Grand lady. Served our family till her dying day. Well I never,' she concluded, shaking her head over the yellowing pages.

I felt that little pang of jealousy again. 'It must be wonderful to have such a strong family history,' I said wistfully, feeling relaxed in the company of this bubbly elderly lady. 'I know so little about mine.'

'It can be a mixed blessing,' Katherine answered. 'Knowledge can bring sadness, too. My parents, well, neither of them lived to a ripe old age. It broke them both when my brother was killed in the Great War.' She bit her lip sadly, but a moment later, her eyes were dancing again. 'But they were marvellous people. When Philip and I had to get married because I was expecting Adam—'

I think I jerked with surprise. Shock almost and certainly amazement. The nearest I had come to physical contact with the opposite sex was dancing with Edwin – and when I had cried in Daniel's arms out in the darkness and the rain at my birthday party. Making love was something I had only ever dreamt about, something mysterious and wondrous you did for the first time on your wedding night. To learn that Katherine Pencarrow, or Warrington as her maiden name had been, had sinned back in Edwardian times, I calculated, was a stunning revelation. But my mother, too, had sinned with a man other than her husband and I had been the result. As I stood there with my hands plunged into the washing-up water, it seemed to bring it home to me. And I couldn't help remembering those minutes when Daniel had held me, his lean, hard body against mine. I really didn't hear what his granny said next.

'Well, that was another superb meal!' she pronounced after Sunday lunch the next day. I had procured a leg of lamb but instead of roasting it, I had braised it in red wine with fresh rosemary, a couple of Oxo cubes and some shallots. 'A very fitting feast to celebrate my announcement.'

She smiled around the table, her head held high with regal satisfaction as she drew everyone's surprised attention. Daniel's parents looked suitably baffled, but Daniel himself merely paused for a second with his hand in midair as he lifted his glass to his lips, met my eye across the table and then proceeded to sip at his wine. He knew his grandmother of old, his look said. He loved her dearly but he was used to her making dramatic gestures out of something trivial.

'I'm not getting any younger,' she began, and held her hand up at the chorus of protest. This was obviously going to have nothing to do with me, of course, but there was a gravity in her tone that intrigued me. 'I'm nearly seventy,' she insisted, 'and dear Marianne died at only sixty-two and my dear Philip at sixty-five. So we must think ahead. When I die, I don't want the tax man to get his hands on the family estate. Look at what happened when the Duke of Bedford died the other year. The family had to sell land and property to pay the death duties, and they'd had to do the self-same thing and sell off half of Tavistock back in 1911. I remember it quite clearly. I know we're hardly in the same league, but I don't want that to happen to you. Above all,' and here she paused to glance fondly about the room, 'I want this mausoleum to stay in the family. It's been the Warrington family home since 1876, and although the name has died out, the family lives on in you, Daniel, and I know you love the place, too. So although I can't promise to survive long enough to avoid death duties, I went to see my solicitor last week and now the London house belongs to you, Adam, and Daniel, Fencott Place is now yours.'

A stunned silence crackled through the air as she grinned at everyone in turn, her chest inflating and then falling with a heavy, ecstatic sigh as if she had achieved something momentous. Which I suppose she had.

Adam and Sheila broke out in profuse thanks.

'Well, you deserve it,' Katherine was saying somewhere in another world. 'You've both worked so hard for the family estate without having a home of your own and…'

Her words drifted over my head. I could only bite my lip as I gazed at Daniel. While the others were talking nineteen to the dozen, he was utterly silent, his face white as he stared, motionless, at his fingers which were still around the stem of his wine glass. I couldn't judge his reaction other than his being in total shock. And I wanted to go to him. Put my arms around him. But I found that I couldn't move either.

The hubbub of animated conversation quietened after several minutes, and all eyes turned on Daniel. He still hadn't moved and was so pale that I was becoming worried.

'Daniel?' his granny prompted.

I saw him swallow hard. 'Thank you,' he murmured at last.

'You, too, deserve it. You've worked so hard to restore the place—'

'But how am I supposed to afford the upkeep?' he suddenly blurted out distraughtly. 'There's so much still needs doing, and then there'll be so much maintenance, and I won't have time for that if I have to get a job to pay the bills. And you know I'm not like Dad. I'm not a financial wizard. I'm just...just... The place will fall into rack and ruin again.'

There was an awful moment when nobody moved. Daniel turned his head away, eyes lowered and his hand over his mouth. His shoulders were rigid and I felt my heart thump in my chest. Only I knew the horrendous details of what haunted him still, and he wasn't ready for this. Instinct led me to go round to him and take his other hand. It didn't occur to me to think how his family might interpret the gesture.

'It's all right, Daniel,' I muttered lamely.

'Have a cigarette, son,' Adam put in, shoving his packet of *Players* down the table in Daniel's direction. 'It'll calm you down.'

'No!' Daniel barked back with such ferocity that I jumped. 'You know how I feel about those things!'

But before anyone else could respond, Katherine was speaking brightly again. 'Oh, no need to worry about all that! I should have said. I've also made over some of my investments to you which will provide a modest income. But after that, it's up to you.' She paused, her head on one side. 'I'm sorry it was a bit of a shock and you not fully recovered from this dreadful accident yet, but it really was time I did it. I do have a suggestion, though.' She took a dramatic breath, her eyes twinkling. 'Tourism in the area is expanding. People are taking holidays here more and more. And they need somewhere decent to stay. This house – I remember it full of laughter and people – and I'd like to see it like that again. Its position is ideal! It'd make a superb hotel! So, what do you think?'

Daniel raised his head, his eyes stretched wide. He blinked, a slow swoop and lift of those long dark lashes, and continued to gaze silently at the old lady's smiling face.

'And Lily here could do the food,' she went on gaily. 'You're such an excellent cook, dear. And with your background, you could take charge of the admin. Daniel could do the maintenance and all that sort of thing, and guided walks across the moor. You'd make a wonderful team. In fact, if I may be so bold, you'd make a very handsome couple altogether!'

I'm sure my jaw must have dropped a mile. Katherine Pencarrow was outrageous! She was grinning at us now, her eyes sparkling with expectation. I really didn't know where to put my face. I couldn't look at Daniel, but out of the corner of my eye, I saw his cheeks, which a moment ago had been the colour of unfired clay, turn a deep scarlet.

'I'm not sure about that,' I heard him mumble in embarrassment. 'I can't think why Lily should want to work with me. She has a good career of her own.'

His voice had become stronger as he spoke, and I felt grateful as I couldn't think of a thing to say myself. But Daniel had successfully diverted the conversation away from our relationship and I managed to collect my thoughts sufficiently to chip in, 'I love my job at the hospital. I couldn't possibly imagine doing anything else.'

'Oh, pity!' Katherine gave a heartfelt sigh. 'But think about the hotel idea, Daniel. It might be just the ticket! Now, Lily dear, what sumptuous dessert have you prepared for us?'

'I'm sorry about Gran,' Daniel said a couple of hours later. 'She means well but…'

I had brought my car round to the front of the house and Adam had carried out my case and put it in the boot for me. I had said my goodbyes and everyone else had gone inside leaving Daniel and I facing each other rather awkwardly.

'She's certainly a bit of a character,' I smiled, attempting to pour oil on troubled water.

Daniel gave a wry grunt. 'She can be too outspoken at times. So my apologies once again. And thank you, Lily. For everything.'

'I've really enjoyed myself!' I assured him. 'It's been great staying up on the moor again. I hadn't realised how much I'd missed it.'

'Oh, well, that's good then.'

There was a tension between us, but it was very different from the antagonism we had once shared, and I recognised that I was reluctant to leave. 'Your family's only staying a week, aren't they? And your appointment at the clinic isn't until the following Friday?'

'I'm sure I can manage on my own the last few days. The ribs are settling down which has been the main problem, so I can hop around the kitchen if need be.'

'I don't like the sound of that. What if you slipped? Tell you what, I'll drive up and stay each night. Cook us a meal. Save you doing that, at least.'

I brightened at the idea and was disappointed when Daniel shook his head. 'I can't ask you to do that after all you've done already.'

'You're not asking, I'm offering. So that's settled, then. I'll come up next Sunday,' I said casually over my shoulder as I slid in behind the wheel. 'Take care of yourself!' And I started the engine.

I watched him in the mirror, a tall, lean, attractive figure balancing on his crutches, and then he was gone as I turned out of the drive. I felt strange and contemplative as I drove across the bleak moor into Princetown and then down to Tavistock. I was saddened that my week at Fencott Place was over because I really had revelled in the lovely old house and opening my curtains each morning to those stunning, far-reaching views. But I had become increasingly intrigued by Daniel's complex personality. I wanted to know more and I was determined to finish typing the book for him. I had lifted the lid and glimpsed at what had made him so dark and brooding, and now I wanted to understand him completely. I still wasn't sure how I really felt about him deep down, but it didn't really matter. He looked upon me as a friend, just as Edwin had done, so that was all there was to it.

'Hello, stranger!' Wendy greeted me buoyantly as I went into the Franfield's lounge. 'Oh, it's seemed so quiet without you! How's old grumpy guts?' she grinned as she linked her arm in mine and led me over to sit with her and Ian on the sofa.

'Much better and much happier to be home, of course!'

'That's good to hear,' Edwin nodded, 'although I'm going up to check him over tomorrow after surgery.' Sadie was obviously off-duty which only happened occasionally on a Sunday and they were sitting up at the table poring over estate agent details.

'You know, you shouldn't talk about Daniel like that,' I reprimanded Wendy mildly. 'He's been telling me some of what happened to him in Korea. He went through a terrible time, you know. It must take a lot of getting over. You see some of these things in films, but it isn't until you associate with someone who's actually been through it that you begin to realise.'

Beside me, Wendy pulled a long face. 'Yes, I suppose so. But it's been over three years now.'

'Maybe, but I don't think you could ever forget something like that.'

'Let's just pray it never happens again.'

I nodded gratefully at Edwin. That tiny barb pricked at me again, but it didn't go deep. In fact, I found myself smiling at him and Sadie as they planned their life together. They looked made for each other, and I felt happy for them.

'I'm gasping for a cuppa!' I announced, leaping up. 'Anyone else want one?'

'Mum's already down in the kitchen making one.'

'I'll pop down and lend her a hand, then!' I cried, and my heart already felt lighter.

Chapter Twenty-Four

'You're certainly looking well after your holiday, Lily!' Mrs Elderman commented the following morning. 'Did you have a good time looking after your friend?'

'Yes, I did actually. There wasn't *that* much to do and we sat out on the terrace whenever we could and it faces south. And I took the dog out every day so I got plenty of fresh air.'

'You look as though you've caught the sun. Very lucky lad, Mr Pencarrow, to have you to take care of him.'

I sat down at my desk and began to organise my work. Thank goodness Mrs Elderman hadn't referred to Daniel as my young man. He was far from that. But Mrs Elderman wasn't the type to pry, though she would be the very person to turn to in a crisis. I liked working with her and felt guilty that I had determined to ring up about that post as secretary at Greenbank. I wouldn't tell anyone, not even Wendy, unless I landed the job.

'Danny's getting along fine,' Edwin reported over dinner that evening. 'Complaining about his mother fussing over him, but then he always does. And do you know, his grandmother's made Fencott Place over to him?'

'Really?' three voices chorused around the table.

'Yes, I was there yesterday when she told him,' I volunteered. 'He was pretty shocked actually. It's a huge responsibility.'

'I suppose it is,' William agreed. 'I wonder what he'll do with it.'

I told them about the old lady's suggestion of turning it into a hotel, which led to a long discussion over the merits of increasing tourism in the area. While everyone speculated on the proposition, all I could think of was whether it was something Daniel would really want to do. Or whether he was the right person to do it.

The days at work passed by quickly in their usual busy and interesting way. I was offered an interview at Greenbank and managed to arrange the afternoon off without arousing suspicion. I found myself wanting to ring Daniel, but I had no excuse to do so. I just wanted to hear his voice. It was stupid. I needed him to mean nothing to me, but the fact was that I thought about him all the time. All the more reason for me to get away and start a new life.

But I couldn't spend that life running away from things, could I? I had wanted to escape from my hurt over Edwin, and now Daniel was unwittingly causing me the same pain. And then there was Sidney and the box in the attic. I knew that one day I would have to open it.

And so I didn't ring Daniel until the Friday evening. My fingers trembled as I dialled the familiar number and I told myself in vain not to get excited. I felt deflated when his father answered the phone.

'Hello, Mr Pencarrow, it's Lily,' I said, trying to hide my disappointment. 'I was just wondering how Daniel is. I promised to come up after you all leave to see if he needs anything.'

'We've decided to leave a day early, so we're going home tomorrow,' was the reply. 'Give me time to recover from the long drive before facing the fray on Monday.'

'Oh, right. Could you tell Daniel then, please, that I'll be up tomorrow afternoon? I work Saturday mornings, you see.'

'I will indeed. I'm sure he'll be pleased. Between you and me, I think he vastly prefers your company to ours. Thank you for all you've done for him.'

'It's been a pleasure. My regards to both Mrs Pencarrows. And I hope you have a good journey.'

'Thank you, Lily. I expect we'll meet you again soon.'

I heard the receiver click. Tomorrow. My heart gave a little jump and I fought to contain it. But it was beating a nervous tattoo as I let myself in the back door of Fencott Place the following afternoon.

'Daniel!' I called, and Trojan came flying up to me in a flurry of welcome.

'In the kitchen!' Daniel's voice answered.

I hurried forward. He was standing on his good leg, crutches propped against the cupboard next to him, as he poured hot water into the coffee filter jug. He smiled at me over his shoulder and I noticed how long his hair had grown, hiding the collar of his shirt. It was lovely, though, dark and glossy and with a slight wave to it.

'I heard the car,' he said by way of explanation, 'so I thought I'd surprise you. It's a bit tricky carrying a mug, though, so you'll have to do that bit. It's just good to be allowed to do something for myself, no matter how small,' he concluded grimly.

I had to smile. 'Oh, dear. Doesn't sound as if last week was very successful.'

'My mother can drive me mad. She still treats me like a little boy, telling me what to do all the time. She just can't accept that I'm a grown man with far more experience of life than she'll ever know.'

'She'll have to read your book, then.'

'I hope she doesn't. I think it'd upset her terribly. They don't know about it, and I'll publish it under a different name if it ever comes to it.'

'You don't mind *me* reading it,' I observed.

I saw his face twitch. 'But…you're different, Lily. You…seem to understand.'

Yes, I supposed I did. Was that meant to be a compliment or a fact? I felt hot under the collar and swiftly changed the subject.

'Have you thought any more about your grandmother's proposal?'

'The hotel idea, you mean? No, not really. I'm still trying to get used to the fact that I own this place now. Maybe I'll be able to think straight when I get this bloody thing off my leg next week. I've really had enough of it.'

'I expect you have,' I sympathised. 'The police haven't been back to you this week, have they, about the accident?'

He shook his head. 'The investigation's probably closed now. I'd love to get my hands on the devil, mind!'

Yes, so would I. But by the same token, Daniel's accident had brought us closer together. Although what was the point if it wasn't close *enough*? I was determined, though, that those last few evenings in Daniel's company would be pleasant ones even though I would deliberately keep my distance.

While I was out at work the following week, Daniel went on with the book, scrawling over untidy sheets of paper. I typed a few pages each evening, but I was way behind him, not that there was any hurry. I had roughly reached the same point he had described to me that morning out on the terrace, the point when he had been taken prisoner.

The first few days had apparently been the most terrifying, expecting to be executed at any moment. Name, rank and number. Second Lieutenant scarcely made you an officer, but the Chinese considered it must make you privy to secret information. And so Daniel had been interrogated, beaten, kicked on the shrapnel wound on his leg. In his own words, everything had been total bloody chaos and he had no knowledge whatsoever of any damned battle plans. It had been every man for himself in the end. His captors had finally been convinced when the lighted cigarette extracted no information from him.

I caught my breath, staring at the typewriter while a sickening wave of horror plunged down to my stomach. Dear God, yes. I remembered those curious marks among the dark hairs on Daniel's chest. Cigarette burns. The shock, the brutality of it, shook me rigid and I sat for five minutes unable to move. No wonder…no wonder Daniel didn't smoke and hated the fact that his father did. Neither William nor Edwin partook of the habit, believing that although tobacco might calm the nerves, it couldn't be good for the lungs despite these new filter-tips. But with Daniel it ran far deeper than that.

I was appalled, almost disbelieving that such evil could be real. But here was the proof. What inhuman, demonic barbarity could take place in the name of war. Such cold-blooded cruelty, even worse than the horrors of the battlefield if that were possible. And Daniel had hitherto kept all this to himself.

I struggled to pull myself together, but when I glanced down at the page again, the writing was blurred and I realised I was crying. Soft, silent tears. My own past, losing Ellen and Sidney and not knowing my true identity, paled into insignificance beside the darkness that had shadowed Daniel's soul. I felt ashamed, but it was a moment of revelation and it somehow gave me strength. But during my interview at Greenbank, the image of Daniel being tortured flashed across my thoughts, haunting me, and I had to ask them to repeat the question.

Daniel had truly expected to be shot when he had proved useless to the Chinese, but the band of prisoners had then been added to a stream of other captives who were being force-marched northward. The stretchered wounded were taken away, never to be seen again.

Those that could walk did so for weeks. The sudden arrival of spring after the bitter winter meant squelching mud caused by the melting of the deep snow and the coming of the rains. Paddy fields fertilised with human excrement stank revoltingly, and fearing his leg-wound would lead to a life-threatening infection, Daniel prayed that the anti-tetanus injections everyone had received back in Britain would at least save him from that painful end. Miraculously, though, the wound slowly healed as they trudged on through the sludge with almost nothing to eat and only hot water to drink. Many fell ill with dysentery and pneumonia – and didn't make it.

They eventually arrived at what was known as Camp One some two and a half months later, in June 1951. Hundreds of Americans had already died there during the winter, mainly from dysentery, beriberi or plain starvation. Now there was the heat, the flies, the lack of sanitation, to contend with, together with the fight against lice, bedbugs, malaria, other fevers, jaundice and the ubiquitous dysentery. A bowl of sorghum twice a day with an ounce or two of beans or turnips, and once a week the meat of one pig shared between six hundred men, was what they were expected to live on. No wonder Daniel considered himself lucky to have survived – and bore such deep emotional scars.

'Come on, Lily, you've done enough,' he said to me on the Thursday evening. 'It's getting late and we'll have to be up early if you're going to drop me off at William and Deborah's before you go to work. And Trojan will need a walk if he's going to be shut up here all day.'

His eyebrows were knitted with concern and I smiled up at him, stifling a yawn. 'You're right. Would you like some cocoa or something before we go to bed?'

It struck me that we were like an old married couple, incongruous when we were sharing such distressing experiences through the medium of the written word. But the next morning, Daniel resembled a young boy in his excitement at the prospect of being rid of the plaster-cast. I had to chuckle at the youthful glint in his eyes as we drove down into Tavistock.

I hurried back to the house at lunchtime, arriving at the gate the same time as Wendy was approaching from the other direction.

'Oh, it's great to have you back again!' she grinned as she danced me up the path. 'I've missed you so much! Do you want to come to the pictures with Ian and me tonight? And there's a dance at the Town Hall tomorrow.'

'I'm sure Ian won't want me tagging along.'

'Oh, he doesn't mind. And dances are the best places to meet people. We've got to get you a boyfriend somehow!'

'I'll come to the dance, then, if you really don't mind. But I promised I'd drive Daniel home this evening.'

Wendy pulled a face. 'He's jolly lucky to have had you to look after him. *I* would never have done. I hope he appreciates it.'

'Yes, he does. He's said so many a time. We get on pretty well, actually.'

'There's no accounting for taste!' Wendy teased as we went inside.

Everyone was eating sandwiches from a piled plate on the table in the lounge as the stairs down to the kitchen were very steep and could be dangerous for Daniel on his crutches. He beamed up at me as I sat down beside him. I thought I'd never seen him look so happy and boyish.

'I can't wait to get this thing off this afternoon and have a good old scratch!' he announced gleefully.

'Well, you just be careful,' Edwin warned. 'And no overdoing it too quickly.'

'Yes, doc,' Daniel answered with mock deference, and then burst out laughing. 'I don't think I'll be training for the Olympics quite yet!'

'The clinic starts at two o'clock and your appointment's not until three,' I reminded him. 'So if we're going to give you a lift to the hospital, you'll have to hang around.'

'I'll just have to sit and watch you, then, won't I?'

he murmured, throwing me a sideways glance that unnerved me.

In the event, Edwin lent him a book to read while he was waiting. 'As long as it's not *War and Peace*,' he said under his breath, the significance of which I was to discover later.

It was a joy, though, to witness the euphoria on his face when he and Edwin walked back down the corridor towards me after his appointment. His gait was a little slow and tentative and he was using the stick he'd been supplied with, but his eyes were gleaming.

'So how's the patient, Dr Franfield?' I asked eagerly.

'Fully mended,' Edwin declared. 'The muscles are a bit wasted as you'd expect, but do those exercises and you'll soon be as right as rain. And the ribs and everything else are fine, too.' He clapped Daniel on the shoulder. 'Take care, old chap. Now, I must see my next patient.'

Daniel sat down and waited until I could speak to him again. We had thought to bring his other shoe and a pair of trousers without the leg seam unpicked and I showed him where he could change.

'How does it feel?' I enquired when he reappeared.

'Wonderful!' he sighed blissfully. 'A bit weird, but wonderful! Ed said if I go carefully and use the stick,

I can walk back into town. I could do with calling in at the barber's, and Deborah will be there to let me back in to the house.'

'Are you sure?' I frowned. 'The hill's very steep.'

'I promise to be careful. And if I feel tired, I'll perch on someone's wall for a rest. So I'll see you later.' He paused, his eyes rakish. 'Carrots.'

I closed my lips as I tried not to laugh. Oh, yes! The old Daniel was back!

'What are you going to do now without the jeep?' I asked as I turned into the gravel drive at Fencott Place that evening and turned off the engine. 'You really need a car out here.'

'I'm sure I'll think of something. The insurance has paid up, not that the jeep was worth much. I suppose I could take the Bentley out of mothballs,' Daniel shrugged carelessly. 'Damned thing guzzles petrol, mind, and while this Suez business is going on—'

'Bentley?'

'Mmm. Apart from her half of the house which reverted to Gran – and which is mine now anyway – my great aunt left everything to me. Not that she had very much. The jeep, the Bentley and the necklace were about the sum total.'

'But…a Bentley—'

'Oh, it's very old. Been up on chocks in the barn

since the beginning of the war, more or less. But I could give the garage a ring and see if they could get it going again. After all, if I'm going to be a hotelier, I might need a decent car to pick people up in.'

I gave a half wry, half bemused grunt. 'You're a dark horse sometimes, Daniel! And will you, then? Become a hotelier?'

He puffed out his cheeks. 'I've absolutely no idea. I don't even know if I'd be allowed with the house being leasehold. And I don't know if I'd want to. Anyway, all I can think of just now is lighting the boiler in the boot room and when the water's hot enough, enjoying a long, long soak. Six weeks without a bath is long enough for anyone. I don't know how you've put up with me!'

He threw up his head with a full-throated laugh and I couldn't help giggling in return, pinching my nostrils between my forefinger and thumb.

'Didn't you notice me wearing a peg on my nose all the time?'

'Get away with you!' he grinned back, a carefree light in his eyes I had seldom seen before, making him more handsome than ever. My heart lurched, and I was glad to be able to say, 'I think you'll have to take Trojan for a walk first. I can hear him barking his head off.'

'Yes, so can I. Will you come with us?'

'I'd love to. But I must get back after that. With

the evenings drawing in, I don't want to be driving across the moor in the dark.'

Daniel's face became serious again. 'No. I wouldn't want the same thing happening to you as did to me. And that was in the middle of the afternoon. So go carefully, won't you, Lily?'

His expression took on its usual intensity, and for a moment, I hoped… But he said nothing more and then got out of the car. I followed, deliberately tamping down my emotions. Just good friends. Perhaps it was best that way.

Chapter Twenty-Five

'The band's great, isn't it, Lily?' Wendy called as she swept past me in Ian's arms. 'You having a good time?'

I had no chance to reply as she was whisked on up the dance floor, so I nodded vigorously, my face in an enthusiastic grin. I dropped breathlessly into my chair, exhausted from three strenuous dances with a quite amenable chap who had been paying me particular attention but had now gone off to play the field. I didn't mind as I sipped my cooling drink. If I was offered the job and moved away from Tavistock, there was little point in developing a relationship with someone in the town.

Besides, as I had danced with the fellow, I couldn't help wishing that it was Daniel who had been holding me, one hand resting in the small of my back and the other joined with mine. I had never known Daniel to dance at any of Deborah's parties, so I wasn't sure he knew how. He always lounged against a wall, quietly observing the frivolities but never joining in as if he couldn't let go of his inner tensions. And as I was the only person in the world to have read his book, I was also the only one who could really understand.

But it seemed he still didn't want to get too close to another human being. I had wanted to go up to Fencott Place on the Sunday to do some more typing. I was totally absorbed in the story, not just wanting to find out more of what had happened to Daniel but because I admired the way he wrote and depicted all the other characters as well. But he had rejected my offer, saying I had done enough for him already. So I had insisted on taking the next few chapters with me and apart from helping with the Sunday dinner and doing my ironing, I shut myself away in Deborah's office with her typewriter.

Once arrived in Camp One, the captives had been segregated according to rank, and Daniel had found himself with other junior officers, some from the captured Glosters but, as everywhere, they were far outnumbered by the Americans. The Chinese programme of *re-education* began at once, a systematic attempt to convert these western capitalists to communism. Half of the four hours of daily lectures was conducted by a handful of English-speaking Chinese trying to convince the allies of how *backward and oppressed* they were, and the other half was in Chinese of which nobody understood a word. Yet if any man looked bored or as if he wasn't paying attention, he was beaten and kicked until he looked visibly interested again. It was laughable, Daniel had written. They were told that the Chinese people welcomed discussion, but that if any prisoner stubbornly refused to accept that communism was the only correct philosophy, he would be punished.

Daniel had been among the hecklers during the lectures. I smiled grimly to myself. I could just imagine it. He wasn't the sort to be cowed by authority. Resistance was higher among the British and they paid for it. It wasn't long before, along with others, he was sentenced to solitary confinement in jail, little wooden boxes so small a man couldn't lie down properly. What with the sweltering heat, being handcuffed, the crawling lice and appalling diet, it was pure hell. Some didn't survive this barbaric treatment, and when Daniel was released after two months, he swore he'd never commit another crime.

Meanwhile, conditions at the camp had improved minimally. Sanitation was a little better as was the food, and a hospital was established for the many who were still falling ill, although medicine was virtually non-existent. To top it all, as the prisoners' uniforms disintegrated, they were replaced with

the Chinese yellow, quilted suits. It was utterly
humiliating but, with winter coming on, they had
no choice. The diet was so disgusting that many, the
Americans in particular, lost the desire to eat and
died of starvation. It was easier to die than to live.

One thing that helped raise morale was that they
were allowed to play football. Those that were fit
enough played every day. It became an obsession
and Daniel, or the character in his book, found it
was a way of releasing his frustration, although in
time, the game became like some torturing ritual.

I sat back from the typewriter with a sigh. So
that was why Daniel had refused so curtly to play
for the Princetown team. Football reminded him
too painfully of his time in captivity. Yes, I could
understand that.

The memory of when I had met him in Bolts sent
my thoughts back to when I had lived with Sidney in
Princetown. Of how the antagonism between Sidney
and me had turned to an odd sort of friendship. But
there were so many secrets, so many unanswered
questions. Perhaps the answers were in that box.

I broke out in a hot sweat. I had encouraged
Daniel to open up his heart, face his demons, when
I didn't have the guts to face my own. My heart
began to beat nervously. How could I be a whole
person again unless I learnt all that I could about my
past? Gloria had said I would know when the time

was right. Well, I had friends now to support me, an adopted family, and anything I discovered would never change that. So perhaps...

I gathered up the chapters of Daniel's book and took them up to my room. When I came back down, Wendy and Ian were just coming in from a walk, followed a few minutes later by Edwin who had been to the hospital to check on a patient.

'I'll make some tea now you're all back,' Deborah announced, rising from the sofa.

'I'll come and help,' I offered, and as I reached the door, I turned back to William and said casually, 'You know that box of Sidney's effects you put in the loft for me? Well, would you mind getting it down again some time, please? I'd like to go through it properly now.'

'This is quite exciting, isn't it? Like going on an adventure!'

It was Tuesday evening and Wendy and I were sitting cross-legged on the rug in my bedroom with the box in front of us. It wasn't very big and I had always kept all the photographs from it in my drawer with one of my mother and another of my brothers in frames on my bedside table. But there were lots of other papers to go through and, of course, the diary. While Wendy's face was aglow with curiosity, I was struggling to summon up the courage to begin.

'I'm not sure about that,' I answered, biting my lip. 'I'm really nervous about what I might find. And I think it's sad that Sidney isn't around to explain everything.'

Wendy's expression changed to one of infinite compassion. 'But if he'd still been alive, he might never have told you anything at all. And anyway, until you look, you won't know if there's anything in this box.'

Yes, I'd been telling myself the same thing for the past two and a half years. And so, with trembling hands, I lifted the lid. That distinctive, musty smell of old papers, especially ones stored in a cold loft, rose into my nostrils. This was it. But dear Wendy, who had become like a sister to me, was there to share the moment.

'These were his payslips,' I said, taking out the bundle I had previously bound with an elastic band that was now in danger of perishing. 'He was paid in cash but we lived so frugally, I'm sure he couldn't have spent it all and I couldn't find anything about a bank or a savings account. You wouldn't mind going through them again, would you, in case I missed anything? And there's all sorts of bits of loose papers in the bottom of the box.'

'Righty-ho,' Wendy smiled back. 'It's a bit like being a detective. Who do you fancy being, Maigret or Poirot? Or how about Sherlock Holmes and Dr

Watson? No, maybe not them. I always think Holmes treats his poor friend like an idiot.'

I chuckled, grateful that I had Wendy to shore up my courage. So I took out the diary and began to read from the beginning. The entries were sporadic, dating from the end of the war. The first few pages contained nothing of interest, and then the word *mother-in-law* jumped out at me, and my heart began to race.

I received a letter from my mother-in-law today. It was stupid of me to have told her my address. I could have come back from the war and disappeared, but I suppose I felt I should make some contact. After all, she still thinks the girl is mine, or at least I believe she does. Cynthia swore that she had never told her mother the truth, although how the pair of us are supposed to have produced a redhead, I don't know. Perhaps the old lady put it down to some throw-back. You do hear of such things. Sometimes I've even tried to make myself believe it, that the child was mine. But Cynthia had worked it out that it couldn't possibly be. At least she was honest in that. It was when the company had sent me up north for those few weeks that she had her fling with Kevin. My own friend! Only it wasn't a fling. They'd been in love for years, she said, but they'd only slept together that one time when I was away and then she had found she was pregnant. So there is no doubt that the girl is Kevin's.

Should I tell Ellen? I've asked myself that question for years. But it would only muddy the waters and ruin her devotion to Cynthia's memory. And it would be admitting to my failure as a husband. I couldn't make her happy. I was too strict, she said, too religious. But what does it matter? She is dead and gone, and I was too proud to forgive her. But I cannot accept the child. Ellen and John, God rest his soul, had already adopted her, so it should remain that way. There is no reason why Lily should know any of this. I shall write to Ellen and tell her I want nothing more to do with them. She will think it strange, but she never liked me and I'm sure will be only too pleased to see the back of me. And then I will move on. Forgive me, Lord, if you do not approve, but at this moment, I believe it is the right thing to do.

That was the end of the entry and I sat back to take stock. It hadn't really told me anything I didn't already know, except that my father's Christian name was Kevin. I wondered what he looked like, some sort of redhead by all accounts. And it was as I had hoped: not some sordid, one-night stand, but a love that had gone on for years. But Kevin had been Sidney's friend, and I felt sorry for that. It must be hard to take such betrayal, worse than if he'd been a stranger. But Sidney was being completely honest with himself in his diary, as if his conscience was speaking directly to his God.

I was beginning to think that, although I was seeing into Sidney's mind, the diary might not reveal very much at all. It made me feel more relaxed about the whole affair as I went to read on. Beside me, Wendy had gone through all the payslips and shook her head. She leant forward to reach into the box again, accidentally knocking the diary, and the newspaper cuttings I had found before fell out onto the rug.

'Oh, sorry, Lily,' Wendy apologised as she retrieved them. 'Shall I look at these for you?'

'Yes, do,' I said carelessly, eager now to get back to the diary.

There was a gap in the dates and Sidney had obviously been busy moving. The next entry was about a month later.

I haven't found a job yet. I don't want to go back to insurance but I don't know what I want to do instead. I still have money from my Army pay, though. Perhaps I should have stayed on in the forces like Kevin did.

Well, that was another snippet of new information. My father was still in the Army, or at least had been at that date. I was feeling far less anxious and increasingly intrigued.

I have completely broken with Ellen Hayes now.

I shan't give her my new address. But one thing has been troubling me. All those years ago, I led Kevin to believe that his daughter died in the raid with her mother. I wonder now if I shouldn't try to find him and tell him the truth. Confess my sin and make amends. I believe his ship is based at Devonport. Perhaps I should drive down and see if there is any way I can trace him. But I don't know if I can face him.

I frowned, and my heart was gripped with some horrible sense of foreboding. My real father believed I was dead! How cruel had Sidney been to let him think that! It was vengeful. So my father had stayed on in the Navy, not the Army. Was that why Sidney had come down from London to Devon? But why had he stayed in the area? And there was another thing. Sidney had told me in no uncertain terms that he didn't drive, and yet...?

I glanced at Wendy and she shrugged at the cuttings.

'Nothing much,' she told me dismissively. 'Some chap was knocked down by a hit and run driver. Seems the culprit was never found.'

'A bit like the devil who forced Daniel off the road,' I commented bitterly. 'The diary's getting interesting, though. You can read it in a minute. Have a look at those other bits and pieces if you want.'

I hadn't explained what I had found. It didn't all make sense yet, like piecing together a jigsaw. My eyes skimmed over the next few entries. Sidney had come down to Plymouth and found digs in the Devonport area so that he would be near the Royal Navy Dockyards. Nothing earth-shattering there, then. I turned over several pages before there was any further reference to my father.

At long last his ship has come in. Three months I've waited and now my patience has been rewarded. Of course, I wasn't sure it was still his ship. We haven't been in contact since I told him about Cynthia and the lie over the girl. Forgive me, Lord, for I was weak when I sinned. I only heard about him through a mutual acquaintance who had no idea what had passed between us. But today I saw him.

My attic room has a good view down over the river and when I saw a frigate coming up the Hamoaze, I fetched my binoculars. I couldn't believe it when I read the name. It was as if I was being called to Judgement. I hurried down to the dockyard gate the sailors seem to use, and waited. Almost all day. But a crew doesn't just abandon its ship when it docks. There are things to do, and when leave comes, it is usually in shifts. I have no way of knowing. Sailors came and went, whether from the ship or not, I couldn't say. Kevin is some sort of petty officer so he could remain on board for days, and the ship could be in port for weeks.

I was about to give up, go home for dinner with my landlady and return later. I would have to keep coming back for as long as it took. Maybe I would never see him and the ship would sail again. I vowed that if that happened, God would be telling me something and I would return to London and forget the past. Begin afresh. But then I saw him. I stood on the corner, hiding behind my newspaper. He walked right past me. And I couldn't do it. I couldn't admit to my shame, not even to this man I had wronged. Because he had done me the greater wrong. So I followed him and discovered where he lives when he is in port. I will go back there tomorrow and observe him, and perhaps God will give me the strength.

'Lily, are you all right?' Wendy's voice cut through my concentration. 'You've gone as white as a sheet.'

I put up my hand. I felt as if I was drowning in some deluge of compulsion. Something momentous was about to be revealed to me, I was sure. I was being rent asunder. Part of me wanted to turn my back on the whole affair, follow that instinct that had made me hesitate for so long. And yet the other part of me was being drawn helplessly into some swirling vortex. There was no going back now. I *had* to know, and turned the page.

I went back today, in the car this time. I parked

at the end of the road and watched. No one came or went, so I gather he lives alone. Eventually he came out at lunchtime. I followed on foot. He went to a pub, had a beer and a sandwich and then did some shopping at a grocer's before going home. I, too, came home to decide what to do. He lives a normal, carefree life. He has a career. While I have nothing but bitterness. Because of him, I don't even have my own dignity. It isn't right! He ruined my life and he is the one who should suffer and pay for it, not me. I...

The sentence was unfinished and there was a line left blank. When the handwriting started again, it was totally different, shaky, wild and uncontrolled as if Sidney had been in the grip of some fevered dementia. As my eyes tried to decipher the scribbled letters, I felt a coldness invade the very core of my being.

Dear God, what have I done? It was the Demon Drink! I should not have opened that bottle of whisky, but it lured me like the Spirit of Satan and I could not resist. The more I drank, the more my wrath took hold of me. It grew inside until the Devil Himself appeared to me, urging me on. I took the car and waited in his street. It was dark and raining and my soul fought with Beelzebub. He placed a curse on me, invoking all that is evil against me, and I was powerless. And when he stepped out into the silent street, the Devil took the wheel from my hands. Oh, dear Lord, why did You not come to me in my moment of need and save me from this terrible thing that I have done? Do anything You like with me now, make me suffer every day of my life so that I shall have achieved atonement when I come to you on the Day of Judgement.

I heard myself cry out, a thin squeal of appalled disbelief. Wendy gasped beside me but I didn't catch what she said as I snatched up the newspaper cuttings. But I couldn't read them my hands were trembling so violently and my vision blurred as the room spun around me.

'Was…was he…a sailor?' I spluttered in despair.

'Who? The man who was knocked down, do you mean?' Wendy answered incredulously. 'Well, yes. Some sort of naval officer, anyway. How did you know?'

'Oh, my God!' My throat had closed so that I was struggling to breathe and my voice had come out in a shrill squeak. 'He was…my father, and Sidney ran him over! Deliberately!'

'What!'

'Yes, it's all here! Look!'

'What on earth's the matter? We could hear you two from downstairs!'

'Oh, Mum, Lily's had a dreadful shock! It really is awful!'

A few minutes later, I was sitting on the sofa downstairs in the lounge, Wendy on one side, Deborah on the other, each with one arm around me. William had pressed a small glass of brandy into my hands, telling me to sip it very slowly, and Edwin squatted on his haunches in front of me, his face anxious.

'I just can't believe it,' I stammered, swinging my head from side to side. I was calmer now, surrounded by these good people who had become my family. How ever could I have thought of leaving them? 'Sidney killed my real father,' I told them.

'No, he wasn't killed, it says here,' William said as he looked up from studying the cuttings. 'Badly injured and expected to remain crippled. But alive.'

I lifted my head. 'Are...are you sure?'

'It's what it says here.'

'So...so...'

Thoughts were spiralling frenziedly in my brain, snatches of things Sidney had said, his religious verve, his condemnation of alcohol. It began to make sense now. I felt giddy, just couldn't take in the enormity of what I had discovered. I had lived with Sidney all that time. Had my life been in danger, too? It was a vile, sickening thought.

'I think you should wash that down with some nice hot cocoa,' William advised solemnly. 'And perhaps a light sedative when you go to bed to help you sleep.'

But it wasn't a pill I wanted that night. Despite everyone's kindness and understanding, through the fog of horror, what I really craved was the comfort of the one person who wasn't there.

Chapter Twenty-Six

I still had a key to the back door of Fencott Place but when I drove up on Saturday afternoon, I didn't feel it was right to use it. I wasn't staying there any more and Daniel was mobile again and perfectly able to open the front door to me. So I knocked loudly and waited under the portico while Trojan barked his welcome from inside.

As I had driven up onto the moor, that sense of timelessness, of the insignificance of my own problems in the scheme of the universe, invaded and soothed my troubled spirit as it always did. It was an amazingly still and balmy day for the third week of October, the sun smiling down warmly from an almost cloudless powder-blue sky. My nerves had been jangling on edge ever since I had started to read the diary on Tuesday evening, but Dartmoor was working its healing magic on me.

Daniel knew about the shocking revelation. I had rung him on Wednesday with the excuse of asking how he was getting on and that I had typed up another chunk of his book and would bring it up on Saturday. And then I had told him the bare bones of what Wendy and I had discovered the previous evening. There was silence at the other end of the phone when I finished, so I had to ask if he was still there.

'I was just thinking what a dreadful shock for you,' he replied ponderingly. 'You might have been looking for answers, but you weren't expecting that.'

He hadn't gushed over with words of comfort, and I was grateful. It wasn't sympathy I wanted. I needed someone to *share* my feelings with. Daniel had been through so much himself and I instinctively knew he would understand.

When he opened the door, he was smiling in that enigmatic way of his that had once unnerved me but was now strangely reassuring. He was looking particularly attractive in a blue shirt unfastened at the collar and tucked into some old cords at his slender waist. I had to pull myself back. He didn't feel the same way about me as I did about him. At least it diverted my thoughts away from my other problems for a few seconds.

'Come on in, Carrots,' he said, raising a cautious

eyebrow. He was testing my mood, but I no longer minded being called by the nickname I had once hated. Now it felt familiar and secure. 'Come through to the kitchen. Kettle's on the go.'

'You managing all right?' I asked as I crossed the hall. 'How's the leg?'

'Fine, thanks. The muscles ached a bit at first but I've been taking Trojan for long walks without any trouble.' He chuckled as the dog pushed his snout into my hand demanding some attention. 'He misses you.'

'I miss him, too,' I answered, ruffling my hand in the thick fur underneath Trojan's ear, a spot he loved. He pushed against me, tipping his head endearingly while I wondered if Daniel had missed me as well.

'You can come whenever you like,' he said quietly, throwing me a sideways look as he poured coffee into two mugs. 'You're always welcome.'

'Thank you,' I smiled in response, setting the manuscript on the table. 'Here's the next consignment of the book.' I paused, feeling I should say something about it but not sure what. 'You...you had a pretty hard time of it, didn't you?' I said lamely in the end. 'No wonder you still have nightmares about it.'

'It's certainly not something I'm ever likely to forget. But it does seem to be helping me to come to terms with it, writing it down. And I really appreciate you typing it up for me. You don't have to go on with it, though, you know. You sound as if you've enough problems of your own. I was sitting in the drawing room. It's really warm in there with the sun. Shall we?'

'Mmm, yes.'

I followed him back through the hall, noticing that he was indeed walking normally again. The sun was blazing into the drawing room through the French doors, one of which was wide open. It felt like summer. Daniel put both mugs on the coffee table in front of one of the sofas and so I sat down next to him.

'You'd better tell me all about it,' he invited, sitting back as if he was preparing to listen for hours.

I drew in a great long breath through my nostrils and released it in a sharp sigh. 'I still can't believe it,' I began with a shake of my head. 'Sidney tracked down my real father to admit to him that he'd lied about my being dead. He came to do the right thing, and then in a jealous rage—'

'A drunken rage, didn't you say?'

'Well, both really. But certainly in a moment of madness, he totally lost his reason and deliberately ran my father over. He could so easily have killed him!'

'He survived then, your father?'

'I think so, yes. Although it suggested in the paper that he was likely to be permanently crippled. I've no idea what happened to him afterwards.'

I watched as Daniel reached forward for his drink, lips pursed thoughtfully. 'And all this was in the diary?'

'Yes. It was weird. Like a sort of confession. Sidney was deeply religious. His father was a Methodist preacher, strict, almost fanatical, I think, and it rubbed off on Sidney. In the diary, it's sometimes really as if he's talking to God.'

'Religion can have a lot to answer for.'

'But without the diary, I'd never have known the truth. It explains so much. Why Sidney was so angry when I suggested he got a car. I suppose he never trusted himself to drive again. And why he was teetotal. He nearly killed me once when he smelt alcohol on my breath. I'd only had a mouthful and it was beer. It was horrible.'

Daniel laughed softly and I realised I was pulling a face. It was a brief diversion before Daniel's expression became serious again.

'It was an explanation you could have done without, though.'

I nodded. 'Yes, I suppose so. But I understand even more now why he hated me so much at first. But it's all, I don't know...' I paused, trying to think of how to express the turmoil of my feelings while Daniel waited patiently. 'I'd come to accept that I wasn't Sidney's daughter after all,' I began again after a few moments. 'But I lived with him for over a year, never knowing that because of me, he nearly killed my real father. It's pretty hard to take.'

'And even though it wasn't your fault, you feel that it was. You feel as if you're treading water and your feet are trying to find the bottom, only they can't.'

His voice was low, intense, his eyes trained on the mug in his hand, and I knew he understood in a way nobody else did. Everyone had been so kind, supporting me and saying that it didn't matter what had happened in the past, I was still the same person they loved. They meant it, of course, but the fact was that, inside, I could never be the same. And only Daniel knew exactly how that felt.

'I feel lost,' I croaked, the words scraping in my throat. 'Incomplete.'

'Yes, I know.'

It was a simple statement of fact. Yes, he *did* know. And suddenly the surge of locked up emotion broke open and there was no stopping it. I knew I was going to cry. Through my tear-blurred vision, I saw Daniel swiftly put down his coffee and for the second time in a few months, I found myself sobbing against his chest. He felt warm and strong and safe, and I didn't hold back. I think I cried for everything that had happened to me over the past few years, from Ellen's death to the devastating revelation in the diary. Daniel held me, not saying a word, not uttering any soothing inanities, but knowing the hurt would only pass in its own good time. And when my tears finally dried, I still lay against him on the sofa, quietly and calmly, and talking into his shirt.

'I've read the rest of the diary since,' I said in a small but steady voice. 'He couldn't find the courage to give himself up or to face the world again. He was riddled with guilt. So he cut himself off, living a life as close to being a recluse as he could. He got the job at Merrivale and living in the isolated cottage at Foggintor was ideal. It was a sort of self-imposed penance. I think he only wrote to Ellen again then as a kind of self-torture. To increase his fear of being discovered. And the real reason he agreed that I could go and live with him wasn't that he felt it was his duty, like he said. Although, of course, at that point he hadn't told me I wasn't his daughter. No. The real reason was that he believed it was his punishment sent by God. Every time he looked at me, he was reminded of what he'd done. I was his hair shirt. His purgatory. The way to pay for his sin and purify his soul. It was no wonder he despised me so much. You know, when I read the first part of the diary, I was really scared. If he could have done that to my father, I wondered if my own life had been in danger. But when I read on, I don't think it was. But to think that I befriended him in the end. Even felt sorry for him in an odd sort of way. And all along, I didn't know that he'd tried to kill my father and all because of me.'

There. I'd said it. What had been pressing on me like a huge, dark cloud. Now it was out in the open.

Daniel had been listening in silence and without moving except for the steady rise and fall of his chest which felt solid and comforting. His left arm was around me and now it merely tightened slightly.

'It doesn't matter, does it, what anyone says? What you tell yourself? You still *feel* guilty. I tried to stop them shooting Tommy, but I couldn't. It wasn't my fault, but I still blame myself.'

I considered for a moment, and then sat up, meeting Daniel's brooding eyes that had turned almost cobalt with emotion.

'We're two of a kind, really, aren't we?' I suggested in a near whisper.

It made him smile. 'If you mean we've both let our coffee get cold, then, yes. I'll make some more. You stay here. I won't be a minute.'

I waited in the silent room that was now so familiar to me. My eyes took in its elegance again, the huge fire place, the worn upholstery, the fine wooden furniture chosen by the beautiful woman in the portrait. And Daniel owned it all. It was part of him, what he was, and I loved it the more for it.

'What are you going to do about it then?' he asked when we were sipping at some fresh hot coffee.

'Do?' I questioned him in surprise. 'There's nothing to do, is there?'

He hesitated, fixing me with his eyes. 'Well, you could try and trace your father. If you wanted to, that is.'

I blinked at him pensively. The idea had been too enormous to contemplate before. 'I don't know. It would be a terrible shock to whoever he is. He thinks I'm dead, and he might not be too happy to learn that it's because of me that he's in a wheelchair. Or at least, so we believe. He could hate me.'

'No one could hate you, Lily.'

His eyes bore into mine, sending a shiver down my spine. I chose to ignore it. We were just friends.

'Anyway,' I said, tossing my head dismissively, 'I've nothing to go on. I don't even know his full name. It wasn't in the newspaper cuttings and Sidney just refers to him as Kevin. And it was ten years ago. I expect he was taken to Greenbank Hospital after the accident, but they wouldn't divulge any details even if they still had it on record. And who knows what might have happened later. He might have moved away or died since then.'

'Or maybe not. The Navy would have records of what happened at the time, but there again, they probably wouldn't release any information.

Pity Ed's Uncle Michael was Merchant rather than Royal Navy, or he might have been able to find out something. But what about Uncle Artie?' Daniel suggested with sudden inspiration. 'He's lived in Plymouth all his adult life and knows loads of people. I remember he had a cleaner once. One of those busy-body types who had to know everybody's business. That was the sort of incident she'd have relished. She'd have gone to the ends of the earth to find out all the details. She had a lifetime of working for people all over the city. She was pretty elderly when she gave up working, but if she's still alive, I bet you she'd remember something about it.'

'Do you think so? Oo...oh,' I wondered, biting my bottom lip and feeling as if I was standing on my head. 'Uncle Artie's coming to dinner tomorrow.'

'Then you could ask him.' And then Daniel pulled in his chin. 'If you want.'

I felt my heartbeat quicken. I was all tangled up inside like a piece of knotted string. Could I ever unravel it? But I was rescued by Trojan bounding up to us with his lead hopefully in his mouth and his eyes gazing balefully up at us.

Daniel laughed and stood up. 'Looks like it's walkie time. Will you come with us, or do you need to get back?'

'No, I'd love to come with you!' I replied, bursting with enthusiasm. 'A walk on the moor is just what I need. My wellies are in the boot of the car.'

'Still haven't bought yourself some proper walking boots, then?' His tone was gruff, but I could see the teasing light in his eyes.

'No, not yet,' I grinned back. 'But I must.' I didn't add that as I had thought I might be moving away, I probably wouldn't need any boots. But I'd learnt the previous day that I hadn't got the job at Greenbank. And in a way, I was glad. What I needed now was normality, not a new life.

We set out westward to the area I myself knew fairly well by now. The Devonport Leat stretched along the side of a gently sloping hill with granite slabs set across at intervals to act as footbridges. There were numerous streams and springs that met up to form Newleycombe Lake, the brook that ran into the top of Burrator Reservoir, and littered everywhere were the curious remains of disused tin workings. It was a bleak and savage part of the moor, but beautiful in its isolation as the sun was setting in a glorious, orange-flamed ball of fire.

'Let's go over to the stone row. You know, where we met,' Daniel suggested after a while. 'We can make a circular walk and come back along the track.'

I frowned at him dubiously. 'That's quite a long way and it'll be dark soon. And what about your leg?'

'My leg's fine. And I've got a torch,' he said,

slapping the pocket of the jacket he'd put on over his shirt. 'Besides, it's going to be a full moon and the sky's perfectly clear.'

'Well,' I hesitated, but I felt safe with Daniel and his intimate knowledge of the terrain. It would be quite an adventure to be out on the moor at night. I used to have that short walk in the dark from King Tor Halt to Foggintor when I came home from work on the train during that first winter. I used to follow the path and came to appreciate those few minutes' solitude before facing Sidney. So to be out in a remote region of the moor in the dark could be quite inspiring. 'All right,' I gave in. 'As long as you don't get us lost.'

He raised a mildly affronted eyebrow but said nothing as we changed direction. The sun had disappeared and the sky almost instantly deepened to a murky grey, the autumn air suddenly cool and damp. I crossed my arms tightly over my chest, glad that I had worn slacks and a thick cardigan over my blouse when I had driven up earlier that afternoon.

I kept by Daniel's side as we crossed the uneven, rising ground. We had both slowed down with the uphill climb and the dusk was making it more difficult to see where we were stepping. The usual sounds of the moor, the stonechats and wheatears chattering among the rocks, buzzards mewing overhead or the occasional cry of a curlew, ceased abruptly, and we

were plunged into a shadowy, fading twilight. I
don't think I'd ever smelt the peat so strongly as I
did then in the evening damp, and when I glanced
over my shoulder, a fragile, pearly mist was rising in
the little valley we had left behind.

Daniel had been right. A full moon was rising
towards its zenith, its silvery incandescence more
radiant as the sky deepened to sapphire velvet
scattered with twinkling stars. It was breath-taking,
eerie, mysterious. And I wouldn't have missed it for
the world.

Daniel suddenly stopped and put a restraining
hand on my arm. 'Trojan, heel!' he commanded in
a hoarse whisper, and the dog obediently came to
Daniel's side and he clipped on the lead. 'Look!'
he grated, and jerked his head to the long, low dip
in front of us. 'There's something going on down
there.'

I squinted into the moonlit darkness. I could make
out the long sweep of the row of standing stones and
followed them up to the circle surrounding the burial
mound. I couldn't see anything else. It was too far
away. And then I saw movement. Yes. There was
someone, something, moving about the sacred site.

'Come on,' Daniel urged, but to my horror, he
was leading me *towards* the stones. 'Keep down low.
We need to see what's going on. It could be to do
with the sheep. A sacrifice.'

I was petrified, my heart exploding with each rapid beat. 'Daniel, it could be dangerous!' I protested in a muted squeal.

He turned to me, the whites of his eyes flashing in the moonlight. 'This could be the best chance we get,' he hissed. 'We've got to stop all this. Look, you don't have to come. You can stay here with Trojan.'

'What!' The idea of waiting there all on my own was more terrifying than going with Daniel. And he was right. There had been some horrible ritualistic sheep-killings on the moor. It didn't do to think what the poor creatures had suffered, and then there were the farmers like my friends, the Colemans. 'No, I'll come with you. But promise me. No heroics, Daniel.'

'Don't worry. I want these people properly prosecuted.'

I followed him, crouching down low as we crept through the long, grey-green grass. My heart was beating so hard that I felt faint and I was stifling one long, terrified whimper. We stole nearer, dropping on our hands and knees to crawl until we were less than a hundred yards away, but keeping on the same contour so that the stone row was still slightly below us. We stopped then, lying on our bellies. Trojan lifted his head, growling softly, until Daniel shushed him and he fell instantly silent.

A dozen figures were moving, gliding like

apparitions, inside the circle, their bodies pale and ghostly in the gloom. With the air so still, I could just catch some murmured chanting, and I shuddered. My God, this was definitely some sort of ritual! But it was 1956, not the Middle Ages! I couldn't believe it, but here was something going on before my very eyes!

Beside me, Daniel fumbled in his pocket and pulled out some binoculars which he proceeded to train on the ceremony below us. I waited literally with baited breath, shaking like a leaf. Daniel gave a wry grunt and his mouth curved at the corners before he handed the binoculars to me.

'See if you recognise anyone,' he whispered in my ear.

I wasn't used to binoculars, especially in the dark, and it took me some moments to adjust the focus. If it hadn't been for the full moon, I'm sure I wouldn't have been able to see anything at all. And then I snatched in my breath. The figures were naked as they swayed about in a circle, and one of them was more than familiar.

'Oh, good Lord! Gloria!' I gasped.

'You know I had the feeling she was trying to warn me off,' Daniel all but chuckled beside me. 'Didn't want me to see her prancing around in the buff. And no sacrificed sheep, of course. All quite harmless.'

'I do hope she doesn't catch cold,' I said in all seriousness, and I heard Daniel splutter as he fought to contain his amusement.

Almost as if they had heard me, the ring of naked, moonlight dancers came together, arms uplifted and holding hands. And then they broke away and wandered over to where they had evidently left their clothes. They dressed quickly and hurried off in the direction of Norsworthy Bridge where we imagined they had parked their cars. I presumed someone must be giving Gloria a lift as she didn't drive. It all seemed incongruous!

'Well, then.' Daniel scrambled to his feet. 'Come on, Carrots. We'd better get back. If you don't fancy driving home, you can stay the night if you'd like. Just give Deborah a ring to let her know.'

But at that moment, I was so astounded that I didn't know what I wanted to do. But I didn't think I could ever look Gloria in the eye again!

Chapter Twenty-Seven

'Kate! Whatever's the matter?'

The following Tuesday I had gulped down my lunch – much to Edwin's disapproval as he said I'd get indigestion – and hurried into Woolworths to see Kate before I went back to work. She always had an early lunch and would be back at her counter. We hadn't met for a couple of weeks and her parents weren't on the phone, and I wanted to tell her about the diary and what I had discovered. I was bursting to impart the news that I had thought really hard about what Daniel had said and had decided to try and trace my father. Uncle Artie had called at the house of his old cleaner. She no longer lived there but the present occupier knew where she was and had agreed to pass on a letter, and dear Uncle Artie promised to write the next day.

All my soul-searching had turned me topsy-turvy. I was bubbling with excitement, but what if my efforts came to nothing or I found that my real father was dead? I would have to brace myself against such disappointment. There again, what if I traced Kevin and he didn't want to know me? Or if I didn't like him? But deep down, I knew I *had* to try. If I didn't, I would regret it for the rest of my days. Who knew, I might discover other relatives along the way? I needed to tell everyone how I felt, hence my desire to speak with Kate. But when I got to Woollies, I found her with eyes red-rimmed and a face as long as ninepence.

'Oh, Lily!' she squealed and then burst into tears.

Oh dear. This wasn't like Kate. She was always so bright and chatty. Fortunately there weren't any customers waiting and although I knew I shouldn't, I went behind the counter and put my arms around her.

'What's brought this on?' I asked, at a loss to know what could have upset her.

She pulled away, sniffing hard, and gave a snorting hiccup as she tried desperately to stop crying. 'It's Pete,' she gulped, squeaking again. 'He's found someone else. At college.'

'Oh, Kate,' I sighed sympathetically. 'I am sorry.'

But my words obviously held no comfort for her as her bottom lip quivered. 'I love him so much,' she moaned. 'I don't think I'll ever love anyone else. And who else is goin' to want an old baggage like me?'

'Oh, Kate, don't talk like that. You're fun to be with, lively—'

'But I'm not pretty and intelligent like you,' she snivelled. 'I thought I'd get your job here as Mrs Kershaw's assistant, but I wasn't clever enough. And now I can't even serve on the counter properly. I keep gettin' the till all wrong and Mrs Kershaw said if I don't pull my socks up, I'll have to leave.'

'I'm sure it's just because you're upset over Pete,' I tried to rationalise.

'Oh, Lily, I don't know!' Kate wailed. 'If my mum and dad didn't need the extra I bring in, I'd chuck it all in. And I'm fed up with the journey on the bus every day. It isn't the same as the train. And I miss Sally so much and I don't see you—'

'I'm sorry about that,' I interrupted guiltily. 'I've been busy with Daniel and other things recently. But I tell you what. I promise I'll come up on Sunday and we can have a good old chin-wag and catch up.'

'Really?' Kate seemed to perk up at once. 'That'd be great!'

'Well, I'd better get back to work. Cheer up! There's more than one fish—'

'All right for you to say that. You've got Daniel.'

'Daniel? Oh, we're just good friends.' I tried to say it flippantly, but I knew in my heart that I was only hiding the hurt from myself.

We had a real girl's day on the Sunday, listening to music and flicking through magazines. I enjoyed myself, but I felt as if it was turning back the clock. I had moved on since those early days I had spent with Kate and Sally. So much water had flowed under the bridge and I was no longer the child who had stepped off the train on that dark winter's evening.

'It's Uncle Artie for you, Lily,' Wendy announced the next evening. 'I think he's got some news,' she warned me, 'but he wouldn't say what.'

My heart jumped into my mouth and I glanced around the lounge. We had been chuckling at *Hancock's Half Hour* and to be suddenly dragged back to reality was a shock. My pulse accelerated wildly and I was trembling as I went out into the hall and picked up the receiver.

'Hello, Uncle Artie,' I said, surprised at how relaxed I sounded when I was tingling with apprehension.

'Hello, Lily, little maid,' I heard his cheerful tone. 'Got a little news for you. Aggie got my letter today and she just rang me. She remembers about your father. She were a cleaner at the hospital at the time and it were all the talk. She's pretty sure his name were Westerham.'

'Westerham?' I repeated inanely. My real father's name was Kevin Westerham. It was like an explosion within me. Somehow knowing his name made him more real, more tangible.

'Yes,' Artie confirmed. 'I've looked in the phone book and rung Directory Enquiries, but I'm afraid there's no K Westerham listed in Plymouth. And anyway, Aggie thinks he went into a nursing home. But at least you've got his name now.'

'Yes. Thank you so much!'

'Not at all. Didn't do much, did I? And it were good to talk to Aggie again. She's getting on, but she's all about, like.'

I had to smile to myself. *All about*. It was one of the local expressions I'd come to know, even used myself at times. *All there and halfway back*, Ellen would have said. It was as if I'd made a complete break with my old life in London, but if the name Artie had found for me led me to my father, it would bring it all back.

There was a list of all registered nursing homes both in Tavistock and Plymouth in the office at the hospital, so I systematically began ringing them all to ask if they had ever had a resident called Kevin Westerham in the last ten years. Several of them didn't keep records going back that far but promised to ask long-standing staff. Others said they would look through when they had time. Nowhere had a definite yes, and I was beginning to wonder if I wasn't looking for a needle in a haystack. I was losing heart. I just seemed to be leaving messages with people who would ring me back if they discovered anything. It was hopeless.

So I went back to concentrating on Daniel's book and the winter of 1951. The prisoners shivered their way through the bitter weather, but by the spring of '52, the Chinese had decided that the Westerners were beyond redemption and instruction became voluntary. Daniel sometimes went to lectures for something to do – and to enjoy the heckling. Boredom, the starvation diet and deep-seated apathy were the main enemies – apart from the rats, lice and disease, all of which resulted in a string of incidents described in the book. The whole ethos was soul-destroying. Morale was occasionally lifted by permission to write a letter home, but none of Daniel's ever got through and neither did he receive any.

A handful of books in English were available, ones which were considered ideologically sound: Dickens – because Britain was portrayed as bleak under capitalism – and some Steinbeck. Daniel had read *War and Peace*, another permitted title, three times. No wonder he never wanted to see it ever again! He had enjoyed rereading *Rebecca*, but the last page had been torn out as it apparently contained some vague anti-communist comment.

At least now the manuscript didn't contain such horrific material as it had at first, but I could imagine the frustration and anger ripping a man apart as the physical and mental deprivations gnawed away day after day, week after week. There was, though, one last incident that turned my stomach again. Prisoners were taken out on forced forays to collect firewood and, on one such occasion, someone had twisted his ankle. My ears pricked up as I remembered Daniel saying something about experience of a sprained ankle when he had rescued me out on the moor, and I wondered if this was what he had referred to. The chap couldn't put his weight on it and instead of carrying on with his own load of firewood, Daniel had gone to his aid. He had been beaten to the ground for his troubles, made to carry both his own and the other man's loads back to the camp, and then was chained in a standing position to a post out in the blistering heat. When he had finally collapsed from heat stroke, he had been taken to the so-called hospital to recover, but the experience had utterly broken his spirit. He resolved to put himself first from then on, to harden his heart to anyone else's sufferings no matter how he hated himself for it. From then on, every ounce of his depleted energies was directed into his own survival.

My heart ached for him. Writing down his experiences had helped him find normality again, but it had also allowed me to understand the gruff, irascible devil I had first met and how it had masked the deeply scarred person beneath. The story was coming to an end, and so was the typing. As I drove up to Fencott Place the following Saturday after lunch, I wondered what I would do when it was finished and I had no more excuse to see Daniel so regularly. Unlike with Edwin, I had never fooled myself into believing there was any future for us. I had sworn I wouldn't let myself fall in love with him and yet, if I was truly honest, that was precisely what had happened, slowly, imperceptibly, but undeniably.

He greeted me with his usual casual smile. 'Come on in, Lily. You haven't brought such nice weather with you today.'

'No,' I agreed. 'I don't suppose Gloria and her chums would have held their ceremony in this drizzle, full moon or no full moon.'

'Well, we are into November now so I don't imagine there'll be any more naked shenanigans until the spring,' Daniel commented, and I could see by his expression that he was still vaguely amused by the events of the previous fortnight. 'I'll be taking Trojan for his walk soon, but I don't expect we'll come across anything so interesting. I assume you'd like to come?'

'Of course.' I would never miss an opportunity to walk on the moor, especially in the more remote areas where Daniel went. 'And I've done it at last. Bought some proper walking boots. They're a bit stiff, though.'

'Good girl!' he grinned at me as if I'd achieved something spectacular. 'It's only taken you, what, three years?' But I knew he was teasing me and I laughed back as he went on with some concern, 'Have you got some good thick socks to stop them rubbing? Don't want you getting blisters.'

'Yes, I have, so I should be all right.'

'Good. Do you want a quick coffee before we go? You can tell me about your search for your father.'

'Not much to tell really. But a coffee would be nice, thank you. Shall I put this in the study?' I asked, nodding down at the pile of papers clutched to my chest.

'Yes, do. Thanks, Lily.'

I went into the study, the one room in the house that always seemed to be in a mess. I cleared a space on the desk to put down the typescript, but in doing so, managed to sweep some other papers onto the floor. I picked them up, shuffling them together. They seemed to be old household bills and so on, but then I noticed that one was a sheet of Daniel's scrawly handwriting. It looked a bit yellowed, but I thought it might be a page from the manuscript that had found its way into the wrong pile, so I cast my eye over it. And my body stilled as I began to read.

Today I met the most extraordinary girl. I think I saw her once before, at the Princetown Carnival. Just a glimpse, like an ephemeral butterfly. She has the most glorious hair, the colour of pure gold, and a gentle, elfin face. She was alone and had twisted her ankle out at Down Tor Circle and so was stranded. She made something move inside me that I haven't felt for a long time. Or at least something I had trained myself not to feel. Concern for another human being. If I was going to survive the camp, I knew I had to harden myself, clad myself in iron, and I succeeded. I was ready to throw it off when I came home, and I tried so hard to when I was back in London. But I needed my shell to keep out the hurt of Great Aunt Marianne's death and Susan's going off with someone else. I feel as if fate has cheated me, and I feel bitter and angry. Most of all, I want to keep away from everyone and to make them keep away from me. That way, no one can hurt me again.

There, Ed. You told me to write down what I feel. But all of this changed today. Or perhaps it has made me even more determined to keep myself shut away. Protected. Safe. The girl must be a plucky little thing. She insisted she could manage but I knew full well that she couldn't. Part of me wanted to leave her there, the impenetrable part of me. But

I couldn't leave her, and the other part of me made me help her. But I couldn't let go of the shield. I wanted to be pleasant and friendly, but I couldn't let my defences down and she must have thought me rude and insufferable. But she was so lovely, so vulnerable and yet so strong. She found the chink in my armour and I rebelled against it. And now I feel pulled in two opposite directions. I hope I see the girl again, and yet I feel afraid.

I stared at the page, totally absorbed. Shattered. Oh, Daniel. That was three years ago, but I wanted to hold him. Heal him. No wonder he had always held me at arms' length. But if I showed him how much I loved him, it would only hurt us both.

I slid the paper back in the pile and went back to the kitchen, my heart beating erratically. I wanted to say something, but he mustn't know that I had seen that sheet of paper. He had probably forgotten he had ever written it.

'I think you were very brave,' I said, hoping my voice didn't sound as nervous as I felt. 'The soldier with the injured ankle, I mean.'

'Brave?' Daniel scoffed. 'Hardly. I did what anyone would. I went to help a fellow prisoner. I'd hardly call it heroic.'

I squared my shoulders. 'I would, given the circumstances. I'd say you're a very brave and sensitive man, Daniel Pencarrow.'

His expressive eyes deepened to an intense violet as they met mine for a few arresting seconds before those long, dark lashes swooped as he blinked at me. My heart stood still.

'What have you been drinking?' he suddenly growled, though it was a low growl, shuttered. 'You'd better have this coffee to sober you up before our walk.'

The hairs were bristling down my neck. 'Where shall we go?' my lips seemed to say of their own accord. I hadn't consciously thought the words, but I was supremely relieved that I had.

'How about out to Drizzlecombe and make a circle back up the Plym Valley?' Daniel suggested. 'We've got plenty of time before it starts getting dark, and if it turns misty, we can just keep to the track.'

'Yes, that would be lovely,' I answered eagerly. One of the remotest areas of the moor. It was exactly what I needed to clear my head.

Chapter Twenty-Eight

'What happened next?' I dared to ask as we followed the track between the scattered ruins of Eylesbarrow Mine. I had been telling Daniel about my as yet fruitless search for my father and then I had broached the subject of his book again.

'After I'd been hung out to fry in the sun, you mean?'

I winced, both at the vision it conjured up in my brain and the searing bitterness in Daniel's tone. 'Yes,' I answered simply.

He gave a sardonic shrug. 'Nothing much. I'd learnt my lesson and I obeyed every damned order I was given after that. And if I saw any brutality being meted out, I ignored it. I felt like a traitor. But I'd been interrogated once and punished twice, and that was bloody well enough for anyone!'

His voice had risen to an impassioned crescendo,

and when I glanced up at him, his jaw was set and I cursed myself for asking. The ensuing silence was taut, but after we had gone another few hundred yards and turned down into Drizzlecombe towards its stone rows, Daniel seemed to have calmed down somewhat.

'I got through that second winter in the camp by dreaming of here,' he volunteered, waving his hand vaguely around us. 'But with no contact beyond the barbed wire, I felt lost and forgotten. And then in the spring, I went down with dysentery. We all had bouts of diarrhoea and various fevers, but until then I'd never had anything really serious. But when I got full-blown dysentery... I tell you, Lily, you want to die. I can't tell you how absolutely bloody awful you feel. You need the lavvy every few minutes, and your insides get so raw and start to... Well, you really don't want to know the details. You get weaker and weaker, and the sooner you die from it, the better. Ironically, though, it was what saved me.'

I frowned as we paused by the massive standing stone where Edwin had once posed with arms outstretched to demonstrate just how colossal it was on the day we had discovered the dying rabbit. 'How come?' I asked.

'Well, we knew nothing about the protracted negotiations, or that the Red Cross had been trying to get us released for months. The first we knew was when a convoy of Red Cross lorries suddenly arrived and the Chinks were releasing everyone who was sick. If I hadn't been ill, I'd have stayed there until the end, I guess.'

'Phew! You must have been relieved!'

He merely grunted. 'That journey was absolute hell. Worse than anything else I'd been through. But we did have clean water and medicine. It wasn't until the hospital in Hong Kong that I really began to feel better. They shipped us home as soon as they could, but I was still pretty weak when I arrived back in London. I only stayed a few days. Not even long enough to see Edwin. I just couldn't face all that noise and... So I came back here.'

'At least your story had a happy ending.'

I noticed him hesitate. 'I'm hoping it might,' he muttered.

My brow furrowed in bemusement. What did he mean by that? But before I could question him, he stopped dead and grabbed me by the arm.

'My God, look!'

His eyes were narrowed keenly in the direction we were going and I, too, squinted ahead. We were walking alongside the stream that was the source of the River Plym. The ground was squelching and boggy, and it was one of the loneliest parts of the moor I knew. You would be unlikely to meet another living soul on a clear summer's day, let alone on such a murky November afternoon. At first I couldn't make anything out from the yellowy brown vegetation and the rocks scattered here and there, but then I caught movement and could see what Daniel was gazing at.

Some way up the valley was a man and he was chasing round after a group of sheep, changing direction and leaping after whichever one came nearer him in its desperation to escape. It struck me as odd. It wasn't the way to herd sheep. I had been with the Colemans before when they were bringing in livestock, and you didn't drive them like that. This man was no sheep farmer, so what was he doing trying to catch one of the petrified animals?

Fear tumbled down inside me.

'That's him, I'm sure it is,' Daniel whispered urgently. 'The chap I've seen before. Come on. We've got to catch the devil red-handed.'

He called Trojan to heel and started to walk stealthily forward. For a few seconds I was rooted to the spot. I don't think I'd ever been so frightened and my whole body shook as I forced myself to follow in Daniel's wake.

The fellow was so intent on the chase that he didn't notice us until we were nearly on him. I could see by then that he was elderly, his face weather-beaten and lined a little like Barry Coleman's. He had just succeeded in casting a net over one of the hapless sheep and was now straddling the poor creature. And then, just as he took it by one of its horns, lifting its head and exposing its neck, he drew out a large kitchen knife.

Oh, dear God. I heard Daniel shout and he catapulted forward at a run. Trojan shot ahead of him, streaking out like a flash of lightning. I caught my breath as the man looked up. Oh, no! What if he killed Trojan with the knife? Oh, please God, no!

My prayers were answered as the fellow let go of the sheep and fled up the narrow gully I knew as Evil Combe. Trojan chased after him, barking at his heels and nearly tripping him up.

'Lily, free the sheep!' Daniel yelled at me over his shoulder and sped on after them.

I stopped by the frantically struggling animal. I was so scared, transfixed, terrified at what was happening ahead of me, but the sheep was suffering and I knew I had to release it. I was wary of its horns, small though they were, and the hooves that were kicking wildly in the creature's panic. And then I remembered that I had seen Barry straddle his livestock from behind and, my heart in my mouth, I did the same. The poor sheep was getting more tangled and I fought to hold it between my legs as I pulled its feet back through the mesh and finally pulled the net back over its head. One of its horns caught again, but an instant later, it wriggled free and scampered away, leaving me holding the net.

I stood for a second and gulped with relief. But it wasn't over yet and I charged after Daniel. The man was moving quickly but was hampered by Trojan leaping joyfully around him thinking what a great game it was. Daniel was flying over the ground, rapidly gaining on them, and I was gripped with terror as to what would happen next. Then I saw Daniel launch himself around the villain's waist in a rugby tackle and bring him down. I raced to catch up, panting and out of breath. The two men were grappling on the ground and I arrived just in time to see the other chap swing round, brandishing the knife. A second later, Daniel cried out and released his hold as the devil scrambled to his feet, still holding the knife aloft.

I froze. There was blood on the blade. Oh, Jesus Christ, what was he going to do now? I didn't think. All I knew was that the man I loved had been attacked by a maniac and I wasn't going to stand there and watch him being killed. I sprang up behind the villain before he realised I was there and threw the net over him. He cursed, struggling like a demon, and, without a thought, I leapt onto his back, tearing at his neck, scratching him, anything to bring him down. I felt the jolt as he crashed onto his knees, and realised with a sense of cold horror that the net had pinned his arms to his sides and in his crazed efforts to escape, the knife had fallen from his grasp.

'Right, you bastard!'

I had never experienced such fear in my life, and neither had I ever been so relieved as I was to hear Daniel's voice beside me.

'Well done, Lily,' he said grimly. 'Are you all right?'

'Yes, but what about *you*?' I squeaked.

He barely flicked his gaze towards his arm. Blood was oozing through a rip in the sleeve of his jacket. I stared at it in horror, and then pushed the felon's head back down as he tried to lift himself from the ground.

'I'll live,' was Daniel's rueful answer. 'I'll take him now. You get that knife well out of his reach and keep it for evidence. And then while I hold him, can you take off my belt? I'll use it to tie up his hands. Now, you bloody bastard, we've got you in the end!'

Five minutes later, Daniel had the fellow trussed up like a chicken and was marching him up the combe to the track at the top. The man knew he was beaten. He said nothing but kept glaring at me with maddened eyes that sent shivers down my spine. I felt my blood curdle.

I knew it was nearly two miles back along the track. It seemed to take for ever. Every now and then, our prisoner made a token effort to run off, but Daniel shoved him forward, convincing him that he didn't have a chance. Daniel's face was like hewn stone and I saw him wince once or twice, but his fury seemed to be giving him strength.

At long last, we got back to the tarmac road and the spot near the bend where walkers sometimes parked their cars. On that miserable afternoon, there was but one vehicle, a large white van. As we came up to it, I noticed it must have been in a collision as it was scraped all along the nearside with a sizeable dent low down on the door.

'Jesus Christ.'

Daniel stopped beside me, the colour draining from his face. He was staring, open-mouthed, appalled, at the van, and then his eyes opened like saucers.

'It's the van,' his white lips mumbled. 'It's come back to me in a flash. This is the van that forced me off the road.'

I frowned, shaking my head. 'No, Daniel. It was a lorry, remember?'

'No!' he cried adamantly. 'It was this van! I can see it now! Perhaps the lorry I rambled on about was the one that found me. You know, the farmer. So...it was *you*, wasn't it!' he screamed, spinning the man round with such force he nearly stumbled. 'You ran me off the road! You tried to kill me!'

'Well, you young bugger!' the fellow spat back. 'You'd found us out, 'adn't you? But you've no bloody idea, you 'aven't! All they dead rabbits! Farmers 'ad to pay, like!'

Daniel's face was savage as he shook the man like a rag doll. 'What the hell do you mean?' he demanded.

'Not sayin' nort more, me.'

'Well, you can damned well tell the police instead! I hope they throw the book at you!'

How is it that in times of crisis you feel utterly drained and exhausted and yet every nerve is like a coiled spring, ready to snap into action? You can almost feel the blood coursing through your body, taut and alive, and yet lifeless and without energy. I had known it before, on the nights Ellen and Sidney had died, and when I had read the diary. I felt it now. I paced the drawing room at Fencott Place, too restless to settle and yet on the brink of collapse.

We had got the man back to the house, or at least Daniel had locked him in one of the old stables and kept guard while I went inside to telephone the police. It was a while before they arrived as they were sending a sergeant and three constables from Tavistock. Two of them took the culprit away and the other retrieved the van for examination while the sergeant took statements from Daniel and me.

Neither of us was really in a fit state to drive but Daniel's arm needed some attention, so I phoned home. Deborah answered and was horrified when I explained briefly what had happened. William was already out on a call, but Edwin was there and drove straight up to us in his beloved Austin Healey.

'It's beginning to become a habit, me patching you up.'

We were in the kitchen which was warm from the range and, having removed his jacket and sweater, Daniel was taking off his shirt and peeling the sleeve over the wound in his upper arm. Edwin had been trying to make light conversation, but Daniel scowled and then winced as the material pulled on the half-congealed blood.

'I didn't exactly plan any of it,' he retorted.

'I don't suppose you did. Now let's have a look.' Edwin frowned as he peered at Daniel's arm. 'Hmm. Lucky you were wearing that jacket. I reckon it saved you from quite a nasty injury. As it is, it's just a flesh wound. A few stitches and you'll be fighting fit. Not that I suggest you do any fighting, not for a while anyway. Hold still and I'll just put in a few little pricks of anaesthetic.'

He set everything on the table and I gave Daniel an encouraging smile. He returned it, but there was a look of irritation in his eyes that said he considered Edwin was making a fuss over nothing. The laceration wasn't serious – I had seen far worse casualties at the hospital – but there was a gaping two inch gash that needed closing. I saw Daniel flinch slightly at the injections, but it wasn't his face I was looking at. I had seen him undressed when he'd been in hospital, but it hadn't seemed right to study his fine physique when he'd been so badly hurt. But now I felt the irresistible draw of his masculinity. His broad shoulders were perfectly muscled and his arms had a slender, wiry strength. His chest was scattered with fine, dark hair and there was not an ounce of spare flesh on his hard, flat stomach.

I felt that tingling sensation plunge into the pit of my belly. Dear Lord, was that love? I'd never really felt like that about Edwin. He was solid and dependable, full of fun. But with Daniel I felt excited, exhilarated, almost feverish. I felt...

'There. All done,' Edwin pronounced. 'Keep it clean and dry, and come to the surgery on Friday morning for me to take the stitches out. Should be healed enough by then. But no doing anything physical that could burst the stitches in the meantime. And here's some penicillin just in case. God knows what germs were on that knife. Make sure you take the full course. I know what you are.'

'Yes, doc,' Daniel murmured, glancing up darkly.

'I'll nip up and get you some other clothes,' offered, jumping up.

'Lily, it's all—'

But I was already out of the door and up the stairs. My head was spinning. God, I loved Daniel. I was enflamed. He was such a good man and I just wanted to open up his heart. And then I remembered the sheet of paper I had found earlier that afternoon. Was there a way I could draw him out? He had come so far since I had first met him.

'Do you want to come back with me, Lily,' Edwin asked as I went back into the kitchen, 'if you don't feel up to driving?'

I considered for a moment. 'If I do, someone will have to drive me back up to get my car tomorrow. So… Well, I think I'd rather stay here tonight. That's if it's all right with you, Daniel?'

Daniel took the clean shirt from me and slowly raised a quizzical eyebrow as he shrugged into the garment. Then the shadow of a smile twitched at his mouth. 'Yes, of course. It'd be good to have some company tonight,' he said quietly.

Edwin cleared his throat. 'I'll be off, then. Nothing strenuous, remember.'

'I'll see you out,' I offered as we went into the hall.

'Thanks for coming, Ed,' Daniel called from the kitchen as he fastened the buttons.

'You and Danny seem…' Edwin spread his hands as I opened the front door. 'I'd never have thought—'

I'm sure I blushed like a radish. 'We're just good friends. *Honestly*,' I insisted. 'And you drive carefully in that nippy little thing of yours.'

Edwin grinned. 'I will. See you some time tomorrow, then.' And he zoomed off into the darkness.

I went back to the kitchen. Daniel was pulling on the jumper I'd brought down for him. 'I'll get the fire lit in the drawing room. Are you hungry yet?'

I shook my head. 'Not really. I'll make a drink, though. Tea or coffee?'

'Tea, please. Tell you what. There's some ham in the fridge. How about making some sandwiches and we can have them later when we feel like it?'

'Yes, all right. I'll do that while you get the fire going.'

He gave me that lazy smile and went out of the room. I still felt strange as I made the drinks and the sandwiches. But it wasn't only the events of the day that were making my stomach churn over and over. I had never felt so close to Daniel as I did now. Could I possibly find the courage to tell him?

It was an hour or so later as we warmed ourselves in front of the fire that the telephone rang. Apart from the kitchen, the old house with its spacious rooms was really cold, so we were in the best spot with one of the sofas drawn up close to the hearth. Daniel reluctantly took himself off to the hall, and

I was pleased when Trojan came and lay down on my feet.

It was some time before Daniel came back. He shivered and knelt down in front of the burning logs. 'That was the police,' he told me, rubbing his hands together. 'The fellow's confessed everything. Apparently he's an old warrener, possibly the last one on the moor.'

'Really?'

Daniel sighed heavily. 'That was the root of it all. The myxomatosis was the last nail in the coffin of a dying trade. It was a complete way of life, handed down through generations. But a very lonely way of life. This chap's lived alone on the moor for decades. Probably been going off his trolley for donkey's years. When myxomatosis got here, it killed not just his business but his entire way of life. He blamed the farmers for introducing it. I suppose some unscrupulous farmers in the country might have encouraged it, but up here on the moor rabbits weren't a particular threat. But this chap was so twisted, he was killing sheep to get back at the local farmers. Totally unfounded, of course. But he was trying to make it look as though the sheep had been sacrificed by some occult group to shift the blame.'

I shook my head, struggling to take it all in. 'Doesn't seem possible.'

'Well, there we are. I feel sorry for the poor man

in some ways. He had his head turned by loneliness, I suppose.'

'Daniel, he tried to kill you! And very nearly succeeded.'

He shrugged ruefully. 'Yes, I know. It was definitely him. His van. Remember I nearly caught him a couple of times before? He recognised me and thought he'd do away with me. I'd become the enemy as well.'

'So what'll happen?'

'There'll be a court case, of course. You and I will have to give evidence. But the poor devil will probably end his days in an asylum. Sad really. Anyway.' He stood up again and gave a deep sigh. 'It's all over now. And I could do with a drink. And I don't mean tea.'

He was out of the room for just a few minutes while I sat staring into the flames. I still felt numbed and yet every fibre of me was poised, strung on edge. When Daniel returned, he was carrying two glasses, each charged with a good measure of brandy. He handed one to me and we sat, sipping at the burning spirit, exchanging an odd word but mainly trying to absorb the enormity of what had happened. Daniel kept feeding the fire and had a good blaze crackling in the grate. Although the rest of the house was cold, we were toasting by the hearth and both of us had taken off our jumpers. The fire and the brandy had relaxed me and I could feel the tension draining away as I sat on the rug at Daniel's feet. My hair had been scooped up in a ponytail all day and now I shook it free and it fell down around my shoulders. A minute or two later, I tensed as I felt something moving. Daniel was stroking my hair so softly I could barely feel it, and my stomach clenched.

'I'm glad you never had your hair cut or permed or anything,' he said from behind me, his voice thick and low. 'It's beautiful, you know. And if I tease you about it, it's only because—'

He didn't get to finish the sentence. He must have moved awkwardly and drew in a wincing breath through his teeth. I turned round at once, kneeling up between his spread knees.

'Are you all right?'

He nodded with a slightly sheepish smile. 'Yes. Sorry. I guess the anaesthetic's wearing off. It's just a bit sore. I'd forgotten about it really, and it just took me by surprise. But…I'm really glad you're here, my little Carrot Top.'

His deep, violet-blue eyes were smouldering into mine, steady and strong, and the fire plunged down inside me. Oh, Daniel. I held my breath as he reached out and cupped my cheek. I was mesmerised, heady with love. Was he…was there a chance Daniel felt the same way as I did? I couldn't stop myself, overtaken by some force far more powerful than I was. I turned my head into his palm. Kissed it.

A small quivering sound fluttered in my throat as I felt Daniel's fingers entwine in my hair, drawing me towards him. And then his lips found mine, so gentle and tender. A thrill of joy, of need, pulsed through my limbs as we kissed, long and deep, and when we finally parted, his eyes were so soft, his mouth lightly curved as I stared at him, breathless and intoxicated.

'I love you, Lily Hayes,' he articulated deep in his throat.

We were so close. I could feel his brandy-scented breath fanning my cheek. He was smiling, his eyes passionate and intense. And I was lost in some enchanted rapture. Daniel loved me. And not in the same fantasy way I had once thought I had loved Edwin. This was real. Pure, hard and strong.

'I could…kiss it better,' I gulped in a tiny whisper. I was shaking, but my keyed up emotions knew what they craved. Daniel's eyes followed me darkly and he didn't move as I began to unbutton his shirt and I slid it back over his shoulder. The neat stitches looked like a train track near the top of his left arm and I tenderly kissed the skin on either side. And then I found myself moving my lips along his collarbone kissing his chest…

His long fingers dug into my shoulders as he pushed me away. 'Christ, Lily, don't! I won't be able… I'd never forgive myself if something happens you regret.'

'I won't regret it,' I whispered. And I knew I wouldn't.

Daniel took me in his arms again, kissing me hard and urgently. His mouth moved down to the well of my throat and my stomach cramped with need. His hand slipped inside my blouse. I'm sure he must have felt my heart beating frenziedly beneath his touch. A warm, delicious sensation burnt through me and I pulled at Daniel's shirt until that glorious torso was glowing amber in the firelight. I traced my trembling fingertips over his chest and then he was undressing me, slowly, touching, stroking every inch of my skin as it became exposed. I flinched as he unhooked my bra and tossed it aside, but the moment of embarrassment was gone as he took my breasts in his hands, so gently, and bent to kiss them before laying me down on the rug. I was aflame, devoured by my love for this good, sensitive man, and he drew me on, alive to the slightest touch, until I was on fire, yearning with desire. He stopped for a few seconds to strip off the rest of his own clothes. I'd never seen a man excited before. I felt scared but fascinated at the same time, but Daniel's body was beautiful, perfect. I lay, rapt and submissive, as he pulled off my slacks and then my knickers, pausing to smile as he ran a tantalising finger over my belly.

'Are you sure?' he rasped, swallowing hard.

I was shaking but I didn't hesitate and nodded silently. And then Daniel was drawing me on to some wondrous world I had never dreamt of, his mouth, his tongue, his fingers stroking, caressing, enticing. He found the sweet, moist core of me, and I knew I was ready to give myself wholly to him. I moaned, feverish, hysterical, but utterly trusting as Daniel came to me. I felt a sharp, intimate pain for just a moment, but Daniel was so gentle and caring, and I welcomed him inside me, healing him, healing myself. He moved in a slow rhythm, delectable and unhurried, building until something unimaginable, bewitching, erupted and exploded within me, sending shockwaves rippling through my entire body. And in that instant, Daniel cried out and shuddered, and I clung to him, knowing at last that this was true, pure love.

He was smiling at me, his brow creased. 'Are you all right?' he whispered.

Just for a moment I wanted to cry, but Daniel was raining tiny, playful kisses on my cheeks, my nose and chin, and I began to giggle instead. Then he turned more leisurely attention to my breasts, sending a riptide of emotion through my flesh before he drew me against him and I curled up next to him, resting my head on his shoulder and with my hand tracing the strong contours of his chest, the faint cigarette-burn scars, everything that made Danie what he was. We lay there, holding each other, not exchanging a word, for some time, totally at peace, until Daniel rolled away to put some more logs on the fire.

He raised his index finger at me. 'Don't go away!' he ordered.

I sat up, tipping my head coquettishly. 'I don't think I'm going anywhere,' I grinned back.

Daniel pulled on his jumper which was sensible as the rest of the house was so cold. I lay back, hugging the dream, the exquisite sensation, to my heart. I had slept with the most wonderful man who had earned my love and respect against all odds. And I was running over with joy.

It was so amazing that I couldn't lie still. I sprang up, facing the roaring fire, watching the dancing light from the flames playing over my skin. I felt strangely free, glorifying in my nakedness, and began to hum, swaying in the firelight, engulfed in a perfect world that contained only Daniel and me. Daniel and me...

'God, stop that or I'll want you again,' his voice came in my ear. 'No, don't turn round. And keep your eyes shut.'

My eyebrows shot up in surprise. But I did as he said, feeling a little giddy with my eyes closed, whether due to the brandy or the intoxication of my love for Daniel, I didn't know. I felt something cold at my throat, and then Daniel moved my hair to one side and was fiddling at the back of my neck.

'OK. Open your eyes.'

I did. And I glanced down. The exquisite Victorian necklace, the one in the portrait, hung around my neck. I caught my breath.

'I hope you'll accept it this time,' Daniel said at my shoulder. And then his voice became oddly ragged. 'You said I should keep it for my wife.'

Slowly, he turned me round, and I gazed up at him, wide-eyed. Could he possibly mean...?

'Will you, Lily?' he croaked. 'Will you spend your life with this miserable old devil?'

His eyes were searching my face, anguished. I blinked at him as a scintillating, joyous whoop burst from my throat.

'Do I take it that's a yes?' he said, a slow smile unfurling on his face.

'Oh yes!' I cried, finding my voice. 'Most definitely a yes!'

He took me in his arms again, pressing my bare flesh against his jumper. 'You do realise you don't have any nightclothes here? I'll have to lend you one of my pyjama tops. Mind you, I'm sure you'll look very fetching in it,' he chuckled softly. 'And I take it I won't have to make up a spare bed for you?'

I threw up my head with a happy laugh and snuggled against him. 'No, I don't think you will,' I replied.

Chapter Twenty-Nine

'What's the matter, Lily? You look as though you've seen a ghost.'

I staggered, groping my way into the lounge. Several pairs of anxious eyes swivelled in my direction, and I sank into the nearest chair.

'Who was on the phone? It wasn't Daniel, was it?' Wendy's eyes opened wide with horror. 'He hasn't...? Oh, the—'

'No, it wasn't Daniel,' my lips articulated. They felt peculiar, like rubber. I had been floating on a cloud since the night Daniel and I had pledged our lives to each other, and now I had fallen to earth with a crash. I had abandoned my search for my father, forgotten about it in my euphoria over Daniel, and suddenly it had been laid at my feet again.

'It was...one of the nursing homes I rang some time ago,' I stammered. 'The woman I spoke to was new, but she's been asking around and...someone remembers. My father was there for two or three years after the accident. And then he palled up with one of the nurses, a single lady who wanted to retire from full-time work. And...' I realised my gaze had been riveted on the pattern on the carpet, and now I raised my eyes to the expectant faces around me. 'He went to live with her. Somewhere in Mannamead. And...he's still there. They have his address. They couldn't give it to me, of course, but if I write a letter, they'll pass it on.'

There was a stunned silence while I read the surprise on every face, followed by a chorus of amazed comments. Their voices became jumbled in my head as I tried to let the information sink into my own brain.

'I'm sorry I could have thought that about Daniel,' I realised Wendy was saying as she came and perched on the arm of my chair.

I gave her a wan smile. 'It's all right. But Daniel *is* back to his old self. If you knew all what he went through, you'd understand. But he's over that now. I just wish...' I felt my forehead pucker in bewilderment. 'I wish he was here now.'

'Shall I ring him and ask him to come?'

'No, thanks. I don't want him driving all that way, but I will ring him.'

'So, what are you going to do?' William asked gravely.

I sat back, rubbing my hand pensively over my mouth. 'Well, of course I'll write. A very careful letter. And...see what happens, I suppose.'

I sucked in my bottom lip and bit down hard on it. I felt confused, a million thoughts, uncertainties, swirling in my head. Disorientated. It had been hard, but I had fought my way through everything, emerging victorious in the end. But at this, the final hurdle, the last piece of the jigsaw, my spirit was faltering. What if my father didn't want to know me? He believed I was dead. Perhaps he would want the past to remain buried. Too many painful memories. Perhaps he might not believe who I was, although I had the proof of it in Ellen's letter and Sidney's diary, and what was I out to gain but my own identity? And what about Sidney's part in his accident? Should I reveal the shocking truth to him? But I had to, didn't I, for it all to make sense?

'We're all here for you, no matter what,' Edwin said almost reverently.

I lifted my head and smiled gratefully at him. Dear Edwin. He never knew that he had once broken my heart, and I wanted it to stay that way. I knew now that Daniel had loved me for a long time while I had held him in contempt, deepening his wounds. It was in the past now, but guilt still twinged at me at times, and I didn't want Edwin to feel like that. Edwin was a dear brother to me now, and there was no need to rake up my former feelings for him.

'Thank you, all of you,' I answered instead. 'But if you'll excuse me, I think I'll ring Daniel now.'

I wrote the letter, choosing my words with ultimate care. I decided not to reveal Sidney's appalling actions, not yet at least. I showed the letter to Daniel before I posted it, and he nodded his approval.

'He'd have to be made of iron not to be moved by that,' he pronounced, and then he pulled me into his arms where I felt safe and secure. 'Even if it doesn't work out, you're still my little Carrot Top, you know.'

Tears had been welling in my eyes, but Daniel's mild teasing drove them away. And then we walked along to the post box. I hesitated with the envelope in my hand.

'We'll do it together,' Daniel smiled with such understanding that yet again I wanted to cry. 'Come on. One, two, three, and we'll drop it.'

And once it was done, he wrapped his arms around me.

I tried to forget about it then, and concentrate on other matters. We had decided there was no point in having a prolonged engagement. We already had a home and only wanted a simple wedding. Daniel didn't see why we shouldn't be married as soon as the banns could be read, but I persuaded him to wait until the spring. We wanted to be married in Princetown's church and any earlier in the year we would run the risk of heavy snow and ten-foot drifts. Reluctantly, Daniel agreed.

'Provided I don't have to wait that long to have you in my bed again,' he remarked with a rakish lift of one eyebrow.

'Kate!'

Her face lit up from the other side of the counter. She was still down in the dumps over Pete and I desperately wanted to cheer her up. I felt I had to damp down my high spirits over Daniel whenever I saw her, but today I had some news for her.

'Kate, come here.' I beckoned her to the gap in the counter so that I could talk to her in a low voice. 'I've got something to tell you.'

'Oh, yes?' She looked at me expectantly and then her eyes stretched wide. 'Oh, my God, you're not... you know?'

I had to chuckle. It was just like Kate to jump to conclusions. She could have been right, though, but since that first time we had been *taking precautions*, as Daniel put it. We wanted to fill that nursery with children, only not yet.

'No, but listen, Kate. We've got permission to turn the house into a hotel.'

'Really?' Kate was clearly amazed.

'Yes. It was Daniel's grandmother's idea. There's loads to do. A new generator, heating, plumbing, fire escapes. And we want to get a residents' licence. And then there'll be advertising, all sorts. But once we've got started, I'm going to need help. In the kitchen, waitressing, cleaning. And it would be good to have someone I know and trust. So…what do you think?'

'What, me?' she gawped.

'Of course you!' I grinned. 'And we could have heaps of eligible young bachelors to stay, and you could take your pick!'

'Oh, Lily! Yes, please!'

'Good. That's one problem solved. Must get back to work now!'

And I left her grinning from ear to ear.

'Someone on the phone for you, Lily. A Betty Harewood?'

Wendy shrugged as she flung herself down on the sofa that evening. I had been dreaming into the fire, thinking of the weekend which I would spend at Fencott Place as usual. Daniel had been persuaded that some degree of propriety should exist between us, so I stayed in Tavistock during the week, but the minute I finished work at lunchtime on Saturdays, I was in my little car chugging up to the moor.

Betty Harewood? I frowned to myself as I went out into the hall. And then my heart clenched in panic. Could Betty Harewood be the woman my father lived with? I was quaking in my shoes as I picked up the receiver.

'Hello, Lily Hayes speaking,' I gulped.

'Betty Harewood here,' a voice announced itself at the other end of the line. 'You don't know me, but Kevin has asked me to ring you. He got your letter.'

'Oh.' A coldness trickled through my veins, and I braced myself. He didn't want to know me. Or didn't believe me. After all that. My legs seemed to be encased in stone and I stared at the telephone table. It needed dusting.

'It was a bit of a shock,' Betty Harewood went on, and I noticed she spoke with a faint Plymothian accent. 'But he would like to meet you. Would you like to come to tea on Sunday?'

'Oh, erm,' I mumbled. My brain seemed to have stopped working and my thoughts reached out for support. 'I...er...yes, please. But...er...would you mind if my fiancé came, too?'

'Fiancé, eh? Well, I'm sure he'd be welcome. Now I'll give you the address.'

A minute later, I stumbled back into the lounge. Wendy looked up brightly as she bit into a Bounty, her favourite chocolate bar. And I burst into tears.

* * *

Everyone was there to see us off on our mission. Deborah and William were, as always, kindness itself, and Wendy hugged me dramatically. Ian and Sadie both wished me well with genuine affection, and Edwin was talking quietly with Daniel.

'Time to go, love.' Daniel turned to me, dipping his head.

'Hope it goes well,' Edwin said with a sincere smile.

I took a deep breath, excited and yet petrified. Daniel helped me into my coat, and we hurried down the long front path to the Bentley.

'You look beautiful,' he whispered as he opened the door for me.

My heart was fluttering in my chest as Daniel drove through Yelverton towards the outskirts of Plymouth and the suburb of Mannamead. I couldn't think of any words, and it was all I could do to hold myself together. So I gazed out at the moor, at familiar landmarks, the distinctive mound of Sheeps Tor dusted with white on that bitterly cold December day. And then we left Dartmoor behind as the road became lined with houses.

'It was good of Uncle Artie to ring and wish you luck.' Daniel broke the silence at last.

'Yes,' I smiled back nervously. 'Without him, this would never have happened. He always seems lonely, and yet he's so kind. What was it happened to him in the Great War?'

It was a way of distracting my own crippling suspense, but the answer filled me with sadness. 'If I tell you, you must never let on you know,' Daniel replied gravely. 'A shell blew up just in front of him. He survived, obviously, but he had shocking injuries to the front of his body and, well, let's just say he could never father children and thought it wasn't fair to any woman. I only know because Ed told me.'

I lowered my eyes. 'Oh, poor man. And there's me apprehensive about meeting my own father.'

'You wouldn't be human if you weren't. Ah, I think we must turn down here. And then just around the corner, and number sixteen.'

Daniel drew the Bentley to a halt and turned off the engine. It was a terraced house in a neat, residential street. Nothing grand but quite respectable. I shivered as I got out of the car, my teeth chattering, and not from the cold. Then Daniel was by my side and took both my hands.

'It doesn't matter what happens,' he said, his eyes deep pools of compassion. 'I love you, and we're going to have a wonderful life together. So.' He bent and placed a tender kiss on my mouth. 'Ready?'

I swallowed, and nodded. And walked up the path on unsteady legs.

Before I could knock, the door opened. I froze on the spot. A man stood there, balancing on some sort of walking frame. He was in his late forties, I guessed, dressed in a check shirt with a plain tie and one of those comfortable, camel-coloured cardigans with leather buttons. He wasn't particularly tall, was of slim build and... I was staring into a mirror of my own silver grey eyes. And he had greying, red-gold hair.

My God.

The world stopped turning and I was in danger of falling off the edge. I think I whimpered and my knees went weak. Only Daniel's steadying hand under my elbow stopped me from falling.

'Lily,' a broken voice croaked. 'My own little Lily.'

And then a bustling, elderly woman came up the passage behind him 'Kevin, dear, what are you—'

'I wanted to meet my daughter standing on my own two feet.'

There was a stubborn tone to his words, and I rejoiced. I could sense myself in him.

Our eyes met. His were tear-filled. And I hugged him across the walking frame. Held him. Not wanting to let go.

'Well, don't stand there on the doorstep this snipey weather!' Betty said from behind him. 'Come on in!'

I glanced back at Daniel, and he winked at me. *It's going to be all right*, his expression said. And it was.

'For sixteen years I believed you were dead,' Kevin, *my father*, told me when we were sitting in the neat front room around a laden tea-tray. 'I suppose Sidney said that to punish me. He could never forgive me for what I did. Rightly so, probably. I wanted Cynthia to divorce him, but she wouldn't. But to think he made me believe you were dead!' he sighed incredulously. 'And we used to be friends.'

I threw Daniel a frightened glance, and he gave an almost imperceptible nod. I took my courage in both hands. 'He wasn't as good a friend as you thought. I've…I've got something to show you. But first, if it isn't too painful, tell me about my mother. Please. Sidney wouldn't tell me anything. He was too embittered.'

My father raised his eyebrows wistfully. 'She was lovely. Pretty, funny. Kind, and very upright. Just as you would expect someone brought up by such good people as John and Ellen. Yes,' he smiled at my sudden surprise. 'I met them at Sidney and Cynthia's wedding. It was the first time I'd met Cynthia, too, and I fell in love with her at first sight. And I soon saw how their marriage wasn't working out. Your mother was a gentle creature and Sidney, well, he dominated her.'

'I could imagine that,' I put in.

'He wasn't a bad husband. He just had very deep-rooted beliefs. If he'd been Catholic, he might have become a priest. He just…stifled your mother. And she turned to me. We…' He paused, his mouth twisting awkwardly. 'We were in love for years. But Cynthia was utterly faithful. It was…only the once. When Cynthia found she was pregnant and realised it could only be mine, well, she couldn't help but be honest about it. Sidney hated her for it. But he had to maintain a façade of respectability. No one else knew. Cynthia sent me a couple of photographs of you. We even managed to meet secretly once or twice so that I could hold you. And then the war came along.'

He broke off with a rueful half smile. He had told me what I had yearned, prayed, to hear. I felt comforted, encouraged. My father was a normal, reasonable man. Not twisted or angry. I owed him the truth. The pulse reverberated in my skull as I handed him the book opened at the relevant page.

'What's this?' he asked, reaching into his pocket for some spectacles.

'Sidney kept a diary,' I managed to wring the words from my throat. 'You should read it, but…I think you should read this bit first, and I'll help Betty with the washing up.' And I shot out into the kitchen with the pleasant woman who had been his nurse and companion for seven years.

Ten minutes later, I could hear the two men's voices in low conversation, and then Daniel came to stand in the doorway.

'You can come back in. And it's all right, Lily.'

I looked at him warily and then followed him back into the room. My father was nodding his head thoughtfully and gave me such a smile as I sat down that my heart melted.

'It's hard to believe, isn't it?' I began cautiously.

'But you must never, *ever* blame yourself for this!' my father insisted. 'I mean, I never had any idea. Though it does explain something. Sidney died nearly three years ago, you say?'

I frowned. 'Yes. It'll be three years in February.'

'Mmm. Yes. That's when it stopped.' He leant forward in his chair. 'Every month, I received cash in the post. Anonymous, but postmarked Princetown. I sometimes wondered if it wasn't from the person who did this to me. Now I know it was. He must have somehow found out the nursing home where I was. But he obviously never knew that I'd come to live here with Betty. The home always forwarded the envelopes, you see.'

My jaw dropped open. So that was where all Sidney's money had gone. I was so pleased!

'That cash came in handy,' my father was smiling now. 'We built on the downstairs bathroom. I can't manage stairs, you see. I sleep in the back room, and I use my wheelchair when I go out. But I'm not a total cripple as you see, so things aren't as bad as you probably expected from those newspaper cuttings. And now I want to hear all about *you* and your young man here.'

We talked on, until it was getting dark and Betty turned on the light. I didn't think we could ever say all we wanted to. And then Daniel looked at his watch.

'I think perhaps we should be leaving,' he suggested quietly.

'Of course, lad,' my father agreed. 'But I do hope you'll come again.' His voice faltered for just an instant. 'You don't know how much this has meant to me.'

I felt my heart tear. 'Yes I do. This is just the beginning, Dad.' I snatched in my breath. That little word that meant so much had found its way onto my tongue of its own accord. 'And I hope you'll both be coming to our wedding.'

Dad straightened his shoulders, lifting his chin proudly. 'I hope you'll allow me the honour of giving you away!'

'Oh, yes! Yes, please!' My words vibrated with emotion and I hugged him once again.

We were coming back into Yelverton. I had been so excited, chatting all the way and hardly able to sit still. But now I had run out of words and was enjoying the elation that consumed me.

'Daniel, can we go home?' I suddenly requested.

'But I *am* taking you home.'

'No, I mean *our* home. Everyone will want to know all about it. Wendy especially will want to know every detail, and rightly so. But…just now, I want to be quiet to take it all in. I want it to be just you and me. That's if you don't mind dropping me into work in the morning.'

Beside me, Daniel chuckled in the darkness as he changed gear to turn up onto the moor rather than continuing towards Tavistock. 'How could I mind if it means I'll have you in my bed tonight? And I'm sure Trojan will be pleased to see me back earlier than expected.'

'Oh, he's a very clever dog but I wasn't aware that he could tell the time,' I answered with a straight face, and Daniel laughed aloud as the Bentley effortlessly took the long, steep climb up onto the moor. The land appeared more bleak and barren than ever, a group of sheep considered hardy enough to winter on the exposed uplands appearing as ghostly shadows in the headlights. We drove through thin patches of mist and as we came into Princetown, ponies were huddling in protected corners of the village. It was all so solid and strong. So eternal. And I was home.

'Gloria was right, you know,' I said as we turned up Tor Royal Lane just before Albert Terrace. 'She told me once that everything would be all right in the end. Almost as if she had second sight.'

'Well, maybe she does. I know I'm pretty sceptical about such things, but who knows? It's a magical place, Dartmoor. Full of untold mysteries. And miracles. It brought *you* to me, didn't it, when I thought I'd never find happiness again?'

I smiled at the windscreen and shifted over in my seat so that I could rest my head on Daniel's arm, absorbing the movement as he changed up after the sharp bend at Tor Royal. I breathed in the familiar masculine scent of him, squinted up at his firm jaw line as he concentrated on the lonely road. When we finally pulled into the driveway, I unlocked the side gates to the old stable-yard, secured them again when Daniel had driven through, and then went to wait on the terrace while he put the car in the barn.

I stood, gazing out over the shadows of the moor. The night was crisp and frosty, nipping at my nose, and a clear, half moon shed a silvery, diaphanous glow over the undulating wilderness that stretched to the black velvet dome of the sky. Daniel came up behind me, lacing his arms around my waist, and I leant back against him, totally at peace.

'Beautiful, isn't it?' he sighed in my ear.

'And to think I might never have known such a place existed,' I murmured back, enraptured. Bewitched. 'Strange thing, fate.'

Yes. Everything had fallen into place. At last, I knew who I was, and where I belonged. And who I loved with a passion that bewildered me.

I felt him kiss the top of my head. I turned to him and smiled, and he took my hand as we stepped across the terrace to the door.

Author's Note

Both the Cribbett family and the Mead family have kindly given permission for members of their families to appear as the real-life characters that they were in the 1950s. Unfortunately, my efforts to trace the family of Mr Bill Gough, the engine-driver, were unsuccessful. I do hope I will be forgiven for repeating some well-known – and previously published – stories about him, and that my portrayal of him will be taken in the spirit in which it was written, that is to say a tribute to a much-loved and respected gentleman.

Readers who know Dartmoor will recognise many of the places referred to in the book, but please be aware of the dangers of the abandoned quarries and take notice of the warning signs. For those who are curious, Fencott Place does not actually exist!

Acknowledgements

Firstly, I would like to thank my marvellous agent who encouraged me to write my first story set in the 1950s, and Allison and Busby for agreeing to publish it! My friend Paul Rendell, Dartmoor guide, historian and editor of *The Dartmoor News*, was, as always, my first port of call for research. I must thank also Roger Paul of the Princetown History Society, Bill Radcliffe of Albert Terrace, and in particular Leslie and Evelyn Cribbett and Ivan Mead for their lifetime memories of Princetown. Kath Brewer told me about when she lived at the cottages at Foggintor and the first stage of their demolition, Elizabeth Stanbrook gave further details of the use of the stone for the television station, and Nick Luff answered my questions on the steam railway.

In Tavistock, local historian Gerry Woodcock put me in touch with Christine Barron, Sylvia Viggars and Ann Yeo who all worked at Tavistock Hospital at the period either as nursing or administrative staff. What a wonderful morning we spent together, ladies!

In more general terms, I must mention my good friend Sir Michael Willatts for his information on vehicles of the time, Auntie Joan Broomfield for her memories of army life in Egypt and the National Army Museum for details of the National Service system.

Last but by no means least, a huge thank you to retired physician Marshall Barr of the Berkshire Medical Heritage Centre for all his detailed descriptions of medical procedures and drugs of the time.

My sincere gratitude goes to each and every one of you!

Hope at Holly Cottage

By TANIA CROSSE

978-0-7490-0835-2

Hardback

The future seems rosy for Plymouth schoolgirl Anna Millington as she studies for her A-levels in order to qualify for teacher training college. But Anna's life isn't all that it appears. Her family hides a cruel secret that resulted from the worst night of the Plymouth Blitz back in 1941, a night Anna remembers all too well as a small child cowering in a bomb shelter. Now, in 1954, the devastating consequences erupt again in tragedy. Anna fears for her own safety and feels forced into abandoning her aspirations for a successful career.

Leaving behind her dear friend Ethel, Anna escapes to nearby Dartmoor, of which she has fond memories from when she was evacuated to Tavistock after the bombing raid that was to change her life for ever. But will her return to the moor bring her hope? Along the way, Anna encounters various other victims of fate who have their own secrets to tell. Will they all have the courage to seek out the happiness they deserve, and will Anna be able to help them – or herself?

An endearing tale of warmth and friendship, love and hope set in the city of Plymouth and the wilds of Dartmoor.

a&b